THE KING'S ADVENTURER

John Smith has rejected the path that has been set
for him – a quiet life as a gentleman farmer in the
England of James I. He dreams of adventure and his
dream takes him across Europe, where he suffers the
triumphs and hardships of war, from military glory
to imprisonment by the cruel Turks. Wherever he
goes there are women who long for him to stay, but
all the time he knows that something else awaits him,
over the seas yet again.

At last, John Smith's destiny takes him to the new
colony of Virginia, where he finds joy and bitterness,
fulfilment and disaster, where he is a distrusted Paleface and a demi-god, and where he is saved from
death by the beautiful, half-wild Pocahontas.

By the same author

MADAME DU BARRY

The Queens of England Series

MYSELF MY ENEMY
QUEEN OF THIS REALM
VICTORIA VICTORIOUS
THE LADY IN THE TOWER
THE COURTS OF LOVE
IN THE SHADOW OF THE CROWN
THE QUEEN'S SECRET
THE RELUCTANT QUEEN
THE PLEASURES OF LOVE
WILLIAM'S WIFE
ROSE WITHOUT A THORN

JEAN PLAIDY

The King's Adventurer

HarperCollins*Publishers*

HarperCollins*Publishers*
77–85 Fulham Palace Road,
Hammersmith, London w6 8jb

This paperback edition 1997
1 3 5 7 9 8 6 4 2

First published in Great Britain in 1961
as *This Was a Man* under the pseudonym of Ellalice Tate
Published by Robert Hale Ltd 1966

ISBN 0 0 00 649911 2

Set in Sabon by
Rowland Phototypesetting Ltd,
Bury St Edmunds, Suffolk

Printed and bound in Great Britain by
Caledonian International Book Manufacturing Ltd,
Glasgow

CONTENTS

AUTHOR'S NOTE

In writing this book, which is based on the life of one of England's greatest adventurers, I have relied on the writings of those whose who shared John Smith's adventures and left an account of them; my chief source is naturally John Smith's own records, edited by Edward Arber, FSA, and A. G. Bradley. Other sources which have been helpful are: *Captain John Smith* by E. Keble Chatterton, *The True Story of Captain John Smith* by Katharine Pearson Woods, *The Adventures of Captain John Smith* by E. P. Roberts, and *Captain John Smith* by A. G. Bradley.

I

The Restless Boy

One of John's earliest memories was the day when his uncle came to the farm, fresh from his battles with the Spaniards. Looking into the blue and red flames in the great open fireplace, little John saw pictures of Spanish galleons proudly sailing up the Channel to be met by the little ships of England.

Everyone listened with breathless wonder, for in the length and breadth of England Drake's defeat of the Spanish Armada was a story which all could bear to hear again and again.

Only a few short months ago the country had waited tensely, certain of victory, it was true, but aware of the might of the Spaniards; knowing, too, that, in the ships which the King of Spain boasted were invincible, came not only soldiers and sailors to pillage the land but the Inquisitors with their racks and *bilboes*, prepared to force a conquered people to accept their way of life and their faith.

Yet Providence had intervened – Providence using England's sailors such as Drake, Effingham and John Smith's uncle.

Oh, to have been one of them! John felt angry with a fate which had made him only eight years old at a time when England's greatest sea battle must be fought.

'One day,' said his uncle, 'you will be a great sailor. Never fear, England will still have enemies when you are old enough to fight them.'

Then his uncle, who was a very merry man, winked

because he knew that John's father did not care for such talk. John was his elder son and as such would inherit the farm; he was ordained to live a quiet life in Willoughby, and bring up his own son to be a farmer like himself, so that in the generations to come there would always be a John Smith to farm at Willoughby.

But John had decided otherwise on that day when his uncle came and told of his adventures with the Spanish Armada.

John's younger brother Francis listened also, but his eyes did not glow with the same fervour.

'When I am a man,' said John, 'I shall go to sea, and no one shall stop me. Francis here can have the farm.'

His uncle laughed and his face, which was the colour of a walnut, creased up like one.

'You're your old uncle all over again, John,' he said. 'If you've the same spirit in eight years' time . . . you'll never be a Lincolnshire farmer.'

Then his uncle told John stories of sailing the seas, of sighting the Spanish enemy on the horizon, of battles and prizes and the Queen's love of all adventurers.

'It's the life for me,' said John.

And Francis, watching, quietly nodded; so did little Alice, their sister. The grown-ups might see their brother John as a boastful little boy; *they* knew that he always meant what he said.

John sat in the classroom at Alford Grammar School, which was two miles away from the farm, and dreamed of adventures. He exasperated his teachers. This was not because he was a stupid boy. Far from it. He was quick and clever and could have been a credit to them. In geography and map-reading he excelled but in most other subjects he was frankly not interested. He was biding his time until the day when he would be old enough to go to sea.

One day, soon after his uncle's visit, he was strolling

home from school, his satchel on his back, when he saw two boys coming towards him.

'On guard!' shouted one. 'Look out! Here comes a Spaniard.'

'Spaniard yourself!' shouted John. 'I'm an English man-of-war. God save the Queen!'

'He tricks us,' said one of the boys. 'He's a pirate flying the English flag.'

The two boys ran to the attack, shouting to each other what they were doing, as they ran. 'I'm going to board her. She's carrying loot . . .'

The lane had become the high seas as they visualized the two great ships involved in the fight. Leaping, whooping, they went on with the play until one of them said: 'My father is home. He has been fighting the Infidel.'

John paused, seeing himself in that moment leading his own company against the Turk.

The others danced round him, catching him off his guard. 'You're dead. I've run my cutlass through your body. You're bleeding. You can never recover.'

And John did not answer; he allowed them to leap on him, to shout of their victory. What was this child's play compared with fighting the Turk!

Two more boys joined them. These were French boys who were being educated with the Bertie children at the home of their father, Lord Willoughby. They had gracious manners, but John and the Bertie boys had long since ceased to despise them because of their quaint English and their less rough manners.

Now they all sat on the bank and talked of the wars in which Lord Willoughby had taken part; and Robert Bertie, the elder brother, brought out a ballad in which the exploits of his father were described. Peregrine, the younger Bertie, listened proudly and the French politely; but John was clearly more excited than any by what he heard.

'Read that part again,' he shouted. 'Can you not see it!

His lordship going into combat. His lordship is a great man.'

He gazed enviously at Robert and Peregrine, and he wished that his own father were not a farmer on the Willoughby estate but a great adventurer such as Lord Willoughby.

The elder of the French boys, the Comte de Plouha, said: 'In my country there is continual strife. There it is Frenchman against Frenchman. Catholic against Huguenot.'

'That is why our father sent us to Lord Willoughby,' put in his brother, 'that we might be brought up in peace. Peace! Who wishes to be brought up in peace?'

'Who, indeed?' cried John. 'As soon as I am old enough I shall sail the seas. I shall fight and win great lands for the Queen.'

The others looked at him. The French boys were too polite, the Berties too fond of him to remind him that, as the son of a farmer, he had little hope of leading the adventurous life of noblemen such as themselves.

Robert Bertie, the eldest of all the boys, thought it was a pity, for John Smith was clearly born to be a leader of men.

That day John was late home from school, and when he reached the farmhouse his mother shook her head in sad exasperation.

'John,' she said, 'you should be helping your father. I do wish you would show a little more interest in the farm. Francis, who is not as old as you, is so much more useful.'

'Francis will be the farmer in the family, Mother,' answered John. 'I shall follow my uncle's career.'

His mother turned away but she did not answer. The eldest sons of the family had always inherited the farm. There had been a time when she had been delighted that her son John should have for his companions the sons of noblemen. Now she was not so sure that this was a blessing. Was John getting ideas beyond his station? They were good, honest people of gentle birth; they owned their farm although it was held by grant of Lord Willoughby who was lord of the manor; and the rent they paid each year was only a quit rent, a token of homage to Lord Willoughby d'Eresby.

The Smiths were honourable, religious people. They respected the nobility and knew their station – all except John, it seemed.

As John went out to join his father in the fields, George Smith watched his son approach. He was a sturdy boy, a little short for his age but making up for that by his strength; he was a handsome boy, and there was nothing feminine about his looks although he had inherited his mother's curly hair. John's eyes were blue, and when he was excited or angry they were the colour of sapphires. The boy held himself with a dignity which, his father noted as he made his way across the field, would have been more natural to one of the Willoughbys than to the son of a farmer. George, who had a feeling almost approaching idolatry for the Willoughby family, had to admit that no one seeing young John with that family would have known that he was not a member of it. John had been born with an easy dignity which was almost regal.

'Well, John?' said George kindly.

'Mother sent me out to help.'

It was useless to say, Have you tethered the goats, have you fetched the butter from the dairy, have you fed the fowls? George knew that John had done none of these things. John had done nothing but dream.

'Son,' said George, 'you should know what is expected of you. Francis does his tasks without being asked.'

'Francis was born to be a farmer, Father.'

'You also, John.'

'Nay, Father. I was born to sail the high seas. I was born to fight for the Queen. Lord Willoughby is home from fighting the Turk. Did you know? Robert has a ballad about him.'

'And you dream of fighting with his lordship one day, is that not it? You dream of high adventure far from the farm?'

John nodded, and a smile curved his lips.

Then George laid his hand on his son's shoulder. 'My son, you are no longer a child, and it is time I spoke seriously to you. You are my eldest child and one day you must farm this land. Learn all you can now. You will find that it will stand you in good stead later on. The time will pass so quickly that it will surprise you. There is something I have to tell you.'

George stopped. He was moved by the beauty of his son, by the rapt enchantment. No, he thought. I will let him dream on; I will not tell him yet that I cannot hope to be with him much longer. There is time. Let him dream his wild impossible dreams for a little while yet. The time will come all too quickly when he must put away his childish fancies and face the cruel realities of life.

But as the years passed, John's ambitions became more insistent. He lacked the placidity of Francis and Alice; he fretted impatiently.

When he was fourteen he asked his father and mother to let him go to sea.

It was in the farmhouse parlour, and the younger children had gone to bed; John, too, was supposed to be in bed, but he had crept down and, candle in hand, had confronted his parents.

'Father,' he implored, 'let me go to sea. Francis will be the farmer in the family. I never could.'

'Come here, my boy,' said George, and John went to his father; he did not notice the grey tinge in his father's face; he was so intent on putting his case to them.

'John,' went on George Smith, 'you are fourteen years

old; almost a man. Many boys of your age are already at work; but we are no ordinary farmers; as you know, this is our own farm; we are land-owners, my son. One day all this will belong to you.'

'Give it to Francis and let me go to sea.'

'You would barter your inheritance for the life of a cabin boy?'

'Most willingly, Father.'

'You know nothing of the rigours of the sea. Sailors are not always singing sea-shanties and winning glory by fighting the Spaniards.'

'I know that, Father.'

'You have no experience of the sea. You know nothing but what you have learned from your uncle and from these ballads.'

'I know that such adventure is for me.'

'You talk like a foolish boy.'

'Tell him, Father,' said Mistress Smith. 'Tell him the truth. The time has come.'

John looked from one to the other of his parents. Then his father stared into the fire and said quietly: 'I am a sick man, John. My days are numbered.'

John stared at his father. He could not take in what was being said because he could not visualize the farm without his father.

'It is true,' said his mother. 'Your father is sick and he cannot live many more years. It is for you, John, to comfort him in the time that is left to him – as we all must do.'

'But, Mother, what can I do? Oh, Father, my dear father!' The boy threw himself at his father who took him into his arms.

'There, there,' he comforted. 'I knew you would be upset. You must not be. We all have to go at some time. My time is nearer than the rest; that is all. I thank God that I have a good wife, two stalwart sons and a dutiful daughter. You are almost a man, John. It will be for you to step into my shoes and take care of the family.'

'Come. Sit here,' said his mother. 'You must not show your grief. It would upset the younger children. Let them be happy while they can. John, you are a man now. It will be for you to take care of us all.'

Then she rose leaving the room and returned after a short while with a tankard of ale. This she gave to her son; and he sat with them, staring into the fire, trying hard to be brave, and finding that he could think of nothing but the fact that this kindly father would soon have left them.

When the boy had gone back to bed his parents continued to sit by the fire. 'He has taken it hard, George,' said Alice Smith.

'I am sorry we told him.'

'It was right that he should know. Once he understands that these daring deeds are not for farmers' sons he'll settle. I'll warrant he'll make a good farmer too.'

'Yes, wife, it is a sad trial for him to mix with these Willoughby lads and the Frenchies and hear their talk.'

'He must understand that he is not of their class.'

'It is asking a great deal. He plays their games, he fancies he is one of them. I have been thinking for some time of sending him away from home. It will be good for him. He could stay with his aunt and uncle in Louth. He could look after that little bit of property we have there. It will teach him his responsibilities. And while he is there he can attend the grammar school. Yes, wife, I think that is what our John needs. You see, my plan will serve many purposes: Teach him independence, for one thing. Appreciation of his home and family for another . . . and it will take him away from his noble friends.'

'I expect you are right, Father,' said Alice Smith. 'When do you propose to send him away?'

'Tomorrow I'll take him over. It is well that he should go soon. We don't want him letting slip out what we've told him tonight to Francis or little Alice. I don't want a miserable household. Tomorrow then.'

And while John lay in his bed thinking of the bravery of his father and the apparent inevitability of a future which was repellent to him, his parents made their plans for sending him to Louth.

Life at Louth was intolerably dull for John. He missed his brother and sister, his home and parents; he was as bored with the lessons at Louth Grammar School as he had been with those at Alford; his aunt and uncle had less patience with him than his parents had had, and he missed the companionship of the Willoughby boys and their French friends.

His great consolation was in day-dreams; he read all he could of the discovered world, and he dreamed of sailing the seas in search of new lands. He knew that Philip, the King of Spain, was ruler of great portions of the New World and that it was the desire of English adventurers to make their Queen a greater ruler than the Spanish Monarch. He longed to join them. He dreamed of sailing up the Thames and being received and honoured by the Queen herself. But greater than any honour he could receive would be the joy of discovery. The important moments would be those when he set sail up the English Channel with the salt breeze in tune with his ambition driving him on.

He forgot that his father was a sick man. He was so young himself, so full of vitality, that death seemed unreal. He had believed in it that night when his father and mother had told him of his father's illness, but he could not go on doing so, and within a few weeks of arriving in Louth he was as determined as ever to live a life of adventure which would take him far from the Lincolnshire farm.

Francis shall have the farm, he told himself. Good old Francis, it will be a fine thing for him . . . and for me also. Francis must have the farm.

He had made up his mind. He would not worry his parents with arguments. He would slip off one morning and, instead of going to school, he would make his way to the coast.

This plan had no sooner struck him than Fate, it seemed to him, stepped in to decide him.

He was on his way to school one spring morning when he met a man with a pack on his back.

It was a glorious morning; the hedgerows were bright with wild parsley and stitchwort; it was a morning when to young John it seemed sinful to sit in a classroom construing Latin.

'Good-day, young sir,' said the man. 'It's a bright and shining one.'

'It is indeed,' said John, 'and I envy you being your own master to enjoy it.'

'So you're on the way to school, eh, with your satchel on your back. Have you some good books in that satchel, eh? Books interest me. I sell them.'

'These are lesson books,' said John. 'My father paid a great price for them. I have to take care of them. They will be for my brother Francis in his turn.'

'Come, show me what you have,' said the book pedlar; and they sat by the roadside while John took out the books and showed the pedlar.

'Are you a boy who loves to read books?'

'No. I want to have adventures which people will write about. I want to go to sea.'

'Then why are you not making your way to the coast instead of to the grammar school?'

'Because that is what I must do.'

'Then 'tis as well. You'll never make an adventurer if you take orders. Adventurers give orders, and no one who wished to go to sea would be trudging the road to school at your age, boy.'

John's heart had begun to beat fast.

The pedlar went on: 'You're a dreamer, boy, and there's a mort of difference 'twixt a dreamer and a doer. Now if you was a doer, say, and I gave you a good price for these books, you'd take it and you'd be on the way to the coast with it and you'd find yourself a ship, and none would say you nay. But you're a dreamer, lad, so you sling a satchel on your back and you go to school; and you live in fancy what you'll never do in fact.'

'What will you give me for the books?' asked John slowly.

It was a long day. He must prowl about the lanes, for how could he go to school without his books? The money was in his pocket. It elated him and at the same time filled him with shame. It was the money which would take him to the coast and put him on a ship; and it was the money he had acquired by stealing that which did not belong to him.

'John Smith,' he said, 'you are no dreamer. You are the one who makes up his mind and acts. John Smith, you are a thief. You have sold that which does not belong to you.'

But it was done now; it had been done on impulse and there was no going back.

'When I discover rich treasure,' he promised himself, 'I will pay my father ten ... no, twenty times the value of the books. He will understand. I did not steal. I borrowed until that time when I shall be able to pay him back!'

He had made up his mind. He would go back to his uncle's house pretending to have come from school. He would gather together his belongings, tie them into a bundle and hide them in an outhouse. In the morning he would slip out as though he were going to school, get his bundle and be away. That would give him a day's start before they knew he had gone.

It was deceitful, but it must be done. John knew that he was destined for a life of adventure and that it was time it had begun.

When he reached his uncle's house his aunt came running out to him. She was agitated, and he knew that something had happened. He had come along quietly, his satchel hidden behind his back lest it should be noticed that it was empty; but his aunt had no thought for the satchel, empty or full.

'John,' she cried, 'come in at once. Come into the parlour. There is bad news.'

John, feeling sick with guilt and horror, followed her into the parlour where one of his father's farm hands was waiting for him.

''Tis bad news, Master John,' he said.

'My father . . .' faltered the boy.

'He is very sick. He is dying, Master John; and he wishes you to return with me and lose no time about it.'

'You'd better leave at once, John,' said his aunt.

And John, bewildered and unhappy, took off his empty satchel, completely forgot the jingling coins in his pockets and prepared to leave for home.

It seemed to John as he stepped into his father's bedroom that he had gone away a boy and come back a man. The man lying in the bed, whose face lightened as his eyes rested on his elder son, was clearly dying; John's mother who sat by the bed looked wan and very ill. Alice was kneeling by the bed, her face buried in the counterpane as she muffled her sobs; and Francis stood by the bed trying hard not to cry.

The tragedy was brought home afresh to John, and he hated himself for his callousness in thinking of deserting them; and he thanked God that he had not met the pedlar a day earlier in which case his perfidy would have been known to his dying father and his grief-stricken family.

Several of their neighbours had come into take their last farewell of him and to add their signatures as witnesses to the will which he had made. John saw the parchment scroll lying on the bed and guessed what it was; and as he looked at it the tears gushed to his eyes.

'My son John,' said George, stretching out a hand, 'I am glad you came in time. It is meet that my eldest should be here to see me go. The time has come, John, as I knew it must. John, from this day you must cease to be a boy. You are a man; you will soon be the head of the house. Oh, John, are your shoulders broad? I believe they are. And they will need to be to bear your burdens.'

'Yes, Father, I am strong enough.'

'Good boy. I can go with an easy mind. I am a fortunate man. I have had the best of wives and three good children. I have good neighbours too.'

As he said this George Mettham, whose land adjoined that of the Smiths, took a step closer to the bed.

'I am here, friend,' he said.

'Thank you. I see you. Master Mettham has promised to give you a helping hand until you are of an age to help yourself, John. He has promised me to be your very good friend. I have appointed him your guardian.'

John said: 'We shall not need a guardian, Father. I am of an age to take care of our affairs, you know.'

George Mettham bestowed a smile on John which to the dying man might have seemed indulgent but which slightly alarmed John. He did not wish for George Mettham's guardianship, and if his father had not been so ill he would have told him so more plainly.

'John,' went on his father, 'I have made my will. The farm will soon be your mother's, and after her it goes to you as my eldest child. There is also the land at Great Carleton – seven acres of it. Francis, are you there, my son?'

Francis sprang to his father's side. 'I am here, Father,' he said.

'You will have to put away childish things now, Francis. You will have to be a help to your brother. The farm must go to the eldest in accordance with the custom of our family. But I do not forget you. To you I am leaving my property in Louth. Be a good boy, Francis. You will have to obey your brother now, for he is at the head of the family. And you must obey your guardian also.'

George Mettham laid a hand on Francis's shoulder, and Francis suddenly burst into tears and threw himself on his father's bed.

'Come, come,' said George Mettham, 'you must not give way to grief. It upsets your father.'

John put himself between his father and their appointed guardian.

'My father knows of our grief,' he said. 'He has always taught us honestly to say and act as we mean. Let the boy show in this way how much he loves his father.'

John's natural arrogance was apparent, and George Mettham restrained his annoyance, promising himself that he would teach Master John a lesson or two at a more appropriate time.

'Alice,' murmured George Smith. 'Where is my little Alice?'

'Here, Father.' Alice lifted her tear-stained face from the counterpane.

'Why, little one,' said George Smith, 'you must not weep for me. Dry your eyes, child, for I have suffered much pain and shall soon be past it. Remember that. For you, little daughter, there is ten pounds in gold. It will be your dowry. And you shall have my second-best bedstead with the feather bed too and the bed-linen and pillows and half my pewter and brass.'

'Thank you, Father,' said Alice. 'But I would rather you did not leave us.'

'But that, my dear ones, is not for our deciding. Now say farewell, for there is little time left to me.'

And one by one the children came to kiss their father. Alice and Francis were led weeping away, but John remained; he, his mother and George Mettham.

That night when John had planned to start on his new life he spent at the deathbed of his father.

There was no question of John's returning to Louth, for there were too many duties on the farm to be performed. John, still dreaming of going to sea, was capable enough. He could not help being interested in animals and the growing of crops; he was by nature practical, and he found a compulsion within him to do well anything he had to do.

No sooner had his father been buried in Willoughby churchyard than John became aware of the frailty of his mother. She had become exhausted through nursing her husband and collapsed as soon as the funeral was over. In nursing her husband she had caught his complaint, and in a very short time the symptoms were apparent in her case.

John immediately took charge; he worked hard himself and made Francis do the same, while little Alice became a nurse to their failing mother.

George Mettham was often at the farm; an efficient farmer he was full of advice; but John had noticed the avaricious gleam in his eyes as they rested on the sick woman, and he knew that George Mettham was waiting for the time when he could be master of the farm and guardian of the young Smiths.

He did not have to wait long. One morning when Alice went to her mother's room to awaken her she found her dead. Thus in the course of a few months the young family lost not only father but mother.

Now George Mettham moved into the farm and took charge. John, who had worked hard for his mother, now lost interest in the farm although it belonged to him.

Francis and Alice who were adaptable found no fault with their guardian. It was only John who disliked him. There was continual strife between them and John's desire to go to sea was greater than it had ever been.

One day George Mettham called him into the little room where he did his accounts and said: 'I think it is time you and I had a little talk about your future. It is clear to me that you have little interest in the farm and that your desire is for a very different kind of life.'

'I want to go to sea, as you know,' said John.

'Your father appointed me your guardian,' answered Mettham, 'and I cannot allow you to go to sea as a common sailor. You are of gentle birth and must never forget it. But I am going to send you to a shipping merchant in the port of King's Lynn, where you will learn about ships and the men who sail in them.'

John was so delighted he all but embraced the man whom, only yesterday, he had told Francis he would never trust.

'When may I leave?' asked John.

'You may start preparing at once,' was the answer.

John ran to Francis and Alice to tell them that he was going away.

Alice began to cry. 'You are all going, one by one,' she said. 'Soon there will be only me left.'

Francis comforted her. 'I'll stay with you, Alice. We'll always be together.'

'And when I'm a great sea captain,' said John, 'I shall give you the farm . . . you, Francis; and Alice can always be with you . . . you with the farm, she with her ten gold pounds and the second-best bed.'

'You'll come and see us as often as you can?' asked Alice tearfully.

'Yes,' John assured her. And he believed that he would sit by the fire, as his uncle had once done, and tell tales of high adventure to Francis, Alice and perhaps their children. He would enjoy talking to the little ones – for perhaps one of them would want to follow in his uncle's footsteps – and there by the firelight he would make their eyes shine with excitement as they admired the mighty deeds of great John Smith.

With what high hope John came to King's Lynn! He would never forget his first sight of the ancient town at the mouth of the Ouse; it was a beautiful spot, he thought, as he came in through the city gates and walked to the dwelling of Mr Thomas Sendall the shipping merchant, with whom he was to begin his career.

Thomas Sendall was a man of great importance in the town of King's Lynn for his was a large business and his warehouses and wharfs were extensive.

John was received into Thomas Sendall's home and treated as a member of the family. He was to be an apprentice, he was told; but John answered that he would only consent to this if it was agreed that he should serve his apprenticeship at sea.

'All in good time,' was Thomas Sendall's hearty reply. 'You should not try to run before you can walk, boy.'

So John tried to be patient. He tried to admire the beauties of the town in which he was now living; he accompanied the Sendall family to St Margaret's Church on Sundays; he practised archery on the market-place near the Corn Exchange; he watched malefactors in the pillory; he attended the pleasure fair on St Valentine's Day.

Thomas Sendall was kind to him; Mistress Sendall wanted to treat him as a poor motherless boy and feed him up – put some strength in him, she said. After the months of neglect which had followed the death of his mother such care was not unwelcome; but very soon John tired of the bluff good nature of Thomas Sendall and the cosseting of his wife. Norfolk dumplings – those lumps of dough served with gravy before each meal – delicious as they were, were no substitute for a life at sea; and all the comfort of the Sendall household seemed frustrating as he sat over his desk in the Sendall warehouse.

One day the kindly Thomas asked him why he was fretting. Wasn't he happy at Lynn? Was there anything he and Mistress Sendall could do for him?

'Only one thing,' said John. 'Send me to sea.'

Thomas shook his head. 'That I cannot do, John. You are a gentleman. You cannot go to sea as a common sailor, and as yet you lack the experience and years to be anything else.'

'I am prepared to go as a common sailor.'

Thomas shook his head. 'I am not your guardian, John,' he said.

'So, contrary to what was promised to me, I must spend my time here as a clerk!'

'Until you have learned a little about the sea and ships.'

'I see,' said John quietly.

Next morning, before the household was astir, he packed his few belongings into a bundle, slung them across his back and tiptoed out of the house.

There were two alternatives: to make his way to the coast or boldly to present himself to George Mettham, tell him that he had been tricked when he had been sent to King's Lynn and demand part of his fortune so that he might set out on his adventures.

He decided on the latter course. He was no penniless boy and he saw no reason why Master George Mettham should benefit because he, John Smith, was fool enough not to claim what was rightfully his.

So he set out for Willoughby.

Alice was feeding the fowls when he arrived. She dropped the bowl, screamed out her pleasure and ran to embrace him.

'John! How happy I am to see you. Francis! Come quickly. Our brother has come.'

Francis, who was in a nearby field, heard her shout and came running into the yard.

'John! This is wonderful. But what has happened? We had no message that you were on the way.'

'Come inside and I will tell you why I am here.'

They went into the farmhouse while Alice hurried to bring ale and meat pie for her brother.

John sat in the old parlour and explained. 'There was no chance for me there. I have been tricked. They had no intention of letting me go to sea. I was destined to be nothing more than a clerk.'

'Were the Sendalls cruel to you?' asked Francis.

'No. They were very kind. But they could not satisfy me with their good nature and Norfolk dumplings. So . . . I ran away. But I must see our guardian. I wonder he is not here. He is in his own house, I doubt not. Well, that is not more than a mile or so farther on.'

'No, John,' Francis explained. 'He was called to London on business. You will have to wait until he returns.'

John clenched his fist and beat it on his knee. 'It is frustration at every turn. I am weary of waiting.' His face lightened suddenly. 'I will go to London and see him there.'

'It would be wiser to wait,' Francis suggested.

'For how long will he be away?'

'He did not say,' said Alice. 'But do stay, dear John. It would be wonderful if we could all be together again, even for a little while.'

'My dearest sister,' John answered her gently, 'there is some compulsion within me which bids me shun all further delay. I cannot stay here, waiting weeks . . . perhaps months. No. I know where he has his lodging when he is in London and, brother and sister, I intend to set out for that place without delay.'

Alice sighed and went away to pack up food for her elder brother, and Francis smiled at John, thinking that life might be easier for him if he would but accept what it offered him and curb his inclinations.

* * *

The journey to London was a long one when it must be made on foot, and John sighed for a good horse. He had little money and slept under hedges and occasionally in barns; once he had the good fortune to meet a wagoner who was going his way, and for a whole day they travelled together. Then their ways parted and John had to rely once more on his own legs.

He had tramped since early dawn and was very weary; and when he reached an inn he wondered if he could afford a tankard of ale and hunk of bread and cheese. After deliberating for some time he decided that it would be a good investment. It was served to him by a rather supercilious man who clearly did not see in John a customer to be respected.

John took a seat outside the inn and savoured his bread, cheese and ale, and never had Mistress Sendall's Norfolk dumplings tasted half as good. As he sat there a party drew up at the inn, and the innkeeper hurried out to greet them, for there was no doubt that these were persons of quality. It proved to be a young gentleman travelling with his tutor and a few servants.

'My good masters,' cried the innkeeper. 'Welcome ... welcome. Pray tell us what service you need, and it shall be yours. Wife! Wife! Where are you, wife?'

The innkeeper's wife was at his side, matching her obsequiousness with that of her husband.

John was amused by the difference in the reception which was given these people and that which had been accorded him; and while he sat there smiling ruefully, the gentlemen of the party leaped from their horses, threw the reins to the waiting grooms and turned towards the inn. John saw their faces then and gave a cry of pleasure as he rose from his seat.

The gentlemen stopped and stared at him; then the younger of them ran forward, crying: 'Why, it is John Smith and no other. John, what do you here?'

'Perry! By all the saints! This is a merry meeting.'

The other gentleman who was hovering in the background was, John saw, Peregrine Bertie's tutor. Peregrine had turned to him. 'My old friend John Smith! Robert and I were talking of him only a few days ago. How glad I am that we pulled up here. We are hungry. John, you will join us.'

The innkeeper was looking somewhat shamefaced at having treated John as though he were not a member of the quality – now he so obviously was; but John was too happy and excited by the encounter with his old friend to bear malice, and he could only think of his luck as Peregrine slipped his arm through his and they went into the inn parlour.

Sucking pig followed by venison and sillabub was a good substitute for bread and cheese; particularly when it was washed down with good mead.

'Where are you going, John?' demanded Peregrine. 'I had heard that you were at Lynn, apprenticed to a shipping man.'

''Tis so, Perry, but I ran away. Had I stayed I should have spent my life at a desk or checking bales of this and that. It was not what I intended.'

'And that I understand full well. So you ran away.'

John nodded. 'I am on my way to London to see my guardian. I will have an understanding with him, I do assure you. I shall demand why I was made to become a clerk when I was promised a place on a sea-going vessel. And Perry, whither are you bound?'

'First to London. Then to Orléans. My father is there and Robert is with him. My father has sent for me that I may join them.'

'What great good fortune is yours!' sighed John.

Perry leaned his elbows on the table and studied his friend. He and Robert had always said that it was a shame John had not been born in a higher station of life. John had been a natural leader in all their games; when he had joined them, fancy in some strange way seemed to become fact. John was a dreamer, but there was a strong sense of the practical in his nature; and when they fought their imaginary sea battles with the Spaniards, it was John whose practical instructions and observations made them seem real. Robert and Peregrine had admitted that playing such games without John always robbed them of their savour.

He said now: 'When you have seen your guardian, what will you do?'

'Ask him for money, and mayhap find a ship.'

There was a brief silence when Peregrine said on impulse: 'Come with me to Orléans.'

John's face grew pink with excitement. 'Is that possible?'

'It seems so to me. You could come in my train. There you will travel free of charge to yourself and see something of the world. It will give you time to decide before making a too hasty decision. Will you do so?'

'Indeed I will,' cried John. 'Oh, what great good fortune that I stopped at the inn for refreshment.' He laughed aloud. 'I hesitated long because my purse was wellnigh empty. On such small decisions rests our fate. Do you not see, Perry, it is such incidents which tell us what an exciting adventure we can make of our lives.'

Peregrine slapped his friend on the back. 'Come on. We should be moving. We have a horse for you. It'll give you more comfort than those overworked feet of yours.'

Then he signed to the tutor to pay the innkeeper and, his arm through that of John, went out of the inn to the London Road.

In George Mettham's lodgings John faced his angry guardian.

George Mettham spread his hands in a helpless gesture. 'I see that there is nothing to be done with you. At great pains I find you an opening in the big shipping firm of Sendall . . . the greatest on the East Coast. And where is your gratitude? You run away.'

'I did not ask to be a clerk, and I will not be.'

'You have been a cause of anxiety to me since the death of your poor father. Had I known what was to be demanded of me I should have been very wary of accepting the charge. Your brother and sister are docile enough; the trouble always comes from you.'

'Then give me what is due to me and let me be gone. I have an opportunity to travel to Orléans with the Honourable Peregrine Bertie, for he is going there to join his lordship and the Honourable Robert.'

George Mettham was silent for a few seconds. He did not want John to know how delighted he was. Here was a chance of ridding himself of the most troublesome of his charges. Willingly would he have sent the boy to sea and hoped he would soon fall victim to storms or pirates, but George Mettham wished to be known throughout Lincolnshire as an honest and upright man, and he feared that if he allowed John to go to sea he would be accused of neglecting his duty to the boy. But if he were going abroad in the company of young Bertie, what could be better?

George Mettham fervently hoped that he would never see John again.

'Well,' mused George, 'since you are going into the service of the Willoughbys I suppose I cannot say you nay.'

'Indeed you cannot,' retorted John. 'I have scarcely any money left and must ask you to let me have some of that belonging to me, that I may equip myself as a gentleman about to enter the service of a great lord.'

'That is fair enough,' answered George. He left John and went into another room. Shortly afterwards he returned carrying coins to the value of ten shillings. These he gave to John with a benign smile.

John stared at them. 'Ten shillings! This is not my inheritance. My father left me pounds, and you offer me shillings!'

'Ten shillings is a very great sum,' replied George Mettham. 'When I was your age I should have considered it a fortune. You are not old enough to escape from my guardianship, I would have you remember. I am still in charge of your affairs and I should not dream of giving you more than ten shillings to fritter away on your madcap schemes.'

'You call this a madcap scheme! To become a member of the household of Lord Willoughby?'

George Mettham shrugged his shoulders. 'That is all you will get from me,' he answered.

John cried: 'It is a very unhappy state to be fatherless ... to be left to the care of those who have little care for anything but the profit that comes to them.'

'You insolent boy! How dare you wrong me so?'

'Do I wrong you?' retorted John. 'Ask yourself that, sir. My father left me land and money. You guard it well and profit by it. As for myself, when I would embark on my new career, I am given ten shillings and told it is a great sum. Have no fear for me. I shall make a fortune of my own. But have a care for yourself. Anger such as yours can be fatal at your age.'

With that John strolled nonchalantly out of his lodgings to join Peregrine at his.

John, smarting from his encounter with his guardian, explained everything to his friend, imitating George Mettham with such comicality that Peregrine was soon laughing with pleasure.

'A fig for your guardian, John,' he cried. 'You have no need of money while you are with us. You shall have some of my clothes. We'll fit you up like a gallant, my friend, and we'll provide you with a horse to ride. Put aside your anger, John. Let us rejoice together that you made the decision to fritter your money away on a tankard and a hunk of bread and cheese.'

The chances of life! mused John, all anger forgotten; his eyes were shining in contemplation of the new life which lay ahead, the life of adventure which at last he had succeeded in finding.

II

The French Adventures

In the farmhouse at Willoughby there was an air of great excitement. Alice had set her serving maids to remove the old rushes and put down new. In the kitchen, great pies were already made, and hams and sides of bacon hung from the beams. Pails of milk stood on the stone floor of the dairy where the maids were making butter. From the kitchen came the smell of newly baked bread and cakes.

This was a rare occasion, for after three years' absence brother John was coming home.

Alice went to the top of the house and looked out of a window across the farmlands. She knew the way he would come riding from London; he had sent a messenger ahead of him to tell them that he would be with them that day.

Alice felt the tears in her eyes; she was thinking what a happy day this might have been if her parents had been alive. She believed, with Francis, that their brother John was superior to themselves. One day he would do some great deed which would resound round the world. She was sure of it; so was Francis.

Alice stood leaning against the window; she was praying quietly: 'Oh, Lord, let me be here to see it.'

Then she smiled a little sadly. What matters it, she asked herself, whether I be here or not? What difference will that make to our John's greatness?

One night recently she had awakened to find her body covered in a clammy sweat; there had been a trace of blood on her kerchief when she coughed. Alice knew, for she had nursed her mother, that it was very possible that she might not live to see John's greatness. Yet her disease might be a lingering one as in her father's case, or a galloping one as in her mother's; she could not know yet; all she knew was that she intended to keep her frightening secret from her brothers. Francis would have to discover one day soon perhaps. Not so John.

She shaded her eyes as she heard the sound of a horse's hoofs. Yes, a rider was coming this way. She stood watching. There he was against the brilliant sky – a gallant figure, a noble knight no less, his cloak flying as he rode, his head set nobly on his shoulders, and his beard – yes, John's beard had grown luxuriant and curly – touching his elegant ruff.

Alice started down the stairs.

She called to the maids: 'My brother, your master, is here.'

He came into the parlour – a fine figure of a man now, no longer the boy who had left them; for John had been but sixteen then and so was now nineteen years old. He strode in with an air, thought Alice, of one who had learned to command men.

'Where is my family?' he demanded. His voice was deep, resonant and authoritative. Alice felt the weak tears in her eyes. Oh that my mother could have seen him now, she thought. He is soldier, adventurer and gentleman.

'John, I am here.'

'Alice! My little sister grown up. Oh . . . and a pretty wench, eh?' He took her hand and as he looked at it, added: 'No wedding ring then!'

'Oh no, John. I am far too busy looking after Francis.'

John clicked his tongue in mock disapproval. 'Well, you are young yet and one day you'll be a wife, I doubt not.'

'And you, John. You have not married. You must have met many beautiful girls.'

'Ah,' said John, 'I am wedded to a life of adventure in foreign lands.'

'I have heard it said that marriage is an adventure,' put in Alice.

'Not for me! For me the battlefields of foreign lands, for me exploration beyond the seas. I'd rather fight the Turk than a wife, I do assure you. And how is our Francis? Has he got him a wife?'

'He too is young yet and there has been much to do on the farm. Doubtless he will . . . all in good time.'

John held his sister at arms' length and smiled into her face; then he kissed her cheek.

'My pretty little sister,' he said. And then he released her with a shout of pleasure: 'Ah, and here is Farmer Francis himself.'

Francis grasped his brother's hand. 'John . . . brother . . . it is good to see you here.'

'I've been hearing news of you from Alice.'

'It's your news, brother, which will be of greater interest than anything we could tell. Our cousins are riding over tomorrow. They all wish to see you. But today we have kept free for ourselves. We want to hear from your own lips, in our own little circle, what has befallen you during the years you have been away.'

One of the maids came in to say that, hearing the master's arrival, the table had been laid and the meal was ready in the great kitchen.

The maid was a comely, cheeky wench, and Alice watched Francis's eyes glint a little as he looked at her. It was not that he was necessarily interested in that girl; the look she had seen was that which might be apparent in the eyes of any young man as they alighted on a comely female.

And John? He looked past the girl. He did not seem to see her. Was it, Alice asked herself, because he had become acquainted with women in comparison with whom country

Bess would seem lacking in grace and charm? It was as if John had no interest in women as women.

'Come, let us go then,' said Francis. 'While we eat, John can tell us what he has been doing.'

'You did not stay long with the Berties in Orléans,' said Alice as they sat at table.

'It was too idle a life,' John told her. 'It was also a little dull. I do not think I was meant to be a courtier. I enjoyed exploring the country and learning the language. Alice, you should hear me converse with the French. I really speak almost like a native now.'

'So you should,' retorted Francis, 'after so long there.'

'Tell us why you left Lord Willoughby's service,' begged Alice.

'Mainly because his lordship could not afford to keep me.'

'Oh come, that could not be. The Willoughbys are very rich,' said Francis.

'Riches,' said John, 'like everything else, are a matter of comparison. Here in the country the Willoughbys are rich compared with farmers like the Smiths. In Orléans, where nobles spend half the day and all the night gambling, they are not so rich; or if they are they soon become poor. Thus it was, his lordship and Perry told me sorrowfully, that they could no longer afford to employ me. I was sorry to leave them but I had found life a little dull. The war of the League was still going on, even though Henri Quatre had been almost universally acknowledged as the King of France; but it was very quiet in Orléans and I saw little fighting. Perry and Robert gave me a purse to enable me to travel in comfort to England, and this I shall never forget for they had very little to spare.'

'But you did not come to England,' Alice reproached him.

'Indeed no,' cried John. 'What would our worthy

guardian have said if I had returned like a beaten dog with my tail between my legs, eh? I decided to see Paris and thither I went. There I met a nobleman from Scotland who was financially embarrassed; and I could not see a fellow countryman – or almost a fellow countryman – in such distress in a foreign land. So I gave him a great part of what I had in my purse.'

'Our guardian is right,' said Francis. 'He has always said that you must be protected from your foolish generosity. He says you'd give away what you needed yourself and then think others should do the same for you.'

'It was foolish of you, John,' reproved Alice, 'to give away money which was intended to bring you safely home.'

'It was not entirely a gift. In exchange I was given letters of introduction to the Court of Scotland.'

'The Court of Scotland,' cried Francis. 'Why, it is said that if the Queen should die – which God forbid – the next monarch will come from Scotland.'

'So,' said Alice, 'you would have done yourself great good by going to Scotland and offering your services to King James.'

'It was my intention, but I could not stomach the thought of returning home without having achieved a little of what I set out to do. So, soon after I had left Paris I changed my mind. I decided to learn a little soldiering. I was in France, and the French needed soldiers. I joined up to fight with King Henry against the Catholic League, for by so doing I was sure I should have the approval of our Queen.'

Francis nodded. 'The Queen encourages her subjects to fight the Catholics in all places where they may encounter them. They say that in the Netherlands the Spanish Inquisitors burn alive and bury alive men and women who won't accept the Catholic Faith.'

'Ah yes,' went on John. 'Our Queen is right. Fight the Catholics here, there and everywhere, but keep England out of war. We soldiers may fight, and we have her approval –

but we fight for the Protestant cause and not in England's name. So I fought awhile for King Henri and, when peace was declared in France, I went to the Netherlands and there I fought once more against the Spaniards.'

'What adventures you must have had!' cried Alice.

John shrugged. 'I faced death now and then – but the recounting of such adventures becomes tedious. I liked not the Dutch Protestants. There was no joy in them. They thought me profane because I was not on my knees praying every hour of the day.'

'I trust you have not become profane, John,' said Alice in dismay.

'Nay,' cried John. 'I'll say my prayers but I want to enjoy life in between. So I left Holland and came to Scotland, and when I reached Edinburgh I presented myself at the King's Court, and with the letters which I had been given introduced myself to various intellectual personages. Alas, I am not the stuff of which courtiers are made, and I quickly saw that a life at Court would be as stifling to me as one here on the farm. So back home I came to make fresh plans.'

'Tell us of these plans,' said Francis.

'They are as yet unformed,' his brother told him. 'I have dreams of sailing the seas, visiting the new land which Christopher Columbus discovered. There must be great riches in such a land. I would like to sail there with a party of adventurers like myself and make that land as much a part of the Queen's dominions as our own Lincolnshire. I would like to take you, Francis, and you, Alice, with me. I would like to farm the land . . . call it . . . New England or some such name.'

Francis's eyes glowed as he listened to his brother, but Alice, watching, thought: Francis, your heart is here in the land which was our father's. As for myself I would never survive that long journey. But John is home and it is pleasant to dream.

*   *   *

37

A few weeks had passed. It was summer and the weather was exceptionally fine. Every day, it seemed, cousins and aunts and uncles came over to Willoughby to see John. Again and again John talked of his adventures. Alice kept the maids busy preparing pies and cakes for the visitors. There were picnics in the woods and merry dancing in the house and in the gardens.

Francis had shown John how the farm was prospering and how each month he was able to withdraw himself a little more from the charge of George Mettham.

'I manage the farm for you,' Francis told his brother; 'for do not forget that our father left it to you.'

'It should have been yours, brother,' John told him; 'and one day it shall be. When I have made my fortune, Francis, I shall make over the farm to you.'

'John, I must change the subject at once, for in a moment you will be offering me the farm now. It would be typical of your careless generosity – and what if I, in a weak moment, accepted it!'

'It is yours, Francis.'

'Nay, since you have determined to be an adventurer, it is better that you should not be a penniless one. Let us talk of other matters.'

'Very well,' said John. 'Yesterday when I was in the woods I found a charming spot. It was a glade pleasantly shaded by trees which grew in such a way as to make a roof. I thought I could build a little hut for myself from the boughs of trees, and there stay awhile in the heart of the forest.'

'John! You are tired of us already.'

'Nay, I could never be tired of you. But I have a desire to be alone. In my wanderings I have been filled with regret that I was not a more diligent scholar. I frittered away my time in dreaming, when I should have been learning my lessons, and now I discover myself to be a very ignorant man.'

'You are well versed in the arts of war.'

'You are wrong there. I know far too little. I have acquired a book during my travels. It is Machiavelli's *Art of Warre*. I wish to study that.'

'John, you are not seriously telling me that you are going to leave the farm for your hut in the woods?'

'Bear with me, brother. Let me choose my way of life, and when I have drawn all I want from my woodland solitude I will return to the farm.'

'You will return to your travels,' retorted Francis grimly.

'Francis.' John smiled affectionately at his brother. 'Take the farm,' he said; 'be thankful that you have a brother who is content to hand it to you. Leave me to my way of life. We cannot mould each other in the way we think he should go. Each man has to work out his own destiny.'

'John, what is your destiny?'

'That I cannot say, for I have yet to discover it. I know that it lies, not at the home farm, but somewhere across the sea.'

'I don't know what Alice will say when she hears you are going to desert us to live as a savage in the woods.'

'Do not fret about Alice. She quickly accepts what must be.'

'When do you leave for the hut in the woods?' asked Francis.

'Now,' answered John.

So he built himself a house among the trees, and there he lived on venison which he caught in the woods; and for water he used that of a stream which ran close to his improvised dwelling. Here he studied Marcus Aurelius and Machiavelli's *The Art of Warre*; and each day friends and relations rode over to the farm to see John and hear first-hand accounts of his adventures.

'What will he do next?' they cried. 'Whoever heard of

such nonsense! The idea of sleeping in the woods like a savage!'

'Perhaps he wishes to understand how savages live,' said Alice. 'He plans to go among savages and cultivate their land for the Queen, I believe.'

'We must bring him home again,' they declared. 'He has been far away from home and has many fine stories to tell; it is inconceivable that he should be allowed to hide himself in the woods. Leave it to us. We'll bring him out of the woods.'

Alice shook her head. 'You do not know John,' she said.

John was reading by the stream wearing nothing but his breeches, for he had washed his fine linen shirt and was sitting naked from the waist up in the sunshine. He yawned. Marcus Aurelius was a little boring; he even tired of reading Machiavelli. He was a man of action; he was one who wanted to learn through his own experiences.

Suddenly he heard the sound of a horse's hoofs, and as he sprang to his feet a dark-skinned man with great black eyes, elegantly dressed and riding one of the finest Arab horses John had ever seen, came into view.

'Good day to you,' said the man.

'Good day,' said John, his eyes kindling with admiration as he studied the horse and rider.

'I know you are John Smith,' said the rider. 'Myself, I am Theodore Palaloga, and I am rider to the Earl of Lincoln.'

'That accounts for your fine steed.'

'A beauty, eh?' Long dark fingers caressed the horse. 'I hear, John Smith, that you had many adventures in the Low Countries, and I would like to joust with you here in the forest . . . a little testing of our skill. You have fought many a battle and won honours therein. It may be that we are well matched.'

John could never resist a challenge and he went to the hut and brought out his lance; then he led the Italian to where his own horse was tethered.

It was a stimulating half-hour, for the men were evenly matched. At length Theodore Palaloga said he could stay no longer on this occasion but would return the next day, when they would continue their tests.

John was delighted, and all that day he found it difficult to return to the quiet contemplation of his books. He was forced to face the truth. He was no true hermit; he was a man of action. He was very impatient for the return of Palaloga, for the horsemanship this man displayed at the Earl's castle of Tattershall was well known for its skilfulness.

The next day the Italian arrived at the appointed time.

'John Smith,' he said, 'I have an invitation for you. When the Earl heard that we had met and were testing our skill he commanded me to ask you to return with me to Tattershall and there rest awhile. The Earl greatly desires to see us joust together.'

John shook his head. 'Thank the Earl on my behalf, but my duty lies here in the woods.'

Palaloga shrugged his shoulders and they continued with the joust; and the next day when he came the invitation was renewed and again refused. But after a week John found the offer irresistible. His friends were delighted, for it was they who had asked Palaloga to entice John from the woods.

For some weeks John stayed at Tattershall and delighted the family and guests of the Earl with his skill at horsemanship.

One day after the displays the company was gathered together at table, and conversation turned to the wars which were raging in Europe.

'The Turks are attacking Hungary again,' said the Earl. 'If something is not done to stop these barbarians, they will soon be in possession of the whole of Eastern Europe.'

John spoke then. He said slowly: 'Here in the Christian world Christians fight each other while, like a mighty sea encroaching on the shore, the Infidel creeps farther and farther into Christian territory. Why do Christians fight each other when the Infidel is at their door?'

All eyes were on John. Although he was but twenty years old and unused to sitting at the tables of the nobility, he could, without effort, dominate any society in which he found himself.

In that moment he was the dreamer in the Alford Grammar School, the boy who on the Louth road had met a pedlar and sold him his school books. He forgot the presence of the noble Earl, the good food and wine, the silver plate before him. John had come to a decision.

'I shall be leaving tomorrow for Europe,' he said. 'I am going to find some means of fighting the Turk.'

It was winter, and John with a few friends from his regiment sought the comfortable fire of a tavern parlour. He was once more in the Low Countries whither he had come after leaving the hospitality of the Earl of Lincoln. His ambition was to join those armies which fought against the Turks, but so far he had not been successful in doing so.

What he hoped to do was join up with troops on their way to Hungary and offer his services to the Duc de Mercœur who was general for the Emperor of Austria in that field.

He had talked to all his companions and had expressed his weariness of fighting against fellow Christian.

'I am not a man,' he declared, 'who concerns himself with dogma. The Catholics have one point of view; the Protestants another. But these Infidels are penetrating more and more into Christian countries. Christians should fight them instead of fighting each other. I wish I could find some of like mind who would travel with me to Hungary.'

He looked around the company. The regiment had been disbanded and they were free to go their various ways; but the fighting in the Low Countries was by no means over, and they would have no difficulty in joining up with other regiments.

One of the men present said: 'I share your views. I do not think it should be difficult to place yourself under Monsieur le Duc.'

John turned with interest to the man who had spoken. He was a Frenchman whose dainty manners had earned him the name of 'Milord of France' among the English soldiers. He had two friends who accompanied him everywhere he went, and was clearly, said the English soldiers, a member of the nobility. He was known as Monsieur de Preau; but then all dukes and counts were called Monsieur in France. They were sure that Monsieur de Preau was at least a count.

'How could this be done?' asked John.

'Oh, but it is simple.' Monsieur de Preau spread his hands. 'Monsieur le Duc de Mercœur has already left for Hungary, but Madame la Duchesse is well known to my family. I myself wish to join Monsieur le Duc in Hungary. I would I had the means to fit myself out for the journey. Ah, but there has been much strife in my country, and those of us who were once rich are no longer so. My friends here and I have decided to go to the Duchesse, tell her of our desire to join her husband, and then I am sure that readily will she furnish us with the means to do so. Monsieur Smith, it would give us the greatest pleasure if you would join us.'

'It seems an excellent idea,' cried John.

'Then allow me to present my friends to you. This is Monsieur Montferrat, Monsieur Cursell and Monsieur La Nélie. If you pack your trunks we could leave at once and together. Have no fear, Monsieur Smith, Madame la

Duchesse is only too happy to help those who would serve her husband.'

The night was dark when the ship which was carrying John and his new friends arrived at the port of Valéry-sur-Somme; there they were to leave the ship and travel overland to the château of the Duchesse de Mercœur.

John was looking forward to the meeting. It would be a pleasure for him to wear some of the fine clothes he had brought with him in his trunks. He had always been particular about his linen, and when Francis had laughed at his fastidiousness John had retorted that a well-dressed man most certainly received more respect than an ill-dressed one. There was more to it than that. John, when dressed in elegant ruff and fine linen, would have been mistaken for a member of the nobility; and he wanted the respect of his fellow men; it was deplorable that a man's garments should be of more consequence to some people than his character, but John was not a man who wanted to reform the world; he wanted to adapt himself to what was, and get the best out of it; and he felt confident that when he was well dressed he would have no difficulty in making a favourable impression on the Duchesse.

John stood on deck watching while his trunks were transferred to the small boat, and Monsieur de Preau was with him.

'But they are not handling our baggage with sufficient care!' cried Monsieur de Preau. 'I will go down to the boat and see that all is well handled. Wait here, Monsieur Smith, while I descend to the boat.'

Monsieur de Preau descended the ladder.

John called after him: 'But Cursell, Montferrat and La Nélie are already there.'

'Irresponsible,' called de Preau over his shoulder. 'All of them. Leave this to me.'

John peered down into the darkness as all his trunks,

containing his clothes and money, were lowered into the boat. He was astonished to see how little luggage the Frenchmen had, compared with his. He could just make out the boat bobbing on the water, and when all the luggage was aboard it John made to descend the ladder.

The Captain was before him. 'A moment, sir,' he said. 'I will first descend and see that all is well. I fear the boat is somewhat overloaded. I must test it.'

The captain descended and after a few minutes John saw the boat moving off into the darkness. He called after it: 'You have forgotten me. I, John Smith . . . I am not with you.'

'We have too heavy a load, sir,' the Captain called back. 'I will take this to the shore and come back for you.'

John stood on deck waiting. He was still waiting when morning came.

John paced up and down the deck; he was becoming more and more worried. He began to remember in detail the contents of his trunks.

'My brocade doublet,' he murmured to himself; 'the breeches of satin; the velvet cloak . . . my fine linen . . .' But in spite of his admiration of fine clothes he was most anxious when he thought of the purse of gold coins which was in one of the trunks.

As he waited there a soldier came on deck and asked what ailed him. John knew the man slightly for they had travelled together since leaving Holland. He was a Monsieur Curzianvere, a French soldier of fortune.

'I am alarmed,' John told him, 'because the captain went ashore several hours ago. He promised to return for me, but he has not done so.'

'It may well be that the high seas prevent his returning to us in the small boat. He'll be coming ere long, you'll see.'

John was relieved, and Monsieur Curzianvere went on:

'It is a glorious thing to return to one's native land. Soon I shall be in Brittany ... my home. Unfortunately my visit must be a secret one as I have been banished from France.'

'You run into danger by returning, my friend,' John warned him.

'Well I know it. But, for a glimpse of family and friends, who would not be ready to face a little danger?'

They were silent for a few moments when Curzianvere said: 'Our four rogues have left us, I hear.'

'Four rogues?'

'Messieurs de Preau, La Nélie, Cursell and Montferrat.'

'You call them rogues?'

Curzianvere lifted his shoulders. 'Did they not pose as members of the nobility? Did I not hear de Preau say he was a friend of the Duchesse de Mercœur? Friend of the Duchesse! He is the ne'er-do-well son of a lawyer, I believe. As for the others they are rogues like himself. What ails you? Have I said something to upset you?'

'Upset me!' cried John. 'These four so-called *noblemen* have gone ashore with my baggage ... all I possess ... and they have been gone some hours. What a fool I have been! They are nothing more than thieves. I must go after them at once. Why, the captain must be in league with them.'

'Tell me how they managed to lay hands on your baggage.'

John told him. The old soldier shook his head, and said: 'It is an old trick. Would I had known what evil they were up to. We must get ashore at once.'

'How so?'

'The captain went with them, you say, and he has taken the only boat. Do not be impatient. The captain will return. He cannot desert his ship for the sake of your baggage.'

'Those thieves will have got clear away with it while I am a prisoner here,' fumed John.

Other passengers joined them. 'Where is the captain?' they demanded. 'Why do we remain here?'

John and Curzianvere explained.

'I guessed those four rogues were hatching some plot,' said another French soldier. 'I know de Preau well. He ran away from his father's house in Mortagne. He wanted to be an adventurer. He'd rather rob his fellow men on the road and the high seas than in the courts of law. Ah, my friend, so you were caught, eh? Come, tell us what was in those trunks of yours.'

John turned impatiently away and, when someone shouted that the boat was coming back, he ran to the ladder and as the captain came aboard roughly seized his arm.

'Where are those rogues?' he demanded, shaking the man to and for. 'Where are my trunks?'

'Sir . . . sir,' cried the captain, 'your trunks are safe with your friends. I will explain . . .'

'Where have you been these many hours?' demanded Curzianvere.

'The sea was too rough for the small boat. I could not return before.'

'And my baggage?'

'As I told you it is with your friends. They have gone to Amiens, where they wish you to join them with all speed that you may travel with them to Picardy and the Duchesse de Mercœur.'

John waited for no more. He released the captain and hurried down the ladder to the boat. As he stepped into it he saw that Curzianvere was beside him.

'I wish to speak with you,' said the old soldier.

'Well?' said John as they rowed to the shore.

'I am an older man than you. I pray you do nothing hasty. Pause and consider.'

'There is one thing I wish to do,' cried John, 'and that is put my fingers about the throat of de Preau and strangle

47

the life out of him before I recover my trunks.'

'It would be unwise. You would then have committed murder, and the recovery of your finery would do you little good. I burn with shame at the scurvy way in which my countrymen have treated you. I would make amends.'

'I would never dream of holding against a country the conduct of four of its subjects. Young I may be, but I trust I am not such a fool as that.'

'Listen to my advice. Do not go to Amiens. They have said they are going there, only to lay a false scent.'

'I guessed it.'

'I heard it said that de Preau is a native of Mortagne. I must pass through Mortagne on my way to Brittany. Let us travel together. I'll warrant you are a little poorer than you were this time yesterday.'

'I have nothing but a coin or two. I should be a drag on you.'

'But I have said I wish to make amends for the ill conduct of four Frenchmen, and although I have little myself I will share it with you.'

As they stepped ashore John swung his fine cloak about his shoulders. It was now the only valuable article of clothing he possessed.

He hesitated. He had nothing more to lose.

'I fear you hesitate to trust a Frenchman,' said Curzianvere.

'I am a wiser man now,' said John, and his anger was smothered by his resilient nature. 'I thank you for your generous offer with all my heart. Come . . . le us be on our way to Mortagne.'

It was many days later when they came to the little town of Mortagne. John had sold his cloak to help buy food, for much as he prized fine clothes his independence meant more to him. They did most of their walking by night as Curzianvere was in great fear of being recognized as an exile for whom imprisonment and possibly death would follow if it were discovered that he had come home. They passed safely through Dieppe and Honfleur, and at length they came to the town of Mortagne.

Curzianvere dared not enter the place, but John could not suppress his impatience to do so, and Curzianvere said he would wait outside the town while John explored the place for any sign of de Preau and his friends.

John made his way to a tavern and sat there refreshing himself for an hour or so while he listened to the conversation about him. It did occur to him to ask if any knew the whereabouts of the four, but since his foreign looks attracted attention he thought it wiser to say nothing, for it would very soon reach the ears of the men he had come to seek if he were to mention his desire to meet them again.

The town was small and, by amazing good fortune, as he came out of the tavern in its main street he came face to face with de Preau and his three friends.

They looked through John as though they had never seen him before.

'I have come to collect my baggage,' said John.

'What is this?' asked de Preau.

'The baggage you stole. Come, I have little time to spare. I want it . . . now.'

'Clearly a madman,' said de Preau turning to his companions with a shrug. 'Poor fellow, let us leave him to his delusions.'

John caught his arm. 'I want my baggage. Come, where is it? You four rogues stole it from me.'

De Preau turned to the others. 'Have you ever seen this man before?' he asked.

'Never in my life,' cried La Nélie, and the others concurred while a few people had come out of the tavern to listen.

'A crazy foreigner,' said Cursell.

'He should be put in chains,' added Montferrat. 'Who knows, he may be dangerous.'

There was a murmur in the crowd. 'It is a dangerous lunatic. What next! Our streets are unsafe for the women and children.'

John was aware that he, a foreigner in a strange town, was the centre of a hostile group.

De Preau was smiling at him cynically.

'My dear fellow,' he whispered, 'your wisest plan would be to get out of this place ... with all speed. Unless, of course, you would like to pass a spell in chains with the lunatics.'

A few years earlier John would have struck de Preau a blow in the face and insisted on the truth of his own story. He had learned a great deal in a very short time. Anger was futile, particularly when the odds were all against one.

He turned from de Preau and pushed his way through the crowd.

Oddly enough, they let him go. They were many; he was alone; yet, even in such circumstances, he was not a man with whom many would wish to pick a quarrel.

He made his way with all speed out of the town and back to Curzianvere who was waiting for him.

When Curzianvere heard of the encounter he was perplexed.

'I must continue my journey,' he said, 'and we must part. You will wish to remain here, and before I go I will give you the address of a friend I have in Mortagne. Go to this friend. Say I have sent you, and tell him how four of our countrymen have cheated you. He will lodge you in his house. His name is Monsieur Colombier.'

John listened to the instructions and took a last farewell of the old soldier, of whom, during their journeyings together he had grown very fond.

* * *

As soon as Curzianvere had left him, John made his way back to the town of Mortagne and quickly found the house to which his friend had directed him.

It was a somewhat large house set back from the road in a pleasant garden, and when John knocked at the door an elderly maidservant opened it.

John bowed and asked if he might have a word with Monsieur Colombier.

'That is something you cannot do,' said the servant.

John said: 'I come from an old friend of his. Pray take me to him. It is important.'

The servant hesitated; then he said: 'Please to come in. You cannot see Monsieur Colombier, I can tell you that. But I will see what can be done.'

She conducted him into a well-furnished room which was very clean, he noticed, and indicated a stool on which he sat. It was some minutes later when the door was opened and another woman came into the room. She was a few years older than John – possibly in her middle or late twenties – but she was decidedly handsome.

'You have come to see my husband,' she said. 'You have evidently not heard that he has been dead for some time.'

John's face fell, for Monsieur Curzianvere had led him to believe that he could expect hospitality from Monsieur Colombier, and he had hoped to hide himself in Mortagne until he had recovered his baggage.

The woman had approached him and stood looking at him; he was shabbily dressed and at first she thought he was some sort of beggar; but she had quickly seen from his manner that there was nothing of the beggar about this young man. He was, if not handsome in a conventional way, extremely personable. She liked his clear and candid blue eyes; she noticed that his curly hair was almost golden in the light from the window.

'Pray do not look so disturbed,' she said, 'if there is

anything I can do to help I will gladly do it. Tell me on what business you have come to see my husband. Since his death I have dealt with his affairs.'

John told her the story of his lost baggage and his friendship with Curzianvere.

'Monsieur Curzianvere was a close friend of my husband,' cried Madame Colombier. 'He was greatly distressed at the time of his exile. I know it would be the wish of my husband that I should offer you help since Monsieur Curzianvere asks it. You shall stay here as long as you wish – and now I believe you must be hungry, so I will send my servant to prepare food for you. A room shall be made ready for you, because you will wish to stay in the town for some time.'

'You are very kind.'

'I am obeying my husband's wishes, I know,' she said demurely. She lowered her eyes. Perhaps she thought they might appear too bright, too brimming with hope and promise for one so recently widowed. John did not notice. He had had little to do with women.

Life in the Colombier household was luxurious, and there was nothing which seemed too much for Madame Colombier to do for her visitor. She would go into the town by day to try to discover news of the four thieves, but since they had met John in the town they seemed to have made themselves scarce. John himself went out only after dark. He knew that if he wished to catch the four men he must not make his presence known in the town. In the meantime it was pleasant to live in such a charming house with such a delightful hostess.

She seemed to delight in discovering what he most enjoyed, and she had a way, which seemed to John almost uncanny, of bringing his weaknesses to light.

'You have lost your clothes,' she said to him on the day after his arrival. 'They were stolen by Frenchmen. Now, I have certain garments of my husband's; I never sold them. They were of his best. I should like you to take your choice from them.'

'I could not think of it!' declared John.

'But you must. Frenchmen stole your trunks, so please let a French woman do a little to repair the damage. Come, I will show you the clothes.'

John could not but admire the fine velvet cloak, the doublet with the slashed sleeves, the lace ruffs. They were a little more elaborate perhaps than he, as an Englishman, considered good taste; but they fascinated him.

She saw his eyes gleam, and laughing, picked up the cloak and flung it round his shoulders. 'It is a beautiful cloak,' she whispered. 'Such swing! I remember my husband, dancing with me, in it.' Her eyes clouded but she was soon merry again. 'We danced like this...' And she took his hand and twirled on her toes. She began to hum a tune and John found that he was dancing with her. They held hands and bowed; and she was flushed with pleasure. She stopped suddenly. 'But this is shocking. I ... a widow ... to dance thus! Come, let us forget my frivolity.'

'Nonsense,' said John. 'It clearly does you good to dance.'

'It does ... to dance with you,' she told him.

John smiled at what he thought of as French flattery. He continually had to remind himself while he was in this house that English manners were a little rough compared with those of the French, and that it was a French custom to be what in English ears sounded over-fulsome.

She turned from him and picked up the doublet with the slashed sleeves and held it up against him. He felt her hands on his shoulders and her beautiful eyes were lifted to his.

'I pray you,' she said, 'put on these clothes. I would see you in them.'

John hesitated. Something warned him not to take the clothes, and yet his vanity assured him that it was folly to leave them mouldering in drawers.

He picked them up and went to his bedroom to put them on.

He had scarcely had time to do so when she came to him.

She seemed breathless with excitement.

'But they suit you perfectly . . . John,' she said. She came near to him, and again he was conscious of her proximity. 'You must keep them,' she went on. 'They are yours.'

'But they were your husband's . . .'

'He would be glad,' she said . . . 'as I am, that you should have what were his now that he is no longer here to enjoy them.'

Then she stood on tiptoe and kissed John's lips, and when she caught him to her in a fierce and hungry embrace, John found himself responding. She was passionate and experienced, and he felt a great willingness to place his hand in hers that she might lead him to new adventures hitherto undreamed of.

John was feeling a little bewildered during the days which followed. He had not realized until now that he could have desires such as these he had heard his fellow soldiers discuss. To John there had been one ever-present dream, which had dominated his life, and although at this time it was shapeless and he himself was not even sure what form it would eventually take, it was constantly with him.

Vaguely he believed that he was going to bring some good to England; that two, three and four hundred years hence people would say: 'John Smith did that.' And that would be a good and honourable act for England.

He had been a child when men such as Drake and Hawkins had inspired Englishmen; he intended that his name should be linked with theirs. He knew the opportunity would present itself one day, and when it did he wished to be ready to take it.

Women had never entered his dreams; he had always believed that they never would. And now here he was, living in the house of a widow who delighted in him and he in her.

It had been significant when he put on Monsieur Colombier's doublet and cloak. Temporarily he forgot the reason for his coming to Mortagne. In that strange and bewildering week he even dreamed of staying for ever in this house and occupying in it the place once held by Madame Colombier's husband.

As for Madame Colombier, she seemed to grow young again. She was a passionate woman and she had long been emotionally starved. She had wanted a lover and would have taken one but for her fear of gossip in a town where everyone knew his neighbour's business. The coming of John seemed a heaven-sent opportunity. Madame Colombier was happy, and so grateful that there was nothing she would not do to gratify the whim of the handsome young Englishman.

One night when they lay together talking in whispers (for she was anxious that her servants should not know that John was her lover) she said: 'John, I would like you to stay here for ever.'

He was startled but he said nothing.

'Why should you not?' she asked. 'I have money. We could live comfortably here. You are a Protestant, I am a Catholic, but we need not let that stand between us. John, you must never go away.'

Her lips were close to his ear; her warm desirous body pressed close to his. John was twenty years old; this was his first love affair; and with his mistress in his arms he thought it might be very pleasant to live for ever in this felicitous state.

*　　*　　*

John awoke in the early hours of the morning. He was cold with terror. He had dreamed that a trap was closing about him and that once it completely enveloped him there would be no escape.

He saw that he was in the familiar room. Madame Colombier lay beside him; he could see the outline of her voluptuous form and, instead of filling him with pleasure, it repelled him because he was only half awake and the nightmare was near.

Here was the trap: This room, this woman with her entwining arms and her unsatiable desire for his body.

What has happened to me? John asked himself. What am I doing here in the house of a dead man, sleeping in his bed, taking what is his?

He knew that he must leave as soon as possible.

'What is it, John?' Madame Colombier stretched out a warm plump arm and was pulling him down to her sensuous embrace; he felt his will being sapped and heard a voice within him asking him why he should be such a fool as to throw away a chance of marriage with a rich widow.

But the call of destiny was stronger than any sensual desire, and disengaging himself, he said: 'I should be on my way.'

She sat up, startled out of her sleepy state. 'What do you mean, John?'

He turned to her and, leaning on his elbow, stroked her long black hair back from her brow.

'I have dallied too long.'

Her eyes were reproachful, but he went on: 'And you have been too good to me.'

'How can one be too good to a loved one?'

'You deserve someone who can make you happier than I ever could. You should marry a worthy citizen of Mortagne. Your period of mourning is clearly over. I should never make a good husband.'

'You are wrong, John. You would make me the best

possible husband because you are the only one I want.'

'There is a torment within me,' said John, 'which would never let me rest. I should leave you to sail the seas. My dear, you are not a woman who should be left.'

She was disturbed and wept a little. He comforted her as best he could but he could not give her what she needed: His promise that he would not go away.

She saw that his mind was made up. Madame Colombier was a practical woman. It was useless to try to keep him when he did not want to stay. A reluctant lover was a poor one.

She was grieved, because she had found him charming – virile yet innocent, masterful yet humble. She would be sorry to say goodbye to her Englishman; but seeing that he was determined to go, she fitted him out for a journey; she embraced him warmly, and when he had left the house he found a full purse in his pocket.

He turned to look back at the town of Mortagne and remembered the reason for his coming there. He had completely forgotten his desire to bring the four rascals to justice.

He laughed at himself. That episode was over. It was imperative that he escape from the velvet bondage in which the passionate Madame Colombier would enmesh him. He must congratulate himself on his strength of mind; he must forget about his trunks. He would now make his way to the coast and endeavour to find a boat which would take him eastward to fight the Turk.

That winter was bitterly cold; the winds sweeping across France from the North and East brought heavy snow and many roads were impassable.

John had visited several of the Britanny ports in search of a ship, but his search had been fruitless.

The money which Madame Colombier had given him

was gone and he was down to his last sou. Often he would gaze across the sea and think of Francis and Alice with plenty to eat and a good roof over their heads in the Willoughby farmhouse which was his.

He should go home, if he did not want to suffer hardship such as this. Francis had never gone without a meal in his life. As his guardian would have said: Francis is a wise man; and you are a fool.

There would be many to agree with his guardian. The prosperous farm, in the kitchen of which was meat and drink in plenty, belonged to John; yet he wandered through France weary and hungry. Why?

'One day,' he said to himself, 'I shall find my way to the Turk.'

As he remembered the games he used to play with the Bertie boys, it suddenly occurred to him that the estates of their French companions were in Brittany and could not be very far from where he now was. If he made his way to the Comte de Plouha he would be able to get help which would enable him to go to Hungary or some place where he could join a regiment to fight the Turk; so he decided to travel with as much speed as possible to the estate of the Comte de Plouha.

He asked the way.

'The Comte de Plouha, Monsieur? Ah, you want the château de Tonquedec. It lies a few kilometres south of St Malo. Between St Malo and Dinan. You could reach it in a day if you had a horse.'

'And since I have no horse, and only two legs, what then?'

'The weather is not good for travelling, Monsieur. And the way lies through the forest.'

John set out and had not gone very far when the snow began to fall. He was blinded by the flakes and as the wind howled and he floundered on he found himself knee-deep in drifts.

He plunged forward, however, deeper into the forest, and although he had no notion where he was, he believed that he must eventually find some human habitation. No one could deny him shelter in such weather, he was sure, and his one desire was to find a house.

He was very tired and seeing a tree trunk lying in the snow he went to this, promising himself a few minutes' rest. Only when he sat down did he know how weary he was. He remembered that during the last days he had eaten scarcely anything.

I must not stay here, John said to himself. It would be dangerous to do so. I must find shelter.

His limbs were numb with the cold and to his horror, when he tried to rise, he found that his legs crumpled under him and he fell back clutching the tree trunk. He managed to hoist himself upon this and lay there, completely exhausted.

It began to snow again; John was not aware of this for he had drifted into exhausted sleep.

When he eventually regained his senses, his limbs felt more comfortable, and then he saw that the snow had made a blanket about him. In terror he tried to rise but he had not the strength to do so; and in a few revealing moments he realized what was happening. Weak and exhausted, far from other men, at the mercy of the weather, he would lie there and be frozen to death and this would be the end of his dreams. He might as well have stayed at home and become a farmer; he might at this moment be in the warm and loving arms of his French mistress. He had escaped from the life his father had planned for him; he had left the comfortable home offered by Madame Colombier. For what? That he might die in the snow.

He did not believe it. He would not believe it. He was so sure of his destiny.

Then John again slipped into unconsciousness and the

snow-flakes fluttered down upon him like white butterflies
... mounting and multiplying.

When John next opened his eyes he was lying before a
warm fire, and a man and woman were bending over him.
The man was chafing his frozen limbs and the woman held
a bowl of hot liquid to his lips.

'Where am I?' asked John; the man and woman shook
their heads, for he had spoken in English; but he quickly
remembered where he was and asked the question in
French.

'We found you in the snow,' said the man. 'Another
half-hour and that would have been the end of you, my
friend.'

The woman said softly: 'So we carried you here into our
house and you are already recovering.'

'My grateful thanks are due to you,' said John. He was
becoming more and more conscious of the poverty of the
place in which he found himself. It was little more than a
hut; he guessed that the man and woman who had taken
pity on him were Breton peasants.

'What we did for you we'd do for a dog, would we not,
Armand?' said the woman.

The man repeated: 'Another half-hour, did I say ... ?
Another quarter of an hour ... and you'd have been dead.'

'I must tell you ...' began John, 'that I am a poor wanderer. I have been without food for days because I lacked
the money to buy it.'

The man nodded. 'These are hard times,' he said.

John lay back on the straw which made his bed, and
closed his eyes; but the woman was kneeling beside him
urging him to drink the broth.

He smiled at her, and the response was so warm and
friendly that she reminded him of someone; he was too
weary to remember whom.

*   *   *

Later he did remember.

The man had gone out to snare a hare or a rabbit for the pot, and John was left alone with the woman.

'You need plenty of good hot food that you may recover your strength,' she told him.

'I shall be all right as soon as I am on my feet again,' John replied.

'You are a strong man. I see that.' She smiled and came a little nearer.

'I am anxious,' he told her, 'because you have done a great deal for me and I have no means of repaying you for your kindness.'

'You must not talk of repaying us,' she said; and again he was conscious of that warm smile. There was no doubt in his mind now of whom she reminded him. It was Madame Colombier, and his recent experiences with that lady gave him a hint of the intentions of the Breton peasant woman. She went on: 'It gives us pleasure to have saved you from freezing to death. Stay with us awhile. There are ways in which you could help my husband . . . and me.'

John stood up and walked about the hut.

'You should not tire yourself,' said the woman softly. 'Remember you have suffered an ordeal.'

'Madame,' said John, 'you and your husband have saved my life, and my thanks are due to you. However, I cannot rest here but must be on my way. I am not travelling in France for my health or for a holiday. I was going to join the army of the Duc de Mercœur when I fell in with rogues who stole all I had. I was travelling to the château of the Comte de Plouha when I was overcome by the weather. So you see, Madame, I must, as soon as my health permits, continue my journey.'

The woman was a little startled by his mention of the Comte de Plouha, and her manner changed. But John was a little wiser than he had been before his encounter with Madame Colombier, and he believed that the woman would soon overcome her awe of a man whom she now knew to have connections with the nobility.

As soon as her husband returned John explained to him that he wished to be on his way and that he believed that if he could reach the estates of the Comte de Plouha, his old friend would give him clothes and money that he might continue his journey.

'You would do well to rest for a day or so, Monsieur,' was the peasant's advice. 'You would not have fallen a victim to the weather if you had been well nourished. Stay here awhile and, if you get what you think you may from Monsieur le Comte, you can repay us. If not . . . we shall still be pleased to share what we have with you.'

John thanked the man warmly and decided to stay for another day and night.

It was close in the hut. John lay on his straw listening to the mingled breathing of the man and woman on another side of the hut. He knew that the woman was awake and that she was thinking of him.

She had already betrayed her feelings, and John was filled with misgivings. The weather was still bad but he knew that he must not stay another day and night in the peasants' hut.

He lay thinking of Madame Colombier, her warm welcome, her almost overpowering devotion. She had been a widow for a long time, and she was a woman who was not meant for widowhood. But this peasant woman? She had a husband. But he himself was younger and perhaps his very strangeness attracted her.

There was a movement from their side of the room.

The woman had risen and he believed that in a few moments she would come stealthily towards him.

John felt the sweat on his brow.

'Hello there! Hello there!' he called.

The peasant rose from his straw. 'What ails you?'

'I thought I heard someone moving about,' said John.

'I rose to get me a drink of water,' said the woman. 'What a light sleeper you are!'

'It's his weak state,' said her husband, and he settled down again on his straw.

John lay still in the darkness.

In the morning he said to the peasant and his wife: 'I can stay no longer. I must be on my way this day. Rest assured that if it is in my power to repay you in some small way for what you did for me, I shall not forget.'

The woman said: 'When you have seen Monsieur le Comte you must come back to see us. We shall welcome you.'

Her inviting eyes held his, and John said, smiling full at her now that he knew he was about to put a great distance between them: 'I shall not forget.'

The next day the weather had improved although it was still bitterly cold. The snow had stopped but lay frozen underfoot. John had come through Dinan and was on the road to Tonquedec when he saw a man in rags coming towards him. A beggar? wondered John, and hoped not, for he had no money to give the man. Beggar or not, thought John, he cannot be poorer than I.

'Bitter weather, Monsieur,' said the man as he approached.

'Bitter indeed,' answered John; and there was something in the man's voice and posture which seemed familiar to him.

John studied the man. His clothes had once been good and he wore a sword at his side; it would seem that the man, like himself, had fallen on evil times.

Then John noticed that there was something familiar about the clothes. He had certainly seen them before. Why, that doublet was one of his own. That jacket was his second-best fawn velvet. Could it be a mistake? Not in the case of a man who was vain about his clothes. John would know that coat anywhere – although it did look as though it had had years of hard wear since he had last worn it.

The man gave a little cry of dismay as he recognized John at that very moment when John recognized him.

'Cursell!' cried John. 'So I have caught you at last. Where are the others?'

'I know not,' said Cursell.

John had drawn his sword.

'I pray you do not be rash,' begged Cursell. 'I have parted company with de Preau and the rest of them. I wished to have no part in their schemes.'

'But you took part in the plot to rob me and are now wearing my clothes,' retorted John. 'I swore vengeance for all you and your confederates have made me suffer, and I'll have it. On guard!'

'Help!' screamed Cursell. 'I am attacked. Murder! Help!' But he drew his sword.

John was an expert swordsman, and so was Cursell; but both were physically weak and for some time they fought on while people from the nearby villages, hearing Cursell's cries, came hurrying to the scene.

John's skill proved to be the greater, and he it was who got in a thrust which sent Cursell to the ground. John stood over him, while the onlookers closed in round the combatants, and one man cried out: 'This is a foreigner. What does he here attacking a Frenchman?'

For a few moments the mob looked angry, but John faced them boldly and said: 'This man is one of a party who stole my property. The clothes that rogue is wearing belong to me. I have been seeking the gang and now I have found one of them.'

'He lies,' said another.

But Cursell, to John's astonishment, cried out: 'He speaks truth. He was robbed by men whose company I shared. But I wanted none of their villainy. They shared his money. I had none of it. His anger is just. It is unfortunate that it should be wreaked on me and not on the others who deserve it.'

'But you are wearing my clothes!' said John.

'My share – all they would let me have, and the only clothes I have now to face the winter.'

John laughed suddenly and, turning to the crowd, he said: 'Am I near Tonquedec, the estate of the Comte de Plouha?'

'A few kilometres on you will find St Malo,' he was told. 'There is Tonquedec.'

'Then,' cried John, 'I shall consider this little matter settled. I have seen the blood of one of the rogues who cheated me. I'll let that suffice.'

The crowd stood back to let him pass, and he went on his way to the estate of his old friend.

As John rode south after his pleasant stay at Tonquedec he travelled like a man of quality. The French friends of his boyhood had not forgotten him; they asked innumerable questions about the Berties and life in England; they were delighted to see him and would have made him their guest for as long as he wished to stay; but John did not forget his real aim in coming to Europe, which was to join the armies fighting against the Turk. 'Very well,' said the Comte de Plouha, 'your best plan is to make your way south to Marseilles. There you will most certainly find a ship sailing to Italy; from there you can make your way to Hungary and Transylvania which I fear are greatly troubled by the Turk.'

So they had fitted him up in a grand manner, and John, delighted to be well dressed again, had set out in good heart to continue his journey, but before making his way to the coast he did not forget the peasants who had befriended him.

Finding a ship was not easy, and he had been in

Marseilles for some days, haunting the waterfront hoping for a passage.

One day as he loitered there he saw a band of men, footsore and obviously weary, coming towards him.

He paused to look at them, and their leader came to him and asked him if this were the port of Marseilles.

John said it was.

'We are to meet a ship here which is taking us to Rome,' John was told.

'You mean you know of a ship that is sailing to Italy?'

'Indeed yes. We have come far to join a ship which will shortly be here.'

'Do you think I might obtain a passage on it?'

'I doubt it not, if you have the money to pay for it.'

John's spirits were lifted. Here seemed a chance of reaching Italy, which could be the first step on the way to Hungary.

Others of the party crowded about him.

The leader said: 'He wishes to join us on our journey to Rome.'

'He does not look like a pilgrim,' said someone in the crowd.

'Ah,' said the leader, 'there are pilgrims of all sorts. Suffice it that he wishes to go with us to Rome and there receive the Pope's blessing.'

John decided to be at the waterfront early next day, and when he arrived there was the ship and some of the pilgrims were going aboard her. John found the captain and had little difficulty in getting a passage when he showed that he had money with which to pay for it.

That day John sailed from Marseilles.

They had scarcely left the French coast when a gale arose, and the captain was forced to take the ship into Toulon harbour.

One of the pilgrims approached John and said: 'What is your country?'

'My country is England,' he replied.

The man stared at him in surprise and then went away muttering.

The high winds made it impossible to leave Toulon for some hours, and during that time John was aware of the strange looks which several of the pilgrims were sending his way.

The man who had spoken to him previously approached him with a companion.

'You say you are English,' said the second man.

'It is true.'

'But that is a land of heretics. The greatest heretic alive is your Queen.'

'The Queen of my country is the greatest Queen in the world.'

The men looked at each other. 'She is the Scarlet Woman,' said one to the other. 'She is a Huguenot or at least applauds the Huguenots. She gives them shelter in her land. They escape from justice to England where they and their wickedness are welcome.'

John said coolly: 'I cannot allow you to insult my Queen and country.' His hand was on his sword hilt. But at that moment there was a shout from the deck.

'The wind has changed. We're away.'

Then the two pilgrims seemed to forget John. They left him and hurried to join their companions on deck, while John, equally forgetful of them, stood watching the coast slip away. They were on their way and he was already a little nearer to his goal.

The wind had risen with sudden fury and the Captain once more regretfully refused to put out to sea. They had been hugging the coast and were not far from Nice when he decided to cast anchor in the shelter of the small island of St Mary.

John listened to the talk of the pilgrims. 'Why does the Lord send such storms to prevent us making our journey? Are we not making a pilgrimage to Rome?'

'It would seem that the devil seeks to prevent our getting there.'

'Nay, 'tis nothing to do with the Devil. God is angry with us.'

'For what reason?' The pilgrims were astonished. 'Are we not devoting much time and expense to the pilgrimage? God would indeed be unreasonable if He were angry with us on that score.'

'Yet we must look for a reason.'

Many pairs of fanatical eyes had come to rest on John. 'Is he a member of the Holy Catholic Church?'

'Is he not a Huguenot – or as near as makes no difference? He is an Englishman and serves a Queen who is the Scarlet Woman.'

'It is the answer. He is the reason for God's anger. While we shelter him we shall be obliged to suffer the anger of God.'

John had caught snatches of their conversation and he now saw that several of them were coming towards him.

'Huguenot!' shouted one.

John's fingers were on his sword hilt.

'Pirate!' cried another.

'I am no pirate.'

'You are an Englishman. All Englishmen are pirates.'

John drew his sword. 'I am at your service,' he cried, 'ready to defend the honour of Englishmen.'

But he was one and they were many; they closed about him and his sword was sent spinning out of his hand. He was sent sprawling to the ground.

'Hey!' cried one of the pilgrims. 'Forget not that we are on a holy pilgrimage. Let us not soil our hands with this man's blood, pirate though he may be.'

'What! You'd let him stay among us, when God has

clearly shown us His anger with us for taking him aboard a pilgrim ship?'

'Nay,' cried the first man. 'Overboard with him.'

John was lifted high in the air. In a few seconds he hit the seething sea.

There was a shout of joy from the pilgrims.

'Let the sea have him. Let him die. So should perish all heretics.'

For a while John believed that this was the end, that he had survived so many adventures only to die before he had come near to achieving his purpose. Then his spirit rose in defiance of the odds against him. Had he not always won when he had swum in races with the Berties or Francis? As he had beaten them, so he would beat the sea now.

He remembered that the island of St Mary was not far distant; he struck out in the direction where he knew it to be.

Then began his battle with the wind and the waves. His cloak impeded him, but it was a fine cloak and he was loth to lose it. The cloak itself seemed a challenge to him. He was going to reach the island with it; he had left all his other possessions behind him on the pilgrim ship; he was not going to be robbed again.

He laughed inwardly as he battled through the waves.

For some time he lay on the beach exhausted. It was not yet dark and he could see the grassy slope of land which led down to the water. He drew himself away from the encroaching sea which washed about his ankles as though it were reluctant to release him.

He was reminded of that occasion when he had almost fallen a victim to the snow-storm, and had been rescued by the peasant and his wife.

But then he had been weak; now he was physically

strong, for his sojourn at the château de Tonquedec had had the effect of nursing him back to health. Yet his position was similar. He had by great good fortune escaped death, but he was cast up on an uninhabited island without food or money; the clothes he was wearing were probably ruined by sea water. It was the infelicitous month of March; he could not take off his clothes to dry them; the storm was still raging violently; and there was no hut or human habitation on the tiny island.

He scrambled up to a clump of bushes and took off the cloak which had so impeded his progress. He could see that it would never be the same again. The velvet was spoiled and the colours of the embroidery had run into each other.

What next? he asked himself. How long can I stay here without food in this vile weather?

With the coming of darkness the storm abated and John lay stretched out by the bushes wondering what the future held for him.

He considered, as he had done on other occasions, that he might be in a warm bed at this moment beside the loving Madame Colombier. Then he fell to thinking of the peasant woman; and he wondered whether there was some quality in him which was attractive to women, or whether these adventures might have happened to any man.

All through that long night he was without sleep. He thought often of Alice and Francis and pictured them in the years to come at the farmhouse, talking of him by the fireside on winter evenings – John, the brother who had dreamed vague dreams of greatness, and who had disappeared somewhere in the lands beyond the seas.

But even that night could not last for ever, and as John watched the sun rise in splendour he saw a sight which delighted him even more. Two ships lay at anchor close to the island. Like the pilgrim ship they must have taken refuge there from the storm.

John seized his cloak, exultantly congratulating himself on that vanity which had insisted that he save it. Frantically he waved and continued to do so until, after great despair that he would never be seen, a boat was being lowered and its destination was soon seen to be the island.

They were answering his signal for help. Once more his life was to be miraculously preserved.

After he had been given warm food and a change of clothes, John was brought before the Captain of the ship.

'Who are you?' asked the Captain. 'And how did you come to be on the island of St Mary?'

John explained.

'And how did you come to be in France?'

'I am on my way to Hungary or Transylvania,' John answered, 'where I hope to be allowed to attach myself to some regiment; I have been unfortunate. I was robbed of all my possessions at St Valéry, after which I made my way to some friends at St Malo.'

'That is my home. What friends were these?'

'The Comte de Plouha.'

'But he is a friend of mine.'

'I pray you tell me your name.'

'It is de la Roche.'

'I remember now. I have heard the Comte mention your name.'

The Captain was delighted. 'I will do all in my power to help a friend of the Comte's. Unfortunately I cannot take you to Hungary, for I am bound for Barbary. Come with us on this trip and, when we return you can disembark on the coast of Italy and thence make your way to Hungary.'

'How can I thank you?' cried John.

'I would make some reparations for the infamous conduct of my compatriots,' said the Captain.

And as they set sail John marvelled once more at his escape from death, and began to believe that it was no idle dream of his that a great future lay in wait for him.

III

The Three Turks' Heads

There had been many adventures since Captain de la Roche had rescued John from St Mary's Island. The trip John had made on the Captain's ship proved very profitable; not only had he learned a great deal about the management of ships but when they had been involved in successful action against a Venetian vessel, Captain de la Roche had insisted on John's taking a share of the prize.

Thus when John had landed in Italy on his way to Transylvania he had been the richer by the equivalent of some five hundred pounds. This was riches indeed, and John could not resist the temptation to see a little of the world. In Italy he had met his old friends the Berties and discovered that their father had died and that Robert was now Lord Willoughby; they asked him to join them, but John was still set upon fighting the Turk.

He travelled to Styria where he met Lord Ebersbaught and through this noble gentleman he made the acquaintance of Baron Kisell who, having discovered something of John's skill and experience in the Low Countries, immediately recommended him to Colonel Meldritch, a nobleman from Transylvania who held a high position in the armies of Rudolph, Emperor of Austria and King of Hungary.

Meldritch was delighted to make use of the services of a man such as John, and at last John had achieved his ambition to fight against the Turks who, at this time, were in possession of great tracts of Transylvania.

The Turks at this time had had such outstanding success that alarm was fast spreading throughout Christendom.

John felt at last that he was engaged in worth-while war-fare. The wars between Christians had seemed to him a futile waste of men when the menace from the Infidel was so acute. Already Transylvania was almost all in their hands and Hungary was threatened. John visualizing the fall of the Austrian Empire asked himself how Italy, Switzerland and those Christians who were fighting each other over matters of doctrine could be so blind as not to see the dangers which beset them.

He gave himself up to this warfare with all the enthusiasm of which he was capable, and thus he soon brought himself to the notice of his superior officers. He devised a method of signalling, by means of torches, to sections of the army which were cut off from each other. He played a trick on the enemy by having bags of gunpowder attached, at regular intervals, to thirty lines of cord about two hundred yards long. These cords were attached to posts some five feet high and when it was dark torches were applied to the gunpowder bags so that an impression was given that hundreds of muskets were being fired. This so alarmed the enemy that they blindly rushed to the attack leaving their camp undefended. This trick proved very advantageous to Meldritch's army.

After this John's name began to be mentioned among the leaders of the armies and it was considered fitting that this ingenious Englishman should be given the title of Captain and two hundred horse to command.

This was the state of affairs when Meldritch's army, with Captain Smith and his cavalry, was drawn up before the town of Regal which was in Turkish hands and which Meldritch was eager to bring back to Austrian rule.

The siege was a long one and it seemed to the besieged and besiegers alike that a decision would never be reached. Regal was situated on a high promontory at the end of a mountain range. The General in charge of the Austrians, Moses Tzekely, having reviewed the situation, was struck by the difficulties which were facing him, and realized that his only hope of success was to wait until more troops reached him and the weather was more favourable to his cause.

The besieged Turks jeered at his caution and shouted insults from the city walls.

One day a messenger came riding out of the Turkish stronghold. He carried a letter to the General from the Governor of the town, known as the Lord Turbashaw.

General Tzekely read the letter in which the Lord Turbashaw stated that he and his people were tired of doing nothing; the ladies found the time hanging on their hands for they had expected to see exciting warfare from their turrets, and all they had seen was an army that was too lazy to fight. Would the General help him to amuse the ladies? He, the Lord Turbashaw, would challenge in single combat anyone whom the Christians cared to send forth, providing he was of no lower rank than a Captain; and the prize should be the head of himself or his opponent.

General Tzekely accepted the challenge on behalf of his army and, when the messenger had returned to the Lord Turbashaw, there was excitement and speculation throughout the camp as to who would be chosen for the fight.

Several gallant soldiers were already presenting themselves to the General, asking for the chance to defend Christian honour, so that the General declared that the only fair way of selecting their champion was to draw lots.

When John heard of the challenge he had immediately come forward; and he was not surprised when he found that his name had been drawn in the ballot.

There was a truce outside the walls of Regal.

On the ramparts sat the veiled ladies and the chief citizens of the town, and at every vantage point were stationed members of the Turkish army. In the plain below, General Tzekely's men were drawn up in their ranks.

It was fitting that the combat should take place in the plain between the armies, that all might witness it. There was complacence among the Turks. They had watched what seemed to them the desultory conduct of the Christian army and they believed that their Lord Turbashaw was invincible.

The hour had come. From the walls of the city the hautboys began to play as the great Lord Turbashaw, in his colourful robes, wearing on his shoulders wings made from eagles' feathers and decorated with precious stones and gold and silver, came into the plain between the two armies. Before him walked a slave carrying his lance, while two more slaves walked beside him. A great cry went up from the watching Turks – it signified admiration and confidence that he would be the victor.

Then from the Christian army came Captain John Smith. Trumpets heralded his advance, but he had only one page who carried his lance.

There was tense silence on both sides as the combatants bowed to one another then bowed to the spectators, took their lances, and rode into action.

John lacked the magnificence of his opponent but his aim was more sure. Within a few minutes he had found a vulnerable spot in the armour of the Lord Turbashaw and his lance had entered the visor and pierced the eye and head of his adversary so that the Turk fell groaning from his horse.

John coolly dismounted, removed the Lord Turbashaw's helmet and cut off his head. Holding it by the hair he went to General Tzekely and presented it to him. There was wild cheering from the Christian armies and a deep silence among the Turks.

General Tzekely said: 'Well done, Captain Smith. This is a good day's work. I shall never forget it. Go, take your trophies. These blood-bespattered wings are jewelled enough to provide you with a fortune.'

But John answered: 'There was nothing in our contract, General, to give me such spoils. Nay, let the jewels go back to his people. I have his head and I shall have his Arab steed which was part of our bargain. That will suffice.'

The truce was over, and the sounds of mourning could be heard coming from the town of Regal while there was rejoicing throughout the Christian ranks.

The next day there rode into the Christian camp another messenger. This was a friend of the Lord Turbashaw, a certain Grualgo. He demanded that Captain Smith fight him for his head; and should he, Grualgo, be the victor he would take the head of John Smith and that of the Lord Turbashaw which was now in Christian keeping. On the other hand, should John win his, Grualgo's head, it should go to Smith together with his horse and armour.

Both sides eagerly awaited the combat. There was the same tension, the same spectators on the city walls, the Christian army drawn up in its ranks, its arms shining in the spring sunlight.

Out came Grualgo, only slightly less magnificent than the Lord Turbashaw himself. To meet him rode John, anxiously watched by his friends. Could it have been luck which had so promptly delivered the Turbashaw into his hands? Could he expect that luck to hold?

The combatants galloped towards each other. Their lances clashed and were splintered, Grualgo in this encounter being nearly unhorsed. But the fight was not yet over, and as their lances were useless, according to the custom both men drew their pistols. Grualgo's shot was stopped by John's shield, and the latter's life was saved by inches. There was a great gasp of relief from the Christian army, dismay from the Turkish as John's shot wounded Grualgo in the arm so that he could no longer control his horse.

The Turk was thrown to the ground. He was now at John's mercy. In a matter of seconds he had lost his head, which John in ceremonial manner presented to his General.

There was mourning in the city of Regal. The people had seen their Turbashaw and the noble Grualgo slain before their eyes. They sent no more challenges. The women had watched the Englishman who, though not tall of stature, was possessed of some strange quality which they sensed; they had been almost on his side during the fighting, they discovered, and all because of that extraordinary charm of his.

'It is because he is the victor,' some said. Others replied that it was because he was a foreigner that he fascinated them.

General Tzekely sent for John.

'Your two victories,' he told him, 'have done a great deal to raise our soldiers' spirits. I am grateful to you. But there is much to be done before I shall be ready to attack the city, and I need your help. You have defeated two of the noblest Turks in single combat. They will challenge you no more; but if you could defeat a third I verily believe that they would consider we had a god among us.'

John was ready. He had begun to believe that he could not be beaten.

'I will send the next challenge,' he told the General. 'And as soon as possible we will stage a third combat.'

He went away and wrote a letter which he had translated into Turkish. It was addressed to the ladies of Regal, and it ran:

'I, Captain John Smith, am not so enamoured of your servants' heads that I would not give them another chance of taking mine, and if you will send another champion to me I shall be pleased to meet him in single combat; and if he should win, he may have my head and those I have already won.'

This was sent, and very soon a reply came back from a Moslem officer named Bonny Mulgro.

Bonny Mulgro was a champion who had never been beaten in combat, and to him was given the choice of weapons. They should be pistols, battle-axes and swords, he decided.

Never during the course of the two preceding combats had there been such excitement.

The combatants met and the pistols were fired without harm to either man; this meant that they were left to fight with the old-fashioned battle-axes and, after that, their swords.

There was a moment during that fight when all but John thought he was beaten. Bonny Mulgro had delivered such a blow at John's battle-axe that it slipped from his hand, and John was left momentarily almost slipping from his horse and weaponless.

There was a shout of triumph from the walls of the town.

'Victory! Victory for Bonny Mulgro!'

Some of the women were silent; they were glad of their yashmaks, they did not wish their men to know that they felt pity for the gallant Englishman who had already been twice victorious.

General Tzekely whispered: 'So this is the end, John. My brave Captain, would I had not suggested you should send a third challenge.'

But it was not the end. John, who was a superb horseman, was firmly in the saddle again; he had simultaneously drawn his sword. Bonny Mulgro came charging furiously forward, his battle-axe lifted, but before it could fall John's sword had pierced his opponent's armour so that the blade penetrated his body under the ribs and, with a cry of anguish, Bonny Mulgro slipped from his horse to the ground.

The Christians went wild with joy. A procession was quickly formed, and the Turks looked on while the ghastly heads of the three Turks, stuck on lances, were paraded before the watchers. Then came the horses on which the Turks had ridden into combat; and, following them, John himself, cheered and honoured by every soldier in the Christian army.

Six thousand Christian soldiers formed his bodyguard, and he was led to that spot where the General was waiting for him.

Tzekely embraced John and presented him with an Arab horse, a scimitar and three hundred ducats.

Shortly afterwards the town of Regal fell to the Christian army, and when Prince Sigismund Bathori came to meet his victorious army he asked that the famous John Smith be presented to him. When this was done he gave John a miniature of himself in a frame of gold and a silk banner on which was embroidered the heads of three Turks.

'My friend,' said Prince Sigismund, 'your fame has travelled before you. I give you permission always to wear engraved on your shield the heads of three Turks, and this shall be granted you according to the laws of heraldry.'

John accepted with pleasure. He had now riches and honours; and the thought occurred to him that it was time he returned home to tell Francis and Alice of his adventures.

IV

The Lady Charatza

John, however, did not return to England at that time – a fact which he was very quickly to regret. Colonel Meldritch was sent to help Rodol who was ruler of Wallachia and who had appealed to Austria for help against the Turks and their allies, the Krim-Tartars.

There were many skirmishes in which the Christians were invariably successful until, before the fortress of Rothenthurm, they were completely routed by the Krim-Tartars. Meldritch swam the river with a few of his men and reached safety, but John was left for dead on the battlefield.

The night was cold and John lay among those dead bodies, scarcely conscious, waiting for the end.

Then he heard the sound of voices and as, during his service, he had picked up a smattering of the language of his enemies, he recognized certain words which warned him of what was happening.

The soldiers were searching the bodies of the dead for booty, so he knew that soon they must find him; and he believed that when they discovered that he was not dead they would hastily dispatch him. They would find much worth taking from his body for, since his triumph over the three Turks in single combat, he had become a rich man and had indulged his love of finery. There were jewels on his clothes, and the stuff of which they were made was of the best.

'Ah,' said a voice close to him. 'Here lies a great lord.'

Another spoke: 'He is not yet dead. See, his eyelids

flutter. Let us dispatch him quickly. The cloak shall be mine, the doublet yours.'

'Nay, not so fast. This, as you see by his garments, is a great lord. A ransom will be offered for him which will be of far greater value than the few trumpery jewels with which he goes into battle.'

'You are right. Come. We will carry him into the camp and see what shall be done with him.'

John winced with pain as he was lifted in their strong arms. He smiled a little grimly; he was only half conscious of what was happening to him, but he knew that his vanity had saved him, here among the Krim-Tartars, as once it had saved him when the pilgrims had flung him into the ocean and he had refused to throw away his handsome cloak.

When John was carried in from the battlefield of Rothen-thurm his wounds were carefully dressed and he was given good food to eat.

He was astonished at this treatment, by a people whom he had always considered to be barbaric in the extreme, until he discovered the reason for it.

One day a Tartar, whom John guessed to be a merchant, came into the tent, where John lay with a few other men who had been picked up on the battlefield and had shared the gentle treatment which he had enjoyed, and made his way to the prisoners.

With him was an interpreter.

The prisoners were commanded to stand; then the merchant prodded them and tested their muscles as though, thought John, they were cattle in a market-place. This he discovered was a true comparison, for it was exactly what they were intended to be.

The interpreter asked them a few questions about themselves which they answered; meanwhile, the merchant nodded his head; and afterwards they were all herded together, and there began the long tramp.

They were not driven hard and they were well fed, for the merchant seemed determined that they should not over-tire themselves, and if he thought any one of them was the least bit exhausted that man would be provided with a mule.

'They treat their prisoners well, these Infidels,' whispered one of the prisoners to John.

John smiled wryly. 'Let us wait a little longer before we congratulate ourselves too heartily,' he said.

'What do you think is to happen to us?'

'It may well be,' said John, 'that we are being taken to the market-place, there to be sold as slaves. That would account for their solicitude, for naturally we shall fetch a higher price if we are in good condition.'

That silenced the other, and John was sorry he had pricked his optimism. He laid a hand on his shoulder. 'Be of good cheer,' he said. 'Nothing lasts for ever, you know. And it is always best to be prepared.'

They continued their march and when they reached the town of Axopolis, John found that his surmise had not been far from the truth.

To stand there, chained like a beast, while one's potentialities were discussed, to suffer this greatest of all degradation. How could a proud man endure it!

The hot sun added to John's discomfort; he could smell the sour odour of unwashed bodies and soiled robes as the turbanned Infidel insolently studied him and his companions and discussed which of them would make the best slaves.

The farmhouse at Willoughby seemed worlds away. Shall I ever see Francis and Alice again? wondered John. Were they thinking of him at this moment as he was thinking of them? If so the last place in which they would expect him to be was a Turkish slave market.

Snatches of talk came to him. 'That one! He looks a

proud one. He will need the lash about his shoulders. That would make him hold his head less high.'

John felt the sweat trickling down his back. His fists were clenched and he longed for an opportunity to strike out. He feared physical torture less than most men, but this insult to his dignity as a man was more than he could endure for long.

An important Pasha was standing before him. John knew that he was important because of the magnificence of his retinue. He was lavishly dressed in a robe of purple, and in his turban were glittering jewels. Two slaves fanned him as he stood before the sweating prisoners. His followers listened in hushed silence when he spoke; and John saw that they applauded his words as though he were some sort of prophet.

'This man,' said the Pasha. 'He has a proud look. What is his race?'

The Tartar merchant came quickly to the Pasha's side. He bowed low and cried: 'Oh, most honoured Pasha; oh, most worthy Pasha, it is to be expected that your noble eyes would discover the most valuable slave in the market-place.'

'I asked, what is his race?' said the Pasha.

'His race, most mighty lord? He is a Bohemian lord of great rank. When his people know that he has been sold into slavery they will send a great ransom for him. Oh, most mighty Pasha, in him you will have a worthy slave. A noble lord . . . a king, among his own people, will serve your mightiness; which is meet, oh noble lord. And when you tire of him, there is his ransom. Oh, most mighty one, Allah gives you wisdom beyond all others who come to the slave market this day. You will bless the day you set eyes on this Bohemian lord.'

'Silence!' said the Pasha, lifting a hand on which the jewels glittered. 'I like the look of this man,' he added, turning to those who crowded about him. 'I believe him to be a great lord. What think you, my friends?'

'We think as you, oh mighty one.'

'Where is my vizier?'

'Here, oh lord, ready as ever to die in your service.'

'Then buy that slave for my household.'

'I live to serve your mightiness.'

Thus John came into the possession of the Pasha Bogall.

The Pasha Bogall was betrothed to a Turkish lady whom he hoped soon to marry. Her home was in Constantinople and she was a person of great wealth, being a sister of one of the most powerful men in the community, the Timor of Nalbrits in Tartary.

Not only was she a lady of wealth but of great beauty, and thus she was beset by many suitors. Her mother guarded her well, but the Pasha Bogall believed that his rank and wealth were favourably regarded.

He was constantly seeking a means of pleasing the lady, but he did not care to travel to Constantinople until he was sure that he would be accepted by her. If he were to arrive there, only to be sent back disappointed, he would lose such face with his own people that he would never recover from the insult to his dignity.

He believed that he would win the young Turkish lady by the magnificence and the diversity of the presents he sent her. And what, he asked himself, could be a more acceptable present to a young lady, who had all the jewels she could wish for, than a slave – a slave such as the one he had recently bought in the market-place and who he had known at once was no ordinary slave but a lord of high rank in his own country.

Cunning lights came into the Pasha's eyes. The slave should serve a double purpose. Not only should he provide a very acceptable present to the lady, but he would tell her that he had captured the man in battle. To have captured such a man would surely add to the Pasha's attractiveness. She would think he must be a very brave and bold fighter.

The idea appealed to him so much that he lost no time in sitting down and writing a letter to the Lady Charatza Tragabigzanda.

'Most beauteous lady,' *he wrote,*
'I have returned from the wars which have occupied me of late, and during one of my campaigns I took as prisoner this slave whom I am sending to you. I trust you will find him a good servant and that he will be a reminder to you of my existence and my devotion. He is a Bohemian lord and his capture caused long and bitter fighting. He is a bold man as you see, and a brave one – the most outstanding of all the slaves I captured during my campaign. It is for this reason that I send him to you – he being almost worthy to be your slave . . .'

The Pasha laughed to himself with glee. He was certainly a clever man. He had little doubt that the Lady Charatza would be overwhelmed by thoughts of his valour; yes, the Christian slave would play his little part in bringing the Pasha to the lady's notice.

Then, said the Pasha to himself, he will be worth the high price I paid for him.

Thus John Smith travelled to Constantinople and the household of the Lady Charatza Tragabigzanda.

John had no idea whither he was being taken. The two guards who accompanied him would say nothing, pretending not to understand when he tried to speak to them in their own tongue; and John, who realized that his knowledge of the language was slight, was not sure whether their silence was due to lack of understanding or orders not to speak to him.

He did not know that the town of narrow streets and wooden houses was Constantinople, and he was surprised when they drew up before one which presented its blank walls to the narrow street.

One of his guards knocked on the low door which was immediately opened by a guard in brilliant uniform wearing a jewel in his turban.

'We come from the Pasha Bogall.'

'You may enter,' said the guard; and John was led into a courtyard.

Now that he was inside he saw how magnificent was the house beyond that blank wall. Around the courtyard were verandas, and beyond them were the apartments. John could see that these must be spacious, and he guessed that he was in the residence of people who were as rich as the Pasha Bogall himself.

He was led into an apartment on the floor of which was a rich and brilliantly coloured carpet; about the walls were silken hangings – elaborately embroidered. There were several divans in the room, and these were all covered in silk cloth. Here he waited until the hangings were drawn aside and a woman appeared.

She was plump and although her yashmak hid her face John guessed her to be of ripe middle age.

One of the guards handed her the letter, which she read; she nodded and looked at John. The guards signed for him to turn round that she might study him from all angles; she pinched his arm to feel his muscles. John frowned; he would never become accustomed to being treated like an ox in the cattle market.

The woman clapped her hands and two men servants appeared. She said something and the guards followed them out of the apartment. Then she signed to John to follow her and, manacled as he was, he did so.

She pushed aside the hangings and he followed her to another veranda into a garden, where brilliantly coloured flowers grew at random among herbs and cypress trees.

Following the woman, he went through the trees to a circular construction which reminded him of an English summer-house.

From within this place came the sound of high-pitched voices. The woman clapped her hands loudly, and the laughter ceased abruptly. She went to the door of the summer-house and stood there speaking. Then she turned and beckoned to John.

The sight which confronted him was one of the most charming he had ever seen. In the summer-house were some twenty girls, all veiled, all graceful in flowing robes, and all young.

Some of them were only children; they sat on the floor, their pretty brown feet bare, their ankles adorned with anklets of silver and gold, and in the hands of one of them was a musical instrument which was not unlike a guitar. She sat in the centre of a group, and John believed they had been singing before the interruption. Seated on a small divan were three of the girls, embroidery in their hands. In the centre of the summer-house a miniature fountain was playing.

The wide trousers and draperies of the girls were the colours of the flowers in the garden, and their eyes, made large and mysterious by the clever use of khol, glowed through their veils as they studied the newcomer.

'Come here, my daughter,' said the middle-aged woman who had led him there; and one of the girls, who had been sitting near the group about the guitarist, came and stood before her mother.

John could see that she was more beautifully dressed than any of the others, that she moved with more grace; among the diaphanous folds of green and mauve silk draperies sequins glittered; there were diamonds and rubies on her slender brown arms and hands. He guessed at once that this attractive girl was the daughter of the house.

'The Pasha Bogall sends you this letter and this man,' said the woman.

The girl laughed; she was clearly very young; she turned to the girls who had come clustering round her, and began talking excitedly, pointing to John. She came close to him and put out one of the dazzling fingers to touch his beard; then she leaped back laughing. All the girls laughed.

Then they were clustering about him, looking up at him with their great, dark, wondering eyes.

'What is he called?' asked one.

John answered for them: 'John Smith.'

'John Smith.' They tried to say it and they seemed to find the effort tremendously amusing.

The Lady Charatza was the first to realize that he had understood what they said.

'You speak our tongue,' she said.

'A very little,' he told her.

'But you know enough to understand . . . a little.'

The others were all listening, including the Lady Charatza's mother.

She turned to her daughter. 'The Pasha Bogall is indeed generous. We shall find the slave useful. Now I shall send him to join his fellow-slaves, and they will acquaint him with his duties.'

'Oh, but he is *my* slave,' cried Charatza. 'I wish to keep him here and talk with him.'

'You are a foolish girl. You know you cannot keep a man slave here in the ladies' apartments. Go back to your pleasures with your friends and girl slaves.' She turned to John and beckoned. 'Come,' she said. And she left the summer-house and began the walk across the garden.

John looked at the Lady Charatza, and he believed she was smiling behind her yashmak. Her eyes looked warm and tender.

He knew that he must obey, so he stepped out into the garden. When he had gone a few paces he turned. Charatza was still standing at the door of the summer-house, following him with her eyes.

John quickly learned that he was in the Constantinople house which belonged to the mother of the Lady Charatza Tragabigzanda whom the Pasha Bogall wished to marry.

He understood that she was in purdah and it was rarely that any men were allowed to see her. She spent her time with her attendants and the Circassian slave girls whose duty it was to sing and dance for her when she so wished.

As for John, his duties did not take him beyond the courtyard; he had merely to obey the superior slaves, and as they were treated with unusual leniency they extended the same treatment towards the lower slaves.

There was sufficient to eat; all that was left, after the ladies had eaten, was given to the slaves; and a pot of stew – the contents of which John did not discover – was brewed each day and, when the upper slaves had had their fill, what was left was given to the lower ones.

It was a strange life for John; it was like living in a perfumed cage. Had he not been still weak from his wounds he would have set about devising some plan for escape; but he knew that for a while he would not be strong enough to carry this out, and that he needed to rest for a few weeks.

In the meantime he contented himself with learning all he could about the city and the house he was in. He gathered that the Lady Charatza was in the charge of her mother who guarded her well, and that it was hoped that she would make a brilliant marriage, which would probably be with the Pasha Bogall.

John felt pity for the lovely girl whom he had glimpsed behind her yashmak, for the Pasha was a boastful man and a hypocrite; John was sure that he was unworthy of this beautiful girl.

The ladies were kept closely guarded. The tall blank wall

prevented any from outside overlooking their apartments which were tucked well out of sight on the garden side of the house. Occasionally they went out, either to the baths or to visit the graves of their ancestors; at the baths they gossiped with their friends, at the graves they mourned the dead; but when they went out they wore long cloaks which completely covered their bodies so that no one could see whether they were fat or thin, aged or youthful.

Some weeks after his arrival two eunuchs, very tall and broad Ethiopians who had been taken in battle, came to the slaves' quarters and asked for the newest of the slaves, the Christian with the blue eyes.

John stood up, and one of the Ethiopians said: 'Come on. You are commanded to appear before the Lady Charatza.'

John was led into the garden and once more he had a glimpse of that strange summer-house. It was enchanting to the eye, with its walls of lattice work which had been gilded and shone like gold in the sunlight. The girls were all gathered there, and as he approached he heard the Circassian slaves singing to the strumming of the guitar-like instrument.

At the entrance of the summer-house one of the little Circassians was waiting to receive him. She bowed and took him by the hand and led him to the centre of the room, where the Lady Charatza was sitting on a cushion, her legs in their pale blue sequin-spattered trousers crossed before her, her slim hands lying in her lap.

He saw that her mother was not present, and he wondered whether she would have permitted him, a man and a slave, to come thus into the secluded apartments.

'Sit,' said Charatza, and one of the girls hastily placed beside her a cushion which was of deep scarlet, embroidered with gold crescents like new moons.

John sat down, and the brightly clad girls formed a half-circle about him and Charatza.

Charatza said: 'I wish to see your eyes.'

He turned to her, smiling.

'They are the colour of the sky,' she announced, and the little girls repeated: 'His eyes are the colour of the sky.' Then the one with the guitar strummed on it, singing: 'His eyes are of the sky.'

'Bohemian Lord,' said Charatza.

'I am an Englishman,' said John.

'Englishman,' repeated Charatza with difficulty.

There was silence, for this was a word which the girls did not know.

Then Charatza began to talk rapidly, and John found it impossible to follow. When she understood this she began to speak again. Still John could not understand. She tried again, and he realized that she was speaking in other languages, hoping to find one which they both knew. Then she said in Italian: 'You have been hurt in the wars.'

John answered her at once in that language. 'Yes. I was taken prisoner on the battlefield and sold to the Pasha Bogall in the market-place.'

Charatza put her hands on her knees and began to laugh. She turned to the girls and said something to them rapidly. Then they all laughed, and the musician began to strum on her guitar and sing, and her improvised song made them laugh all the more.

Charatza clapped her hands and one of the Circassian slaves approached her with a tray on which were sweetmeats.

Charatza selected one, and the others watched breathlessly while she put this into John's mouth, an action which made the girls rock on their cushions with ecstasy.

Charatza said to John: 'You like these sweetmeats ... John?'

He told her that he had not tasted anything he liked so much for a long time.

She put another into his mouth and then, taking handfuls, she made him put them into his pockets, while he thought the girls would grow hysterical, so much did they laugh.

'Tell me of your home,' she said.

He sought for the words to describe England in Italian. He spoke glowingly of his country, of the great Queen who ruled it, of its fields which were greener than any fields in the world. He spoke with feeling and longing for it; he spoke of the flat lands of Lincoln, of the farm, and of Francis and Alice; and although Charatza could not understand half he said she could not take her eyes from his face. Every now and then she would put up a finger to touch his beard, and her black eyes looked long into his blue ones.

It was thus that her mother found them, and there was immediate consternation in the summer-house. Some of the little slave girls ran to hide themselves behind the fountain, where they knelt burying their faces in their hands as though they believed that by hiding their eyes they hid themselves.

Poor Charatza! She was being very severely reprimanded, thought John; and no wonder. She, a Turkish lady of high rank, to invite a slave to sit beside her, to talk to him, to give him sweetmeats and to call him in her quaint Italian John *Occhio Celeste*!

John stood by while the scolding voice of the Lady Tragabigzanda filled the summer-house.

Charatza spoke again and again, and John heard her say: 'But he is mine. He is my slave. Was he not given to me? Should I not do what I will with him?'

But her mother continued to scold, and all the girls drooped on their cushions like wilting flowers after a storm.

One of them was sent away, and in a few moments the two Ethiopians appeared.

John was led back to the slave quarters.

*   *   *

93

Charatza had a will of her own and was determined to see more of her slave.

Sometimes he was set to work in the gardens. Then she would appear at one of the turrets which overlooked the spot where he worked.

'John ... Smith,' she would call gently, and when he looked up she would laugh at him. 'I am here, John Blue Eyes,' she told him.

'So these blues eyes see, my lady.'

'Have all the people in England blue eyes?'

'No. Some are brown, some grey, some dark almost as yours.'

'Only the best have blue,' she said. 'Only lords.'

'I am no lord,' he told her.

'No lord?' She was faintly disappointed.

'Only a common soldier. I was to have been a farmer, and I became a soldier instead.'

'You are a great lord,' she said, 'and they will send a ransom for you.'

'No one will send a ransom for me, my lady. I know no one rich enough to do it.'

Again she was disappointed, but only momentarily. Then she cried out: 'I am glad, John *Occhio Celeste* ... I am glad. You shall stay here always and be my slave.'

Others appeared in the gardens and she stepped back from the turret window.

She thought about him continually. He was different from all others. It was more than the colour of his eyes, than the fairness of the skin and the curly beard. He was young and handsome; he was gentle and courteous; he did not strut as others strutted but moved about with dignity. She could not believe that he was not a great lord, and she had to find out.

She set one of her servants the task of discovering all she could about the strange blue-eyed slave, and after some investigation the woman found that among the servants of

94

other families were slaves who had fought with John Smith; and they talked of how he had, in single combat, slain three Turks and that his emblem which had been honourably bestowed upon him was three Turkish heads; the news was brought to Charatza that he was a great captain whose very name had struck terror into the hearts of Turks and Tartars alike.

'I knew it,' said Charatza. 'My blue-eyed John is no ordinary man.'

She would let no day pass without an encounter between them; she found that her greatest pleasure was to be in his company; and when she was not enjoying it she spent her time in contriving how she could do so.

She was not happy unless she was talking of or to John Smith. She knew that there were many English people in Constantinople, and she believed that it might be possible to discover something of him through them.

Her mother employed a Jew, who lived in the town, to do certain commissions for her, and this man was surely the one to find out all that was known about Smith.

Charatza was shrewd enough to know that she must not betray her real interest in this young man, so she made use of subterfuge.

'We heard from the Pasha Bogall,' she said, 'that the blue-eyed slave is a Bohemian lord. If this is so, should he not be worth a great ransom?'

'You would like to receive that ransom?' her mother asked her.

'I would like to know what he is considered worth. He walks like a lord. He looks like a lord. I am sure he would bring a good ransom.'

The Lady Tragabigzanda smiled. There had been a time when she have been vaguely alarmed by her daughter's interest in the slave; she was delighted now to hear that she was interested in a *ransom*.

'We will employ the Jew,' she said.

'I myself would wish to see the Jew when he has made his investigations,' said Charatza.

Her mother smiled at her indulgently. She had always loved her beautiful daughter more than her fierce son, the Timor; and the fact that so many rich and influential lords wished to marry her enhanced her value in her family's eyes. That she was wayward and wilful was well known, but when she could be placated and granted her wishes it was very pleasant to do so.

'You shall see the Jew,' Charatza was told.

So the Jew was sent for and given her commissions, and he very quickly discovered Englishmen in Constantinople – prisoners, merchants of the English Turkey Company, and travellers; and through these he soon confirmed the fact that John Smith was the son of a gentleman farmer, an experienced soldier, highly thought of by his superior officers, it was true, but one who could not be expected to fetch a big ransom.

Charatza talked with the Jew; she fired questions at him; she wanted to know every detail he had discovered about John Smith, and the Jew, who was a shrewd man and eager to please the Lady Tragabigzanda, was faintly alarmed. It seemed to him remarkable that a lady of Charatza's rank should interest herself to such an extent in a slave – even when she became aware that he was not the noble lord she had at first thought him to be.

The Jew presented himself to the Lady Tragabigzanda and hinted to her that the Lady Charatza was more interested in this man than was advisable.

The Lady Tragabigzanda decided that her daughter must be carefully watched.

The Lady Charatza appeared to be suffering from some *malaise*. She became languid and not interested in singing and dancing. Her laughter no longer rang out from the summer-house.

The Lady Tragabigzanda was not unduly worried. The child grows too rapidly, she told herself. Alas, soon we must arrange her marriage and then she will leave me.

She was indulgent to her daughter, gratifying her whims, seeking to tempt her with sweetmeats. Charatza responded languidly, but she preferred to be alone.

When the ladies wrapped themselves in their all-concealing garments and went to the baths or the graves of their ancestors, Charatza said she preferred to stay in the house and rest. Her slaves would lovingly settle her on her divan and cover her with silken sheets; and when they returned they would find her resting there, with perhaps one of her little Circassian girls fanning her or feeding her with sweetmeats.

What the Lady Tragabigzanda did not know was that, as soon as she and her party had left the house, Charatza leaped from her couch and sent for John Smith, that she made him sit beside her and tell her of his home and his family, and most of all of himself and his adventures. She would make him tell these stories again and again; and she never tired of them.

'We go to the baths,' said the Lady Tragabigzanda. 'My daughter, it is long since you have been. Would you not care to come with us?'

'Nay, my mother,' replied Charatza. 'I feel too weary this day. Next time you go I will accompany you, but today I must rest.'

'Then let it be so,' said the Lady Tragabigzanda.

Charatza lay on her divan and summoned two little slaves to take their stand on either side of her with their fans, and when she was alone she commanded one of them to go and watch for the departure of the party.

As soon as the little one returned with the news that

they had left the house, Charatza sent the girl to summon John Smith to her presence.

Charatza sat on her divan, hugging her knees. Her diaphanous trousers of palest green and silver fell gracefully about her legs, and her little feet were in embroidered silver slippers with toes which curled upwards. She had taken off her veil, because in his country women did not wear them and she wanted to look as much like an Englishwoman as possible. Her dark eyes, large by nature but made to look enormous by the clever use of khol, shone with excitement; her hair hung down her back – blue-black like the wing of a bird; it hung in plaits into which strings of pearls had been threaded.

When John entered she held out her hand to him; he came to her and, kneeling, kissed it in the gallant way which he had learned first in the Orléans establishment of the Berties, then in the household of the Earl of Lincoln, and later in his travels abroad.

Charatza was enchanted with him. She made him sit beside her on the divan. She never tired of looking at his blue eyes.

'You are not a great nobleman, they tell me,' she whispered.

'I have told you that,' he replied smiling.

'Yet you are too good and great a man to be a slave.'

He thought that she wanted him to recount one of his adventures to her, but she was in a different mood on this day.

'Do you think I am as beautiful as an Englishwoman?' she asked

'I do,' he replied.

'As beautiful as your sister . . . Alice?'

He laughed at the thought of quiet little Alice's being compared with this glittering creature. 'Alice is like a wild daisy in an English field,' he told her. 'You are an exotic flower.'

'I would be as this wild daisy.'

'No,' he told her, "you can only be as you are.'

'*Occhio Celeste,*' she whispered, 'how can a man such as you go on living as a slave?'

'It will not be for ever.'

'You spoke fiercely. Do you mean to run away?'

'Would you betray me if I did?'

She turned to him passionately. 'Never would I betray you!'

Her black eyes were close to him. John was aware now that she loved him; so was she.

She knelt on the divan and put her hands across her breasts. She said: 'I am a lady of rank; you are a slave. I worship Allah and you have some strange god whom you call Christ and the Holy Ghost and there is God too. I do not understand. But I would be willing to try to.'

She put a hand in his.

'You will soon leave your mother's house,' he told her. 'The Pasha Bogall eagerly awaits your coming.'

She bared her teeth in a wild gesture. 'I will not go to the Pasha Bogall.'

'Then what will you do?'

'You will not always be a slave, John.'

'No,' he said. 'I shall not always be a slave.'

There was a sound of footsteps outside the summerhouse. John leaped off the divan, Charatza continued to kneel, but the heavy darkened lids quivered over her blazing eyes as the Lady Tragabigzanda came into the room.

There was silence – the silence of catastrophe. The little Circassians began fanning themselves vigorously, because they held their fans and did not know what else to do.

John bowed to the Lady Tragabigzanda but she ignored him; she was looking at her daughter, who was shamefully unveiled in the presence of a man, and a slave at that.

The silence continued for some seconds, then it broke.

'Go! Bring the Eunuchs!' cried the Lady Tragabigzanda;

and the little slave girls, eager to escape, both ran to do her bidding.

Nothing was said until the Ethiopians arrived; then the Lady Tragabigzanda pointed to John. They went to him, stood on either side of him and marched him out of the summer-house.

The Lady Tragabigzanda turned to her daughter.

Charatza had begun to weep, not noisily but in a quiet, hopeless way.

Her mother said nothing; she understood.

There was a last meeting. The Lady Tragabigzanda had agreed to it. It was held in the summer-house and this time Charatza wore trousers of deep purple, and her only ornaments were golden anklets and golden bracelets; she was heavily veiled.

'John Smith,' she said, 'you are going from here. It is the only way. My mother would have sold you in the market-place, and that I could not allow. You were mine. You were given to me and I would not permit that.'

'Tell me what is to become of me,' John asked her.

'You are to go to my brother. I have written a note to him and I am going to give it to you. I do not wish my mother to know I have written this note. In it I have asked him to treat you as kindly as he would treat me, for in hurting you, in humiliating you, he hurts and humiliates me. I want him to keep you there with him. You will tell him your stories as you have told me, and he will in time love you as I love you – because all must love you, Blue-eyed John. He will do this for me, for he is a very powerful man. Take this note. Hide it. And give it to the Timor and no other.'

'You are so good to me, my lady,' said John. 'I shall never forget you.'

'No, you must not forget. I shall come to my brother one day. I shall visit him and then we will go together to your country . . . you and I. I shall never wear a veil again. I shall be as the little Alice . . . I shall be an English daisy.'

'My lady . . . my lady . . .' murmured John, and his voice was broken with emotion. She moved him deeply; more deeply, he realized, than Madame Colombier had ever done. He felt that she was in need of his protection; and if ever she did reach her brother and begged him to take her away, he knew he would do so.

He had a fleeting picture of himself arriving at the farm with a Turkish bride. It was such an incongruous picture that he could not clothe it with any reality.

'Perhaps,' he said, 'you would be happier if you tried to forget me when I am gone.'

She shook her head and her eyes shone through the yashmak bright with tears. 'There is only one happiness for me, John. It is with you. So I tell my brother this, and command him as he loves me to love you too. I command him to make you free but to keep you with him, to talk to you of Allah and of our customs, to make you one of our people. But if he cannot do it, then I will become one of yours. You must go now, John. My *Occhio Celeste*!'

And so John took his farewell of the Lady Charatza, and next his skin he carried the note which she had given him for her powerful brother, the Timor of Nalbrits.

V

The Timor of Nalbrits

As John travelled eastwards his spirits were high. Travel always appealed to him, and he had realized that he had been drifting towards a very dangerous situation in the company of the Lady Charatza. Life had not been a hard one in her mother's household but his spirit resented his captivity and, as he made the long journey first across land and then by sea, he was alert for some means of escape.

He did wonder what Charatza's reaction would be if he effected that escape. Sweet child, he reflected, she did not realize that it would be the best thing that could befall them both. She had allowed herself to become possessed by romantic dreams which had no hope of becoming reality. Yet he would always remember her grace, her charm, her sweetness and her affection for him, and wished that he could have rescued her from the fate which would most likely be hers as wife to the Pasha Bogall.

There was, however, no chance of escape. He was heavily manacled and, if he did get away, would be immediately betrayed as a slave by his chains.

His first call was at Varna, and from there he crossed the Black Sea, sighted the Crimea, entered the Sea of Azov and eventually reached Nalbrits, the territory of Charatza's brother, the Timor.

John studied the country through which he travelled with great interest. During this long journey he had been treated with consideration, but he had come to know that this treatment was accorded all slaves who were to be offered for sale or as gifts, that they might arrive in worthy condition.

The country to which he had come lay between the Don and the Volga, and as he passed through it he was depressed to see the poverty of the people. The Turks had conquered this land and it was clearly in the grip of tyrants. The land itself was well cultivated but this was the work of the miserable people who were slaves to the Timors and were forced to work hard for only enough food to keep them alive. They were almost without clothes, and wore sheepskins clipped together by thongs. They lived in huts made of logs, miserable airless places which would either be bitterly cold or stiflingly hot.

Nalbrits was a fortress and, as they approached this, John had his first glimpse of the Timor's castle. Standing as it did among those miserable log huts, it seemed twice as magnificent as it would anywhere else. But it was a stately building by any standards. Built of white stone, its roof was flat, its walls high, and it was entered by means of a pair of heavy iron gates.

The Timor was lord of this domain. All the soldiers who were lodged in the fortress must obey him; his slightest wish was a command, and to disobey meant instant and cruel death.

The iron gates were opened for John and his guards, and as they passed through a courtyard where Turkish and Tartar soldiers stood on guard, one of the guards approached John and said to him: 'The great lord Timor awaits you. He has heard of your coming.'

John was led into a passage, left between the walls, to another and smaller courtyard, through a door and into an apartment where, like a King surrounded by courtiers, sat the Timor of Nalbrits.

One glance at him was enough for John to recognize him as the brother of Charatza. He was tall; his eyes were black and his features well formed; but all the gentleness of Charatza was lacking. This was understandable, reasoned John in those few seconds; Charatza was a young girl living in purdah; the Timor was a great soldier and land-owner.

He said as John approached: 'So this is the Christian slave.' He looked at John, and his mouth was a grim line of cruelty; his eyes mocked. 'We have news of you, slave,' he said. 'You dared to lift those insolent eyes of yours to my sister.'

John knew then that the Lady Tragabigzanda had written to her son to announce his coming, and that she had probably asked him to see that the Christian slave was never again allowed to come near Constantinople.

'I have a letter for you,' said John; and he brought out that which Charatza had given him and which he had carefully guarded all this time.

The Timor looked surprised but he took it and read it; his expression did not soften, and when he had finished reading he laughed.

He took a step closer to John, and John saw that his fists were clenched and shaking and he thought for a moment that he was about to be struck as the glittering eyes surveyed him hotly.

'The Lady Charatza would have you treated kindly,' said the Timor in a voice which was almost a whisper. 'She would have you learn to be a good Turk and then be sent back to Constantinople. The Lady Charatza is suffering from madness, and it is a madness which you have brought with you from your evil lands. We will show you, slave, how we will make a good Turk of you!'

He took John's beard in his hand and tugged it viciously. John would have struck him had he not been manacled.

'Tear off his garments,' shouted the Timor. 'Every one. Call the barber.'

When John stood naked before the Turks they jeered at his white body and still manacled he was obliged to suffer their insults. He was forced on to a stool and held by several guards while his hair and beard were shaved off.

'Bring him the garments of a slave,' cried the Timor.

And a dirty piece of rough goatskin with a hole in the centre, through which his head was forced, was put on him and tied about his waist with a strip of hide.

'Now, what a handsome Christian lord he is!' cried the Timor, and all those about him dutifully laughed.

'But we must mark him for the slave he is,' cried the Timor, 'and the slave he will always be.' He looked at John, who still held his head high and managed to appear dignified even in his present plight. 'Christian dog,' went on the Timor, 'you will be set to work in my fields, so we shall not keep you chained, but think not that you can escape from us. We shall decorate you, slave . . . so that wherever you go all shall know you for what you are. There are no ladies here to fancy you and make life easy for you.'

The blacksmith had appeared carrying a spiked iron collar which was riveted about John's neck. It was thick and heavy and John almost reeled under the weight of it. On the iron collar was stamped the mark of the Timor.

'Wherever you stray,' warned the Timor, 'you will be found and sent back to me. If you are wise you will not attempt to run away. I have ways of making life unpleasant for those who attempt to trick me.'

John did not speak. Even his great spirit seemed to be crushed by this treatment. The evil-smelling goatskin irritated his flesh; the iron ring cut into his neck and shoulders. He wondered how he would be able to bear the weight of it and work as he guessed he would be expected to.

He felt a mad urge to strike out at the mocking face which was so like and yet so different from that of Lady Charatza, and he might have done so had his hands not still been chained behind him.

'Take him away!' cried the Timor. 'Take him to his fellows and let them know that it is my command that he be the lowest among them.'

So, amid the jeers of all present, John was led from

the apartment and taken down a winding stair to what resembled a dim hole beneath the castle. The floor was of earth; it smelt evilly of the unwashed bodies of slaves, of decaying food and excrement. Squatting about on the floor were creatures who he felt astonished to realize were men. They all wore goatskins tied about their bodies, and each wore the iron collar riveted about his neck.

A guard removed the chains which bound his hands and pushed John among them, telling them of the Timor's command.

'Dogs!' he cried. 'Here is the lowest dog of you all. Treat him as such. It is the word of my lord the high and mighty Timor. Should any seek to become a friend of this Christian dog, let him beware.'

Then the guards had gone, and John was left alone in that dim dungeon while many pairs of eyes watched him cautiously and cunningly.

Now, thought John, I have touched the very depths of despair.

In all his travels never had he known such wretchedness. He was forced to work hard and, as there was much land to be cultivated about the castle, he and his fellow-slaves were set to sowing and reaping in the fields. For this John was grateful. The hard work he accepted; he was glad to be in open air for long hours of the day after the dark cave in which he spent the rest of the time. His fellow-slaves had attempted to carry out the Timor's commands and treat him as *their* slave, but it was not easy to do this and one cold glance from those blue eyes could strike fear into most of them.

For some days John ate nothing. He was near starvation before he could bring himself to touch the foul food which was their daily lot.

This was made almost intolerable by the sight of the wholesome food which was served to the Timor and his high officers. Slaves assisted at the slaughter of horses, sheep and goats and in preparing them for the Timor's table. But slaves who attempted to eat any of the good food would be tied to a post and whipped to death. The Timor delighted in the milk of mares, and it was the task of certain slaves to milk the mares. The temptation to drink this delectable beverage, which was known as *Koumiss*, was an added torment.

In the nostrils of the slaves would linger that most appetizing of smells which came from the kitchens when a special drink was being prepared for the Timor. It was made from brown beans which were roasted and then ground to a powder and called coffee.

John had never heard of this beverage, but the aroma almost drove the slaves frantic with the desire to taste it. They wished that the Timor would take sherbet instead of coffee, for this lacked that aromatic smell.

And when this delicious food had been prepared for the Timor's table, the slaves would prepare for themselves the stew which was always made of the same ingredients: the entrails of goats and horses chopped up and boiled with a white grain which was called *cuskus*.

This food was revolting to John's European tastes, but the manner in which it was served was even more so.

The food was boiled in a great cauldron, and when it was ready for consumption the higher slaves would come in and sit round it, putting their hands and arms into the brew to take the choicest pieces. When they had had their fill the Christian slaves were allowed a turn at the cauldron.

Hands and arms, filthy with the sweat of weeks and the soil of the fields, were thrust into the stew.

It was a long time before John could bring himself to eat. Eventually he realized that his strength was waning and he must eat of the foul brew or die.

After days without food he began to eat with the rabble whose turn to put their hands into the pot came last.

When he lay on the earth of the cave-like room he thought again of Francis and Alice in their beds at the farmhouse, and he longed to be with them. He believed then that he would give up all his hopes of achieving lasting fame to be back with them.

If I could escape this life, he told himself, I would ask nothing but to be a farmer, serenely ploughing my fields, leading my humdrum life, one day exactly like another. Oh, Francis, you were the wise one.

But sometimes, when he was in the fields, he thought of escape, and his spirits rose and he knew that he would not endure this life for ever.

Then he would be aware of the heavy iron collar about his neck, and he knew that he would be a fool to attempt escape unless some great opportunity presented itself.

He lost count of the days. He believed he must have been several months in captivity. The Christian slaves no longer tried to bully him, for they recognized him as a leader among them.

Sometimes they whispered together in the dark of their cave.

'Is there no way out?' they asked. 'Are we to spend the rest of our lives in misery?'

John answered: 'There is a way out, but as yet I cannot see it.'

They knew him for John Smith, the champion who had slain three Turks in single combat, and they looked to him for guidance.

He began to find life more tolerable. He thought of plans for escape, examined them and rejected them. There must be a fair chance of making good the escape. He did not even know the country in which he was living. He would not know in what direction to go, even if he could get away. How far would he get, wearing the Timor's iron collar?

'But there is a way,' said John. 'I know there is, and one day I shall find it.'

The Timor was not unaware of this lowest of his slaves. He could not prevent himself from watching John. When he rode about the fields to see how work was progressing he sought out John and took especial pleasure in setting him the most arduous tasks.

It was not lost on the Timor that John had the respect of his fellow-slaves, and he suspected that the Moslem slaves also held him in a certain awe.

When it was brought to the Timor's knowledge that this John Smith was that legendary figure who had slain three Turks in single combat, he was infuriated still further.

He strode about the castle, a whip in his hand, and he sought John Smith. He never passed him without giving him a lash with the whip he carried.

'Dog of a Christian!' he would cry. 'Work, idle slave.'

He longed to kill John, but he could not bring himself to do so because he wanted to torment him and he believed that any of his slaves must be better off dead than alive.

The harvest had been gathered and it was threshing time. The Timor's vast lands had given a good yield and there was much work to be done. The Christian slaves were sent to his barns to work at threshing. This was a slow process because the Turks knew nothing of flails and threshing bats were used.

One day John was working some two or three miles from the castle; he was alone in a barn, and finding the process of working with the threshing bat an irksome one, for he could not accustom himself to its use.

He was suddenly aware of the stillness all about him, and the thought occurred to him that if he were ever going to escape from his bondage he would never have a better opportunity than this. He wondered what would happen to the slaves when there was no work to do out of doors, and he shuddered at the thought of being kept within the castle walls all day.

Escape! The very word exhilarated him as a draught of French wine or English ale would have done. Escape? But how in a filthy goatskin and a thick iron ring about his neck, proclaiming him the Timor's slave?

He would need a horse. He had no chance of getting away on foot. But even if he had a horse, what chance had he, dressed as he was with the mark of bondage about his neck.

And then suddenly he heard the sound of a horse's hoofs. He went to the door of the barn and saw that the Timor was riding towards it. He looked a fine figure on the beautiful mount; in his hand he carried the usual whip.

John felt sure that he was coming to the barn because he was aware who was working there. John felt no fear, but a great rage took possession of him.

The Timor leaped from his horse, tied it to a staple and came into the barn.

His dark eyes were glistening as he stood watching John at work with the threshing bat.

'Dog!' he cried. 'Christian dog! So you idle your time away, eh?'

John did not answer, but went on working.

The Timor leaned against the door, playing with the whip.

He went on: 'So this is the dog who tried to seduce my sister, is it?'

John felt his heart leap with exultation. The Timor would not have referred thus to his sister if they had not been out of earshot.

Still John did not answer.

'This is the dog who presumed to be her friend. And she sends him to me that I may make him a good Turk! I would she could see you now, dog. Ah, would that she could see you now!'

John went on working.

'This is the dog who cut off the heads of Allah's servants. This is the slave who would wear the heads of the Faithful on his shield. Dog! Vile slave! Come here that I may put this whip across your back.'

John straightened, and his blue eyes met those of the Timor. Had the Timor not worked himself into such a fury he would have paused to consider the cold, hard glitter of those blue eyes.

'Come quickly, dog. There is nothing to be gained by delay but more lashes of my eager whip.'

John did not move; he was thinking quickly. He knew that he was some distance from any other living person; he and the Timor were alone.

The Timor, maddened by his hesitation, came nearer. John felt the stinging whip about his shoulders and then he leaped at the Timor; he wrenched the whip from his tormentor's hands.

John was weak from his inadequate diet; he wore the heavy iron collar about his neck, but he was a desperate man. He knew that he had to win this fight or face a slow death before which he would suffer the utmost torture which man could devise.

He succeeded in flinging the astonished Timor to the ground and, before he could rise, John had picked up his threshing bat and given him a hearty blow on the head.

He went on beating the Timor about the head until the man's brains spattered the floor of the barn.

He stood for two seconds staring at the results of what he had done, then hastily threw off his goatskin and undressed the Timor. Having exchanged clothes, he hid the body under straw in a corner of the barn together with his old goatskin, and filled a sack with corn.

He came to the door of the barn and looked out.

The horse was impatiently pawing the ground where the Timor had left him; there was no sign of any human being.

John untied the horse, mounted and, without knowing in what direction he went, except that it was not the way back to the castle, he rode away.

John did not draw rein until the horse was near exhaustion; he dared not. He guessed that he would have to traverse many miles before he left the Timor's country behind him, and that if he encountered any person he would immediately be recognized and betrayed.

Sweating, praying, he went on and on until he knew that the horse could go no farther.

Then, finding himself in a strange, wild country dotted with scrub on which berries grew, he dismounted. The foam-flecked horse began to devour the berries, and John was fearful lest they should prove poisonous. To his great delight he found a stream nearby and when the horse had drunk John fed him from the sack of corn he had brought with him and then, tying him to a bush, he lay down and himself ate some of the grains of corn.

All the time he was giving thanks to God for what might be his deliverance; he asked for help and, above all, courage, because he knew that his trials had only just begun.

He had killed the Timor and escaped from the castle, but what ordeals lay before him he could only imagine.

In the first place he had no idea where he was. During his imprisonment he had tried to find out the exact position of the Timor's castle, and he had been told that Nalbrits was situated in the country of Cambia close to the River Manytch. He was still well within the territory of the Turks and Tartars and, until he had escaped from it into that of the Christians, his life was in peril. Had it not been for the iron collar about his neck he would have felt optimistic; but how wise the Timor had been, to mark his slaves thus!

He pulled at the collar in desperation and then laughed at himself for a fool. He would need the aid of a blacksmith to remove it.

He must therefore forget his collar. He could do nothing about it without help; this meant that all the time he was in the land of Turks or Tartars he must not go near enough to any person for the collar to be seen.

It grew dark and he slept; he was awakened early to see the horse, refreshed, pawing the ground and eager to be off.

It was a fine horse, for the Timor had been proud of his horses. It was great good fortune that he had seen fit to use one of his best on that day when he had come to the threshing barn.

The berries had had no ill effect on his mount, so John ate some himself. They were refreshing and, after eating a little corn and watering and feeding the horse, he mounted and went on his way.

He rode westward, eyes strained to the horizon.

Another day passed; he was still in the wilderness but at least it had the thirst-quenching berries to offer him and the horse.

On the third day the country changed a little; it was less wild, but he regretted the loss of the berries.

That day he saw in the distance an encampment, and he pulled up short.

He presumed it to be a Tartar encampment, for the Tartars were a wandering people who never built township but travelled about the country taking all their possessions with them. He guessed that this was why he had not seen any villages on his three days' journey.

He was very keen-sighted and he could distinguish the wickerwork huts which were easily transportable. These the Tartar tribes carried with them on their travels and, when they came to a spot where they decided to stay for a while, they erected them and camped in a semicircle.

John saw smoke rising and knew they were cooking food. His mouth watered. The bag of grain was serving him well, and he thanked God that he had had the foresight to stop and fill it, but he was beginning to feel the need for a different sort of food.

So great was his hunger that he had started towards the Tartar encampment and had gone half a mile before he halted. His iron collar had seemed to become heavier, and it was as though it warned him of his folly. He pulled up, turned his horse and galloped off in the opposite direction, eager now to put as great a distance as possible between himself and the Tartar encampment.

But he was thoughtful as he rode on. How long could he go on in this way? How long could the horse?

What would be the end of this escapade? Death of thirst and starvation in the wilderness; giving himself up to the enemies of Christians?

He almost turned again and rode to the Tartar encampment. But dismounting from his horse, he tied it to a bush and knelt down and prayed.

'Oh God,' he said, 'give your servant courage. Show me the way back to my own people. Give me strength to continue until I find the way.'

Then he remounted.

A calm had come to him. He rode on, alert, eyes strained.

Late that day he thought he saw a rough path in the distance. In a short time he had reached it. He was right. It was a rough sort of road. This was a sign. This must be a road which travellers had used before him.

He had heard certain of the Timor's prisoners talk of a road which they called the Castragen. Once a man was on this road he could discover whither he was going, for there were signposts on it, placed where the path divided into two or more. On these signposts were pictures indicating the sort of country to which the signs pointed.

Did this rough path lead to the Castragen?

It was almost dark but he would not stop yet; and taking a westward direction he rode on for several miles. At length to his great joy he saw a signpost. It had three arms and there was enough light to show him the pictures there. One was of a black man with the sun overhead; another showed a crescent moon and the third a cross.

The crescent arm pointed to the direction from which he had just come and he knew that this indicated the Mohammedan countries; the black man and the sun must mean Asia; and the cross could only mean the Christian countries, so if he followed where that arm pointed he would surely come to Russia or Muscovy.

He wanted to cry aloud with joy. The horse had begun to whinny and was moving forward. John saw to his delight that there was a stream near the signpost.

Both drank their fill. Afterwards John fed the horse and bathed himself in the cool waters.

Then he knelt down by the stream and gave thanks to God.

There were still many trials before him. For sixteen days he rode on; the grain had all been eaten and he and the horse had to rely on berries and the occasional stream which they discovered often just in time. Sometimes they had to eat grass. John dared not approach to ask help from any while he wore the iron collar and was in Mohammedan country.

At every branch or each cross-road he found the sign-posts, and always he followed the cross; and at the middle of the sixteenth day he came to a fortress and, exhausted as he was, he felt a wild exultation, for on the rough wall he saw the sign of the cross, and he knew that he had reached Christian territory.

He did not doubt for a moment that he would receive help, for he knew it was a point of honour that any Christian prisoner escaping from Mohammedan territory was to receive shelter.

He forgot that he was wearing the dress of the Timor, and when he rode up to the fortress he had some difficulty in making himself understood. Now he was glad that he was wearing the iron collar for, as soon as he called attention to it, the guard's face lightened; he nodded with understanding and signed for John to wait.

Eventually he was led through a courtyard and into a rich apartment where he was received by the Governor of the town.

John quickly uttered a sentence in English, then Italian, then French.

The Governor smiled. He knew a little French and, although their accents were quite different, they managed to make contact.

John soon explained that he had escaped from the Timor of Nalbrits, indicating his iron collar. The Governor then sent for a smith to strike off the iron collar, and this was done. By that time the Governor's wife had appeared. She was a woman in her mid-thirties and, when she saw John in his tattered Turkish garments, his neck bruised and raw from the collar, his hair and his beard, which had now grown again, unkempt and dirty, she shrank back.

John was about to speak to her, but he was suddenly so overcome by weakness that he swayed and would have fallen had not the Governor caught him.

John awakened to find himself in a bed, while a woman sat beside him. There were other women in the room, and when he opened his eyes the woman by his bed began to speak.

John was for the moment uncertain where he was; then he remembered the Governor's wife.

She was smiling at him, and she lifted a dish from a table and held it out to him.

He took it. It was some savoury stew and never in his life had food tasted so good.

She watched him, nodding as he ate. Then she beckoned to one of the servants who came to stand beside the bed holding doublet and breeches, all in very fine cloth. The Governor's wife pointed to them and then to John.

He understood, smiled and nodded.

She took the bowl from him and held up a finger. Then she brought him grapes. With the utmost pleasure she watched him eat them.

He wanted to thank her, but he did not know the words in Russian. Her name sounded like Callamata and he called her the Lady Callamata, which pleased her greatly.

She went away after a while and when she returned the Governor was with her.

'My wife has taken a fancy to you,' he told John. 'She was overcome with pity for your plight. She has unguents with which she wishes to heal your neck, where the skin has been chafed away.'

'I am indeed grateful to her,' said John. 'Pray tell her so. She has made me feel as though I have risen from the dead.'

'Your horse is being attended to. He is in a sorry state. But you will not be needing him for a while. He will have time to recover.'

'I must be on my way,' said John.

'My wife will not allow it until your neck has healed and she has assured herself that you are fit for the journey.'

John felt weak with gratitude, and for a few moments he could not speak.

'In truth,' went on the Governor, 'you should rest here until the next convoy is ready to leave. These are rough lands, my friend, and travelling alone is unsafe. You are a brave man – that is clear – but you have suffered a great deal and may well be weaker than you suspect.'

So John stayed a few weeks at the fortress of Æcopolis under the protection of the Governor, and during that time the Lady Callamata nursed him, provided him with clothes and herself superintended the food which would give him back his strength.

John learned a few words of Russian mainly that he might tell her of his gratitude and how in the years to come he would always remember her kindness.

There came a day when the convoy was ready to leave; and John went with it. His beard neatly trimmed, his curly hair glinting golden in the sunshine and his blue eyes tender, he took his leave of the Governor and his wife.

The Lady Callamata stood shading her eyes until she could see him no more; then she turned away and hurried into the house; and her servants noticed that she was sad for many months after the departure of the blue-eyed Englishman.

And by easy stages John made his way to Leipzig where Prince Sigismund then held his court; and when the Prince heard that Captain John Smith had arrived, he cried: 'Bring the Captain to me at once. We must do honour to this brave English gentleman who, while he served with my army, slew three Turkish warriors in single combat.'

Prince Sigismund embraced John and announced that wherever he went in the Prince's domain he was to be honoured as the Prince's dear friend.

So John lingered awhile in Leipzig, savouring the honour which was done him. Nalbrits seemed far away and little more than a bad dream while here was reality.

He could walk through Leipzig in his fine garments, for Sigismund had insisted on rewarding him for his services; he was known throughout the town as the Prince's honoured friend, the bravest man in the Prince's army. The name and exploits of Captain John Smith became a legend.

But John grew restive.

'It is natural,' said Sigismund. 'You have your home in England. It is long since you have seen your family and friends.'

'Yes,' said John, 'it is long indeed.'

'Then go to them,' said Sigismund, 'but before you leave

I have a little present for you. It is a small reward for what you have done in my service.'

And John received from him a present of fifteen hundred gold ducats.

The Timor's lowest slave was a rich man.

VI

The Meeting with Gosnold

There was festivity in the Willoughby farmhouse, and all the villagers had come out to see the wedding of Francis Smith.

In and out of the house the guests had been dancing, and now they were assembling on the lawn outside the farmhouse to watch the morris dancers while Francis and his bride looked on with smiling faces.

Peregrine Bertie, who had looked in to wish the married couple luck, sought out Alice whom he had not seen among the revellers.

He went into the kitchen, but there was no sign of Alice there. Peregrine looked round the big and comfortable room with its long table at which Francis and his sister, and all their servants and labourers had their meals. The remains of the feast which the guests had enjoyed, reminded him of long ago when as boys he and his brother would come into the farmhouse and sit at that table with John, while Mistress Smith served them with the soup or cakes hot from the brick oven.

I wish I could see John again, he was thinking.

But where was Alice?

He went through the kitchen to the brewhouse and there he found her sitting on a stool, staring straight ahead of her; her cheeks were flushed and, coming upon her suddenly and seeing her in repose, he noticed how thin she had become.

'Alice?' He spoke her name tenderly and as she swung round the flush deepened in her cheeks.

'I wondered what had become of you when I noticed that you were not with the guests.'

'So you noticed,' she answered. 'I hope you were the only one who did.'

'The others probably thought you were in the kitchen busying yourself with some task. I came to see.'

'Thank you, Peregrine.'

'You are tired?'

'Always it seems I am tired now, Peregrine.'

'You have had so much to do.'

'Oh no, do not let us delude ourselves. I can say to you what I cannot say to Francis. I have not many more months left to me.'

'It is not so!'

She held up a hand. 'Did I not see the going of my mother and my father? I am happy today. Francis has a good wife. She will take care of him. She will do all that I have been able to do for the farm, so Francis will not miss me as much as I once feared he would.'

'This is no way to talk on your brother's wedding day.'

'It is always best to face the truth. I faced it long ago.'

'You must get better, Alice. You will, now that you have Francis' wife to help you. You have worked too hard. What will John say when he comes home and finds you like this?'

'Ah! John! I think often of him.'

'As I do. Robert and I often speak of him. I wonder what has become of him. It is so long since he went away.'

'Nearly five years. When he comes back he will see changes.'

'Everything seems different since the Queen died.'

Alice nodded. 'England cannot be the same without her. There is a different spirit abroad. I wonder what John will think of England when he comes home.'

'You think he will come soon?'

'Yes, said Alice. 'I think he will. There were two things I have prayed for. One was to see Francis happily married, so that he would not miss me when I left him. The other is to see John before I die. I think my prayers will be answered.'

Peregrine looked at the frail girl beside him and he shivered. It seemed such a short while ago that she was running about the farm, gay, attractive and so full of life.

But she was right when she said the old days had gone forever. The policy of the Court had changed; the almost legendary Queen was dead and an unimpressive Scottish monarch had taken her place – a man who provided little inspiration to adventurous Englishmen.

'I hope you are right and that John will soon come home,' he said fervently.

It was several weeks after Francis' wedding. Francis was a blissful husband and Alice was content, for the young bride was eager to learn and eager to please.

Now that the work of the house was shared, Alice seemed a little better. Francis rejoiced at this, but Alice knew that she was smitten by the disease which had carried off her mother and father, and that the respite was temporary.

She was working in the dairy when she heard the sound of a horse's hoofs clattering on the stones of the yard and then a voice crying: 'Is anyone at home today?'

She dropped the butter pat on to the floor and sped into the yard, where she was immediately caught up in the wild embrace of a handsome man.

'Alice!' he said. 'You are Alice?'

'Oh, John, did you not know me?'

'But you would seem to have grown smaller. Is that truly so?'

'And you have changed. How magnificent you are! How bronzed! You are a man now, John. I feel as though I'm going to faint ... No, it is nothing. I am better now.'

'I should have warned you of my coming.'

'It is wonderful that you are here. I must call Francis and his wife at once.'

'Francis and his . . . *wife*!'

'Yes, he has a wife. And you?'

'Still a bachelor.'

'It is strange that Francis should be a husband before you.'

'Nay, Francis was meant to be a husband. I never was.'

'Perhaps, now that you have come home, you will settle.'

He touched her cheek gently. 'Ah, Alice, I cannot believe I shall ever do that.'

He lifted her up in his arms and he was alarmed by her frailty. He thought, If it were I who weighed little more than a bird it would be understandable, but Alice . . . oh, my little sister, has death marked you too as it did our father and mother?

He was glad he had come home. He reproached himself for not coming earlier, for in spite of his resolutions he had dallied after leaving the Court of Prince Sigismund.

He carried her into the farmhouse. It seemed smaller than he had imagined it – strangely homely when he compared it with the Palace of Prince Sigismund, so luxurious and comforting when compared with his quarters in the Timor's castle.

'Francis,' she called. 'Francis! Where are you? John is here . . . at last.'

The farmhouse had changed since John had come home. Now there were frequent visitors. If John had a great deal to tell of his adventures, his friends and family had a great deal to tell of what had been happening at home.

The death of the Queen, although it had occurred two years before, was still the main topic of conversation.

John visited the Willoughbys and there discussed the new England.

'You see, John,' Robert told him, 'this new Scotsman

has no spirit of adventure. Do you remember how delighted was the Queen when her sailors tweaked the beard of the King of Spain? Now that King of Spain is dead; so is our Queen herself.'

'But there is still Spain,' cried John. 'There is still England. Rivalry exists between us on the high seas. They are colonizing half the world. Would this James of Scotland have us stand aside while Spaniards, Portuguese, French and Dutch divide up the world between them?'

'He declares himself to be a man of peace.'

'A man of peace!' snorted John. 'How can he be that in a world of conflict?'

'There is trouble brewing, John. There are many of us who sigh for the old days when the spirit of adventure walked the lanes of England, when royal smiles were for the bold and brave. Now it is said that this King reserves his smiles for pretty boys. Raleigh, whom the Queen delighted to honour, is out of favour with the reigning King.'

'What? Sir Walter!'

'Aye, Sir Walter. He is a prisoner in the Tower of London . . . accused of plotting against the King.'

'But this is monstrous. If the Queen could be aware of this . . .'

'If the Queen could have foreseen events she would never have nominated James as her heir. So Sir Walter Raleigh is languishing in the Tower, occupying himself, so they say, in writing a history of the world. He failed, as you know, to establish a colony in the land which he named Virginia after the Queen.'

John nodded; then his eyes blazed. 'He would not have failed had he been well supported. I remember the excitement when he returned with potatoes and tobacco, and how strange we all thought them – yet now we would seem to have taken to them somewhat heartily. Why did he fail to establish a colony in Virginia, do you think, Robert?'

'They say the climate was too rigorous for Englishmen to bear. The heat of the summer, the cold of the winter. We live temperately here, remember. Then many of them fell victims to hostile natives.'

John's eyes narrowed. 'I think it may have been that he chose his colonists from the wrong quarter. He took gentlemen with him who hoped to discover gold and fortune, and rogues of whom the country wanted to rid itself. If I were founding a colony, Robert, I would take men who were prepared to work. I would take farmers to till the land ... I would take carpenters to build houses. And women ... women who would be ready to stand by the men and work with them, and raise families.'

'Oh come, John, don't talk of founding a colony. You have had adventures enough to last you a lifetime. You must stay with us for a while. There is Alice, for one thing.'

'Alice,' said John, and his expression grew melancholy. 'Robert, do you think that she is going the way my parents did?'

'She grows more frail every day. But she is delighted to have you with her. I think that she would be content if you stayed at home. John, could you? It might not be for long.'

John was silent. Then he said: 'Tell me more of England.'

'Oh, once England was merry. She no longer is. There is dissatisfaction everywhere. Its roots are in religion. The Catholics would seem to be ready to spring at our throats. There is political unrest as well as religious unrest. The Queen was beloved of the people because she always understood that it was through the people that she ruled. There may have been times when she was arrogant with those in her immediate circle, but never did she forget to placate the people. It is said that James believes in the Divine Right of Kings to govern and that he condones what his ministers do – providing he is fond of the ministers.'

'But England will be always England. We are a seafaring

nation. No Scotsman can change us. We'll always be Englishmen.'

'John, you've something on your mind.'

'I cannot stop thinking of Raleigh . . . and Virginia.'

But he was also thinking of Alice, and he was telling himself, It will not be long. It would be cruel of me to leave her when she so clearly wants me to stay.

John stayed at the farm during the summer and autumn, helping to bring in the hay and thresh the corn. As he worked with his flail he thought often of that threshing barn, miles away in the east of Europe, and he marvelled at the great fortune which had been his.

He wondered what had happened when the Timor's body had been discovered, and what Charatza had said when she heard the tale. Often he thought regretfully of Charatza, a dainty exotic figure on her gaily coloured cushions, and wished that their lives had worked out as she had planned, that the Timor had been of as loving a disposition towards him as his sister had been, and that she had come to visit him and they had escaped together.

That would have been too fantastic for reality.

Charatza was probably now the bride of the Pasha Bogall, and doubtless she would have forgotten all about her blue-eyed Englishman until she heard that he had slain her brother. But she would understand he had been ill-treated, and she would forgive him.

It was preposterous to think of Charatza and absurd to remember Madame Colombier who had doubtless consoled herself with a new lover – perhaps a husband – by now. If he were a wise man he would marry as Francis had done, and together they could farm the land. So many times during his adventures in Europe he had come face to face with death. Why not settle down to a comfortable life? Had he not savoured adventuring with all its thrills and dangers to the full?

Yet he continued to think of Raleigh in the Tower and the colony of Virginia which might fall into the hands of the Spaniards, the French or the Dutch if no Englishman made an effort to preserve it.

Yet Alice was clearly delighted to have him at home, and each day it seemed more and more clear that she would not long be with them.

He would sit by the fire on those autumn evenings and tell them of his adventures; and how, even when he had reached Leipzig and Prince Sigismund had rewarded him so handsomely, he had not come home immediately. He explained that he had felt he must see Germany and Spain while he was in Europe, and he told of what he had seen in these countries.

And having travelled through Spain he had wished to see Africa, because at that time war was being waged in Morocco since the ruler, Muley Hamet, had died and his sons were fighting for the possession of the throne.

The Moors he had discovered to be a people with a civilization of their own, though to John's mind as Infidels they were barbarians and, he believed, treacherous.

He told how having reached the port of Saffee he had been invited aboard a ship by her captain and, while he was enjoying the captain's hospitality, a storm blew up and it was necessary to let anchor and cable slip and go to sea. 'Thus,' said John, 'I was, whether I wished it or not, forced to take a sea trip.'

It was during this trip that there was a fight between the ship on which John was sailing and two Spanish men-of-war.

'Many gave us up for lost,' said John. 'There were these two mighty galleons bearing down on us, and we but a little trading vessel! But there were some of us aboard who ached to do battle with the Spaniards, and when they called for us to surrender in the name of the King of Spain we shouted back: "We'll see you in hell first. We are Englishmen. We'll not be driven off the sea by Spanish Dons!"'

John's eyes blazed at the thought of the battle. 'So the men cheered and the trumpets blared forth and our men shouted "St George for England!" Then the guns blazed and we worked like demons ... or gods. And for all their big guns we had the Dons beaten. Their ships were big, but cumbersome, and our little one could turn and tackle with a speed that confounded them. We came safe into the port of Saffee after the battle, with twenty-seven slain and sixteen wounded. I heard that we accounted for more than a hundred Spaniards.'

'And when you came into port you decided to return home, John?' asked Francis.

'Ay. I had thought about you all and wanted to see the farm again. I felt I'd faced death so many times that I couldn't always expect to escape. So here I am ... safe, and all in one piece.'

'Are you in one piece, John?' asked Alice quietly. 'Methinks your heart stayed behind in your adventures.'

'What mean you?' asked John.

'That your heart is not here with the quiet life. You dream, John, as you ever did.'

'Alice, I have promised you and myself that I shall rest here until ...'

'Until?' she prompted.

'Until I feel the urge to travel again.'

Alice smiled; she understood that he would stay as long as she lived. She was grateful but she said: 'I would not be one to hold you here, John, if the urge to go wandering again were to come to you.'

'I know it, Alice,' he said.

But he made a vow with himself that he would not leave Willoughby while she lived.

It was less than a week later when one of the maids went to awaken Alice but found her as Alice had once found her own mother.

As John stood with Francis and his sister-in-law about that second-best bed, he marvelled that death should have taken this girl who had lived so quietly, and again and again should have looked him in the face and passed him by.

He was overcome with grief and mourned her as sadly as did Francis, who would miss her so much more.

But he knew that the bond which held him to the farm was broken; the time had come for him to go travelling again.

It was Robert Bertie, Lord Willoughby, who heard of the expedition which a certain Captain Ley was proposing to take to Guiana.

He rode over to the farm to talk to John about it.

'I haven't forgotten what you said about Raleigh and Virginia,' he began. 'Well, here is a chance. Captain Ley is looking for men like yourself. He plans to take an expedition to Guiana and claim it for England. He is at this time endeavouring to bring together a group of men who will join in this enterprise. If he can form a company and so raise the money he needs to fit out the expedition, he will be ready to set out. I thought it might be the kind of enterprise which would interest you.'

John was undoubtedly interested. He was eager to leave the farm, which seemed to him full of memories of the dead, for he felt he could only be sad there; and he believed that it was the wish of Francis and his wife to find a bride for him.

John visualized himself slipping into marriage, which, he knew, would immediately curb his freedom. He was aware of the inviting looks of the daughters of his neighbours, and the project of going to Guiana seemed far more inviting.

'Why do you not go to London,' said Robert, 'and meet Captain Ley? I will give you a letter of introduction to him. You could then see what you think of his project.'

So John took the letter of introduction and rode to London.

That November London was a city of rumours. On the 5th a conspiracy had been discovered to blow up the Parliament. This, it appeared, had been plotted by a group of Catholics who, displeased with the new king and his ministers, sought to blow them up when they were all assembled for the opening of Parliament. Robert Catesby, the leader of the men, had already been arrested, as had several other conspirators including a certain Guy Fawkes who had been caught while on his way to ignite the gunpowder.

John walked through the narrow cobbled streets over which the gabled houses almost met, and could not avoid the unsavoury smell of refuse which clogged the gutters. It was very noticeable after the fresh air of the country.

He looked at the goods displayed in the shop windows and the markets, and he returned the smiles of the shopkeepers' wives and daughters who appeared in the doorways as though to tempt him to pause and inspect the wares displayed.

He kept his hand on his sword though as he walked through those streets, for he well knew that he might be set upon by rogues even in daylight. He also kept a sharp eye on his purse.

He found the house of Captain Ley, but when he presented himself he was told by a serving man that the Captain was with his friends in a nearby tavern, *The King's Head*, and that if John went there he could no doubt discuss his business with him.

John made his way with all speed to *The King's Head*, and when he arrived and told the innkeeper that he looked for Captain Ley he was conducted to the inn parlour where several men sat at a table.

'Captain John Smith,' announced the host.

And Captain Ley rose to embrace him.

'I have a letter of introduction from Lord Willoughby,' John told him.

'But Captain Smith needs no introduction,' replied Captain Ley. 'We have heard of the captain who slew three Turks in single combat.'

He made John join him and his friends at the table and called for ale.

When this was brought, Captain Ley introduced John to his companions, among whom were Richard Hakluyt the geographer and author of *Principall Navigations, Voiages and the Discoveries of the English Nation*, Henry Hudson, the Arctic explorer, and Captain Bartholomew Gosnold.

On the table were spread out maps and other papers.

John said: 'Lord Willoughby has told me of your project to take an expedition to Guiana, and I am interested.'

'Nothing,' said Captain Ley, 'could please us more. It is men such as yourself whom we welcome most heartily to join us in the enterprise.'

John sat quietly listening. Hakluyt talked of navigation, and Ley explained what he wished to do in Guiana.

'The English flag must be kept flying there,' he said. 'I plan to take willing people with me . . . to transplant them, one might say, and make a corner of England in that land.'

'What of the climate?' asked Captain Gosnold.

'Doubtless it differs from our own, but where on the face of the Earth could we find a climate as temperate as that of England?'

'Where indeed?' said Gosnold. 'The climate may present surprises. Now the Virginian climate is known to us . . .'

Captain Ley smiled. 'Gosnold hankers for Virginia,' he explained to John. 'He feels that he could right Raleigh's mistakes.'

'I have never visited Virginia,' said John, 'but I share Captain Gosnold's interest in the place.'

Captain Ley smiled at him. 'Virginia later perhaps. For the time being let us give all our thoughts to Guiana. Captain Smith, will you join our expedition?'

John did not hesitate. 'I will,' he answered.

John who had put up at the inn and joined his new friends when, the next day and the next, they met to discuss the venture, began to understand what a great deal of work was necessary to plan such an enterprise. Previously he had gone off on his adventures alone. It was a very different matter to transport several shiploads of people. First the money must be raised; then the people selected; stores must be considered; and unforeseen eventualities arranged for.

The idea of colonizing fascinated him. He began to feel that he had wasted years of his life, wandering about Europe learning the business of a soldier. He longed to organize a colony, to set the English flag flying over some hitherto unclaimed tract of land.

His friendship with Bartholomew Gosnold grew. Often they sat over a tankard of ale in the inn parlour before the others arrived or after they had left.

'I have sailed along the coast of Virginia,' Gosnold told him. 'I cannot think of any spot on Earth more suitable for colonizing.'

'But the climate?'

'We could cope with that.'

'And the natives?'

'From what I saw of them they were a friendly people – copper-skinned in headdresses of feathers, and their faces often painted in red, blue and white – presumably to make them appear ferocious to their enemies. I feel they would be friendly and tractable, for there appeared to be but few of them.'

'I should not be displeased,' said John, 'if Captain Ley decided to take his expedition to Virginia instead of Guiana.'

Gosnold nodded; but it was useless to talk of Virginia to Captain Ley. His heart was set on Guiana, and as they had agreed to join his expedition they must accept his decision.

Therefore both John and Captain Gosnold, understanding the need to obey one leader without question, gave themselves up to making the expedition to Guiana a success.

A day came when the planners were all gathered together in the inn parlour and Captain Ley did not arrive. There was some consternation because the Captain always arrived punctually for the meetings.

They waited with some apprehension, but not for long. As they sat there, a servant of the Captain's was ushered into the parlour.

'I come from Captain Ley, my masters,' he said. 'The Captain was struck down with a grievous sickness in the night and is therefore unable to attend you this day. He asks that you discuss your business without him.'

They did so, but it was clear to all that Captain Ley was the leading spirit and they felt that the meeting was far from successful.

Two days later Captain Ley was dead.

For a few weeks the meetings continued, but very quickly it was discovered that the project could not go forward without Captain Ley.

The last meeting broke up; and it was then that Gosnold and John spoke to each other of what had been brewing in their minds since the death of Captain Ley.

'Why should we not plan for our own expedition?' said John.

'I see no reason why we should not do what Captain Ley has done. But ours would not be an expedition to Guiana.'

The two men looked at each other and smiled; and simultaneously they cried: 'Virginia!'

VII

A Gallows for John Smith

The year that followed seemed to John the most frustrating through which he had ever lived. Never before had he realized the difficulty of making others see one's point of view.

To him it seemed so obvious that there must be a Virginian colony for the glory of England. Others were less sure.

He tramped the country looking for recruits. He did not want too many highly born gentlemen who were looking for a gamble; nor did he want those frequenters of taverns who thought they might be escaping from a country which had little to offer them, to a paradise where they would live for ever in comfort and luxury. He wanted good honest workers; he wanted carpenters, blacksmiths, farmers, doctors; and he also wanted men who could govern.

John was certain that he was possessed of this quality. He was already beginning to look on the enterprise as his. That was all very well when he had been dealing with Gosnold, who was a gentle person, a man who knew how to captain his ship and take her safely across the Atlantic, but who, provided he was given a free hand to do that, was ready to leave the governing of a colony to others.

John must have money; he must have backing. One could not set off light-heartedly on an adventure of this sort. The lives and future of many people were at stake.

He planned then to form the 'London Virginia Company' in which he asked people to invest their money. They would be the shareholders, and as such have a say in matters of policy.

The King and certain of his ministers, who must give their support to a scheme of this sort before it could be carried out, at first frowned on the enterprise. They could see no reason for antagonizing Spain. Spain looked upon the new world as hers. It had been discovered by Christopher Columbus as far back as 1492 under the aegis of Ferdinand and Isabella, King and Queen of Spain. James was content to remain in his little island.

But the spirit of the great Elizabethans was still abroad and there were many English who rose in revolt against such a policy.

It was known that in Virginia mighty forests existed and their timber would be of great value; it was known that tobacco could be grown there. Was it not possible that there might be gold and other precious minerals?

Eventually John and his supporters managed to interest certain rich men in the scheme; the royal charter was reluctantly given, and the 'London Virginia Company' came into existence.

Now the task of fitting up the ships must be considered.

This took time and, chafing against the delay, John visited Willoughby to stay for a brief visit with his brother and sister-in-law, for he believed that when he said good-bye it might be for a very long time.

Francis talked earnestly to him on the day of his arrival.

'John,' he said, 'I have done well since I farmed here, and I have saved money. As you know, I have my Louth property which brings me in a good revenue.'

'So, Francis, you are a rich man?' murmured John.

'I am comfortably situated, John. I know what this venture means to you. I know that many have put money into it, and that if you did likewise it could mean that you had a bigger say in its conduct than you now have. I suggest that I buy the farm from you. This would leave you with capital to put into this enterprise.'

John considered this for some few minutes; then he took Francis by the hand and shook it warmly.

'I had intended to give you the farm,' he said.

'I know it. Well, I will buy it and you will become a shareholder in the "London Virginia Company". What could be more satisfactory?'

'Then let it be so,' said John. 'Francis, one day you must put a man in charge of the farm and come out to Virginia. I promise you, you will find it easier to prosper there than you do here. I'd ask you to join us now, but I know you would not leave your wife, and moreover in the first expedition there will be no women.'

'It is as well, John, that you have no wife. You might not be so wholeheartedly eager to leave England if it meant she must stay behind.'

'I shall never marry,' said John determinedly. 'See, I am twenty-six years of age and have managed so far without a wife.'

'A wife might be a comfort to you.'

'Virginia shall be my wife, Francis.'

Francis looked at his brother with affection.

That, he thought, could be so.

The expedition was ready to sail. It consisted of three ships. The largest of these, the *Susan Constant*, was a vessel of one hundred tons in the command of Captain Newport, who had distinguished himself in the service of Drake and Raleigh; the second was the *Godspeed*, forty tons, in the command of Bartholomew Gosnold; and the third, the *Discovery*, a pinnace of twenty tons, was under Captain John Ratcliffe.

The party numbered one hundred and forty-three people, and about a hundred of these were colonists. Seventy-one persons travelled in the *Susan Constant*, fifty-two in the *Godspeed*, and the remaining twenty in the *Discovery*.

On December the 8th of the year 1606 the pioneers

assembled at Blackwall in preparation to sail the next day.

It was on this day that John began to feel his first misgivings. He had naturally assumed a leading position in the enterprise for he and Gosnold had, after all, been two of its originators; and his adventures in Europe had made him accustomed to take command. There was a little group of men who seemed determined to oppose him at every turn, and these were men who had been highly regarded by the Company and would most surely have a place on the Council which was to be appointed on their arrival in Virginia.

The names of those chosen by the Company to be members of the Council had been written on a paper which was enclosed in a sealed box. This was to be opened on their arrival. John could not conceive that his name would not be one of those; yet at the same time he thought it very possible that some of those men whom he was already beginning to distrust would be mentioned also.

There were one or two men whom he singled out as potential enemies, and the chief of these was Edward Maria Wingfield.

Wingfield was an arrogant man with an inflated idea of his own importance. Moreover, he was a staunch Catholic and higher in the social scale than almost every other member of the expedition, for he was related to the Poles, and John was not unmindful of that family's one-time friendship with Spain. The only other member of the party who could count himself of more noble birth than Wingfield was the Honourable George Percy, who was a brother of the Earl of Northumberland. Percy, however, was of a mild nature. Not, John considered, likely to prove of great use to the expedition, he was clearly a man who cared about the success of the new colony and, since he was a mild mannered person who would not interfere, his presence was welcome.

But John determined to keep a sharp eye on Master Wingfield. Staunch Catholics were suspect and it seemed a pity in John's opinion that Wingfield should have been considered as one of the leaders.

They had all taken the sacrament together and in the little church at Blackwall prayed very earnestly for the success of their enterprise; and as they went aboard John decided to have a last check-up on the stores of the *Susan Constant*.

It was here that Wingfield and another of the emigrants, Captain Gabriel Archer, came upon him.

Wingfield said with studied nonchalance: 'And what do you here, Captain Smith?'

John explained in his exuberant way: 'Why, if we are short of anything 'tis better to discover it now than when we're days out to sea.'

'Of what should we be short?' asked Wingfield.

'How can I tell until I have made an inspection?'

'I did not know, Captain Smith, that you had been appointed to take charge of stores.'

John's eyes blazed suddenly. 'It was Captain Gosnold and myself who first thought that this journey should be made. I believe I have a right to interest myself in any part of it.'

'Captain John Smith,' said Gabriel Archer, 'the Captain, I believe, is a title you earned in the army. This is not the army. We are on board ship, and on board ship there is but one person from whom passengers and crew take orders: The Captain.'

'I believe,' retorted John, 'that neither you, Captain Archer, nor you, Master Wingfield, are captain of the *Susan Constant*?'

'You know full well it is Captain Newport.'

'Then I take orders from Captain Newport and no other.'

With that John turned and continued his inspection of the stores.

But the incident rankled. It boded ill for the journey which was to begin the next day.

* * *

The three ships were delayed in the Channel for three weeks, the winds being unfavourable. During this time relations between John and Wingfield and Archer did not improve. Moreover, many of the would-be colonists were sick even as the ships lay in the Channel, and they asked themselves: If this is life at sea when the coast of England is in sight, what is it going to be like miles out on the ocean? If this is how we feel during the first weeks, how are we going to feel after months of it?

There was no doubt that some of them would have asked to be taken ashore that they might abandon the project, but for John, who talked vigorously to them and managed to kindle in them a little of his own enthusiasm.

'The Company is not sending you out for a holiday trip,' he told them. 'If you are not the sort of people who can face a little hardship with courage, then go home, for you are not the kind we want to people the new colony of Virginia.'

And there was something in John's manner, in the fiery blue eyes, and the excessive vitality, which inspired these people. Not one of them left the ships.

There was one, however, whom John did try to persuade to return. This was the Rev Robert Hunt who had joined the expedition because he said that, although there were many clever men within it who would look after the physical needs of the colonists, their spiritual needs must not be neglected.

John had liked the spirit of this man with the gentle eyes and expression of infinite sweetness. Robert Hunt had been a welcome addition to the party as the ships lay in the Channel during those three frustrating weeks, waiting for the gales to stop, but John had his doubts as to the advisability of his remaining with the expedition.

He found Robert Hunt on deck one day, his face pale, his body doubled up with pain. Robert was clinging to the rail, looking at the coast of England.

'What ails you?' asked John.

'I am a little sick. I shall be better when we are out in the open sea.'

John realized then the physical frailty of the man and he was alarmed.

'This,' said John, 'is slight discomfort compared with what we shall have to endure later. You are wise enough to know that.'

'I fear so,' said Robert Hunt. 'And these people will need someone to lead them in prayer.'

'But you are not strong enough to undertake this task.'

'I have had a call from God,' the Rev Robert explained, 'and that is why I am here.'

'We could easily put you ashore,' said John. 'And perhaps we could persuade another chaplain to take your place.'

'I shall remain. I feel a certain power within me. This is the task allotted to me. God will give me strength to stay with you as long as I am needed.'

John stared back at the English coast. This was the spirit that was wanted; and when he thought of the bickering of men such as Wingfield, Archer and Ratcliffe, who appeared to be anxious that they might be jostled out of the high places they intended to take for themselves, he knew that men such as the Rev Robert Hunt were badly needed by the expedition.

'I shall pray,' said John soberly, 'that you will be with us for a very long time.'

There was great relief when, after three weeks, the ships set out for Virginia.

As they sailed across the Atlantic the friction which had begun to show itself while the ships lay in the Channel intensified.

Many of the would-be colonists had never been to sea before and they had little idea of what was in store for them. They were seen on the built-up decks of the two larger vessels, their faces bleak, their eyes almost fanatical. It came into John's mind, and into those of others of the leaders, that the colonists might one day demand that the ships turn back for England.

The constant lurching and rolling of the ships distressed these people; many of them suffered acutely from sea-sickness. The situation was not helped by the members of the crew who, aware that they were having a somewhat quiet journey across the ocean, were inclined to sneer at the landlubbers. The stewards and coxwains, the cooks, the trumpeter and the sailors, and even the youngest of the boys, took especial delight in showing their contempt; and when the colonists heard the nautical language of the crew they felt they were among strangers.

This amused the crew. They in any case were not going to settle in some strange heathen land, for Captain Newport, when he had landed the colonists and stayed with them awhile to settle them in their new home, would be returning to England with accounts of Virginia for the Company – and, it was hoped, a good cargo of valuables.

Robert Hunt, in between bouts of sickness, was, John realized, at this stage one of the most useful people aboard. He was ready to deliver a sermon at any time, and the people listened to him more eagerly than to anyone else.

It was ironical but true, thought John, that when people feared themselves to be in danger of death – as these people clearly did – they were at their most eager for spiritual guidance.

They had been a month or more at sea when John began to be a little worried about the stores.

They had been well stocked and carried with them sugar, prunes, spices and rice; they had beef which had been roasted and was pickled in vinegar; they had mutton which had been minced and stewed and put into earthenware pots with air-tight covers; they had butter in similar pots and quantities of salt fish; there were biscuits and oatmeal and bacon; there was wine and *aqua vitae*; there was marmalade besides almonds and comfits. Many who saw this food declared that it was enough to keep them free from hunger for the rest of their lives. This, John pointed out whenever possible, was because they were unaccustomed to seeing such large quantities of food. They must remember that they were a large party; and that they were not at all certain what they would find in Virginia.

John's plan was to land in Virginia with stocks to keep them going for the many months which would elapse while they looked round and perhaps had to till the soil to provide a harvest. But it was difficult to make the others understand this.

Wingfield who, on account of his noble birth, was looked to as one of the leading figures of the expedition, was so careless with the stores that he would take from them without keeping count of his withdrawals. As for Captain Newport, his one aim was to take his ship safely to Virginia; he did not concern himself – nor had he time to do so – with other matters.

Thus the main conflict sprang up between John and Wingfield and his supporters.

Wingfield called together a private council of his friends, among whom was Gabriel Archer.

'Who is this man, Smith?' demanded Wingfield. 'He would command us all. We have heard that he had great adventures in Europe and slew three Turks in single combat. Even if this was true, which I doubt, this would not entitle him to slay us.'

'You have reason for doubting that Smith slew the Turks, Master Wingfield?' asked one of those present.

'I have reason to believe he is a boastful, blustering man who would stop at nothing to win glory for himself. I went into the hold last night to take something from the stores, and I found him prowling about there. I asked him what he did, and he answered me most sharply; and I verily believe that if Captain Archer had not been with us he would have drawn his sword and killed me – and probably thrown my body overboard.'

'Could he do such a thing?'

'What could be easier? Does he not boast of killing three Turks?'

'It would seem,' said Archer, 'that we have a traitor and an assassin in our midst.'

'Be of good heart,' said Wingfield. 'He will not concern himself with the colonists. He cherishes them. His anger is turned against any of us who, he thinks, could be elected President by the Council when we arrive. He is determined to be President and rule the colony. For that reason he plans to kill all of us who might stand in his way.'

'What should be done about this?' asked Archer.

'We should take every means to balk him. None of us is safe while John Smith prowls about the ship.'

'What do you suggest, Master Wingfield?'

'That we put him in irons until we can execute him.'

'He would have to be tried before he could be executed.'

'It is true, but since we are unsafe while he walks abroad I believe that he should be clapped into irons immediately.'

'Could we do this without the command of the Captain?'

'Leave the Captain to me,' said Wingfield. 'Captain Archer and I will make him aware of the villainy which is being concocted on his ship.'

Shortly afterwards Wingfield sought out Captain Newport.

'Captain,' he said, 'certain of us have discovered a mutineer among us. It is John Smith whose arrogance you have doubtless noticed. We learn that he plans to murder myself and Captain Archer, and others whom he fears may stand in his way.'

'Mutiny!' cried the Captain. 'I'll not have mutiny in ships

under my command. Clap the fellow in irons and keep him there until this can be proved against him.'

'What is the penalty for such conduct, Captain ... assuming, of course, that the fellow is proved guilty?'

'Hanging by the neck until he dies,' retorted the Captain grimly.

Wingfield nodded; he was satisfied.

John was furiously angry. Here he was, a captive, when his presence was needed aboard.

He knew that the stores were not being kept as they should be; he knew that there was sickness and discontent among the colonists. And he lay, a prisoner in irons.

Wingfield was certain that he could prove his case against him, and so he set one of the carpenters to make a gallows.

This was done at a spot whence John could hear the continual hammering.

'A charming fellow, this Wingfield,' said John to himself. 'I see that we shall get on well together in Virginia.'

He was unafraid because he did not believe that the gallows would ever be for him. He had faced death on so many occasions that he did not believe it would catch up with him now. He had his enemies, it was true, but he also had his friends.

The Rev Robert Hunt came to talk with him. He was very sad that John should have been so accused, and he came to pray with him.

'Curb your anger, John,' he said. 'They will never be able to prove you guilty of these charges. The Lord will guard you now as he has on other occasions.'

'Master Wingfield's venom shocks me,' said John, 'but what disturbs me most is the thought that these men who plot against me are more concerned with gaining power than with the good of the colony. How can we face all the difficulties which must be ours, if we are going to fight among ourselves?'

'John,' answered the Reverend Robert, 'forgive me for asking this question, but will you give me a truthful answer? I think it is important. You are a natural leader. It is no flattery to say this, for it is clear to all and perhaps most of all to you yourself. They say that you wish to slay all those who you fear may be elected to be President of the new colony, so that there will be only yourself to take the post. It is foolish to say you plan to kill them, John, but how much does this Presidency mean to you?'

'A great deal,' answered John.

'I know it, John. Now search your soul and tell me this. Would you be President because of that love of power, that desire to organize all within your orbit, that desire to lead ... or would it be because in your heart you know that you are the best man for the task, and that only you can give the colony what you think it needs?'

John was silent for a while. Then he said thoughtfully: 'I think that both these notions enter into my motives, Reverend. I want power ... yes ... for the good of the colony. I know that *I* am the man to make the colony great. But I want power because of the love of power which is within me. Those are my reasons.'

Robert Hunt nodded. 'You are a truthful man, John. You must pray to God to subdue your love of power for its own sake.'

'I will,' answered John. 'And I say this, I think with truth, that if I believed that Wingfield or Archer, Kendall or one of the others would make a better president than I, I would say, "Stand down, John Smith. It is the colony that counts, not your pride."'

'I believe you, John. I pray that all will be well. Virginia needs you.'

They prayed together while not far off they heard the tap of hammer on the wood of the gallows on which certain members of the party hoped John Smith would hang.

* * *

Captain Newport was not concerned with the fact that there was friction between the leaders of the expedition. John Smith was in irons and he would doubtless be brought to the gallows when they reached Nevis Island in the Leeward Group; Newport had noticed John; it was impossible not to notice him, and he was inclined to think that John, being so young, should have been content to listen to the advice of men who were older and presumably wiser than himself. If John Smith was condemned to the gallows, Captain Newport did not think that fact would greatly affect his own task.

What he was worried about was the health of the colonists, who were already pining for England; life at sea was arduous for all, and for those unaccustomed to it wellnigh intolerable. Some years before a certain Captain Lancaster had kept his crew in good health during long sea voyages by a daily ration of lime juice; but the 'London Virginia Company' had not provided this for the crews and passengers in the three boats, and as they had lived so long on the ships' victuals the effects were now being felt.

He did not wish to land sick and dying people in the new colony, so he decided that he would give them a little respite from the sea journey by a stay among the West Indian Islands.

This plan was received with joy by all on board except John, who, chafing in irons, was unable to leave the ship.

Although he understood the need for a short stay he began to grow alarmed as the time went on and the colonists and the leaders of the expedition seemed to become more and more enamoured of these islands.

At the island of Mona hunting parties were organized from the ships, and one of the colonists, a man of noble family named Edward Brookes, died during the hunt.

John had so loudly voiced his disapproval of this delay that his enemies decided that now was the time to bring him to trial. The gallows were ready. Let them make an end of troublesome John Smith.

'I shall need to be judged by my friends as well as my foes,' cried John.

'Perhaps,' Newport said, 'we should have this man tried in London. In which case he would remain our prisoner until the *Susan Constant*'s return home.'

'Nay,' said John. 'That's folly. When you reach Virginia you are going to need the help of every able-bodied man, and one who has travelled as widely as I, and endured many adventures, may well be useful to you. Try me here and now. But I warn you that you will never persuade me to use your gallows.'

The Captain was faintly amused. For the first time he was impressed by the young man; arrogant he might be, but he had a good spirit and he was right when he had said men such as himself would be needed in Virginia. He was young and overbearing but, thought the Captain, keep him in order and he certainly would be the kind of man who could be useful to the new colony.

John had now won a certain support from Captain Newport, who was the most important man in the expedition.

When he was brought to trial, Wingfield and Archer rallied his enemies against him, but John had the support of his friends and it was impossible to prove he had attempted mutiny.

Captain Newport eyed him sternly. He said: 'He shall not go to the gallows as the charge has not been proved against him, but he should be kept in irons, and his friends should be distributed among the three ships so that, if there should be anything in this story of a conspiracy, they can conspire no further.'

John was angry. He could be of little use in irons. And the ships continued to linger in the West Indies.

On the island of Moneta they discovered wild fowl, so plenteous that they were able to catch them in their arms;

and when they climbed to the top of a small hillock they found eggs of many varieties lying on the ground. These they collected, and loaded several of the small boats with fowl and eggs and this for a few days made a change of diet which was acceptable.

On they went to the Virgin Isles; here they found strange animals such as none of them had ever seen before. They were horrified by the iguana, but they trapped fish by the thousand, and pelicans and parrots; and these they ate with great relish, so that when they left the West Indies, although the journey had been considerably delayed, the health of everyone was improved, and Captain Newport, good captain that he was, felt the time had been well spent.

But as they came into the open sea great winds had arisen and the three Captains, Newport, Gosnold and Ratcliffe, were uncertain at to where the winds had carried them.

Ratcliffe was of the opinion that they had been blown miles off their course and that they would never reach Virginia.

'Let us return home,' was his verdict.

John, chafing in irons, heard of Ratcliffe's desire, and his anger was of such intensity that he strained so recklessly to break out of his bonds that the iron cut into his flesh and the Reverend Robert Hunt beseeched him to regain his composure and good sense.

But John was furious. He cursed Ratcliffe who, when he heard of this, declared that John Smith should have been strung up on Nevis Island and that he would do all in his power to see that he did not escape the gallows for ever.

The winds were still raging and the colonists were very frightened; John heard them praying for a wind which would carry them straight back to England. He tried to reason with those to whom he was able to speak but they would not listen.

Night came and John could not sleep, for he believed

that the captains would lose heart if they failed to sight land soon. John thought of the stock of food which had been used in such a carefree manner. Was there enough to last if they must begin the journey back to England?

Fervently he wished that he were in sole charge of the expedition. It was maddening to think that after all his plans he was here in irons while other people had it in their power to shatter his dream – and just at that moment, when he was sure it was about to become reality.

During the night the wind dropped and, with the coming of morning, John lay gazing across the sea in that direction where he believed the land of Virginia lay.

He stared with excitement, for as the darkness fell away – surely what he saw was land.

For a few seconds he continued to stare in silence. Then he shouted. 'It's land! Land in sight! Land to the West!'

The three ships sprang to life in a moment.

There, before the Captains and the crews, the leaders of the expedition and the colonists, stretched out that fair land which Raleigh had named after the Virgin Queen – Virginia.

VIII

Up the James River

John tugged at his irons. This was the most frustrating position in which he had ever found himself. Never, he believed, had he suffered so acutely, even when, instead of the irons about his ankles, he had worn the Timor's iron collar about his neck.

There lay Virginia, the land of his dreams, and others might explore her while he lay a prisoner.

Some men had gone ashore. He lay, gently rocked by the boat, and cursed his fate. His should have been the feet that first trod that soil. That was *his* colony. Had he not said to Francis: 'Virginia is my wife, my children, my home?' And now he was unable to reach her, to embrace her, to swear to honour her. That was left to others, who would treat her lightly; who would not cherish her as he, John Smith, had sworn to do.

In the distance he heard the sound of musket shots. They could not be shooting the natives! That was not the way.

'Oh God,' he cried, 'how could you do this to me!'

Later his friend, George Percy, came and sat beside him.

'What has happened?' asked John.

'We went ashore – a party of us. Oh, it is a fair and goodly land. It is a land of meadows and tall trees, of rivers which run through the woods; a land of sunshine.

'A land where we can build houses, where we can grow corn?'

John's eyes gleamed.

'A land which we can call a corner of England?'

'A land of sweet flowers,' went on George, 'of cedar and

cypress trees, of fruits which are larger and finer than those we knew in England.'

'We must make friends with the natives,' John interrupted. 'That is of the utmost importance. Forget not that only they know the country. We shall be strangers to it. We shall need to trade with them. We must make sure they understand that we come as friends and not as enemies. I heard the sound of musket fire. Pray tell me what this meant.'

'When we were ashore they shot their arrows at us.'

'You should have told them you came in peace.'

'There was no time. We were returning to the ship when we saw them. Tall handsome people with skins the colour of copper. They seemed to be painted in some peculiar way – in red and white. They looked very strange to us, and I saw this was because their heads are shaved on one side and their long black hair on the other side of the head is gathered into a knot on the top – except one long lock which hangs down their backs. They seemed to be wearing feathers on their heads but there was little time to observe more as they were creeping towards us on hands and knees, and they carried bows and arrows in their mouths.'

'You should have found some means of making them understand.'

'We faced them with our muskets.'

John stamped his foot in such impatience that the iron cut into his skin afresh. 'That is not the way.'

'They sent a shower of arrows at us. These are dangerous weapons.'

'Anyone hurt?'

'Archer was hit in his hand; it is a slight wound, we hope, but one of the sailors caught an arrow in his body. He is rather more hurt. We then let them have it from our muskets. You should have seen their panic. I imagine that they have never seen anything like that before. They moaned and gabbled, and ran as fast as they could back

to the woods. That will teach them a lesson – not to interfere with the white men.'

John shook his head. 'It is not the right way.'

'I have a strong feeling,' said Percy, 'that you will find
yourself elected as one of the seven members of the
Council.'

'Much good would that do me, trussed up as I am,'
retorted John.

'Tonight, aboard the *Susan Constant*, we assemble to
open the sealed box.'

'And I,' replied John, 'shall have to remain a prisoner in
irons while this interesting ceremony takes place.'

'I tell you this, John,' said Percy; 'if your name is one of
the seven, which I believe and hope it will be, they'll be
unable to keep you a prisoner any longer. If it is the will
of the Company that you shall be a member of the Council
they must free you.'

'Alas,' said John, 'the directors of the Company are in
London, and London is far away. We are here in Virginia,
and here it is my powerful enemies who will decide my
future.'

'You'll not let any man but yourself decide your future,
John.'

Then John laughed exultantly. 'Do you know, George,'
he said, 'you are right about that.'

In the cabin of the *Susan Constant* the leading members
of the party were assembled under the direction of Captain
Newport. John was not present, being still in irons.

Captain Newport addressed the assembly.

'The moment has come,' he declared, 'to open the sealed
box and discover whom the Company has chosen as
members of the Council. We shall then elect the first
President of Virginia and learn what orders have been
given us. The first act will be to read the names of the
Council.'

He unsealed the box and all eyes were on him as he took a paper from it and read out the names. 'Edward Wingfield, Bartholomew Gosnold, John Ratcliffe, John Smith, George Kendall, John Martin and, for the time that he shall remain in Virginia, Captain Christopher Newport.'

There was silence. Then Wingfield burst out: 'I am willing to work wholeheartedly with all members of the Council save one. John Smith, the man who is now in irons suspected of treason, cannot be a member of the Council.'

Newport said wryly: 'We are the servants of the Company. It is essential that we obey their orders.'

'But this man has been discovered to be a mutineer . . .' stammered Wingfield.

'Not proven,' retorted Newport. Now that he had brought his ship into port, the Captain was ready to give his great energy to his second task, which was to leave the colony in good order before he returned to England. 'There is much work to do here,' he went on. 'We have already seen that the natives may well prove far from friendly, and we need every able-bodied man we can lay hands on. Smith may be overbearing, but let us remember that he could be one of the most useful members of the community. He certainly does not lack courage and I am inclined to think that what you have mistaken for incitement to mutiny was merely an excess of zeal. He shall be released within the next few days from his irons and shall be given his freedom. Gentlemen, we must sink our differences. I now propose to lay before you the Company's instructions.'

The colonists, he informed them, were to explore the country and, as it had been discovered that four rivers flowed into Chesapeake Bay, they were to explore these, discover the most fertile spot and there build their first town. They were to examine the surrounding country for precious minerals, and they were to send rich cargoes of their findings back to England.

'There are many instructions here,' went on Captain

Newport, tapping the box, 'but, before we continue with them, let us set about this business of electing our first President.'

The matter was quickly dealt with and, as George Percy, the most nobly born, was clearly a man who did not seek office, the next most noble was chosen; and as he was a man who obviously longed ardently for the position and was possessed of a strong character as well, Edward Maria Wingfield was elected First President of Virginia.

Wingfield as President was in no hurry to release John who had the maddening experience of knowing that exploration of Virginia had begun while he was not allowed to take part in it.

George Percy, Gosnold and the Reverend Robert Hunt brought him news of what was happening.

He heard that a party of explorers had gone a few miles inland and discovered some natives gathered about a fire, roasting oysters. The explorers were carrying their muskets, and the fame of these weapons, which seemed as magic to the natives, must have travelled before them because at sight of the newcomers they leaped up and fled.

The explorers then took their places and ate the oysters.

'Such oysters,' reported Gosnold, 'that our men said they had never seen before. They were larger than those we know. And going on a little farther our men discovered oysters and mussels lying on the ground for them to pick up. They brought a large number back and we shall feast well on them. This is a land of plenty.'

The days passed and still John remained a captive. Meanwhile, the colony had decided on a site for their first town. It was at the mouth of that river which they had called the James River. And as they had succeeded in making contact with the natives, Captain Newport, who was of the same opinion as John regarding the way the settlers should conduct themselves with the natives, asked to see the Chief among those who inhabited that spot near to which he intended to set up the town.

He discovered that the chiefs were called Werowances and that they were the equivalent of kings of their territory, that there were many Werowances, but there was one great King who was king of them all.

The rivers which flowed into the bay were known to the natives as the Potomac, the Rappahanock, the Pamaunke and the Powhatan; and the land in which the colonists proposed to build their town was known as Powhatan.

The Werowance from whom Newport gleaned this knowledge was chief of a small territory known as Paspahegh in the great country of Powhatan; and Captain Newport offered him a hatchet in return for the land on which he would build his town.

With this bargain the Werowance of Paspahegh was delighted. He had dressed himself with the greatest care to greet the strange Palefaces. On his head was a crown of deers' hair which had been dyed a deep scarlet, the colour of blood, and in this had been fixed two feathers shaped like horns. His body was painted blood-red and his face blue; the legs of fowls had been stuck in his ears and about his neck were rows of beads. He wore nothing else but an apron of buckskin; and this costume may have been intended to strike awe into the spectators; the explorers, however, found it amusing.

But the meeting was a friendly one and the Werowance of Paspahegh was joined by the Werowance of Rappahanock who, it appeared, endeavoured to outdo the glory of his brother chief's costume.

Captain Newport was delighted because the natives were proving friendly. The next task was to set about the building of the first town, and for this they would need the skill and ingenuity of them all.

Captain Newport remembered that there was one man

who might be very useful and whose skill was not being made use of.

He gave the order: 'Release John Smith at once. We have need for his services.'

So at last John came out of captivity; at last he was free to set foot in Virginia. Thus he was able to take his part in the building of the first town.

This town was called Jamestown, after the King of England.

Now there was great activity. Everyone was put to work. There were tents to set up; there was the land to prepare; there must be a stockade in case the natives ceased to be friendly. A fort was built and a few guns mounted on this. In those early days this was Jamestown.

Certain men were set to fell the trees, for Captain Newport had planned that his first cargo was to be of timber.

He decided that before he returned to England he must see a little of the country for himself that he might report on it to the eager shareholders, and he called John Smith to him.

He said: 'John Smith, I am grieved that it was necessary to put you in irons.'

'Not more grieved than I, Captain,' John answered promptly.

'It is a sorry state of affairs,' went on the Captain, 'when men engaged in an enterprise such as this fall out. I am aware of your good qualities, and I want to ask you to curb your petty annoyance which the manners of others may cause you. John Smith, I want you to remember the colony.'

'I shall never forget it,' said John.

'I do not think it is necessary for me to say more,' added the Captain. 'I am going on a journey up river and I propose to take with me the Honourable George Percy, and Captain Gabriel Archer, and I think I shall take Master Thomas

Wotton as he is a medical man. There will be a few others too and about fourteen sailors. Would you care to join us?'

John's eyes sparkled as he said nothing could please him more.

'I thought you would not hesitate,' said Newport, with a smile.

So they set out and sailed up the Powhatan River which they had renamed the James River.

This was the month of May, and the men experienced the full beauty of Virginia in springtime. John was exultant. This indeed was Arcadia. The trees were exceptionally tall; there were oak, beech, pine and cedar. Flowering shrubs grew prolifically in the woods and the blooms were of many brilliant colours. There were black birds with red wings, there were blue birds, humming birds and woodpeckers. They saw turkeys, squirrels and conies.

And they were warmed by a sun that was by no means fierce. The skies were blue, the forests green and the air filled with the song of the birds.

'A paradise!' cried John.

During their first day they saw natives on the river bank who came to peer through the trees at the strange craft and the strange men.

John cried: 'Let us do it this way.' And Newport who had begun to understand him and feel a certain amused tolerance for his youthful enthusiasm, replied: 'Try it your way, John.'

John was out of the boat. In his hand he held a string of red glass beads which glittered in the brilliant sunshine, and in spite of their fear the natives came close. John held the string out to them and indicated it was for them if they would come and talk.

Four of them came towards John and stood looking from him to the beads.

John gave them the beads, and they all crowded round

to study them. He then pointed to the boat and up-river. One of the natives had very bright alert eyes, and John addressed himself to this one. He bared his teeth and nodded. John thought he understood. Then he beckoned to the barge and Captain Newport and Gabriel Archer came ashore.

The natives appeared as though they would run, but when they saw that none of the men carried arms they were placated.

John took a pen and paper, and with the pen he drew pictures on the paper. He drew the natives and themselves; this made them look at each other and then look at the paper, and execute a few dancing steps which appeared to indicate the utmost amusement. John then drew the bay, the river, and the bank on which they stood.

Three of the natives looked blank, but the bright-eyed one began to dance, and it was clear that he understood. Then John pointed to the barge and indicated that they were sailing up-river. He wanted to know what they would find. He handed the pen to the bright-eyed native.

When he took it the others stepped back in fear, but he immediately began to mark the paper with the pen and his delight was obvious when he saw that he could do the same as the Paleface.

He understood what was wanted. In a very short time John had a rough map and some idea of what he must expect on the James River.

John invited the bright native into the boat, because he believed that in this man, who was obviously of a high intelligence, he might have found a useful guide and interpreter.

The man hesitated, but his curiosity, which was probably the reason for his unusual intelligence, got the better of his fear, and to the astonishment of the English and the Virginians, he agreed to come aboard.

This was success beyond any hopes, and Newport's

manner towards John ceased to be slightly amused and was even a little deferential. It was clear that John Smith was possessed of extraordinary gifts.

John himself took charge of their new guide and showed him the barge and all on it which he thought would be of interest to him. His manner, Newport noticed, was carefully calculated to win the friendship and trust of the guide, and this he succeeded in doing.

'Now,' said John, 'it should be less difficult to make friendly contact with the natives, and this I propose to do at the earliest moment.'

That moment was not long delayed. The guide, whose name was Nauiraus, had even picked up a few English words and John had learned a few of the natives ones so that he had no difficulty in telling him that he wished to meet the tribes. Nauiraus understood, and at one point he was put ashore with presents for the chief of a certain tribe; anxiously John awaited his return, fearing that he might be so overcome by the value of the beads he carried that he would keep them for himself.

But in a short time Nauiraus returned to the barge and told John, by signs and an occasional word, that he would be welcomed by the Werowance of the territory through which they were passing. So, armed with beads and brightly coloured toys as gifts, they went ashore.

Nauiraus conducted them to a village of wigwams, and before the largest of these sat the Werowance of the tribe – tall, copper-skinned, in buckskin apron and headdress consisting of feathers and the dead bodies of rats and other small animals. His face was painted blue with white stripes across it. Seated on their mats in a circle about their Werowance sat the braves of his tribe.

They were received in friendship, and the chief was wearing a string of beads which John had sent by way of Nauiraus as a present.

But the Virginians did not wish to take presents without

giving presents in return. They brought mats for their visitors and, when they were seated, roasted deer was set before them with oysters, mulberries, strawberries and nuts which tasted like sweet acorns. They were also offered pipes of tobacco, and when the smoke from the pipes of the copper-skinned people mingled with that from the Palefaces' it was clearly deemed a sign of peace.

The Werowance showed that he would give sweet nuts and beans in exchange for more beads and toys.

John was delighted. This was exactly what he had hoped to bring about: peaceful trade with the natives and an understanding that the white man did not come to rob them but only to share in a land of plenty which had more to offer than those, who already lived in it, could possibly need.

The news spread through the forest: 'The Palefaced men are among us.'

Everywhere Werowances wanted to have a share in the excitement. The Palefaces must visit *them*, must bring them presents, must sit with them, eat with them, smoke the pipe of peace with them.

And when they had been received by several smaller Werowances, a more important one wished them to visit him. This was Powhatah, who was chief over a large territory, and to whom it appeared the smaller Werowances paid some homage.

The ceremony of meeting the great Powhatah was a little different from those somewhat jolly occasions which the contacts with the smaller Werowances had been.

Powhatah was not as ready to accept the Palefaces as the other chiefs may have been. He believed they might have come to raid the copper mines, which were farther up the river, and take away copper which Powhatah needed for his own ornaments and implements.

However, Powhatah received the beads and other trinkets with appreciation, and in return gave food and tobacco. But he would have them know that he was a great ruler. He embraced Captain Newport as the leader of the Palefaces, and this meant that he was ready to be friends. He took them to show them the magnificent falls of the James River. These were so beautiful and awe-inspiring that the Englishmen could only stand and silently wonder at them. Then they realized that they could not navigate them, and that if they wished to proceed farther it would have to be by land.

'It is imperative,' John said to Newport and Archer, 'that we keep friendship with this Werowance who is clearly the greatest we have so far met. He is a little less inclined to accept our friendship than were the others, and, I fancy, is a little suspicious of us. Let us therefore invite him to a feast. We have pork with us, let us cook it with beans and, as tomorrow is Whitsunday, let us celebrate the occasion with this feast.'

'Let it be done,' said Newport; and the invitation was issued by way of Nauiraus, and most gleefully accepted by Powhatah.

During the feast which took place by the rapids, Nauiraus was seated beside John as was his custom.

'Tell the great Werowance,' John indicated, 'that we wish to travel into the copper country.'

Nauiraus told Powhatah, who was silent for some time. Then he spoke and the tone of his voice sounded ominous.

'No,' said Nauiraus. 'Not good.' He then began to make signs which indicated that there were mighty warriors in the copper country. They came to fight Powhatah at the fall of the leaves. There was much slaughter. They would slaughter the Palefaces as they did the great tribes of the Powhatan country.

Powhatah wished to end the subject but Newport and John would not do so. Therefore, before the pipe had been smoked, Powhatah rose, and with his friends he left the Englishmen.

Nauiraus shook his head and murmured: 'Bad. Bad.'

John was disturbed. He said: 'We should not have persisted. He showed us clearly that he did not wish to discuss the matter further and I'm afraid we have offended him.'

'We have been away long from the fort,' said Newport. 'I am beginning to be a little uneasy. I do not think Wingfield understands the natives as you have proved yourself able to do. I fancy he is ready to trust them too readily, merely because they accept a few beads and give him a pipe or two of tobacco. I think we should return to the fort and on another occasion venture further afield.'

John saw the sense of this and agreed.

'Before we go,' said Newport, 'we will mark this spot for England.'

The pioneers stood round Captain Newport as he set the wooden cross in the ground. On it was inscribed: *Jacobus Rex* 1607.

They stood in a circle about the cross and, as Newport lifted his hand, they shouted in unison: 'Long live the King. St George for ever!'

The natives, who had been watching at some small distance, were stricken with wonder at the sudden shouting of the Englishmen.

Later they came forward to inspect the cross; but none would touch it, fearing it to be magic.

They began to mutter together, pointing at the cross, and even Nauiraus showed his suspicion of it.

John sought to explain to him, and hit on the idea of telling him that the two arms of the cross represented those of the Palefaces and Powhatah; this was a sign of love and friendship.

The face of Nauiraus cleared and he hastened to reassure Powhatah, whereupon the great Werowance immediately insisted that the ceremony be repeated and that he take part in it.

So there was nothing for it but to uproot the cross and begin again. Powhatah stood up in his magnificent head-dress and cloak of turkeys' feathers, that he might appear grand among the Palefaces and, when the Englishman shouted 'Long live the King and St George for ever,' Powhatah and his braves leaped into the air and shouted with them.

This would have been a very happy occasion in spite of the first disagreement about the copper country, but unfortunately a native was caught trying to steal a hatchet. With a cry of anger one of the sailors struck him on the arm in order to retrieve the hatchet, and at that another native struck the sailor.

This was a small affair but it was evidently considered a great breach of etiquette by Powhatah and his tribe, who once more departed from the scene with affronted dignity.

'It is certainly time we returned to the fort,' said Newport.

So they began the journey back. The Werowance of Arahetec, who had entertained them on their way up-river, was eager to do so again. He had very much enjoyed their 'Hot drinks,' Nauiraus told them; and he now asked to see and hear the Paleface weapon in operation.

This was explained by much pointing, gesticulation and laughter, and at length a musket was fired; but at the sound of it the Werowance put his hands to his ears, and with his braves was ready to run back to the familiar cover of the forest.

This Werowance thereafter lost a certain amount of his pleasure in the Palefaces because he could not take his eyes from the muskets, and it was quite clear that he believed they contained some malevolent spirit.

Their next encounter was with a female Werowance – a lusty creature who was more like a man than a woman – very much decorated with beads and copper ornaments which comprised the main covering of her body. She received them with pleasure, sat with them, ate with them and smoked with them; she too demanded to see and hear the devil-machine, but when the musket was fired she sat, impassive and scarcely moving an eyelid.

Lastly they came to Pamaunke, the territory of a chief named Opechancanough, and Nauiraus told John that it was the will of this great Werowance that the Palefaces should visit him.

Opechancanough was one of the greatest of all the Werowances, second only to the ruler of them all whose real name was Wahunsonacock but who was known as Powhatan after the whole of the country over which he held sway. Opechancanough would be ruler on the death of Powhatan, and therefore it was necessary to be very friendly with him.

They left the boat and were conducted to his wigwam in the centre of his village. There sat Opechancanough. He had evidently dressed himself with the utmost care; his headdress of feathers and dead animals was an object of lively interest to all; his face had been painted a brilliant blue, and there were copper beads about his neck, while from one ear hung a great copper ring and from the other the tail of a dead animal. Sitting on his mat he received them with a dignity which was so obviously assumed to impress the Palefaces that the latter could only be amused by it.

But when Nauiraus told him of their reception by the other Werowances, Opechancanough unbent a little, and food was brought and the pipe smoked while white and red skinned men watched their smoke ascending.

John, however, was aware of a change in the demeanour of the natives. They were uneasy, and he wondered why.

He turned to Newport and said: 'Something has happened to change their feelings towards us. I sense it.'

'I shall be glad to see the fort again,' replied Newport uneasily. 'We have been too long away.'

'We will make our farewells to Opechancanough as quickly as possible,' replied John; 'we are only a day's journey from Jamestown.'

They took their leave of Opechancanough and went back to the barge.

The natives stood on the shore watching them and, as they slipped down the river, John called to Nauiraus, but he did not come.

'Nauiraus!' called John. 'Where is Nauiraus?'

To his dismay he soon discovered that Nauiraus had not come on board with them; and John, who was beginning to learn the ways of the Virginians, felt this to be full of significance.

He was now as eager as Newport to return to the fort.

They were welcomed with great relief by Wingfield who was quite clearly under some stress.

'The natives have attacked,' he said. 'I doubt not that they will soon return. They crept on us unawares while most of the men were at work in the fields. It was left to the rest of us to defend the place.'

'How could it have happened?' cried Newport. 'Was not someone on watch all the time?'

Wingfield looked rather sheepish. 'We thought them to be our friends. They had been . . . and then suddenly there was this attack. As I said, they crept upon us unaware.'

John let out an oath. 'Small wonder!' he snapped. 'Look at the weeds and grasses about the stockade. They could creep right up to us and not be seen in all that long grass. One would have thought that the first precaution would have been to keep the grass about the stockade short.'

Wingfield accepted John's criticism with a meekness which was surprising; and Newport thought: Wingfield is incompetent. It is a great pity that he was elected President. As for John Smith, he is doubtless the most capable man in the expedition, but he is one who will not suffer fools gladly nor keep a curb on his tongue. Oh, there'll be trouble here . . . great trouble.'

'Get that grass cut at once,' Newport ordered. 'We'll see that the guns on the palisade are constantly manned.'

Wingfield called one of the men and passed on the order.

'Now,' said Newport, 'tell us the details. Anyone killed?'

'A boy; and seventeen men wounded by their arrows. I myself narrowly escaped death.'

A reward for incompetence! thought John, and the retort trembled on his lips – and he would have uttered it had he not received a warning look from Captain Newport.

'An arrow caught me.' Wingfield laughed on a somewhat hysterical note. He touched his long beard. 'This saved me. The arrow went through it and did not as much as prick me.'

'Let us thank God for that piece of good fortune,' said Newport.

'Soon it would have been the end of us, had not those on the pinnace seen what was happening. They fired and that terrified the savages, who scattered.'

Newport was silent, and Wingfield went on: 'I cannot understand why their attitude should change towards us. They were friendly. They brought us presents, and we gave them beads and toys. Why should they suddenly cease to be friendly?'

John could restrain himself no longer. 'They saw the grass grown high about the palisade. Savages have no respect for fools.'

Wingfield flinched slightly but he accepted the rebuke without protest.

'If,' went on John, 'we are to live in peace with these people we must have their respect. We must show them that we are their equals in all matters – nay, we must prove ourselves their superiors. This means that we must watch, not only them but ourselves.'

'John Smith is right,' said Newport. 'He has travelled much and learned much.'

John turned in exasperation to Newport. 'Nauiraus would have been invaluable to us as a go-between. He was the best thing which came out of our journey, and now ... we have lost him. Out of such small matters as uncut grass can grow tragedy.'

John strode away. Both Wingfield and Newport looked after him.

Wingfield was silent; he felt too ashamed for speech; Newport was thinking: Soon I must leave for England. What then?

IX

Tension in Jamestown

June was almost over, and the *Susan Constant* and the *Godspeed* were loaded with a cargo of cedar and sassafras. The leaders of the expedition had been invited to attend supper in the captain's big cabin on board the *Susan Constant*, for the next day Captain Newport with two ships was sailing for England.

There was a feeling of tension everywhere. Even the men who were returning home were disturbed, because they knew that the Company would be disappointed with what they brought from Virginia; they were expecting gold and precious stones – and cedar and sassafras would be poor substitutes.

But those who were left behind were more uneasy.

The Virginians had attacked again and they were recognized as members of the tribe of Paspahegh; but once the grass had been cut around the palisade and they had experienced gunfire, they were less bold.

Several of them had been killed, and the sound of the wailing in the woods after this event filled thoughtful men such as John with apprehension. He felt that all his endeavours during the journey up-river had been nullified by the stupid conduct of those who were left behind.

But John was happier in some respects than he had been since the journey began. Wingfield, who was by no means an evil man, but only a self-opinionated and sometimes not very clear-sighted one, recognized his folly in allowing John's somewhat domineering characteristics to blind him to his virtues. Wingfield believed that the colony needed men such as Smith, and he was ready to forget their differences. He realized that John was not one to bear grudges; he had no time for that. John had one desire, and that was to make a successful colony. If the remembrance of a slight hindered this, John would be first to forget it.

Newport had also recognized John's outstanding qualities and was determined to have him reinstated, with the taint of mutiny wiped from him forever. Therefore he arranged that there should be a further consideration of his case; this took place, and John was completely exonerated and recognized as an honourable member of the Council.

John expressed his delight by his exuberance for work and voicing his own opinions; and Newport was conscious of a great relief.

As for Wingfield, he now believed that Gosnold and Archer were the men most likely to disagree with him, and did not stand in the way of John's being reinstated.

So now the company about the table was a little sombre.

'I shall be back with supplies in twenty weeks,' said Newport.

'We have only enough stores for some fifteen,' said Gosnold soberly.

'Ha!' cried John. 'We'll do a little trade with the natives, and if stores get low we shall have to allocate them with care.'

'I like it not,' said Gosnold.

But John would not be dismayed. They would continue to build the colony until the return of Captain Newport with provisions.

They took the Holy Sacrament, and prayers led by Robert Hunt were said for the safe voyage of the ships and the safety of those who were being left behind.

'Come,' said Newport to Wingfield, when they were saying their last farewells. 'Cheer up, man. You will weather all the storms till my return with the ships.'

'I trust not Gosnold and I trust not Archer,' murmured Wingfield. 'Gosnold could make trouble if he would. As for Archer, he would if he could.'

'Watch John Smith,' advised Newport. 'There is a man with dreams in his eyes and practical wisdom to go with them. A rare combination. I leave the happier, knowing that he is a member of the Council.'

'Doubtless I misjudged the fellow,' mumbled Wingfield, 'but he'd be more useful if his opinion of his own virtues were more modest.'

'Nay,' said Newport, 'there is a man who will achieve what others believe to be impossible, simply because he believes that with John Smith all is possible. Give him authority. Listen to him. He is one of those who will save Virginia for England.'

The next day a little group stood on the shore and watched the *Susan Constant* and the *Godspeed* sail away.

With the departure of the ships it seemed as though immediate ill-fortune struck the colonists.

The weather had been changing. The sunshine which had reminded them of the finest summer days in England had grown fierce beyond anything they had previously experienced. There was no longer the same freshness in the air. The Virginian spring was passing, and taking its place was the burning heat of summer.

Many of the colonists had been unaccustomed to physical labour and would have found outdoor work in an English summer arduous; they had much to learn of the Virginian climate.

They who had revelled in the heat now deplored it, as each day the blazing sun awakened them. The river had almost dried up, to disclose a malodorous slime.

John, watching them anxiously, calculated that as this was only the beginning of July there was the rest of the month and the whole of August to be lived through before they could hope for the cooler weather in September.

He rowed out to *Discovery* one day to look at the last of the grain, which was stored in the hold of the pinnace.

It was a hot day he would never forget. He looked back at the land shimmering in the heat, the tall trees, the fair meadows and the flowers which were more brilliant in colour than those they had seen on their arrival.

He had been anxious about the winter but it had not occurred to him that the summer might be their undoing.

He realized now that the corn they had sown would not be reaped in time to save them from hardship, and he cursed the folly of the leaders of the expedition who, while he was in irons, had tarried on the journey. If they had not lingered in the West Indies they would have sown their corn when the Virginians had sown theirs. There would be a rich and early harvest for the natives, which the settlers would miss.

John respected Captain Newport and he knew that, had he not given his passengers a respite from the sea, many of them might have died; but it was a big price to have paid.

He went down to the hold and untied one of the sacks in which the grain had been stored.

'That,' he murmured, 'will keep us alive for many months.'

But as he looked at it, he saw a movement, and when he looked closer the whole sack was heaving. There were more weevils there than grain.

Feverishly he tore open the rest of the sacks. They were all alive with weevils.

John stood for some time blankly staring.

What now? he asked himself. How can we keep alive until the return of Newport?

There was only one answer. They must bargain with the Virginians. Virginian corn must keep them alive until the ships returned.

He rowed himself back to the shore. He must call a meeting of the Council immediately and tell them what he had discovered. Food would have to be strictly rationed at once.

As he clambered ashore he saw two men carrying in another. He went over to them and asked what had happened, and his heart had sunk still further thinking this was another victim of a Virginian arrow.

'He complained of sickness and headache,' said one of the men, 'and then . . . he just collapsed.'

John examined the man, and fresh fear came to him. He had seen men look like that before. This one was the victim of a particularly virulent fever which was highly contagious.

He knew that this was an even greater blow to the colony than that which he had discovered in the sacks of grain in the hold of the pinnace.

Death stalked through Jamestown. It was impossible to work. Day after day more and more men were stricken with fever; and each day the heat grew fiercer.

The stockade was no longer a fortress; it was a hospital, as one by one men were laid low with fever and the few healthy ones who remained untouched by it must do the necessary tasks, which included burying their dead.

The groans of men could be heard throughout the nights and John, as he saw man after man stricken down, asked himself how much longer it would be before the natives got wind of the position within the fort and decided to make an end to the usurpers of their soil.

Starvation was facing them, and it was impossible for any to go and attempt to trade with the Indians; a few struggled feebly on tilling the soil, half-heartedly knowing that the corn had been sown too late; but lethargy had crept into the settlement. 'Our days are numbered,' they said to each other. 'Why should we seek to prolong our lives since they must be lived in misery?'

It seemed that there was but one among them who never seemed to lose hope, who stubbornly refused to accept defeat. He irritated the others almost beyond endurance, although he had the grudging admiration of them all.

Virginia was his wife, his home and children; and John Smith was a man who would have suffered any torment to protect his family.

'We must continue to keep Jamestown in existence,' he told them again and again. 'We did not take into consideration the fierce heat of the summer. But it must pass. The autumn will come, and that will be as beautiful as the spring.'

But one day, when John Smith himself attempted to rise from his bed, his legs doubled under him and he fell back. He was sick and dizzy and, like so many others, he understood that day that the fever had come to him.

The news spread through the settlement. 'John Smith is stricken with the fever. Who will deal with our rations now? Who will tell us that naught is of significance, save the colony? What of John Smith now?'

For three days he lay on his bed unable to move, and it seemed to him that death was as near to him as it had ever been. But he had become accustomed to eluding that icy grasp.

'I will not die,' he repeated to himself again and again. 'I must live. I must preserve Virginia for England.'

One of the colonists, who had expressed a great admiration for him, made himself his nurse, and from this man he learned what was happening in the settlement.

'There is continual discontent,' he was told. 'They are asking how they can hope to exist on half a pint of wheat and half a pint of barley boiled in water – and that is all they may have for the day.'

'They are fortunate to get that!' retorted John.

173

'Now that you are stricken, there is murmuring everywhere. Some of them want to offer all our guns and hatchets to the natives in exchange for food.'

John began to sweat afresh at the thought of such folly.

'That must be prevented,' he said, 'by any means.'

'Ay, Master Smith, and luckily so far nothing has been done to bring it about. They are afraid of the arrows that may strike them down before they have time to make their bargain.'

'It must be stopped. It must be stopped!'

In his fever John said it over and over again, and it was like the beating of drums in his head.

That night it seemed to John that a figure came into his tent, and he knew it for Death.

He felt as he had at that moment when the Timor had stood before him, the whip in his hand. And John Smith wrestled with Death as once he had wrestled with the Timor of Nalbrits; and in the morning, when his nurse came in to look at him, he found John lying in his bed exhausted and pale ... so pale that for a moment he thought he was dead.

But John Smith was not dead. He was pale because the fever had left him, and when he spoke his voice had the old clear and authoritative ring.

John Smith had thrown off his fever; once more he had wrestled with Death and won.

He was exhausted, but in a day or so he would be at work.

The news spread through the settlement. 'The fever has left John Smith. He is on the way to recovery. Soon he will be among us once more.'

But many groaned and said: 'The rations will be less than ever. We shall be made to work, sick as we are. We shall be told that we should eagerly give all we've got to the colony. Oh, John Smith will soon be among us again to harry us.'

Nevertheless, there was a feeling of relief. Every man among them knew that, if they dared to hope they would survive this terrible disaster which had fallen upon them, they could only do so if John Smith were there to command.

John was on his feet again, but there were more disasters to come. The August heat was even greater than that of July, and another enemy appeared to torment the settlers: malaria.

Bartholomew Gosnold was one of the first to be smitten. John nursed him, but it quickly became apparent even to John's ebullient nature that Gosnold could not survive.

John was with him at the end, when Gosnold talked of their meeting in the London inn when the project had been born.

'So this is the end of it, for me, John,' said Gosnold. 'We never thought it would end this way, did we? If it had been an arrow from one of those savages one could have accepted that. But here in my bed . . . Who would have believed it?'

'You must not worry. You must rest. Remember I am here, Bartholomew, to take care of you.'

'You . . . John Smith, are invincible. You were stricken but you recovered. There is something within you, John, which we lesser men do not possess.'

'Nay, I am less advanced in years – that is why I rallied.'

'It is your invincible spirit, John. Oh, now that I am on my death-bed I am sorry I quarrelled with Wingfield. He is not worthy of his task, but at heart he is a good and religious man.'

'Think not of him.'

'I must think of you all . . . you who will be left to build Virginia when I am gone. They are now accusing Wingfield of eating well from the stores while the rest starve. 'Tis not true, John. He is incapable of such an act.'

'I know him to be incapable of it. The men are weary. They would as lief accuse you or me.'

'Not you, John. They have seen that in you which we all admire. It is apparent in adversity. We were wrong, John. We should have made you the first President of Virginia.'

Gosnold turned his head away wearily, and John wiped his brow.

He sat by the bed awhile, even though there was much to do elsewhere. This was a special occasion, this was the passing of an old friend.

After a while he stood up and bent over Gosnold. He touched his brow and lifted his eyelids. Then he knelt by the bed and prayed for the soul of this man, and that some miracle might happen to save them all and Virginia.

During August, Ratcliffe and Martin went down with malaria; and John himself, with the aid of Thomas Wotton, the doctor, undoubtedly saved their lives.

The position was growing worse. Each day John checked off the supplies and counted the days. He was longing for the end of August.

But September came in as hot as August, and often men could see a painted body emerge from the long grass about the stockade, for there was now no one to cut the grass and it offered excellent cover for any marauding force.

Every minute they expected to hear the wild war whoop and they asked themselves what would become of them? How could they hope to defend themselves?

Inside the settlement was sickness and despair; and outside a brooding ominous quiet.

One day soon they will come, thought John; and he tried to prepare the colonists for such an event. They listened half-heartedly. Savage warfare seemed little more terrible than what they had already suffered.

Complaints rose against Wingfield, and the Council

unanimously agreed that he must be deposed.

The obvious man to elect in his place was John, but there were still many who reminded each other that on the way out he had been suspected of mutiny; he was too overbearing, they said; it would be work, work all the time, under John Smith, who did not realize the importance of a little leisure.

So they elected Ratcliffe as their next President, for they said he was not a man to bestir himself greatly and would be but a figure-head. Whereas whether John be elected President or not he would work just the same for the colony.

They chose John as their spokesman to go to Wingfield and tell him what had been decided. John was loth to do this, in view of what had already passed between them, and he feared that the ex-President might believe that he was glorying in his defeat.

However, since he was elected to do the job, he did it.

'I come with unpleasant news,' he told Wingfield. 'The Council have deposed you.'

Wingfield nodded. 'I understand,' he said. 'I have done my best. But who could hope for success in such a venture! Everything was against us.'

'They have elected Ratcliffe in your place.'

'Then they must be mad. You are the obvious man for the Presidency.'

'They think otherwise.'

'I tell you they are mad.'

'You have changed your opinion.'

'I am a man who will change his opinions when his eyes are opened a little wider.'

'Thank you,' said John. 'I fear we misjudged one another.'

They shook hands before they parted. John had the idea that Wingfield was not sorry to relinquish the task which had been too much for him.

*   *   *

To the great relief of all, in the middle of September the heat abated.

Everyone's hopes soared. John rallied the little company together, for Ratcliffe was quite content to leave everything in his hands. Now that the heat had passed they must get out into the open air; they must build their houses and clear the ground for more corn.

He could see the need of spiritual guidance for these men, who were not only sick in body but in mind. He heard them at every turn talking of England with a yearning which showed a madness in their eyes. They remembered the cool refreshing rain, the sun which was never so fierce as to be uncomfortable. They talked of all they had left behind; and even those who had come from the direst poverty in England feigned to believe – or perhaps actually did believe – that they had left a life of luxury for this new and terrible land.

John superintended the building of a barn, and here the Reverend Robert Hunt preached many a sermon.

The time had come when it was absolutely essential to trade with the natives. John must buy food, and he set out on a journey up-river accompanied by one or two men who he felt could do more useful service with him than they could in the colony.

The Virginians met him. They watched him slyly and, when he offered beads and needles and pins, they showed him small pieces of bread and a few handful of beans.

John understood. They believed the colony to be starving; therefore it seemed to them that John would be ready to give a great deal for a little food.

He made signs to them and spoke one or two words which he had learned from Nauiraus.

'More,' he said. 'More!'

The Virginians added one more handful of beans to the little pile.

John turned to step back into the boat.

The painted faces expressed surprise. They looked at each other. The power of John's personality was felt by them.

Quite clearly he had, after all, not come to beg but to bargain. They wanted beads, pins and needles as much, it seemed to them, as John Smith wanted their venison and beans.

It had been a mistake. If they wanted these treasures of the Palefaces they must pay for them.

John returned to the settlement with a boatload of provisions.

With what relief did they watch the passing of September. The health of everyone improved and Jamestown took on life again.

John made more and more expeditions up-river and returned with such cargoes of corn and beans that he was able to build up a small store.

Then, with the coming of the colder weather, cranes and swans, geese and ducks appeared in great quantities on the river. These made an appetizing and varied diet for hungry men who needed to build up their strength after weeks of semi-starvation.

John's eyes were for ever on the future, and he wished to build up the stock of food. The summer heat had caught them unready; John dreaded the winter, which he believed might be as cruel in its cold as the summer was in its heat.

So he continued to make journeys into the Powhatan territory, and again and again he came back with corn for his store.

But it seemed that, when John was not with them, mischief grew among the colonists; and the yearning for England had become so acute in some of them that they could think of nothing else.

John had intended to go farther up-river and trade with certain of the Virginians whom he had not seen since his first forays into the land with Captain Newport; however, he changed his plans and returned to the settlement some five or six days before he had intended to.

As soon as he returned, he knew that something was wrong, for he read it in the shamefaced looks of the men he saw.

'Has aught happened during my absence?' he asked.

'Nothing, Master Smith,' he was told.

But he was not sure of this.

'Where is Master Wingfield?' he asked. But Master Wingfield was not to be seen. Nor was Captain Kendall.

The Reverend Robert Hunt came hurrying to him. 'There is trouble, John,' he said. 'I thank God you have returned.'

'What is this trouble?'

'A plot between Wingfield and Kendall. I have only this day learned of it, so secret have they kept it. But the blacksmith, whom Master Wingfield accuses of insubordination, has told me of it. They have stored food in the pinnace, and they plan, with a few chosen men, to slip away to England.'

John's face darkened with anger.

This was a dastardly act, for when they sailed away they would take with them food which he had risked his life to get from the savages.

'John,' said Robert Hunt, 'they will already have been informed of your return, and it may well be that they are attempting to slip away at this moment.'

John did not hesitate another second. He summoned a few of the men who he knew would serve him with their lives.

'To the guns!' he commanded. And with them he hurried to the guns on the palisade and trained them on the pinnace.

He roared instructions and, to his delight, he saw Wingfield, Kendall and some of their confederates appear on the deck of *Discovery*. 'You mean-souled creatures!' shouted

John. 'So you would slip away to England! You would desert your companions! I give you two alternatives: You will stay here or you will sink.'

They knew John, so they believed he meant what he said. Shamefacedly they realized that he had foiled their plans. As they stood there, disconsolate and uncertain, John sent out boats to have them brought in.

They were going to stand their trial for treason to the Company.

This, John reasoned, was the most dangerous of all their troubles: disloyalty and treason within.

He was going to deal with them harshly.

There should be a trial, and punishment should be severe, for John must be free to go on his expeditions and know that there was peace in the settlement.

The blacksmith who had struck Wingfield was sentenced to the gallows but, as he was about to ascend the ladder to the tree-top from which he was to hang, he turned to John and said: 'I could give you information which would surprise you, and I would do so in exchange for my liberty.'

John hesitated for a second or so. It was not he who had wished the blacksmith to hang; that had been the verdict of the Council. He was acutely aware of the value of lives, and they had lost too many, during the plagues of fever and malaria, lightly to throw away even one.

He said: 'Let us give the blacksmith his life in exchange for this information.'

So the blacksmith was taken into the Council chamber and there he spoke.

'You gentlemen know that there is one great enemy of England and England's colonizers. And why? Because this enemy wants the whole of the New World for itself. I speak of the Spaniards. Captain Kendall has been a very pleasant gentleman. He has been helpful in building the town. He is a Catholic, gentlemen; and in the pay of Spain. He is with us for one purpose; and that is to wipe us out as soon as he can, so that there is no English colony in Virginia. I have heard him talking to Master Wingfield. I have seen them together and I have watched them. It was for this reason that I struck Master Wingfield. These men are Catholics and they work for Spain.'

The Council was astounded and, if there was one among them whose anger almost choked him at the mention of Spain, that man was John Smith.

Surely this was the greatest misfortune which could have befallen them.

Captain Kendall! A man whom they had all respected.

John insisted on a thorough investigation. He called Wingfield to him, for much as he disliked Wingfield he did not believe he would be guilty of working against England.

Yet he had planned to escape in the pinnace.

'Did you know that Kendall was a Catholic?' asked John.

'Of course I did. We are both Catholics.'

'I do not wish,' said John, 'to persecute colonists for their religious opinions. But if as Catholics you were prepared to work against England, that is another matter.'

'I would never work against England.'

'Yet you were about to abandon us.'

'Only because I believe that we cannot continue through the winter. I have said this many times.'

'It is a policy of defeat, and we have no use for men who hold such views.'

'We must be reasonable,' retorted Wingfield.

'So you planned to desert us.'

'To sail to England and report the true position, and to return with food.'

'Captain Newport will do that.'

'We cannot wait for Captain Newport. Moreover, he may have been wrecked on the way home. The winter is almost upon us.'

'You must tell me everything that Kendall has said to

you. He is a fellow Catholic, but it is important that, if he is working for Spain, he should not be allowed to live here among us.'

Wingfield was silent. Staunch Catholic though he was he was horrified to have been involved with a man who supported the great enemy of England. He could not bring much tangible evidence against Kendall, but Kendall was suspect; and John realized that they could not afford to have among them a man of Kendall's abilities who might conceivably be working for Spain.

After much heart-searching as to the justice of this, John came to the conclusion that even justice must be set aside. The colony might be in danger, and the colony was all-important.

Therefore he advised that Kendall be put to death, not because he was proved to be a Spanish agent, but because he was suspected of being so and could not prove he was not; and they dared not run the risk of those suspicions being justified.

Kendall was shot. Wingfield was made a prisoner in the pinnace, and tension brooded over Jamestown.

Wingfield now being dishonoured, John's position was made more secure by the Council. He was completely cleared of those charges which had been brought against him and awarded damages – a somewhat farcical proceeding because money could mean little in a community such as that of the settlement.

John was constantly aware of the need to keep the store of food high. He was determined to make provision against the winter.

He took the shallop, which had been made after their arrival in Virginia, up-river to a spot which was called, by the Virginians, Kecoughtan because he had been told by those natives from whom he had bought corn that there were great stocks of it at this place.

They reached Kecoughtan and, to their surprise, although they saw grain heaped up on the banks of the river there were no signs of anyone near.

As John and his men left the boat, he warned them: 'Have your muskets ready. I like this not. It may well be that a trap has been set for us.'

They went cautiously into the woods and when they came to a clearing John halted, ears strained for the slightest sound. Suddenly the chanting of voices could be distinctly heard; it rose to a shout and was followed by what could only be called a roar.

'Hold your fire,' commanded John. 'Wait for orders. We cannot be sure what this may mean.'

There was a rustling in the undergrowth and into the clearing rushed about sixty Virginians; they were dancing as they came and, watching them, John did not believe that in those first seconds they were aware of the Englishmen.

Their faces were painted in various colours – some red, some white, some blue and some black; they were dressed in what John knew now to be their ceremonial garments; they carried clubs which they brandished fiercely as though at some invisible enemy.

Before this throng walked two of their number who between them were carrying a grotesquely painted wooden figure.

When they saw the Englishmen they all stopped and uttered a wild cry of rage, and John realized at once that he and his men had stumbled into some religious ceremony, and that the fact that they had witnessed part of a sacred rite would infuriate the savages and determine them to slaughter the white men without question.

As the leader of the group let out a great war-cry, John gave the order to fire.

The men who were carrying the image were killed by the volley; they lay on the grass beside the wooden figure;

and as gunfire never failed to terrify the Virginians, the others ran.

John went forward and picked up the image. It was in the form of a man, and on the face had been painted a grimace of infinite cruelty.

'I do not like the look of him,' said one of the men.

'It is meant to inspire fear,' answered John. 'Let it be a lesson to us. They can only respect what they fear. Back to the shallop as quickly as possible! They may overcome their terror of our gunfire when they discover that we have their image.'

They went with all speed back to the boat, John carrying the wooden figure.

John, who by this time had begun to understand the character of the inhabitants of Virginia very well, kept the shallop in the same spot and waited. He had come to bargain for grain, and he was not going back to Jamestown until he had it.

He believed that very soon someone would be sent to ask for the return of the idol.

He was not wrong. Within an hour two of the most luridly painted of the party, who had fled at the sound of gunfire, cautiously approached the shore.

John hailed them. He held up the image, and the two men threw themselves on to the ground.

Clearly, thought John, we have in our possession one of the greatest of their gods. I must make good use of such an opportunity.

The two Virginians began to wail as they lay on the ground, and John, who had learned a certain amount of their language, knew that they were asking what they must bring the Palefaces for the return of the image.

John was exultant. He knew that he could demand a high price.

He went ashore and squatted on the grass beside the savages, who eyed his musket fearfully.

'Let six of your number bring enough corn and any food you may have to fill this boat. When that is done I swear by my God to return to you the image.'

'It is great Oke,' they told him. 'He could bring great misfortune to you.'

'He has no power to harm the white man,' John told them gleefully.

'We shall die unless we return him to his temple.'

'Bring the food I ask and he shall be yours.'

The men went away and in a very short time six others were seen bringing grain and venison to the boat.

John watched them, loading it, and all the time he stood, holding Oke under his arm while he kept a firm hand on his musket.

When the shallop was loaded he gave them the image.

It was an excellent bargain, and when he added beads and a few hatchets to give good measure, the Virginians were delighted.

And, squatting on the grass, one of them began to sing. The music of the Virginians sounded like cacophony in English ears, but John and his men applauded enthusiastically when the song was ended. Then certain of the men danced for the Englishmen, and pipes were brought out that they might smoke together.

The shallop, crammed to the full with provisions, rocked gently in the river; the smoke from the pipes circled above the party.

It was time to leave for the settlement.

'Paleface, my brother,' said the leader of the men. 'Paleface give back great Oke, and Oke will not harm them.'

'We are brothers,' replied John. 'Pale face – Copper face. We are brothers.'

They took their leave of the Virginians who stood on the bank watching the boat make its way back to the settlement, listening in wonder to the sound of English voices raised in song.

John said: 'So that which might have cost us our lives brought us what we set out to obtain.' He sighed. 'These short expeditions for food teach us little of the country. Soon Captain Newport will be back with us, and he will ask us what explorations we have made.'

'How could we be expected to explore?' asked one of the men. 'It has cost us all our time and ingenuity to keep ourselves alive.'

John's eyes were gleaming. 'The sickness has passed,' he mused. 'There is a goodly store of food in the settlement. On my return I shall prepare to make a trip in a hitherto unexplored direction. There is a tributary of this river which I have long wanted to navigate. Yes, before Captain Newport returns I must make a trip along the Chickahominy River.'

X

Up the Chickahominy River

John addressed the Council.

'In a short time from how, Captain Newport should be arriving from England with fresh supplies and we shall be expected to have information for him to take back to the Company. I therefore propose to set out on an expedition to explore the Chickahominy River. The time is ripe. Our Tuftaffaty humorists here in Jamestown have been feeding royally of late on good bread, peas, pumpkins, persimmons, fish and divers wild fowl and beasts. We have heard less of their desire to return to England. I could safely leave the settlement at this time and I plan to leave immediately.'

The Council agreed to this decision. It was true that they were expected to explore and report on the fertility and potentialities of the land, and they were all agreed that there was not one among them who possessed John Smith's ingenuity, resourcefulness and yearning for discovery.

'Very well,' went on John, 'I will make my preparations and leave tomorrow. I propose to take seven sailors with me and a carpenter – for he may be useful – and perhaps one of the gentlemen. I intend to ask Master Jehu Robinson if he would care to accompany me.'

With the Council's approval John lost no time in putting his plan into action. Jehu Robinson was delighted with the honour of accompanying John on a voyage of discovery. Thomas Emry, a carpenter, was also chosen with seven sailors, among whom was George Cassen – a man who was eager for adventure but not quite so eager to take orders.

It was December and the river was teeming with wild

fowl and birds which had come in from the sea for shelter. The barge travelled up the river, which was bounded on either side by high cliffs.

They had travelled some fifty miles when the character of country and river changed; the cliffs gave way to woods and the river had grown more rapid and some great trees had fallen into it so that it was impossible for the rather cumbersome barge to proceed. Here was the first obstacle, and John was wondering whether it would be possible to remove the trees, when a canoe containing two natives came winding its way between obstacles, and skilfully negotiating the rapid currents of the river.

'Canoe!' cried John. 'That is what we need.'

He hailed the natives.

They paddled close to the barge. John showed them beads and toys, of which he always took a good supply on all his trips. With the words at his disposal and a few gestures he explained that the trinkets were for the natives if they would take the white men up the river in their canoe and act as guides.

The natives looked at each other, and that expression which denoted pleasure began to creep across their faces. They hung the proffered beads about their necks and beckoned John into the canoe.

John turned to Jehu Robinson and Thomas Emry, saying: 'You two, come with me.' To the sailors he added: 'Stay here and await our return. Do not leave the barge. I believe this part of the country to be very thickly inhabited and it is possible that the natives may be hostile. But you will be safe if you stay in the barge.'

Thereupon John, accompanied by Jehu Robinson and Thomas Emry, got into the canoe and very soon it was carrying them swiftly up-river.

The sailors watched the canoe until it was out of sight, then settled down to await its return.

* * *

Half an hour passed and they grew tired of waiting.

George Cassen, who had stepped into the position of natural leader, said: 'It's all very well for Captain Smith. He is always the one to have the fun. We're left behind to do nothing. I'll warrant there are some birds and game to be had over there.'

The others looked towards the land, where the trees grew thickly, and whence every now and then they would hear the rustle of undergrowth or the cry of a bird.

'We have our muskets,' said one.

'We could slip ashore, shoot some game and have it cooked ready for the Captain by the time he returns,' suggested George Cassen. 'I'll swear he'd not be angry if he found a good meal waiting for him. What say you?'

'The Captain gave instructions,' one of the men reminded them, 'to stay aboard.'

'Very well,' said Cassen, 'you stay. What about the rest of you? Are you frightened of these copperskins?'

'Nay,' cried the others. 'Let us go. As George says, the Captain will be pleased if he finds a nice pot of stewed fowl waiting for him on his return.'

So the men scrambled ashore – except the one who had first demurred – and they soon disappeared into the woods.

Left alone he strained his ears listening, and suddenly he heard a wild native war-whoop, and he began to sweat with fear, for he dreaded an affray with the natives while Captain Smith was not there to command.

He was glad that he himself had obeyed orders and remained aboard, and he wondered what he would do if the others failed to return.

He then heard a scream of terror and saw the sailors running through the wood towards the river. George Cassen was at the rear, and behind him came some twenty natives, ferocious in their war-paint.

The man who had stayed at his post was tense, preparing to help the sailors clamber aboard. They reached the barge

– one, two, three . . . yes, six of them. But before George Cassen could run down the bank he was seized.

His body was thrown into the air and caught by several of the natives who, with demoniacal laughter, disappeared with him among the trees.

The five sailors clambered aboard. They were sweating with fear and their exertions.

'Another minute,' said one of them, 'and that would have been the end of us. But for my sharp ears . . . we'd have been caught . . .' He stopped. 'Hey, where's George?'

He who had remained behind said slowly: 'They caught him. I fear we shall never see George again.'

All the men turned to stare at the trees, but there was no sign of George Cassen or his captors. They shivered and did not meet each other's eyes. They knew the treatment which the natives gave to their enemies when they felt the inclination to do so. This might have happened to any one of them.

The man who had remained behind said: 'The Captain has gone up-river. He has only Master Robinson and Thomas Emry with him. It's the Captain they're after. And the woods are full of them.'

'What should we do?'

'I think we should sail back with all speed. I doubt if we shall ever again see any of the others who set out with us on this trip up the Chickahominy Rover.'

George Cassen was surrounded by grotesquely painted faces; fierce eyes under headdresses of feathers and dead animals watched him.

'Where is the great Paleface Werowance?' they wanted to know.

Cassen caught his breath. So they knew John Smith was nearby. It was John Smith they wanted; he, the great Werowance of the white men, he, the great magician. They respected him because they feared him; but doubtless they believed that a hundred of them were more than equal to his strength and cunning.

Cassen shook his head. 'We come alone. No great white Werowance came with us.'

The natives talked together and, after a few minutes, two of them came to Cassen and seized him; they tied him to a tree while others lit a fire close by.

Then one of the natives brought a mussel shell and showed it to him. Cassen grinned nervously, not knowing what was expected of him.

'Which way went the big Chief Werowance?' asked the man with the mussel shell.

Cassen said: 'No Werowance. We come alone.'

Cassen felt a sharp pain in his hand. His bleeding thumb was thrown into the fire, while those who had formed a circle about the tree began to dance with glee.

In a matter of seconds he was set on by others, all armed with mussel shells; and his hands and feet were soon lacerated and bleeding stumps, for all his fingers and toes had been hacked off and thrown into the fire.

Now they danced round him with renewed frenzy. 'The Werowance, the great chief, where went he?' they cried.

They were approaching him with their mussel shells. He screamed: 'Up the river. He has gone up the river with two others and two of your people. He has gone in a canoe. He cannot have gone far.'

They smiled and began dancing around him; he had told them what they wanted to know, but they would not be robbed of their pleasure. He was falling into unconsciousness when, with their mussel shells, they flayed the skin and hair from his head and hung up his scalp to dry on a nearby tree. He did not know what further foul atrocities they committed; he did not feel the fire which consumed his body and the tree to which he was tied.

* * *

Meanwhile, John went up on the river and when he had proceeded some twenty miles he said to Jehu: 'It seems quiet here. I think we might go ashore and perhaps cook a little food.'

Jehu and Thomas Emry agreed that this was an excellent idea, so they left the canoe, and with the two natives scrambled up the bank and went a little way into the woods.

'Here is a good spot,' said John. 'Let us set the pot to boil here. I will leave you two to look after it while I explore awhile. I shall not be long. I'll take one of the guides with me and leave the other with you.' John paused and listened. 'It seems quiet,' he went on, 'but we should be prepared. If any natives should appear fire a shot in the air and I will return at once. I shall make sure not to go beyond earshot. I'll take the French pistol with me. Come,' he said to one of the guides, 'we'll go along.'

They went off into the woods, and John talked with his guide as best he could for he had now made himself fairly fluent in the Powhatan tongue. The guide was both friendly and intelligent, and John was thinking of suggesting that he should return with them to Jamestown, when he heard a sudden war-whoop. He stopped short. There was no warning shot, which Robinson and Emery had promised to give.

He guessed what had happened; they had been surprised, and either killed or wounded before they had time to fire their muskets.

Could it be that the two natives had betrayed them, had led them into an ambush? John's prompt actions had saved his life many a time, and now in a second he had taken off a garter and bound his guide to his left wrist.

He turned and, dragging the native with him, made with all speed back towards the spot where he had left Emry and Robinson; but even as he took his first step an arrow brushed past him, and a native appeared, bow and arrow in his hands. John's pistol barked and the native was lying on the ground. Hastily he reloaded, but now he saw ten or more warriors coming towards him.

Ruthlessly he held the guide before him to act as a shield while he reloaded and fired again. More natives had appeared, waving their tomahawks and screaming the war-cry.

John was cornered but it never occurred to him to give up. He shot down another of the braves who was coming at him with his tomahawk.

'Great Werowance,' cried the guide, 'even you cannot fight so many. You must give in.'

'That I will never do,' said John. He was moving backwards as he spoke and his feet touched something which was soft and cold. He did not look down, but he felt the cold come over his ankles. The guide screamed, and those natives who had been creeping towards him stopped to stare.

Then John understood he had stepped into a quagmire and was rapidly sinking.

'Help us,' cried the guide, 'or we perish.'

Soon the thick mud was up to their waists.

One of the natives moved forward. 'Let the Paleface give us his devil-machine and we will save him.'

John hesitated. The guide implored: 'Great Werowance, it is the only way. Give up your machine ... or our lives.'

The mud was rising higher and John, looking about him and feeling his body growing paralysed with the cold, took a chance and threw his pistol from him; when it disappeared in the mud, there was a great shout from the natives. They wanted the great white chief, in person, to show their friends. In a few seconds, muddy and numb with cold John and his guide were dragged from the quagmire and stood on firm ground; but John was now at the mercy of his enemies who, with a shout of triumph, seized him and dragged him through the trees to that spot where the pot still simmered over the fire which Robinson, Emry and the native had made.

Lying by the fire was Robinson's body; it was pierced by at least twenty arrows.

For a moment John stared in dismay and grief, then sank to the ground, for his legs were half frozen through his immersion in the quagmire. He covered his face with his hands, oblivious for a while of everything save that his friend was dead.

The natives watched him. His obvious unawareness of their presence was unexpected, and the unexpected always threw these people off their guard. They did not know how to deal with a man who found time to mourn his friend when his own life was in the most imminent danger.

Then two of then began to rub his legs tenderly as they might a child's, and slapped and pummelled his arms until the life came back to them.

John smiled at them then, and his startling blue eyes made them look away from him. They did not know why, and this in itself disturbed them.

One had an arrow set to his bow but others shouted angrily at him and, when John could stand, they dragged him away through the woods.

At a clearing not far distant a band of painted warriors came breaking out of the forest. They were headed by one whom John knew by his headdress to be a great Werowance, and as he drew nearer John saw that it was Opechancanough himself whom he had met on a previous occasion and whom he knew to be a brother of Powhatan, the greatest Werowance of them all.

John concluded that this party was on the hunt and that he was their prey. He wondered what had happened to the barge, and was fearfully anxious.

'Well met, great Opechancanough!' he cried.

Opechancanough was silent, and John's heart sank. This

silence could mean that the chief planned to put his captive to death.

John tried again. 'What means this? We come in peace. My friend has been slain by your people's arrows. Is that what happens to those who smoke the pipe of peace with you?'

John's voice rang out, clear and angry, and again the eyes beneath the brilliant headdresses shifted uneasily. They believed: This Paleface has magic. He will not die, for his devils will come with their magic and save him.

Opechancanough, however, was less suspicious than his men. His face beneath the brilliant feathers was touched with the light of intelligence; he believed that a hundred braves could put to death one man, even though he was the Great Paleface Chief.

'Two Palefaces die,' he said. 'They cook by a fire and they die by the arrow. Now you are with us, great Chief of the Palefaces.'

'Ha,' cried John, 'but I have my friends close at hand. I did not walk here. I came by barge.'

Opechancanough said: 'The boat has gone back. We took one Paleface.'

John thought: So this is the end. The risk I took was too great. I am here, some sixty miles from any white man. What now?

What now indeed! Here was death again, so close that he could hear it whispering in his ear, its breath mingling with his own, for Opechancanough had made a sign, and several of them were coming towards him.

He knew the procedure. It would begin by his being tied to a tree.

He put his hand into his pocket to steel himself for some resistance; he was not sure what it was going to be; all he knew was that he was a man who could not mildly accept death.

His fingers closed about an ivory compass, and he drew it out and looked at it.

Those who had been about to seize him hesitated; they had been afraid to approach him while he held a pistol in his hand; but what was this new object? It had a look of magic.

John saw Opechancanough's bright eyes fixed on the compass.

'What?' asked Opechancanough.

John held it out to him but Opechancanough did not take it.

'It is a compass,' said John. There was silence all about him, broken only by the sudden cry of wild fowl and the rustle of some animal in the undergrowth.

'Is it magic?' asked Opechancanough.

'Yes,' answered John. 'It is magic indeed, because this needle will always point to the North. See! No matter how you turn the compass about, the needle always points to the North.'

Opechancanough had come closer; he was completely fascinated. He tried to touch the needle and could not understand why he could not do so, when he could so clearly see it.

'I use it,' said John, 'to sail the seas. Always it tells me where I am. Great Chief, it is a gift for you. I pray you accept this compass.'

Opechancanough held out his hand, and John laid the compass in it. The warriors gathered round and tried to touch the needle. One after another they came up, and they were bewildered because they did not understand what prevented them from touching the needle.

John saw that the thoughts of them all had been turned from torture and death. Often they had seen bloodshed; never had they seen a compass.

'It is magic,' they muttered. 'See, but not touch. That is Paleface magic.'

Opechancanough was becoming less afraid of the compass. He turned it round and round in his hands and he nodded with glee. 'Always North,' he cried. 'Always North!'

Then John said: 'You know of no lands but those of Powhatan and there are many lands greater than Powhatan. There are many seas and many peoples; and Earth, the planet on which we live, is like a ball with many lands and much more water.'

They listened gravely; and John went on talking to them all of the action of the sun, moon and stars; of how ships were steered by the stars; and again and again he brought their interest back to the compass.

And at length Opechancanough walked away, his head bent in thought, and he was still holding the compass. He wanted to see if it worked at some distance from John, or whether it was merely a piece of ivory when removed from his side.

Those who had been standing near took this as a sign that the Werowance was no longer interested in the victim, and they fell upon John and began once more to tie him to a tree.

But holding up the compass Opechancanough called to them to desist, whereupon they released John.

Opechancanough shouted orders, and two men seized John by the arms, while two lines of warriors formed a bodyguard, their bows and arrows ready to shoot him should he attempt to escape.

Opechancanough lifted a hand and they began to march through the forest.

John knew that the news was spreading like a forest fire: 'The great Paleface Werowance is our prisoner. He comes this way.'

Through the woods they met parties of warriors on the march, and he believed that they had determined to catch him and had sent hunting parties for this purpose.

When they reached the village of Orapakes the women and children came out of the thirty or forty wigwams which made up this village, and the children were shouting that they wanted to see the great Paleface Chief.

The men of the villages had put on full war-paint; their heads and shoulders were a brilliant scarlet and they were adorned with feathers, shells and the skins of snakes. They stamped their feet and danced when John was led among them. He was taken to one of the biggest of the wigwams and there he was left, while men danced about that wigwam and the children called to each other that they would play the game of the great Opechancanough and the White Chief.

As he waited there two women entered the wigwam and knelt before him; they carried a large wooden platter on which were venison and cakes made of corn. In spite of his anxiety regarding his fate John was hungry and fell upon the food ravenously.

The women watched, smiling at him and each other with their soft dark eyes.

John remembered then other soft looks which he had received from women during his life, and he began to wonder whether these gentle creatures might be ready to help him as others of their sex had done before them. But outside he could hear the songs of the warriors and the stamping of feet; he did not believe these two soft-eyed women could do much for him even if they wished to.

He was so tired that when he had eaten he fell into a sleep of exhaustion and was awakened to find someone standing beside him as he lay there on the floor of the wigwam.

It was Opechancanough himself.

'You are rested?' asked Opechancanough.

'I thank you, yes,' answered John.

'We could be brothers,' said Opechancanough.

'We are brothers,' was the answer. 'We have smoked the pipe of peace together.'

'It was in another season.'

'But we are brothers for ever.'

'The white man kills our braves with the devil-machine.'

'There should be no killing. No killing of your braves with the devil-machine; no killing of Palefaces with bow and arrow.'

'You be my brother,' said Opechancanough. 'But other Paleface . . . no!'

John was silent, eyebrows raised.

'We have the big magic man,' said Opechancanough. 'They have him no more. We will go to their village with our bows and arrows. No more Paleface village.'

'No more Opechancanough,' retorted John grimly.

'You will be my brother. You will tell. You will say, "Go this way. This best way." You tell Opechancanough how to kill all Palefaces, and you are chief . . . like Opechancanough . . . like all chiefs of the Powhatan land.'

John was alarmed. He knew that an attack was being planned; that they were making ready to descend on Jamestown; and it was for this reason that, knowing he was in the woods, they had made such a big attempt to take him prisoner.

He must save the settlement. But how? No matter what happened to him or any of them, the settlement must be saved.

The two women came into the wigwam; this time they brought wild fowl and beans. They knelt before him as he ate. But he was no longer hungry and he told Opechancanough that he had had enough food.

'You like?' asked Opechancanough indicating the women.

John nodded.

'Yours,' said Opechancanough. 'Be my brother and you shall have many wives. You shall have land. You shall be one of us . . . one of Great Powhatan's Werowances.

You shall fight with us and we shall be as brothers.'

John pretended not to understand. 'Always I wish to be the brother of Opechancanough,' he said.

Opechancanough went and left him for a while, and when he was alone he tried to make some plan for getting the news of the proposed attack to Jamestown.

While he tormented himself with these thoughts the two women came back into the wigwam; they sat, one on either side of him and touched his face; their gentle eyes were pleading with him. He wondered what their rewards would be for success, what their punishment for failure.

'The Paleface Chief is beautiful,' said one.

'He is our brother,' said the other.

Then the first one rose and began to dance before him. There was no mistaking the nature of the dance; it was provocative in the extreme; her beads jangled about her neck, and the copper rings danced in her ears; her great eyes were languorous with desire and promise; while one danced the other caressed him.

He was touched by their beauty; they were such gentle creatures. He could have felt as tender towards them as he had towards Madame Colombier and Charatza; but all the time he was thinking of the settlement and wondering how he could get a message through to them.

'Our brother does not desire us,' said one of the women to the other. 'Let us bring him more food.'

They went out together and John lay thinking of what might be happening in the settlement, and as he thought the memories of those two sensuous bodies kept coming back to him.

'The Colony is all-important,' he said to himself. 'Any one of us must die willingly for it; the colony is Virginia, and Virginia is England.'

The women came back with more platters of food and the seductive dancing and caresses began again.

* * *

The women were seated on either side of him; he talked to them; he told them of the great engines they had at the fort, which could kill from a great distance. He hoped they would pass on this information; they merely smiled at him and sought in a hundred ways to seduce him.

Then into the tent came one of the braves, and in his hand he carried a tomahawk which he waved wildly. He was crying: 'Death to the Paleface! Death! Death!'

He came towards John, but John was ready for him; he stepped swiftly aside, and the man ran headlong into the other side of the wigwam. John then seized him and wrenched the tomahawk from his hand as Opechancanough came in.

'He sought to kill me,' said John.

Opechancanough explained: 'It is because his son is about to die. He was one whom you wounded with your devil-machine when we took you in the woods.'

'Could I be taken to this young man? I may have some magic which would save his life.'

'Let him be brought to my son,' pleaded the man; and Opechancanough, always eager for magic, agreed that John should go to the man's wigwam.

John was led to it and there on the floor, covered with a deerskin, lay the dying young man.

'I could cure him,' said John. 'But I need medicine. I have this at the Paleface village, but I do not carry it with me. Let me go there and I will bring back that magic which will cure him and make him well again.'

'Let him go,' begged the young man's father. But Opechancanough shook his head.

John said quickly: 'Very well, as you will not let me go, I pray you allow me to send a letter to my friends. I will ask them to place what I need on a certain spot, and you will see that it is done.'

'But how can you do this?' asked Opechancanough. 'Can you make paper speak?'

'It is part of the Paleface magic,' John told him.

He was allowed to write the letter, and this he did while Opechancanough looked on in wonder. In the letter John told his friends at the settlement to make great efforts to defend themselves, as an attack might be imminent. He also wanted a bottle of *aqua vitae* and a few bandages left at a certain spot, to be picked up by the messengers. They were to fire the guns and make as much noise as possible, so that the messengers would believe the place was heavily fortified.

Two messengers were then sent off with John's letter and told to give it to the first white man they saw and to explain whence it came.

Opechancanough was sceptical and impatient to see the result of the magic paper.

Before the messengers returned the young man died and his father once again broke into the wigwam where John was kept, for the purpose of killing him; but the man was sternly reprimanded by Opechancanough whose great desire was to keep John alive at least until he had decided how he could best make use of him.

Three days after they had left, the messengers returned. They were so terrified that at first it was difficult for them to explain to Opechancanough what had happened.

They heard such a roaring from the fort; they had seen the devil-machines in action. The fort was full of them. They had wrapped the paper round a stone and thrown it into the fort, and they had seen one of the Palefaces pick it up and look at it. Soon after that they had heard the terrible noise and seen the flashes of fire.

They had hidden themselves in the woods, and when they returned to look in the place where the Great Paleface Chief had told them to look, there were these things which he had told them they would find.

The messengers were still trembling with awe. They had taken part in magic. They had carried the paper which could speak.

Opechancanough also was overawed. 'We must set our magic against Paleface magic,' he said.

John had been taken from the wigwam to another dwelling. This was shaped more like a barn and, like the wigwams, it was made of branches from the trees, which had been bent and tied together; it was roofed with mats made from the skins of deer and other animals; and in the centre of the dwelling was a great hole to let out the smoke from the fire beneath.

It was early morning when John was awakened by the entry of his guards. They touched him gently with their feet and indicated a mat which had been placed against a wall. John understood that he was to sit upon it, and he did so.

No sooner was he seated than one of the tallest of the braves entered; his body was covered with oil and charcoal, so that he was entirely black; his headdress, ear ornaments and necklaces were made of the stuffed bodies of dead animals, and in his hand he carried a rattle.

His body writhed as though, thought John, he was suffering from the influence of some virulent poison; he began to wail, and John saw that he was putting a circle of meal about the fire. He did not look at John but, still writhing and chanting, went out as suddenly as he had come in.

He was immediately replaced by more natives, and John recognized among these the priests whose habitual residence was the temple of the gods.

These intruders danced as the first man had done; they uttered strange incantations and began to sing, and at the end of each song they put down a few grains of wheat some distance from the circle of meal.

More grotesquely painted and adorned natives came in; some carried pieces of deer flesh and cakes, some tobacco which they threw into the fire.

This ceremony went on all through the day and with the

coming of night Opechancanough himself came into the dwelling.

'I pray you,' said John, 'tell me the meaning of the ceremony which has taken place this day.'

'We would set our magic against that of the Paleface,' answered Opechancanough. 'We are asking our gods what manner of man you are. We would know if you are our friend or our enemy.'

'You have no need to ask your gods,' retorted John. 'I will tell you. I am your friend.'

Opechancanough gave him a long and steady look. 'Of that,' he said, 'we must be sure.'

More food was brought to John – a great deal more than he could eat; but he was urged to do so by the women who waited upon him.

It entered his head then that they had decided to kill him and that before they did so they would torture him. They wanted him to be strong, so that he could longer endure the torture, and their sport would not be curtailed by his inability to bear it.

At the same time they were convinced that he was possessed of powers above those of ordinary men. He knew this by the gifts which were brought to him and the covert looks in the eyes of men and women as they met his gaze; but it was the children who betrayed this fact more than any. They came into the barn to play with him and show him their copper beads. 'Are you greater than Great Oke?' they asked him; and, because he knew that they would tell their elders what he had said, he replied: 'I have knowledge beyond that of Great Oke.' At which the children waited for the heavens to open and the wrath of Great Oke to smite the Paleface. But no such thing happened, and so they were sure that their captive was a god whose power equalled or even might outshine that of Great Oke himself.

In these winter evenings the fire would blaze and many standing outside watched the smoke from the dwelling of the Paleface rise to the sky. Some would creep into the barn to sit with John and question him. One man showed him a bag of gunpowder which he had stolen from the white men.

'Tell me, Great Paleface Chief,' he asked, 'when must I sow this to reap a good crop?'

John patiently explained all that they asked him, and he made his answers as truthful as he could – when truth would not lessen the awe in which they held him, and therefore the settlement.

Opechancanough himself would wander in and they would sit together while the Werowance of Pamaunke told of great hunting expeditions in the forest in which he had taken part, and how he built a circle of forest into which he and his fellow hunters drove the deer. He showed John his deerskin which he wore then he went hunting, and how he hid his face behind the stuffed head so that he deceived the deer, who thought him one of themselves.

But for the threat of death which constantly hung over him, John could have enjoyed those days and nights which he spent as the prisoner of Opechancanough.

Some days after the ceremony of the grain had taken place, John asked Opechancanough what the result had been. Had Oke yet told them that the Paleface was their friend? He must do so in due course, because it was the truth, and the gods would surely speak truth.

'Oke does not answer,' Opechancanough told him. 'Your Paleface magic puts a barrier between Oke and his servants.'

'Come, smoke a pipe with me and I will return to my people. I swear that there shall always then be peace between your people and mine.'

But Opechancanough was silent, and the next day he told John that he had decided to take him to the greatest Werowance of all – the mighty Powhatan.

XI

Pocahontas

So they began the trek to Werowocomoco, where the great Powhatan was living at this time.

John, guarded by two hundred braves, arrows ready at the bow to kill him should he attempt to escape, was led through the forest. At the villages through which they passed, the men, women and children left their wigwams to come and stare at the great Paleface Chief of whose capture they had heard; they wailed, sang and stamped their feet; and some stared at him in awed silence. The tale of his magic had spread through the land.

And so they came to Werowocomoco.

John saw the Great Chief's house among the wigwams; it was a long building, the shape of a barn, made of branches interwoven and covered with bark. The door was a curtain of deerskin; and there was a hole in the roof through which John could see smoke rising to the sky.

He noticed that the demeanour of all had changed a little – even that of Opechancanough – and he guessed this was because they were coming into the presence of the greatest of all the chiefs – the overlord, the mighty Powhatan.

The curtain of deerskin was pushed aside and a few selected guards went with him into the house.

There was a loud shout from all within as he entered, and he saw that, drawn up in rows, were what appeared to be hundreds of warriors, all in their war-paint; he saw women, with their heads and shoulders painted red, their heads decked with the white down of birds, and about their necks great chains of beads.

His gaze was immediately directed to the great Powhatan, who was more gloriously bedecked than any. He was reclining on what John presumed to be his throne, and which reminded him of a bedstead. Behind his head was a pillow of leather roughly embroidered with pearls and white beads. His face was painted blue with white stripes, calculated, John supposed, to strike terror into all who beheld him. On his head was a headdress of the finest feathers of brilliant hue, and from one ear hung a copper ring and from the other a small live snake which curled about his neck and now and then touched his lips as though to kiss them.

He stared at John, and John returned his gaze with friendship but with indifference to the awesome spectacle which he presented.

On either side of him stood a woman, one far gone in pregnancy; they wore more copper beads than the others, and the deep scarlet of their faces was relieved by a little white paint. John believed these must be two of his wives, and other women who ranged themselves about him might either be wives or concubines, for they had clearly been selected for their beauty and voluptuousness.

Then John's eyes were caught by a small figure reclining at the feet of the great chief. This was a girl who was on the verge of womanhood. Her small bare breasts were like buds that were about to open; she wore nothing but the usual buckskin apron and a few rows of white and copper beads about her neck. Her long black hair had not been oiled or dressed, but hung about her head as did the hair of children.

For two reasons she caught and held John's attention; one was because she sprawled there at the feet of Powhatan in a manner which indicated that she was a specially privileged person. Thus he presumed her to be a daughter of Powhatan, for there was an innocence about her which told him she could not be a wife or concubine. The other reason was the expression in her great, dark eyes. All were studying him, he knew, even as she was, but none in this place looked at him as she did. There was fear in her eyes, and he believed it to be not of him but for him. That young girl, alone in this vast assembly, was afraid that he was going to die wretchedly, and she alone knew the meaning of compassion. John remembered then that that was something he had never before seen in the face of one of these people.

Powhatan was claiming his attention.

'Paleface, you come to visit us and we bid you welcome.'

'I thank you, mighty Powhatan.'

Powhatan lifted a hand and women came forward with a platter on which was venison, fresh from the fire, and special cakes made of their corn to eat with it.

A mat was brought and John was signed to sit facing Powhatan. They ate of the food and, while he ate, John was still conscious of the eyes of the young girl fixed upon him.

It was not easy to swallow in such circumstances, but John knew that he must do so; any show of fear would have immediately signed his death warrant.

When he had finished the food which had been set before him, Powhatan lifted a hand and a woman appeared with a bowl of water and a bunch of feathers that he might wash and dry his hands.

John saw that the woman who did this service was no other than the Werowance of Appamatuck whom, on his expeditions in search of food, he had previously met. He realized then that this was indeed a royal occasion.

Now the time had come for the pow-wow.

Opechancanough now sat beside his brother, and they conversed together. Then Powhatan addressed John.

'I am the greatest chief in all the countries,' he said.

'You are the greatest chief in the Powhatan country,' John replied. 'In the world beyond the seas there are greater chiefs. There is the King of England from whom I come. He lives in a great palace, and there are windows in that place, made of glass, which you have seen on the compass I gave to my brother Opechancanough. He sees through them as though they are nothing. And yet they are something.'

'It is so,' said Opechancanough, and he showed Powhatan the compass.

'Tell me of this King,' said Powhatan, when he had marvelled at the compass.

And John told of the ceremonies of the Court in London while Powhatan listened entranced. John also told of the voyage he and his friends had made, and still Powhatan listened.

Then Powhatan lifted a hand for silence, and he told of the hunting he had done in his territory and the scalps he had taken. He had heard that his subjects had slain the Palefaces, and so they could be killed by bow and arrow like other men and animals. He did not believe there were greater Werowances in the world than he was.

John insisted that there were, and that very soon a great Werowance would come sailing to the settlement from England. He would come in a few days, and then he would set out to look for Captain Smith.

Powhatan wanted to know how he could cross the seas, and John told him of sailing ships, and how they set out, and how their captains planned their courses, using compasses.

Powhatan seemed to listen with a contented smile on his face. Then suddenly his manner changed, and he became angry. He had made his decision. He signed to two of the warriors to bring a great stone and set it before him. The four men came forward, carrying clubs on their shoulders; and Powhatan signed for them to take their stand about the stone.

John saw that the young girl was looking at him in great

terror. He thought she was going to burst into tears. He saw her lips move, and it appeared as though she were saying something about the Paleface.

She had risen on her haunches and her hands were crossed on her little breasts. She rocked to and fro as though in anguish. No one else appeared to notice her; all eyes were fixed on John Smith.

Powhatan again lifted his hand, and John was roughly seized by three of the strongest of his guards.

He was dragged to the stone and held down on it while one of the guards passed a buckskin thong about his body and slipped it under the stone. He was now held down so that he could not move.

He knew what was going to happen. It was one form of execution. The brains of the victim were beaten out on the stone – a merciful death for which he must be thankful, for these people had other ways of disposing of their victims.

He lay there, and it seemed that time was passing very slowly. He was aware of the stuffy atmosphere of the barn-like building, of the mingling smell of sweat and paint and the oil they used on their hair. Only a few more seconds of life were left to him. He waited for the death blows from those murderous clubs which were now raised and waiting to descend, when a piercing cry filled the place. 'No! Stop! Stop! It must not be.' It was the shrill voice of a young girl.

The clubs were poised in mid-air. John saw the anxious eyes of those men who were prepared to murder him turned on Powhatan. He himself looked to Powhatan. Clinging to the robes of the great Werowance was the dark-eyed girl whom he had noticed lying at Powhatan's feet.

She was saying: 'No, no! Give him to me, my father. Give the Paleface to me. I wish him to be my slave. Do not kill the Paleface!'

Powhatan growled: 'Go from me.' But even as he

frowned at her there was a gentleness in his face. John marvelled, even in that moment, that he should see tenderness in these people; but he had seen it twice since he had entered this place – first in the compassionate eyes of the girl, towards him; now in the expression on Powhatan's face, when he turned towards his daughter.

But Powhatan would not relent, for to do so would show his softness to his people.

He threw the girl off so that she fell from him, sprawling on the floor close to where John lay. For a few seconds they looked at each other and he saw that her eyes were brilliant with an expression which he could not entirely understand.

Powhatan lifted his hands to the executioners and once more the clubs were threatening. In a second they would descend and that would be the end of John Smith.

He closed his eyes and waited. Then he felt something soft and warm on his face and on his body. He opened his eyes and saw a small face near his own, and he realized that it was the girl who had thrown her body over his.

'No!' he cried. 'No. They will kill you. It must not be.'

She answered: 'If they will kill you they must first kill me.'

Once more the executioners uncertain stood, their clubs raised. They dared not strike, for to strike would mean dashing out the brains not only of the Englishman but of Powhatan's daughter.

Powhatan signed for the men to wait. Now the girl was sitting astride John's body; her eyes were ablaze with triumph and she looked so beautiful that Powhatan could not take his eyes from her.

'This man is mine,' she said. 'I claim him.'

Powhatan said: 'You have as yet saved his life, daughter. What would you do with this man?'

'He shall be my slave. He shall tell me stories of the Palefaces, and make copper beads for my neck.'

Powhatan was silent.

'You have said you love me,' went on the girl shrilly. 'All I want is this Paleface. Only that he shall be mine.'

'You would have bought him with your own life,' said Powhatan.

'Then I have paid for him.'

Powhatan addressed the assembly. 'My daughter, Pocahontas, has bought this Paleface man by offering her life to Oke. He is hers. Release him and give him to my daughter.'

Pocahontas had leaped up; her face was shining with joy; she jumped up and down with pleasure and put the palms of her hands together in an ecstasy, while John was untied and took his stand beside her.

She measured herself against him.

'You are not a big man, Paleface,' she told him. 'Some of my uncles are bigger. But your eyes are of the sky.'

John took her hand and kissed it. This made her laugh and there were sounds of merriment all about them.

'Come with me,' she said; and she led the way out of the hall.

Although John had escaped death and he was now the property of the young girl who had saved his life, it was clear that he was not free to make his way back to Jamestown.

His guards had followed him when he left with Pocahontas and, when she led him to a small wigwam in the woods close by, these guards still stationed themselves outside it.

'How can I thank you for what you have done?' he asked her.

'Thank?' she said. 'There is no need to thank. I am glad you speak our tongue. I wish you to teach me the Paleface tongue.'

'Gladly will I do so,' he answered.

'Can you make beads?'

'No.'

That amused her. 'You shall not make beads. You shall speak with me. You shall tell me of Paleface lands. That is what I wish.'

Then she stroked his beard, touched his face with her long brown fingers and embraced him. 'You are mine . . . always mine, for as long as we live.'

It was rarely that John's emotions got the better of him, but the youthful innocence of this child and the ordeal through which he had passed temporarily unnerved him. He felt a new emotion sweeping over him, and on impulse he put his arms about the girl and held her to him.

Her face was close to his; her long hair mingled with his. He held her thus for some seconds and she remained passive. It was he who broke away.

She said: 'I like it when you hold me thus. I feel happy then.'

She ran her fingers through his hair, comparing the crisp curls with her own straight locks; the blond with the black.

'Oh,' she cried, 'but indeed you are a Paleface.' Then she whispered: 'You are a god. How did you come into the world? One of your gods got you on your mother who is mortal. That is why you walk on Earth. You are half god.'

He wanted to contradict her, and he almost did, because he was grateful to her and had a feeling that there should always be truth between them; but even in such a moment he remembered the settlement and the need for her people to hold him in awe, that they might hesitate before making war on Jamestown.

So he did not answer but contented himself with stroking her hair.

She said: 'You will tell me stories such as those you told my father and my Uncle Opechancanough. You will tell me of the land across the seas whence you came.' She drew away from him suddenly and her eyes darkened with fear.

'You will wish to sail across the sea one day. But you may not do so. You are mine. For always, you are mine.'

'If I ever sailed across the sea . . .' began John.

And she finished for him: '. . . You will take me with you.'

He tried to imagine her in London or on the farm. It was not easy. No one living in England had ever seen anyone like her.

He laughed, and she said: 'When you show teeth so it means you are happy?'

'Yes,' he said. 'I am happy now.'

'Because I have bought your life? Because you belong to Pocahontas?'

Again he was aware of an emotion hitherto unknown to him; he took her hand and kissed it that she might not see the tenderness in his eyes, for tenderness was universal and that she would recognize. He did not want her to see that which as yet he did not fully understand.

She said: 'Now I will show you that you are as my own.'

He answered: 'How will you show this, my little one?'

She put her face close to his, as a child might, and peered into his eyes. 'To you I am Pocahontas. Yes?'

'You are indeed Pocahontas.'

'But it is my name for strangers. My second name. My first name would not be used before you, for to use the first name of the Werowance's daughter in the hearing of strangers would be to harm her. Pocahontas is my second name. But I tell *you* I am Matoaka in my father's house. You see? I have told you my name . . . you, a white man. And it is said that to do so could bring me evil. But I would have you know you are not a stranger. To you I will be Matoaka . . . if you wish.'

He answered: 'It was Pocahontas who offered to die if I died. I shall always be grateful to Pocahontas.'

'And you do not wish Matoaka?'

'To me you are Pocahontas for ever.'

She flung herself against him, and his arms tightened about her.

She cried out: 'It is what I wish. Now I shall be Pocahontas to you ... to myself ... and to all for evermore.'

Then she marvelled once more at the blueness of his eyes, and he was reminded of Charatza, who had also liked that blueness; but this child moved him a way Charatza had never done.

Suddenly she leaped out of his arms and scolded herself.

'But you need to eat. You must have food, and I do not give. Oh, what a stupid one! My slave must eat. I will make him grow tall as a Sasquesahanock. And we shall go through the woods together, Pocahontas with her Captain John Smith ...' She spoke his name slowly, stumbling over the unfamiliar syllables. 'They will say, "Oh there is Matoaka who is now Pocahontas to us all, and with her is her Paleface who is her slave ... and yet he is a god."'

She ran to the door of the wigwam, and he heard her calling in her shrill high voice for food.

And when it was brought she had two mats set for them, facing each other, and together they ate; and he taught her to laugh and speak a few words of English.

'I wish,' she said, 'to be as a Paleface woman; then I think my Captain John Smith will love Pocahontas very much.'

She was constantly with him during the following days. They were watched, and he was continually under the eye of the guard; often he wondered whether Powhatan might not regret the impulse which had made him grant him his life.

During the next day he was required to move from the wigwam to a dwelling nearer Powhatan's house. This was much smaller than that in which Powhatan lived, but was divided into two compartments by means of a curtain of skins thonged together.

John wondered for what reason he had been brought here. Was he about to be murdered? Did Powhatan wish to know more of what his daughter said to her slave and he to her?

Each day she ate with him; and when night came she wrapped herself in a skin and slept near the deerskin mat which served as a door. He believed she too suspected that Powhatan might regret his leniency and send someone to murder him, and was determined to prevent this.

As soon as it was light she would bring water in which corn had been boiled and they would eat cakes made of the corn.

She sat on her mat opposite him and bade him tell her how women ate in his land. Her efforts to imitate an Englishwoman amused him and she was happy to see him laughing.

When they had eaten she would have water brought for him, and she herself would hand him the feathers with which to dry himself.

He must talk to her of his life and adventures, so he told her of the farm in Willoughby and of Francis and his wife, and of his sister Alice who was dead. Then he recounted his adventures in Europe and tried to describe the country to her; but she was impatient to hear about the people. Her face darkened with anger when she heard how the Timor of Nalbrits had ill-treated him, and she rose from her mat to dance with joy when John described how he had slain this man.

At the end of those strange days, when both knew that life would never be quite the same for them again, she was speaking a few words of English and she knew the details of many of John's adventures.

During the nights John had strange dreams. He dreamed that he escaped with her, out of the Powhatan country to the settlement, that he took her aboard the *Susan Constant* which had come into the bay, and that they sailed to England together.

And in this dream he took her into the Willoughby farmhouse, and Alice was there, so were his father and mother; and he said to them: 'Here is Pocahontas. She saved me from fearful death and she has made me her servant.' And they took her into their arms, and they embraced Pocahontas likewise, and it was like bringing a bride home to the farmhouse.

In this dream he was conscious of a strange happiness which he had never experienced before.

When he awoke he saw her small body curled up in the rug by the door, and he lay for a long time watching her.

She awoke and for a few seconds they lay looking at each other.

Then she said: 'You smile, John Smith. You have happy dreams?'

'I dreamed of you,' he told her.

'Then that was happy dream,' she answered simply. 'But you are a hungry Paleface. I must feed my slave.'

They had eaten and she herself had taken away the platter. She had left him but a few minutes when he heard a great wailing outside; this was followed by shrieking and the stamping of feet.

John guessed that some further ceremony was about to be performed and, as he pondered this, a warrior came bursting in. It was a tall figure which confronted him, made black from head to foot with oil and charcoal; the man began dancing about John, writhing and twisting his body into contortions which John guessed at once to mean he was being threatened.

John yawned and closed his eyes as though he did not find the phenomenon alarming or particularly interesting; and then the writhing figure gave a great shout, and into the room burst some ten warriors, all black from head to foot, all writhing and screaming.

John now recognized the one, who had first entered, as Powhatan himself; the others were his picked warriors.

What did they plan? wondered John. To kill him in the absence of Pocahontas? He would make a stand, of course, and he might account for two or three of them before they finished him; but he was not going to show them what they expected to see – signs of fear – for it was always dangerous to show these natives that. Now they expected him to be terrified; so he showed complete indifference.

They were clearly nonplussed; and then Powhatan, because he had to take some action while the eyes of his warriors were upon him, called a halt to the dancing and sat down on the mat which Pocahontas had vacated.

'Captain John Smith,' said Powhatan, 'you wish to return to Paleface village?'

'Yes,' said John.

'Then perhaps I let you go.'

John's heart leaped with exultation. 'When?' he demanded.

'When you promise.'

'Pray tell me what conditions you seek to impose.'

'You are as my son,' said Powhatan, 'because my daughter loves you. You are one of my Werowances.'

John bowed his head.

'So, for my son I have trust. You will go back to the village and you will give me for your release two of the engines of war, two of the big devil-machines called culverins. You will give that, and you will give one of your big stones for grinding knives.'

John was silent. It was impossible to explain that the culverins belonged to the Company, and that the last thing he wanted to do was to arm the natives with weapons equal to their own.

Powhatan watched him broodingly. His anger was ready

to flare up. John knew that, if he did not promise, he would not live long enough for Pocahontas to rescue him again.

He said: 'Very well. Give me my liberty, and you shall have what you ask.'

Powhatan was delighted. He sent for pipes, and they were smoking together when Pocahontas returned.

She was surprised to see her father there, and threw herself down on the floor beside him; her small face cupped in her hands and propped up by her elbows, she studied with pride and affection her blue-eyed slave.

But her expression changed when she heard the conversation. John Smith was going away. He was going back to the settlement. She was going to lose him.

'No,' she cried. 'But he is mine. I offered my life for him, and you gave him to me.'

'You are but a child,' said Powhatan. 'Captain Smith will give us two devil-machines for his liberty.'

'So you care more for the devil-machines than for your daughter!' she cried.

Powhatan put out a hand and touched her smooth head; she lay still glowering at her father, but the gaze she turned on John was full of anguish.

He spoke then. 'I shall not be far away,' he told her. 'We are friends. Often we shall meet. Do not forget I am your slave. Do not forget our friendship is for ever.'

'I would rather there were not even those few miles between us.'

'Ah,' said Powhatan, 'my daughter grows too big for children's games, and is not yet of an age to join the women.'

'I am of that age!' said Pocahontas defiantly.

'Then we must find a husband for you.'

She retorted quickly: 'I am too young to be the wife of one of our men. But old enough to be a Paleface one.'

John marvelled at Powhatan's patience with this

daughter; clearly he loved her most dearly of all his numerous children; she, Pocahontas – Matoaka, as she would be to her father – stood apart from the others in Powhatan's eyes.

It was not merely John then who had noticed this. She was different from the others. She need not have made him swear never to forget her. He never would.

A hunchback came into their presence.

'My servant, Rawhunt,' said Powhatan, 'whom I trust as I trust few. He will go with you, back to the Paleface village, and he will be in command of those who go with you. They will bring back the devil-machines and the grindstone.'

'You may trust me,' said John. 'But I shall need to take venison and corn with me.'

'I trust Captain Smith as I trust no other Paleface,' answered Powhatan. 'Now. Be ready. You shall start at once and you shall have the food to take with you. I wish much to have my devil-machines.'

John stood up. At last he was at liberty. Then he looked at Pocahontas who was still stretched on the floor watching him.

It was over then, those few hours of intimacy. Was it but three days ago that they had brought him to the dwelling of Powhatan and those executioners had stood above him, clubs raised to murder him?

He could scarcely believe it. He felt he had lived through so much since then.

'I am ready,' said John.

'And so are Rawhunt and those who are to accompany you.'

Powhatan went out, followed by Rawhunt. John went with them to the door but there he paused and turned to look back at Pocahontas.

She had risen; and now she ran to him; she threw herself into his arms so that he could feel her heart fluttering against him. He laid his face against her hair and she clung to him.

'This I like,' she cried. 'This and nothing else.'

He answered: 'We shall meet again.'

'Where you are I would be,' she told him.

'Who knows?' he answered. 'Perhaps it will be so.'

Then gently he withdrew himself from her embrace, and went out into the cold crisp air.

Strange that, freed from captivity, he should feel this vague longing to return to it, this faint but definite regret.

XII

The Return of the 'Susan Constant'

As John came towards the settlement, Rawhunt and his guards beside and behind him, he was seen from the stockade.

He heard someone shout: 'It is John Smith, John Smith come back from the dead.'

John smiled grimly. So they had believed he was dead.

As he came into the settlement he saw the signs of neglect everywhere. It was five weeks since he had left to sail up the Chickahominy with Robinson, Emry and the rest, and in that short time the colony, which had been prosperous and well stocked with food, was clearly on the edge of collapse again.

The colonists, headed by Ratcliffe and Archer, came hurrying out to meet them, and when they saw the food which John was bringing with him he guessed from the glint in their eyes what had been happening to the stores.

He was anxious that they should not betray to the natives how eager they were for the food, so he handed it to the storekeeper and asked him to put it with their stores. Later they would eat.

'You yourself look well fed,' said Ratcliffe.

'I have been a prisoner of Powhatan,' John told them. 'I came near to death but, as you see, not through starvation. I do not need to ask what has been happening here. I see that work has been neglected and that food has not been carefully distributed. Five weeks I have been away. One would think it were five months.'

Ratcliffe looked at Archer. They resented his implication that they were unfit to govern.

'But I do not wish to hear a chronicle of your sufferings, before the ears and eyes of these men. I have promised them two culverins and a grindstone in exchange for my liberty.'

'Two culverins! You must be mad!' said Ratcliffe. 'You would give them our weapons that they might turn them against us?'

'Leave this matter to me,' said John. 'Let us not quarrel in front of these people.' He turned to Rawhunt and the guides who had been waiting for him at some distance. 'Come with me,' he said. 'I will show you the culverins which you are to take back to Powhatan.'

He led the way to the platform where the demi-culverins had been mounted.

'There,' said John, 'they are yours. Take them.'

Rawhunt and his men tried to lift them. The weight was somewhere in the region of two tons and they found they could not move them. They looked at the culverins in dismay, and John said: 'Ah, they are too heavy for you. They are full of great balls. If I shoot these out they will be a little lighter. Then perhaps you can manage them. Watch! I will fire them at yonder tree.'

He did so and there was an ear-splitting roar as the branches of the trees crashed to the ground. Rawhunt and his men covered their ears and eyes, and ran as fast as they could away to the forest.

It was an hour or so later when they came creeping back.

'Captain Smith,' Rawhunt said, 'we dare not return to Powhatan, though we know that the devil-machines will not move for us.'

'Go back to Powhatan,' said John. 'Tell him that the devil-machines would not move for you and that they were so angry, because you tried to take them, that they sent out fire which blasted the trees in the forest. Tell him too that the grindstone could not be moved either. Instead I will give you some beautiful ornaments. Some are made of glass, and that is a magic thing, as you saw on the compass, but this is a gentle magic and if you do not break it, it will hurt no one. Take back these trinkets for Powhatan and his wives and tell him that I am his very good friend.'

So Rawhunt went back to Powhatan, and John once more had his liberty; yet the culverins remained to guard the settlement.

Archer and Ratcliffe were angry. They knew that they had failed. They had to admit to themselves that during John's absence affairs had grown almost as bad as they had been during the heat of the summer. Few people were working; and the stores were low again. And here was John Smith ranting and raving through the settlement, telling them all that they were an idle bunch of fools.

'And what has *he* done?' demanded Archer of the weak Ratcliffe. 'He went off on a tour of exploration and, owing to his carelessness, Robinson, Emry and Cassen lost their lives. In my opinion he should be tried for murder.'

'That is an excellent idea,' cried Ratcliffe. 'We will condemn him to the gallows and that will be the end of our jaunty captain.'

They called together the members of the Council.

'Captain Newport's ship is due in any day,' said Ratcliffe. 'We shall hold out until they come bringing us fresh provisions. But are we going to allow this overbearing Captain Smith to give a bad account of us? Are we going to allow him to tell the Captain, and through him the Company, that he brought us stores, that he kept our cupboards full, but when he went away on his explorations in five weeks we were plunged into want again?'

'Captain Smith is too full of his own importance,' Archer supported him. 'He carelessly led Robinson, Emry and Cassen to their deaths. I believe he should be found guilty of causing the death of these men.'

They called in John and made the accusation against

him, and Ratcliffe and Archer so swayed the Council that John was voted, by a majority, guilty of causing the deaths of the three men, and was sentenced to be hanged immediately.

John listened to his sentence almost incredulously; but he was so used to coming close to death that he had ceased to feel very perturbed about it.

Now he rose in his wrath and, pushing his way out of the Council's presence, he called to all the colonists to listen to him.

There were not many of them now – only thirty-eight – for many more had died during John's absence; and when they gathered round him and looked into that strong and resolute face, even those who believed that now he had returned they would have to work harder, knew that if they were to continue to exist they needed John Smith. They had no respect for Ratcliffe who had proved himself to be a weak man, so they listened to John.

'You fools!' he cried. 'When I left you you were prosperous. But what have you done? You have squandered your food; you have feasted today and forgotten that tomorrow brings famine. You have neglected your work. You are asking for death. You complain of Virginia. My friends, Virginia complains heartily of you. Those greater fools in there have just condemned me to death. They want to hustle me to the gallows. If you are of an opinion that I deserve death in this way, if you do not want me here among you to go among the natives and bargain for food, if you have had enough of John Smith, then stand with them. If you do not agree, I will defy them to take me to their gallows, and we will snap our fingers at those fools who call themselves President and Council of Virginia.'

One man shouted: 'Indeed they are fools. When John Smith leaves us our troubles start.'

The others took up the cry. 'John Smith is back. We'll get through.'

John laughed exultantly.

'Courage,' he cried. 'We are not defeated. Nor shall we ever be unless by our folly we defeat ourselves. My friends, I have been a prisoner in Werowocomoco; and there I have seen stocks of food which would keep us from hunger all through the winter. Some of those stocks shall be ours, I promise you.'

'Hurrah!' cried the colonists. 'John Smith is back. The starving time is over.'

Ratcliffe and Archer heard the shouts; and they knew that the time was not yet ripe for hustling John Smith to the gallows.

John's first task was to make a thorough examination of the stores; he was horrified to see how low the stocks were. This would mean that he would have to go bargaining almost immediately, unless Captain Newport arrived with fresh supplies.

He stormed about the settlement, cursing those whom he considered responsible and working out a new system for the distribution of the food which remained.

'It is but January now,' he cried. 'The winter has only just begun. How do you imagine we are going to get through it if we persist in such folly? You know the dangers of the sea. What if Captain Newport's store ship has met with some accident? That, my friends, is not an impossibility, and it is something we have to be prepared for.'

There was a murmur throughout the assembly.

'He is back. There is no doubt about that. There will be no peace now until the stores are replenished and all the houses are built.'

John insisted that they all attend the service which the Reverend Robert Hunt would hold that very day. John was as eager for their spiritual as their physical welfare for he firmly believed that the two went hand in hand.

So it was back to the old routine; the great consolation

being that, under the rigid rule of Captain John Smith, starvation was more likely to be held at bay.

Two days after John's return Robert Hunt was coming out of his barn-like church when he saw a strange party approaching the settlement. They were native women and they all carried baskets on their heads. They moved with grace, and he wondered what was the meaning of this.

He went to meet them, and the leader of the group, a girl of some thirteen or fourteen years, said to him: 'I seek Captain Smith.'

'I will bring him to you,' answered Hunt; he saw then that the baskets contained meat and corn, and he believed that they had come to bargain for some glass beads or some such trinkets.

When John heard that the women had come, he guessed who their leader was and hurried out with great gladness.

He was not disappointed.

She would have run to him and thrown herself into his arms, but John, fearing that this gesture might be misunderstood by some of the members of the settlement who had heard of the women's arrival and had come out to see them, managed to hold her off by taking her hands, as she came towards him, and kissing them.

There was no lack of warmth in the glance he gave her and Pocahontas was satisfied.

'I feared what you would find on your return,' she said. 'I hear that there is little food in the Paleface village, so I bring this for you.'

'Pocahontas, you are my good angel.'

'What is this good angel?'

He explained, and her face was suffused by the warmth of her tenderness towards him. 'Always ... your good angel I will be,' she told him.

He said: 'Come into the settlement, my dear Pocahontas, and I will show you many wonderful things.'

John's eyes saw that the baskets were loaded with good food – enough to feed the whole colony for several days – and on impulse he said: 'You have brought that which we need most. How can I thank you?'

'I need no thanks,' she said. 'What I have is yours. I wish only to please Captain John Smith.'

'You please him . . . you please him mightily.'

Other members of the colony were pressing round, and it was necessary to introduce her.

John said: 'This is Pocahontas, the beloved daughter of Powhatan, to whom I owe my life.'

'But she is beautiful!' said Ratcliffe.

'It is long since I have seen such a fair lady,' put in Archer with a leer.

John's eyes were like sparks of blue flame. 'The Lady Pocahontas is my friend,' he said. 'She is the daughter of a Werowance and not to be submitted to the insults of commoners.'

Pocahontas, looking from John to the others, understood a little of what was passing between them. She said fiercely: 'My friend is Captain John Smith. I am friend only with those who are his friends. Those who are not, I hate and betray to Powhatan. He will tie them to a tree and burn them by a slow fire.'

John's expression softened. None would dare touch her. She was all gentleness towards him, but to them she would be a wild savage if any dared that which was distasteful to her.

'You have made a good impression, Captain Smith,' said Ratcliffe with a sneer. 'It is clear the lady has a very high opinion of you.'

'High opinion?' asked Pocahontas.

'He says you have become my friend.'

'He speaks true. Captain Smith is my friend. I die for him and he die for me.'

'There must have been a charming idyll between our

gallant Captain and the savage Princess while he was her father's prisoner.'

'You have heard,' said John tartly, 'that we became friends; and I should advise you to watch your tongue.'

With that he led Pocahontas away. He showed her the wooden houses which they were building; and pointed out the culverins which had been too heavy for her father's servants to take away. He introduced her to certain of the colonists, who found her charming, particularly when they heard she had brought baskets of food.

Then John took her to the storehouse and selected a string of glass beads which he placed round her neck.

'It is for the food?' she asked, and her eyes flashed.

'It is for many things,' he told her.

'Then I do not take. It is not to bargain I come. The food is a present ... from Pocahontas to Captain John Smith. There must be no payment.'

'These beads,' replied John, 'are a present from Captain John Smith to Pocahontas. He does not wish to bargain any more than she does.'

'Then I take,' she said softly, and she lifted the beads and held them against her cheek.

He walked with her to the edge of the forest, and her women walked behind them, their empty baskets on their heads.

She said as they parted: 'It pleases you, John Smith, that I come with food? So again I come.'

'It pleases me to see you,' he told her, 'whether you come with or without food. It is you I rejoice to see.'

'Now,' she replied, 'I am happy.'

John kissed her hand and stood watching her as she with her women disappeared among the trees.

Within a few days Pocahontas again appeared at the settlement, followed by her little band of women; again they brought baskets of food, and there was great rejoicing through the settlement; it meant that for the colonists the fear of starvation was removed a few days distant every time Pocahontas visited the settlement.

Captain Newport was overdue and it seemed often that the stores would not hold out until his arrival. The weather was bitterly cold. But through the trees at regular intervals came the girl who became known as the Princess Pocahontas. Always the ceremony was the same. She would ask for Captain John Smith, and to no other would she hand over her baskets.

She would walk with him round the settlement and speak with some of the colonists. If any were ill she would ask after their health in a polite and charming manner; yet it was clear to all that she had eyes and ears for none but Captain John Smith.

They waited for her coming; they blessed her when she came, wrapped in a cloak of skins or feathers.

In those cold January days the colony was saved from starvation because of the love of Powhatan's daughter for Captain John Smith.

Edward Wingfield was still a prisoner on board the pinnace, and when John visited him there he found him a sick and unhappy man.

He had a story to tell which was alarming.

'There has been a plot afoot,' he said, 'to return to England. It may well be that your return was just in time as it was previously. Ratcliffe, Archer and some others planned to take the pinnace to England and leave the rest of us here to the mercy of the savages, or starvation.'

John's eyes kindled with fury.

'Would they had never come!' he cried.

When he left Wingfield he approached Ratcliffe and accused him of treachery.

'You forget, Captain Smith,' sneered Ratcliffe, 'that *I* am President of this colony.'

'Which is indeed a great misfortune for the Colony.'

'I'll have you dragged to the gallows yet,' cried Ratcliffe.

'Make sure that you yourself do not end up there,' retorted John.

'It grieves you, does it not,' said Ratcliffe, 'that we are not all simple savage maidens, to fall down and worship you.'

'It grieves me that such men as you and Archer ever came to Virginia. It was not meant for such as you.'

'Nay, it was meant for noble Captain Smith. He alone is worthy to set foot in Virginia . . . he who goes off and has such exciting adventures, and is always triumphant and victorious . . . according to himself.'

John was at Ratcliffe's throat and was shaking him to and fro, when there was a sudden shouting close at hand. The shouting increased; they were shouts of joy.

John threw the bulging-eyed President from him and listened.

He heard the words: the *Susan Constant*!

Then he forgot his disagreement with Ratcliffe, and ran down to the shore. There was no doubt the ship was in sight, that ship they knew so well: the *Susan Constant*. Captain Newport had returned to Virginia.

There was no time for anything but rejoicing as the *Susan Constant* lay in Chesapeake Bay and the little boats brought the crew and Captain ashore. With them they brought not only the much-needed stores but more colonists; and this party was generally called The First Supply.

Captain Newport seemed delighted to have made the journey in safety and to see Virginia again.

'I had a companion vessel, the *Phœnix*,' he told them. 'She should not be long delayed.'

This was wonderful news. Not only the *Susan Constant* but the *Phœnix* was come to succour them.

As Captain Newport sat at a meal with the Council members he said: 'The Company was not very pleased with the cargo I took home. They criticized you for not being more bold in making discoveries. They are sure that there is gold or precious stones in Virginia.'

'It has been as much as we could do to keep alive,' retorted Ratcliffe. 'We have had differences among ourselves.' He look at John. 'These, I think, grew out of our anxieties. We were worried because we feared starvation. To know that we have food in the storehouse puts a different complexion on matters, eh, Captain Smith?'

John replied that he believed it did.

But when John was not present, Ratcliffe told Newport that he was finding it increasingly difficult to work with John.

'Never,' said Ratcliffe, 'did I encounter such arrogance. He has been a captive of the savages, as he told you; and because he escaped death and appears to have made them believe he is a demi-god, I verily believe he thinks he is one.'

'He was ever a man with a high opinion of himself,' agreed Newport.

'The savages believe that he is President of the community,' added Ratcliffe. 'He must have told them so.'

Newport nodded. He remembered that they had put John Smith in irons on the journey out.

On the very day of Captain Newport's arrival Pocahontas came to the settlement with her baskets of food. John met her and said: 'You shall meet one of our great Werowances. He has sailed his great ship here, and he brings us food and many things we need from England.'

Captain Newport took the hand which was proffered to him and bowed over it. He was astonished by the charm of this girl which set her apart from any of her people. He had heard that she brought food to the settlement but he was none the less astonished when he saw her do so. It amazed him that John Smith had been able to inspire such devotion.

'He is a Werowance of the sea,' John explained. 'He has brought yonder great ship many miles across the ocean.'

'He is indeed a great Werowance,' said Pocahontas, but it was clear she could not feel the same respect for Captain Newport as she did for John Smith.

John was aware of this, and he said: 'He is my Father.' This, in her language, meant that Newport was far above him. But she merely smiled; she did not believe that any man could be above John Smith.

Those who had come with her eyed Captain Newport with great interest; but even they did not believe that he was a greater man than Smith.

One of them said: 'The winds are bitter and we pray Oke to tell the North Wind he must not blow so long and so cruelly. Oke hears us not. Would Captain Smith ask his god to whisper to the North Wind?'

'You see,' said Ratcliffe to Newport, 'Smith is a demi-god among them. One would not think that you were a great Captain and I the President of the colony. What are we in the eyes of these savages compared with Smith?'

Newport laughed, but Ratcliffe was delighted to see that he was a little piqued.

John made the acquaintance of the new colonists, and there was one man, a certain Master Scrivener, whom he found greatly to his liking. Master Scrivener was a gentleman who shared John's ideals. That much they discovered on the first day of their acquaintance.

If they had sent more men like Scrivener, thought John, it would have been good for the colony.

He feared, though, that he had certain gentlemen gamblers and tavern loafers among this lot, when what he needed was good workmen. Perhaps, he decided, one of the most frustrating difficulties in founding a colony was the lack of understanding between those who were on the spot and those at home who gave the orders.

Powhatan, having heard that the great Werowance had arrived from over the seas, greatly desired to meet him, and a few days after the arrival of the ship he sent presents for Newport and an invitation for him to visit Werowocomoco.

So, with John and a few chosen people among whom was the newcomer Master Scrivener, they sailed up the river, stopping to trade as they went, on their way to visit Powhatan at Werowocomoco.

Newport's vanity was touched by the idea that he was the great Werowance from over the seas, and he began to assume a somewhat regal manner. Like Ratcliffe he had become a little jealous of the respect which John inspired, and he sought to turn that respect away from John and towards himself.

He had brought from England many bright articles which, it was believed, would find favour with the Virginians. He had a white dog, a red suit of clothes and a hat as presents for Powhatan from the King of England.

When they arrived at Werowocomoco, Powhatan received them with much ceremony in that barn-like dwelling where John had once come very near to death. It was a similar ceremony – the braves, painted in all their glory, and Powhatan seated on his bedstead with his wives and concubines about him. Pocahontas was there, and her gleaming dark eyes obviously saw no one but Smith.

It was an occasion filled with memories for John, and he warned Newport not to take Powhatan's offers of friendship too seriously. He remembered how he had been fed and almost fêted one moment, and condemned to death the next.

Newport was impatient of any warning. He was going to show them all that he was a more important person than John Smith.

Presents were exchanged, and the time came when it was

necessary to bargain for the corn which they had come to buy.

Powhatan was wily. He saw that Newport was a proud man and he said to him: 'Great Paleface Werowance, I am the greatest Werowance in my country, and I know you are, on the sea. My greatness forbids me to bargain as common men may do. Let us go to work like Werowances. Set down the goods you have to sell, and I will give you what I believe to be their worth. It is the way of great chiefs.'

John, who had had to interpret this speech, warned: 'Do not trust Powhatan. He is wily and he is trying to cheat us in some way. I know the expression which comes into his face when he does so. Insist on bargaining, or leave it to me.'

'Captain Smith,' retorted Newport, 'this is a matter which you must leave to me. It is better thus when there is dealing between Powhatan and myself. I too am not eager to bargain.' And to John's dismay he signed to his men to bring out the goods he wished to exchange for food – copper kettles which made Powhatan's eyes gleam with acquisitiveness; copper bells and hatchets – always much desired.

'Tell him,' said Newport, 'that they are for him, and that he may give me what he believes to be their value in corn.'

'This is folly!' cried John.

'Remember,' snapped Newport, 'that you are here as my interpreter.'

John shrugged his shoulders and translated; whereupon Powhatan signed to his men to bring out a certain amount of corn.

Newport stared at the corn. This was incredible. It was not a twentieth of what he expected, being only some four or five bushels.

John, seeing the sly expression in Powhatan's eyes and the dismay in Newport's, took some bright blue beads from his pocket and set them flashing in the winter sunshine.

'What are those?' cried Powhatan.

'Oh,' John replied, putting them back into his pockets, 'I do not bargain with these.'

'Why do you not bargain?'

'They are precious jewels, because they are the colour of the sky.'

Powhatan's eyes had begun to shine.

'I would buy them.'

'But they are not for sale. Only the greatest Werowances in the world may wear blue beads.'

'I am a great Werowance.'

'Only in Powhatan. You could never buy them.'

'Why not?'

'You have not enough corn here to pay for such valuable beads.'

'I will give you a hundred bushels.'

John shook his head, and could not resist a sly glance at Newport who was still staring at four or five bushels which was all he had to show for that great heap of copper.

'Two hundred,' cried Powhatan.

John still shook his head.

'Three hundred.'

John hesitated. Three hundred bushels of corn for a few glass beads! It was too great a temptation to miss.

'Come,' cried Powhatan.

'There is a condition.'

'What is this condition?'

'Only Werowances and their families may wear beads which are the colour of the sky.'

'Only Werowances and their families shall wear these sky jewels,' declared Powhatan.

'In that case . . .' John handed him the beads and Powhatan held them up, his eyes glistening with delight. He hung them about his neck, and all his braves stared at them with fascination and wonder.

The party returned to the settlement with a boatload of corn, a triumphant Smith and a crestfallen Newport. Nor was that the end of the affair for, within a few days, other Werowances arrived at the settlement with loads of corn which they were eager to barter for 'jewels of the sky'.

Now it had become a fashion all over the country. No Werowance was happy unless he was the possessor of bright blue beads – the sign of greatness.

Thus once more John Smith filled the granaries of Jamestown.

The incident did not endear John to Captain Newport, and there was a great coolness between them. This increased when John discovered that the Captain had been foolish enough to promise Powhatan a present of twenty swords.

John could not restrain his feelings. 'It is the height of folly,' he stormed. 'To what purpose do you think Powhatan will put these swords?'

'It is the Company's order that we shall be friendly with the natives,' said Newport; 'and if they ask for a present which we can give them, it would be unfriendly to refuse.'

'So we give them weapons with which to destroy us?' cried John. 'You, Captain Newport, will return to England. You and the Company will discuss together as to how the settlement should be run. But we, sir, have to live here. We have to bear the fruits of your folly!'

John turned and left Newport seething with rage against him.

Thus the coming of the *Susan Constant*, although it relieved the anxieties as to food, brought its own tensions.

Captain Newport was continually reminding the Council that the Company was far from pleased. They had expected cargoes of gold and precious stones which the Spaniards had brought back from South America. They were dissatisfied with cedar and sassafras.

John found great comfort in those days from the new

arrival, Master Scrivener, who had quickly become his friend. Scrivener was a man of such outstanding qualities that he had been immediately elected to the Council. It was a great relief to John to talk to this man and to see how quickly he grasped his ideas, and was in complete agreement as to what the colony needed, and shared John's enthusiasm in trying to bring it about.

Scrivener possessed the qualities of leadership; he was in fact a man with whom John could feel at ease.

One day as they walked together through the settlement a colonist came running to them, carrying something in the palms of his hands. He was almost hysterical in his excitement.

John said: 'What have you there? Calm yourself, man, and tell us.'

The man could only gibber and hold out the palms of his hands for John to see.

In them was a fine yellow powder.

'Captain . . .' stuttered the man. 'I have found it. It is here in Virginia after all. Gold!'

Now there was a fever of excitement throughout the settlement. Men left those essential tasks of building and tilling the soil to hunt in the river bed for this fine gold-coloured powder which they believed to be gold.

There was one alone who was sceptical. 'So far,' said John, 'although important work has been neglected in the search, we have discovered nothing but this yellow dust.' All over the settlement in the surrounding country men were digging. Specimens of the yellow powder were carefully carried on board to be taken back to England to be examined. Captain Newport and his crew were caught up by the fever. They had intended to sail in February, but they remained all through March. John was disturbed, for the digging and sifting was hungry work, and there were still the crews to feed on the supplies which had been brought for the colonists. John sighed as he went about the settlement and looked at the half-finished buildings. If there was indeed gold in Virginia, he was convinced that they would have found something more than this yellow dust which he believed to be a deposit of the soil, indigenous to the country.

In April Captain Newport, his ship loaded with this gold dust, left for England; with him he took Wingfield and Archer, who had both had their fill of the new colony and were glad to return with Newport.

As soon as they had departed John ordered the resumption of building and the regular work of the settlement, appointing a few of the men to continue in their search for gold.

Shortly after Newport had sailed away, another ship was sighted on the horizon. This was the *Phœnix*, which had been blown off her course and thus delayed in her arrival.

Her Captain, Nelson, proved to be an excellent man, more modest than Newport, and honourable. He was not eager to win glory for himself but merely to do his duty. Newport and his crew had often bargained with the colonists for the goods which they had brought out; this seemed to John and many others a nefarious practice since the goods had been supplied for the colonists by the Company. Captain Nelson did no such thing, but handed all the stores over to the storehouse.

It was pleasant to have a man of Nelson's calibre coming from England, and John entrusted him with an account of the colony to be put before the Company; for he guessed that Newport, Wingfield and Archer might give a very garbled account of this which would be most unfavourable to himself. He also wrote a letter for Henry Hudson, the Arctic explorer who, he knew, was greatly interested in colonization, as he hoped Henry might learn something from his, John's, experiences.

So the *Phœnix* returned home, taking with it Martin

whose health had suffered considerably and who needed medical attention. Martin had not been a trouble-maker, but he was a weak man and he had become a little unbalanced by the frantic search for gold. John was glad to be rid of him.

It had come to the Company's ears that there had been certain skirmishes with the natives, and orders had been brought, both on the *Susan Constant* and the *Phœnix* that on no account were settlers to harm natives. John groaned in exasperation when he read these orders.

'How,' he demanded of his good friend, Scrivener, 'can we hope to run a settlement under orders from those who know nothing about it?'

But Ratcliffe, still President, gave the order that the Virginians were not to be attacked. It was not long before the natives became aware of this. In the settlement were hatchets, copper kettles and swords, all greatly desired by the chiefs. They sent their warriors to creep stealthily into the settlement, snatch one of these treasures and make off with it.

Ratcliffe shrugged his shoulders. 'It must be endured,' he said. 'Those are the orders of the Company.'

Powhatan, shrewdly aware of the situation and summing up the character of the great Werowance of the sea who had allowed himself to be so easily cheated, lost his respect for the Palefaces. He even forgot the might of Captain John Smith. He sent his warriors, not only to pilfer, but to insult; whenever they met Palefaces they were to jeer at them and rob them of what they carried, because it was safe to do so. No harm would come to them. The Palefaces, after all, must be cowards who went in fear of the warriors of Powhatan.

John and Scrivener were working in the fields one day – for John made a point of doing any kind of work which came to hand, because he wanted the men to know that he was ready to do anything that he asked them to do –

when Scrivener said to him: 'Captain, there are natives creeping up on us. I see four of them.'

John straightened himself. 'And the orders of the Company are that we allow them to insult and rob us, while we do nothing. My friend, I have had enough of the Company's orders.'

'I am glad to hear it, Captain.'

'Wait until they come closer,' said John. 'Then spring at them and lay about them. We will teach them a lesson.' John was relieved when he saw that several of the colonists were at hand.

'Paleface, give me your knife,' said one of the natives insolently.

'Come here and get it,' John challenged him.

Swaggering before his companions, the man approached. John's fist shot up, caught him under the chin and sent him swaggering back. His companions let out a war-cry, but Scrivener was giving one the same treatment as John had given the first, while John dealt with the other two.

So astonished were the natives that they were caught off their guard, and John shouted to the colonists to make all four prisoners. This the colonists were very ready to do, for they were weary of having to accept insults.

President Ratcliffe was startled when he saw the four prisoners being marched back to the settlement.

'Is this the way you obey the Company's orders?' he demanded.

'*I* am giving orders on this matter in future,' said John.

Ratcliffe, who was alarmed by the way matters were going, said nothing, and the four natives were bound and kept in custody.

When the news reached Powhatan that his men were prisoners in the settlement, he was furiously angry and sent a company of braves, complete with war-paint and bows and arrows, to attack the colonists and bring the four men back.

'It will be an easy thing,' he told one of his chiefs. 'The Palefaces do not make war on us. It is their law.'

'Great Werowance,' replied one of the chiefs, 'these men made war on Captain Smith, and that is not the same as making war on other Palefaces.'

'Go,' said Powhatan. 'They will give you our men. It is the Paleface law.'

John was ready. When he saw the savages creeping through the long grass towards the settlement he set the culverins blazing and led a small company out against the marauders armed with muskets.

'It is the devil-machines,' cried the natives to each other; and they fled, terrified as always by gunfire.

They realized that they might insult and rob other Palefaces, but not Captain John Smith.

Powhatan listened in silence to their report. He shook his head.

He said: 'My daughter has spoken truth. Captain John Smith is a god. We must not offend Captain John Smith. But I have sworn that the Palefaces shall release the men they hold, and if we cannot do it with bows and arrows we must do it with gifts. One does not go to the gods with bows and arrows.'

Then he sent for his daughter.

'You must go to the Great Captain Smith, Matoaka, my child; and you must tell him that Powhatan is his brother. You will take with you a gift of venison, and you will say that Powhatan asks in return for the release of the men who are now prisoners in the Paleface village.'

So to Jamestown came Pocahontas, and with her was Powhatan's special servant and messenger, he whom he trusted beyond all others – the hunchbacked Rawhunt.

Pocahontas decked herself in her best finery to make this journey, for she wished to look beautiful in the eyes of Captain John Smith.

She wore her leather moccasins and deerskin cloak, and

about her neck she put the blue glass beads which proclaimed her as the daughter of a great Werowance; and thus she set out to meet John Smith.

As she walked through the settlement men stood aside for her. To those newly arrived on the *Phœnix* she was a bizarre and beautiful figure. She scarcely looked at them; there was in her expression a rapt contentment. Soon she would be in the presence of the man she not only loved but reverenced.

He embraced her, and for a few seconds she clung to him almost childishly, her reverence forgotten in her passionate love.

She said: 'Powhatan sends me for the prisoners.'

'He is a wily man,' replied John, 'to send such a messenger.'

'You will give me the prisoners?'

John hesitated. He said: 'Pocahontas, my dearest child, I have to teach your people that they must respect my people.'

She answered: 'They will do this when they understand your people; and it is peace, not war, which will bring that understanding!'

'Ah, my dear one, if they all had your understanding!'

'It is you who have taught me understanding. You have taught it with love. Thus it should be between our peoples.'

'Is that possible?'

Then she laughed in the way he had taught her to laugh, in the way she believed the Palefaced women, whom she had never seen, laughed. 'It is not possible. I have been taught by a god. It cannot be so for all.'

'I am no god, Pocahontas. Why, you are above me, for you are the daughter of a Werowance – a King's daughter, as we would say in England, and I but a commoner. Were we in England we could scarce be friends, so great is the difference in our rank.'

She looked frightened. 'I will be this . . . commoner, then. You must teach me how.'

'What! You would give up your rank?' He took the blue beads in his hands and made as though to break them. For a moment her eyes were apprehensive; then she smiled.

'Break them,' she said, 'if that makes me this commoner, so that you may love me and we may always be as one.'

John turned away quickly. She was not a child. She was fourteen, mature even for one of her race. He thought: So at last I love a woman. And this woman loves me.

'Pocahontas,' he said, 'my dearest lady Pocahontas! Take the prisoners back to your father. But tell him this: I give them only for you. I give them because you have such a place in my heart that I could deny you nothing.'

As the weeks went by, Ratcliffe left the governing of the colony more and more to John. Ratcliffe had to admit that the manner in which John had dealt with the natives had meant that the colonists were no longer plagued by petty pilfering and sly attacks. The men were working well under John, and as the winter passed a new prosperity came to the colony.

John delighted more and more in the presence of Scrivener, for he realized that he could go on voyages of exploration and leave the management of affairs in Scrivener's capable hands. Scrivener, though a man of initiative, was quick to see that John had a genius for leadership, and he was eager to follow his advice in all things; this meant that John could go on a voyage and return after a few weeks to find the settlement as it would have been had he remained there.

'One of the best discoveries I have made since I came to Virginia!' he announced on one occasion.

With the coming of spring he declared that he would go off on a voyage to explore Chesapeake Bay, and with him he took among others a young doctor named Russell who was eager to see the country. The inclusion of Russell in the party proved extremely fortunate.

They sailed through a sea which they soon realized was full of fish, so full that they could reach out and touch them. They tried catching them with their hands but the slippery fish eluded them.

'Try with a frying-pan,' cried John; and this was attempted, but the fish slithered into the pans and then leaped high to escape.

John brought out his sword and managed to spear the fish. The others did the same, and very soon the appetizing smell of cooking fish filled the barge.

Nothing delighted John more than to find food locally; it was so much more satisfactory than dipping into the stores which had been brought out from England.

He said: 'Let us take a boatload of fish back to the settlement. We have evidently struck rich fishing grounds and it would be foolish not to make use of them.'

So his crew began to spear the fish and take them aboard, John working harder than any of them.

'Why,' he cried suddenly, 'here is a strange-looking fellow.' The others crowded about him. It was a fish such as they had never seen before with a long tail and a spiky back.

John grasped it to take it off his sword, when the long tail swished out and wound itself round his arm. John cried out in pain and pulled hard at the fish. He managed to remove it, and threw it from him.

He stared at his arm; there was hardly any sign of blood or a wound, but the pain in his arm was excruciating.

'Well,' said John, 'he gave a good account of himself. Let us avoid his sort in future.'

He tried to forget the affair but the pain would not let him, and in a very short time his arm had swollen to twice its normal size.

'There is no doubt,' said John, 'that that fish has a sting

which is poisonous. The swelling grows almost as one watches it. I fear, my friends, that I have been poisoned and this is the end of me. Bury me near this place, and call it Stingray Point, after this calamitous event.'

The men gathered round him; they had already begun to mourn him.

But Doctor Russell said: 'Pray do not dig the Captain's grave yet, for I believe it is possible to remove the poison from his body.'

He took John's hand and lanced the place, where the sting had penetrated, to about an inch. He washed it carefully and put in what he called a precious oil, which he carried with him for such an emergency.

The effect was almost immediate, and the swelling began to disappear.

John was exhilarated.

'Let us cook the stingray,' he cried. 'Let us eat him for our supper. Here at Stingray Point.'

And they were very merry that night, all rejoicing at the good fortune of having Dr Russell with them to save the Captain's life.

They were no longer merry when they returned to Jamestown. Scrivener had fallen sick, as had many of the colonists, particularly those who had recently arrived. John found the settlement in a state of revolt.

The reason for this was that, without Scrivener's excellent supervision, Ratcliffe had been recklessly using the supplies; he had also set the colonists to building him a house which he required should be like an English residence and worthy of the President of Virginia.

John was met by a deputation.

'We will no longer tolerate Ratcliffe as President of Virginia,' he was told. 'We have decided that there is only one man worthy of the post, and we have sworn that if you came back alive we would no longer hesitate to bestow it upon you. We proclaim John Smith, President of the Colony of Virginia.'

John received this news with mingled feelings. At one time he had longed to be the President, but the honour had been too long delayed. Now his thoughts were on further voyages of exploration. He had realized that he was a man who found it difficult to work in a team; he was an individualist and he had come to the conclusion that the ideal state of affairs would be for him to conduct voyages of discovery while the President remained in the settlement to control events there.

But he saw there was no help for it but to accept the honour. Thus, belatedly, Captain John Smith became President of Virginia.

XIII

Powhatan's Coronation

As soon as Scrivener had recovered his health John set him in charge of the settlement and went off on further voyages of exploration. During these he made the acquaintance of the Sasquesahanocks tribe which contained the tallest men any of the travellers had ever seen. These men, who were like giants to the English, and whose looks seemed ferocious, turned out to be the mildest of all the tribes they had encountered, and far from resenting the explorers they welcomed them to their territory.

Watching a service – John did not care that a day should begin without prayers – these giants were so impressed by the singing of hymns and the incantations uttered that they believed these strangers were a race of gods; and the Werowance, who was tall even among his giant tribesmen, presented John with beads and a bearskin and begged him and his party to stay with the tribe and be its protectors against the evil spirits which ranged their forests.

It was pleasant dwelling among these gentle giants, and John bade them farewell with reluctance, telling them that he would come again.

He then made further explorations of Chesapeake Bay and was able to make maps to send home.

When they returned to the settlement it was to find that Scrivener had acted as John had known he would; all was in order, the harvest gathered in, and the granaries full.

John now took over his duties as President and, as an old soldier, trained the most likely men on the plain outside the fort once a week. Every Saturday certain of the natives would lie in the grass to watch the manœuvres which were unlike anything they had ever seen before. There was Captain Smith himself shouting orders while the men wheeled and marched with a precision which, to the Virginians, seemed remarkable.

John named the plain, Smithfield, after himself, but perhaps inspired by the famous district of that name in London.

And that September Captain Newport returned to Virginia with the Second Supply.

When John greeted Captain Newport he knew that Newport still harboured resentment against him.

'Well, Captain Smith,' he said, 'so you are the President now. May I tell you, Master President, that the Company is ill pleased with progress in Virginia?'

'And were they pleased with the yellow dust you loaded on to your vessels when you were last with us?' asked John.

Newport flushed darkly. He had been made to look a fool because he had loaded his ship with useless dust, and he did not care to be reminded of the derision which had greeted them in London.

Once again this upstart, John Smith, had been proved right. He was the only man who had scorned the idea of the yellow stuff's being valuable. It was unpleasant to be reminded.

Well, thought Newport grimly, John Smith has not given any great pleasure to the Company either.

'I trust,' said John, 'that you have brought me the kind of men I need. I want carpenters and builders, that we may complete the building of the town. I want blacksmiths.'

'The Company have decided that they must have some profit from this land,' replied Newport. 'They say that, since you cannot find gold, the colonists should be put to work. I have brought Dutchmen with me to start factories for the making of soap and glass.'

'How can they be so foolish! England can buy from

Holland all the soap and glass she needs, far more cheaply than she can produce it here.'

Newport shrugged his shoulders. 'These are orders.'

'But you know full well what we need. Could you not have explained? You have seen what conditions are here. You are the only man who can explain to those madmen in London. I rely on you, and you bring me Dutchmen!'

'Captain John Smith,' Newport warned him, 'you take too much upon yourself. You are President now, I understand. Make the most of the position. You may not long hold it.'

'That will not be the disaster to me, Captain Newport, which you anticipate. The Presidency is a thankless task, I assure you. We are directed by people from afar who understand nothing ... nothing. It will not grieve me greatly if I am relieved of this burden and am free to carry on my explorations.'

'And what do you discover on your exploration? The Company says there must be gold here, and that you are too indolent to discover it.'

'The Company is composed of fools!' cried John.

'I will convey to them the President's opinion,' replied Newport. 'In the meantime I have instructions. King James, having heard that Powhatan is the King of this territory and wishing for peace among the nations, commands that he be given a coronation and that he be proclaimed King under our Sovereign Lord James the First.'

'Powhatan have a coronation! Then they're madder than I thought.'

The coronation of Powhatan was a bizarre affair. In the first place Powhatan had been very suspicious.

He refused the invitation to come to Jamestown for the ceremony, expecting some treachery.

When Pocahontas came to the settlement John explained to her that it was a ceremony which all kings were proud to undergo, and that it was a great honour which the King of England was bestowing on the King of Powhatan.

Pocahontas listened gravely, and as her great desire was to make friendship between John's people and hers, she herself went to her father and begged him to submit to the ceremony.

'These Palefaces have bewitched you, my daughter,' said Powhatan.

'Nay, my father,' she answered. 'I understand their language better than most of our people do, and I understand them.'

'Captain John Smith has set a spell upon you.'

She lowered her eyes. 'That may be,' she admitted.

There were few people with whom Powhatan could be tender, but his daughter was one of them.

'Little one, my Matoaka,' he said, 'we will find a husband for you. Choose him, daughter. The finest brave in the land ... he shall be yours. I will give you a wigwam like to my own, and you shall wear half as many blue beads as I wear myself.'

But she shook her head and turned away. Powhatan understood, and he was disturbed.

After a while she answered: 'My father, go to the Paleface village and be crowned as their Kings are crowned.'

But he still refused.

Pocahontas sought her brother, Nantaquaus, and begged him to go to Powhatan and persuade him to be crowned as the Palefaces wished. And, with Nantaquaus on one side of him and his daughter on the other, Powhatan at length agreed, although he would not go to Jamestown. Therefore it was decided that the coronation of Powhatan should take place at Werowocomoco.

But when the English party, led by John and Newport, arrived at Werowocomoco, it was to find that Powhatan had gone off on a hunting expedition, whether in fear of treachery or because he thought it was unwise to appear too eager to receive honours from the English King, none knew.

John was received by Pocahontas, a new dignity upon her. She wore a cloak of ostrich feathers, and her long hair, which she had refused to have oiled since John had told her that Palefaced women did not, hung about her shoulders. She looked regal and her manners, half savage, half English, were beguiling, so that all were charmed by her.

As was her custom she received John as though he were the great chief and found it difficult to take her eyes from him as he stood before her. She explained her father's absence and begged him with Captain Newport to sit on the mat which was before a fire in the centre of a field.

As they walked to it she said to John: 'I hear that a Paleface woman came with the great ships.'

'Did you hear this, then?' said John with a smile. It was true, for in addition to his Dutchmen Captain Newport had brought a certain Mistress Forrest, a lady who had accompanied her husband, Thomas Forrest and his brother. Nor was Mistress Forrest the only woman who had come, for she had brought with her her young maidservant Anne Burrowes. Mistress Forrest was not young enough to have caused any excitement among the men, and Anne Burrowes scarcely old enough, and their coming had not caused as much stir as that of the resented Dutchmen.

'I hear much from your village,' she told him. 'You like this lady.'

'She is very brave to come here. Yes, I like her.' Then he laughed. 'She has a husband who likes her even better, and for whom I fancy she has a great fondness since she is ready to endure the hardships of Virginia for his sake.'

Then Pocahontas laughed with him and there was great joy in her laughter.

She left the visitors sitting about the fire, eating food which had been brought for them, and entertained by her many half-brothers and sisters and those braves who had not accompanied Powhatan on the hunting expedition. She herself disappeared, and soon there was a wild shouting from the woods. John leaped to his feet, suspecting that Powhatan had returned with the intention to attack, but, instead of the warriors, out of the woods danced Pocahontas, leading thirty young girls.

Now John saw her as the beautiful savage. She had cast aside all the English manners which he had taught her. She wore bucks' horns on her head and an otter's skin about her waist. Her hair was loose in wild disorder; there was a quiver of arrows on her back and a bow in her hands.

The girls danced in a frenzied fashion about the fire, and one of their number came and stood before John Smith and sang while the dancing continued.

'Captain John Smith is a Werowance of Powhatan.
Great Powhatan has made him so.
He is our brother,
But he takes no wife from among our people.
All Werowances must have wife.
So should John Smith.'

Then the dance began again and, one by one, the girls danced up to John and, placing her arms about his neck, whispered: 'Am I your love, John Smith?'

The members of the party looked on with amusement at the somewhat embarrassed Captain. But when it was Pocahontas' turn to put her arms about his neck and ask the question, John heard himself answer: 'You know.'

The English party slept that night in the fields, and John was deeply disturbed. He slept fitfully and when he dreamed, it was of Pocahontas, not the gentle Pocahontas, but a wild unbridled savage who entwined her arms about his neck and asked him fiercely, 'Am I your love, John Smith?'

They were awakened in the morning by the sounds of distant shouting. Powhatan had returned to Werowocomoco.

Then the coronation began.

It was all according to Whitehall. There was the scarlet carpet and the throne. The Virginians stood about in all their war-paint, watching in an awed silence but ready, should their great chief be attacked, to rush into action.

With great suspicion Powhatan regarded the red robe which he was asked to wear, and it was only when Pocahontas assured him that it could not harm him, and wrapped it about herself, that he would continue. He refused to kneel before Captain Newport.

'Slaves kneel,' he said. 'You would make a slave of me.'

He cried out in anger when he was anointed, and Pocahontas and Nantaquaus hastened to assure him that all was well.

But he refused to bow his head to receive the crown and had to be forced to bend – being pushed forward by several willing hands.

The crown on his head, fifty soldiers fired their pistols, which made such a noise that Powhatan shouted in his rage and his braves stood ready, on the alert, bows and arrows in their hands.

John reassured him that the show was in his honour, and at last Powhatan began to be rather pleased about it all.

He embraced John and Captain Newport.

'We are brothers,' he said.

Then he sent one of his men into his wigwam, and when the man came out he was carrying a pair of worn moccasins and an old deerskin cloak.

These Powhatan wrapped about Captain Newport's shoulders.

'You give me coronation,' he said, hugging the crimson robe which he liked better every moment, 'and I give you coronation.'

He thrust the worn shoes into Newport's hands; the coronation was over.

But the effect was not.

Powhatan pondered the matter. He was a greater Werowance than he had thought, because the King over the waters sent him a coronation. Clearly the Palefaces thought highly of him and, if they did this, it must be because they feared him. He was going to demand more for his corn than hitherto; that was not all.

He sent a messenger to the settlement.

'I now great King,' was the theme of this message. 'I have coronation. English King lives in house with glass holes. English King has doors which open and shut. Great King Powhatan does not want wattle house any more. He will sell corn to the Palefaces, and for this corn the Palefaces will build him a house with glass holes and doors that open and shut.'

It was an ultimatum. It was the price he asked for the food which the colonists so badly needed.

'This,' cried John to Newport, 'is the result of your coronation. Had you not told him such things existed, he would never have known they did. Then he would have been content to give us corn in exchange for glass beads. Now he demands a palace.'

'I obey the Company's orders, Captain Smith,' said Newport. 'I think you would find greater favour in their sight if you did the same.'

'If I obeyed their orders there would not much longer be a colony in Virginia.'

Captain Newport shrugged his shoulders. He was now only concerned with taking his ship to England. He was loading it with cedars.

XIV

Outside the Wigwam of Opechancanough

John stormed away to compile his answer to the Company's foolish instructions. This he addressed to the Treasurer and Council of Virginia (in London). He railed against their folly; he pointed out that they knew nothing of the country which he and the colonists were striving to live in and make prosperous for England. He deplored the coronation of Powhatan, from which he believed trouble would spring. Strongly he criticized Newport and Ratcliffe. He deplored the fact that the Dutchmen had been sent, and not the workmen he so urgently needed. He explained that it was largely due to this lack of understanding that the colonization of Virginia had so far been disappointing.

He signed this document, Captain John Smith, President of Virginia.

And impulsively he carried it out to Newport and delivered it to him to be taken to the Company in London.

'Here,' he cried, 'is my answer to the criticisms from London. I do assure you it is a rude answer.'

The settlement heard that John had answered the adverse comments, and they all speculated as to what would happen when 'the rude answer' was received in London.

John was glad to see Newport sail away, particularly as he took Ratcliffe with him. It did not occur to John to wonder what kind of report Newport and Ratcliffe would give of him; he had no time for such conjectures. For trouble in plenty, as he had anticipated, had been left behind by the Second Supply ship.

*   *   *

The winter was approaching again and the President was once more concerned regarding the depleted state of the stores. As yet the colonists could only live by trading with the Virginians; but Powhatan had given the order that there must be no corn for the Palefaces until he had his palace; and so, raging against the folly of London, John had no alternative but to send valuable workers to Werowoco-moco to begin building the house Powhatan demanded.

Although glass and soap were now being made in the settlement, John had always been sceptical about these enterprises, and three of the five men he sent to build Powhatan's house were Dutchmen. These men had names which were unpronounceable by the English who had immediately anglicized them. So the Dutchmen had become known as Samuel, Adam and Francis.

What John did not know was that the Dutchmen who had come to Virginia had not done so for the sake of adventure, nor to take part in making the colony great. They came as spies for their own country, and their motive was to ruin the English colony. Other countries had their eyes on the New World, and Holland was an ambitious nation. Therefore John could not have played into their hands more successfully than he did by sending these three men to build Powhatan's palace.

No sooner had they arrived at Werowocomoco than they persuaded Powhatan that there was trouble in the English settlement, and that he should either refuse to trade with them – which meant they would soon be too weak to retaliate if he attacked – or if he did trade, he should ask for swords and weapons of war instead of glass beads.

Thus, when John came with his barge and a supply of trinkets, Powhatan received him gravely.

'I have little corn to spare,' said Powhatan. 'It has been a bad harvest.' (This was a lie, but John stifled the retort which rose to his lips.) 'I might find corn in exchange for swords. I could not for any other goods, for we have beads in plenty.'

'Has the great Werowance forgotten that he is my brother?' asked John reproachfully.

'The Paleface Werowance forgets this: He comes among us with his devil-machines.' Powhatan's eyes were fixed on the muskets which John and his men carried, and his eyes were sly. 'Let the Palefaces put away their devil-machines before they come trading,' Powhatan continued. 'Then I know they are my brothers.'

John was alarmed. He read Powhatan's thoughts; he wished the English to come into his territory unarmed; and he would have a reason for this.

John took his leave of Powhatan and returned to the barge, deciding to come back when Powhatan was in a better frame of mind. He returned an hour or so later to find that Powhatan had left the village and gone into hiding in the woods with his wives, children and warriors.

John said to his party: 'I like not this. I do not know what has happened to Powhatan, but it bodes no good. We must perforce take what stores we have been able to buy and return to the settlement.'

When they had taken the stores on board the river was too low to be navigated, so they knew they must wait until the next day. They made a fire on the bank and settled down to sleep.

'Keep your muskets to hand,' warned John. 'You may need them.'

While the others slept from sheer exhaustion John lay awake, listening to every sound in the woods. The night was bitterly cold and very still; he felt sure that if an attempt were made to surprise them he would hear the natives approaching.

Suddenly he sat up, his senses alert, for surely he had heard the sound of a footfall in the woods. There was a rustle of leaves, the crackle of dry grasses and twigs.

John rose and crept into the woods. He hid himself behind a tree, his musket ready for immediate action.

There was no doubt. Someone was stealthily creeping through the woods.

John waited, and then he made out a cloaked shape darting through the trees in the sure-footed manner of the natives. The figure came close. John put out a hand and grasped it as it passed close to the tree behind which he had hidden himself.

The cloak fell open.

'Pocahontas!' cried John.

She was sobbing in his arms.

'You must not stay here,' she cried. 'John . . . go quickly. My father and his warriors, they are preparing for battle. They come to kill you. They have your weapons now. They have the swords which Captain Newport gave to them and devil-machines which have been brought to them by your enemies. The Dutchmen who come to build the house with glass holes have been to Jamestown while you are away to tell them that you ask for swords and muskets. These they have brought to my father. John, do not stay here. Go quickly.'

Astounded by the treachery of the Dutchmen though he was, John's first thought was for the safety of Pocahontas.

'My dearest one,' said John, 'you have come through the dark woods to tell me this. How can I thank you! How can I show you my gratitude?'

'You must show nothing and give nothing, for if Powhatan knows I come thus, although I am his daughter he will kill me.'

John took her face in his hands and kissed her tenderly. 'It would seem,' he said, 'that you are ordained to save my life.'

'To serve you . . . with all my heart,' she said, 'and always to offer my life if it can buy yours.'

'Oh, Pocahontas . . . My dearest, my love, what can I say to you?'

'Say this . . . "I will go away now, but one day we shall meet again. We shall be together." And now there is little time to lose. I have listened to his plans. He will send you food and, while you eat, his warriors will encircle you. They will fall upon you and kill you all, for it is their wish that there shall be no more Palefaces in Powhatan, and he knows that first he must kill Captain Smith. Go . . . go now. They come soon. They bring you food. Listen! I hear them coming now. I have been longer in the woods than I thought. It was so dark for a while I lost my way.'

'My dearest . . .'

But she shook her head. 'There is no time. Go . . . go quickly.'

Then she threw herself against him in a passionate embrace. He held her to him, and it was she who, oppressed by the urgency of danger, tore herself away and ran back through the woods.

John went to his men and told them what had happened.

Some of them scrambled up and prepared to leave, but John shook his head. 'We cannot go by barge on account of the lowness of the river. If we attempt to hurry away they will know that we have been warned, and they will believe we are afraid. There is only one thing to do: Remain here, but let them know that we expect their attack and are ready for it.'

It was very shortly afterwards that eight Virginians arrived carrying hot dishes in which were venison and maize cakes, cooked and ready to be eaten.

'Great Paleface Werowance,' said the leader, 'we bring you gifts of food from Powhatan, who thinks you are hungry because the river is too low for your barge to sail.'

'My thanks to the greatest of Powhatan Werowances,' said John. And he called to his men to gather round. 'Let us sit in a circle, and our guests shall first eat the food which Powhatan has so kindly sent to us.'

'The food is for you, Captain Smith!' was the astonished answer.

But John, believing that he would know whether or not the food was poisoned, by the way in which the Virginians took it, insisted on their eating first. And, believing it was a Paleface custom, they did so without any show of alarm. John suggested they should all take their fill, for a good meal would put heart into all of them.

When they had finished, John said to the leader of the men: 'Take my greetings to Powhatan and tell him that we await his coming. We have our devil-machines in our hands and there is no fear in our hearts.'

The natives slunk away without a word. John and his men waited, but Powhatan, realizing that someone had warned John of the coming attack, lost heart. Who could have warned him? It must have been some supernatural force. Captain John Smith was no ordinary mortal.

But the Dutchmen were at his side. 'John Smith is not immortal,' they told him. 'He is a man of abounding energy, experience and resourcefulness. Without him the colony would be lost. If you wish to destroy Jamestown and drive the Palefaces from Powhatan territory, you must first destroy John Smith.'

Powhatan pondered this. He then sent messengers through the forests, calling all tribes. He had a message for them, a command which must be obeyed before all others. It was: 'Bring me the head of the Paleface John Smith.'

John, ruefully sailing down the river, his barge containing not a quarter of the grain he had hoped to bring back, decided to go ashore in the territory of the great chief Opechancanough.

Opechancanough, who had that day received the command for John Smith's head, from his brother, Powhatan, was filled with savage exultation. The great god Oke had clearly destined him to be the one who would deliver the land from the Palefaces; for what were the Palefaces without John Smith? And here was the Captain at his mercy.

I must use great cunning, Opechancanough told himself; and he had always prided himself on his cunning.

The taking of John Smith would have to be planned; they must not forget that the Englishman was part god himself. Therefore Opechancanough made his plans with care.

When the Englishmen came to barter, the business was never a hurried one. There must be a few days' feasting, that it might appear they regarded each other as brothers.

John was pleased, for he believed that the hostility of Powhatan was not felt by Opechancanough; and with his mind on the Dutchmen's treachery he was considering how he could punish them.

It was on the third day after his arrival in Opechancan-ough's territory when the chief invited him to his house to bargain for corn. John, leaving Master Fettyplace – a mariner whom he trusted – to look after the barge, went along to Opechancanough's wigwam accompanied by the fifteen men who made up the rest of the party.

Opechancanough seeming bland enough was waiting for them, for this chief, possessed of greater imagination than most of the Virginians, was better able to cloak his feelings. He did not betray by even a look that seven hundred of his braves, all painted for war, were creeping on the hut and would soon be ready to break in and slaughter all the Englishmen, making sure of preserving John Smith's head which he would send as a present to Powhatan.

Dr Russell, however, who was of the party, had lingered a little behind the others; thus he saw the warriors advancing towards the wigwam.

Pretending he was unaware of what they were doing, he burst in on John, Opechancanough and the others, and sidled up to John.

'Captain,' he whispered, 'the wigwam is surrounded by hundreds of warriors. They are in their war-paint and have come here to kill us.'

The others who heard this gasped in dismay, and John looked inquiringly at Opechancanough who had not fully understood what had been said. But the Virginian chief could not meet John's eyes, and John knew that Dr Russell had made no mistake.

John turned to his men. 'Well,' he said, 'we are sixteen and they may be hundreds. What of that? We are Englishmen, and they are savages. My friends, we will fight like men, and like Englishmen at that, and you will see that sixteen Englishmen are a match for hundreds of savages. They will see this too, and at the sound of our fire they will be sore affrighted. And if we are to die, let it be as men . . . not as sheep.'

He turned to certain men of the party on whose bravery he relied. 'Guard the entrance,' he commanded.

Then he went to Opechancanough and looked straight into his eyes. Opechancanough flinched; that was enough to show John that he still believed in the supernatural powers of Captain John Smith.

'So,' he said, 'you are a cheat and a liar, Opechancanough. Your word no longer counts. You feign to be a friend. You ask us to your house, and you think to trap us here and murder us.'

Opechancanough did not speak. He remembered that he was almost alone with sixteen Palefaces, one of whom was the great John Smith. Outside were hundreds of his warriors, but the walls of his house divided him from then, shut him in with John Smith who all men knew was no ordinary man.

John went on: 'You are a Chief in this country, Opechancanough. And your people have made me a chief under Powhatan. We are, then, two chiefs. I challenge you to single combat. You will bring as many baskets of corn as you have armed warriors and I will stake their value in copper. The victor shall take both corn and copper.'

Opechancanough could not follow this challenge. His one desire was to get out of the wigwam, into the open where he had but to give the order and hundreds of his men would be eager to give him John Smith's head.

Opechancanough hesitated, but John knew that delay was dangerous, that at any moment those warriors would burst into the wigwam. He therefore held his pistol with one hand and seized Opechancanough's long lock of hair in the other.

Then he dragged Opechancanough into the open.

There was a gasp of dismay from his followers as they saw their chief dragged by the hair in the hands of the Englishman with the dazzling blue eyes.

Those who had doubted the immortality of John Smith no longer did so. The warriors had never before seen a Werowance so treated. As for Opechancanough, he was as surprised as they were, and he believed that only a god could treat a Werowance as he was being treated.

John stood facing those seven hundred warriors, his own party ranged behind him.

'Lay down your bows and arrows,' commanded Smith. They all obeyed.

Still holding Opechancanough by the hair, Smith talked to them in their own language.

'I do not come to harm you. I come to trade with you as brothers trade. Be fair with me. Be honest traders and I promise you no harm shall come to you. I have found some of you to be base traitors, men who give your word and do not keep it.'

The Virginians were ashamed and would not meet each other's eyes.

'If you shed one drop of blood this day, if you attempt to steal from us, remember this: I, John Smith, will be revenged on you. If one warrior, or woman, or child of the Pamaunke tribe steals from a Paleface or draws the blood of a Paleface this day, I shall not rest while one man of the Pamaunke tribe is left alive. It was this tribe which once made me its prisoner. They captured me in a quagmire. Then they brought me to Powhatan and, so they thought, to my death. But did I die? No, there was a miracle which some of you have seen. So here I am to tell you this: I come in peace to trade. If you are wise men you will remember.'

One of the warriors cried out: 'We will remember it, Great Paleface Chief!'

'Then,' said John, 'it is well. Load my barge with corn, for which you shall be paid. Fail to do so and I shall load it instead with your dead carcases.'

The Virginians were eager now to placate John Smith. They wished to trade with him. They had corn to spare and they were ready to begin as soon as he was ready to do so.

John was indeed ready.

Later that day the barge, loaded with grain, sailed down the river to Jamestown.

XV

Farewell Virginia

In great triumph John prepared to return to Jamestown. The barge was loaded with the stores they had come to collect; and even those men who had worked with him and lived with him so long, having witnessed the scene outside the wigwam of Opechancanough, were inclined to believe there was something of the superhuman about John Smith.

As they neared the settlement John sensed that all had not gone well during his absence. To his astonishment he saw that the work which he had expected to be done had been left undone. He noticed the hungry looks of the men when they saw that he had returned with food.

This was like those homecomings in the days before he had Scrivener to leave in charge of the colony. Had Scrivener failed him?

He called to one of the men: 'Tell Master Scrivener that I have returned and would have speech with him.'

The man shook his head and said: 'That I cannot do, President. Master Scrivener is no longer with us.'

'What?' shouted John.

'He was killed some weeks since, during the great storm, when crossing the river in one of the boats. There were nine others with him. The boat came ashore. We found their bodies later.'

John stood speechless. Scrivener! he thought. Not Scrivener, who had been his greatest friend, the man whom he had trusted more than any other. Was there no end to the blows he must accept?

For a moment he seemed defeated. He could not accept

the death of Scrivener with that calm with which he had faced Opechancanough and his ferocious braves, and a sudden mist of tears swam before his eyes. Through a haze he saw the neglected settlement, the colonists who were desperately longing for England, the stores which were continually being diminished; he thought of the newly discovered treachery of the Dutchmen, who were still with Powhatan. He thought of the hostility which he had had to face, from natives who at one time he had believed were his friends.

And so he stood in silence.

Then he said gruffly: 'I ever regarded Master Scrivener as myself.'

He walked hurriedly to the settlement.

In a short time John had overcome his despondency. He had lost his best friend but the colony remained.

He himself would now stay in Jamestown and see that the colony grew healthy again. First he had the food stored and checked, and then worked out the rations, the distribution of which would be supervised by himself. There was going to be no more slacking. He announced that work would proceed regularly each day, and that those who failed to work – unless through sickness – would not share in the daily ration. Each day he himself would be seen working with the colonists. He made a point of doing a little of each type of work, so that no man could say their President would shun work which he imposed on others. He insisted that all must attend a daily service. He deplored the blasphemous oaths uttered by many of the settlers, and he made a law that these oaths should be taken account of and, at the end of the day, for each one recorded a can of water should be poured down the sleeve of the offender.

John himself was not guiltless, and submitted willingly to having a few cans of water poured down his sleeves.

The colonists grumbled, but they had seen enough of disorder by now and they had begun to realize that they could only live in some sort of comfort if they obeyed a set of rules; and that their President was the only man among them who could save them and the colony from perishing.

With John Smith among them the most timid of them ceased to fear the savages; and they discovered that there was a certain contentment in working together. Jamestown was taking on more and more the shape of an English town. This had been more obvious since the arrival of Mistress Forrest, who insisted on having a clean house and introduced a certain gentility into the community, which had not been there before.

John was pleased to notice that since she had come among them the manners of the settlers were a little more refined and, when one of the colonists, John Layden, told John he was going to marry Mistress Forrest's maid, Anne Burrowes, he was delighted.

Anne was only fourteen years old, but it was inconceivable that she should remain long unmarried in such a womanless community; so Jamestown had its first wedding, and John looked forward to the time when they would be ready to receive more women in the colony. He anticipated with pleasure the days when there would be children among them.

Then with God's will they would increase and multiply.

He knew that many of the colonists longed for that day; so the marriage of little Anne was a spur to them all, and Jamestown was a happier place because of it.

George Percy had taken Scrivener's place with John, but Percy, although a good, honest and conscientious man, lacked the abilities of John's dead friend.

To Percy John confided his misgivings regarding the Dutch traitors who were still with Powhatan. This was particularly alarming as various objects were continually being reported missing from the stores, and these objects were usually gunpowder and muskets.

It came to John's ears that among the Virginians one had been seen who bore a marked resemblance to the Dutchman they called Francis, although he had been disguised and wore a feather headdress. 'But,' was the comment, 'I could tell a Dutchman anywhere.'

John gave the order that the man suspected of being Francis should be tracked down and brought to the settlement, and there was a great keenness among many of the settlers to find him.

John was with the Colonel one day when a man rushed in to announce that he believed he had seen Francis, skulking near the storehouse.

'After him!' cried John, and on the spot he organized a party to go in pursuit, placing himself at the head of it. The search led them some distance from the settlement, and John sent the party ahead while he made to return. On his way back he came face to face with a Virginian whom he recognized as the Werowance of Paspahegh, who stopped him to converse. Suspecting treachery, John, after speaking a few words, made to pass on, but as he did so, the Werowance made ready with bow and arrow. But he was not quick enough. John turned and grappled with him; the bow and arrow dropped from the Virginian's grasp and the two went rolling on the ground. Fortunately for John the river was nearby and he manœuvred that they should fall into this, for he thought, as an expert swimmer, he would then have the advantage.

Had it not been for John, the Virginian would have drowned. John seized him by his hair and, holding the man's head above water swam with him to the bank. There John stood with his foot on the Virginian's neck and took a dagger from his own belt.

'Spare me, oh great Paleface,' cried the Werowance of

Paspahegh. 'Spare me and make me your brother.'

John considered this. 'If I spare your life I shall make you my prisoner.'

'Do what you will with me but spare my life,' was the answer.

So John took the Werowance of Paspahegh back to Jamestown as his prisoner, and a few minutes later his party marched in bringing with them the Dutchman Francis.

The Werowance had been brought into the Council room, and thither they also brought Francis.

'Traitor!' cried John. 'So you have worked against us. You have worked with Powhatan.'

The Dutchman cried out: 'No, Captain. It is not so. As soon as we reached Powhatan's territory he made us his slaves. Desperately we tried to escape, and our only way of doing so was to disguise ourselves as one of them. I hoped thus to reach the settlement.'

The Werowance, who had been listening, suddenly stepped forward.

He said: 'Captain John Smith, you save my life. Now I repay. This man is traitor to Captain Smith. He works for Powhatan. He comes here and steals devil-machines for Powhatan. He is bad man to you, Captain Smith.'

Francis looked as though he were going to leap at the Werowance, and for a moment it appeared that the two men would be at each other's throats.

But two of the guards seized Dutch Francis and pinioned him.

'He should be hanged forthwith,' said one member of the Council.

John hesitated. 'He is a good workman,' he said, 'and we have already lost too many through sickness. We are in desperate need of good workmen.'

The Dutchman fell on his knees and swore that if he were allowed to live he would be loyal; he would work as directed, and the Captain would never regret his magnanimity.

'Take these two men to prison,' said John thoughtfully. 'Keep them well guarded, and I will consider what should be done.'

John's first act then was to send a messenger to Powhatan demanding that the other two Dutchmen should be delivered to him. In exchange he would give them the Werowance of Paspahegh who was his prisoner.

Unfortunately, while Powhatan was considering this the Werowance of Paspahegh escaped from his guards and made off to his own people.

Such an eventuality naturally stiffened Powhatan's attitude, who in any case found the Dutch traitors too useful for him to be willing to part with them.

Now there was continual strife between the Virginians and the settlers; the former were constantly creeping about the town and finding their way into the storehouse where they continued to pilfer.

John knew that he had to have an understanding with Powhatan before there could be peace. He believed that they had been too lenient with the Virginians – under orders from London – and he was certain that, if he could have his way, he could subdue the savages.

During one foray he captured two Virginians who he felt might be useful hostages; and the men were kept in a hut which, on account of the cold weather, John caused to be heated by means of a pan of charcoal. One of the Virginians was overcome by the fumes and lay as one dead. The other, who was his brother, set up such a great wail of misery that John and some of the colonists came hurrying to the hut.

Seeing what had happened, John called for brandy and vinegar, and there before the wondering eyes of the savage he revived his brother.

This brother fell on his knees and touched the floor with his forehead; then he looked up at John as though he were in the presence of a god.

John made a decision. 'Go,' he said, 'and take your brother with you. You have suffered enough. Tell the warriors that there is mercy to be had for those who wish to live in peace with the English.'

So the brothers left, and soon the countryside was ringing with the great story of how one had been raised from the dead by Captain John Smith.

Captain Smith was not only a demi-god; he was a great medicine man.

Powhatan heard the story and was a little shaken.

Pocahontas and her brother Nantaquaus, implored him to make peace with the white man, but Powhatan looking at his daughter who was ripe for marriage and, remembering her continual refusal to enter that state, hardened his heart and said: 'He bewitches all. He is no god. He is sorcerer who has magic, but he is no god.'

And he would not release the Dutchmen nor make peace with the English.

The warlike forays continued, and John decided that he was going to have peace in the land even though it meant flagrant disobedience of the Company's orders.

He picked a few men and, armed with muskets, he set out.

He sent the Virginians scurrying from the first village he came to, and set fire to their wigwams.

The sound of musket fire was heard for miles and the smoke of burning villages filled the air.

The Virginians were terrified; they had seen the great devil-machines in action. They had now learned what it meant for those who were not prepared to live in peace with Captain Smith.

John took many prisoners whom he hoped he would

soon be able to release, for the problem of feeding them was going to give him great anxiety; but although he killed only some six or seven Virginians, he had nevertheless succeeded in filling them with terror.

A few days after his campaign had begun, the Werowances begged for a pow-pow.

This took place outside Jamestown, and John spoke first.

'This is a land of plenty,' he said. 'Plenty for you. Plenty for us. Let us share it. Let us be friends. It is for you to say whether you will be the friend of John Smith and live in safety, or be his enemies and see your homes burned, your warriors slain.'

'Let us have peace with Captain Smith,' cried the Werowances in unison.

The pipes of peace were smoked. Even Powhatan was subdued.

At last there was harmony between the natives and settlers.

During the peace, the colony under John's careful guidance prospered. The Virginians appeared to have no desire for strife.

Powhatan remained at Werowocomoco and the Dutchman Francis, who had been let out of prison to work, took the first opportunity of rejoining his countrymen under the protection of Powhatan.

Some of John's friends wanted to go after him, wanted to bring the three traitors back for execution, but John was never a man to bear resentments. He believed that by showing his strength to the Virginians he had clipped the power of the Dutchmen. They only had a chance when Powhatan believed the settlement weak.

'They deserve to hang . . . or worse.' Even gentle George Percy said that.

'Nay,' said John. 'Let be. If I want the Dutchmen I shall have to send a party of men to get them. I need workmen here in Jamestown far more than I need traitors with pulled teeth.'

So the Dutchmen were allowed to go free, and the work went ahead.

'Now,' said the colonists, 'we have a President who will make us a great colony. Soon men and women from England will be coming out to join us. Then we shall live as at home, and the town will grow big. There will be other towns. The James River will be as old Father Thames.'

It was during the month of August that the fleet of ships arrived. Four of them came sailing into the James River, and all the colonists went down to the shore to greet them.

Here were hundreds of colonists – and supplies of food. John, watching, knew from the fact that they had sent so many and such grand ships, that the Company had decided to make changes.

There was feasting and revelry.

It was learned that seven ships had sailed out of Plymouth three months before, that a hurricane had struck them and it was not certain what had become of some of the others. It was believed that some had taken refuge in Bermuda, there to await a favourable wind.

Four days later more ships arrived.

It was with a feeling of dismay that John discovered among their passengers those trouble-makers, Ratcliffe, Archer and Martin.

The voyage had been a hard one and there were many sick on board all the ships, but they were a proud sight and John was filled with pleasure as he surveyed them, although he guessed that his 'rude answer' had probably resulted in a further and perhaps more caustic reply.

Ratcliffe sought him out at the first opportunity.

'So,' he said, 'the Captain as President pleased them at home even less than the other Presidents. And now they have sent a noble lord to do the job.'

'I have heard of this,' replied John equably.

'They send my Lord De la Warr, and with him will come Sir Thomas Gates and Sir George Summers – noblemen, you see, Captain Smith. Doubtless they will please the Company better.'

'I doubt that any will please the Company, but we can always hope and pray.'

'So, John Smith, this is the end of your reign.'

A retort rose to John's lips, for he believed that this man had played a big part in maligning him with the Company, but suddenly he felt his anger leave him. The Presidency was a thankless task and he believed that his real mission in life was to explore fresh lands.

He was silent, contemplating the future. Why should he not take a few kindred spirits and range the country? Why should he not discover more lands? The Company wished to be rid of him. They knew nothing, in London, of conditions here in Virginia; he had worked for the colony; again and again he had risked his life for the colony; but the people at home did not want bravery; they did not want courage and resourcefulness. Perhaps he and they were searching for different things. He wanted a new land, a land which would be part of England. They wanted gold and quick profits.

He was smiling to himself as he left Ratcliffe.

John, some seventy miles up-river from Jamestown, lay meditating in an open boat. He was no longer President of the Company for George Percy had been elected to that office until the arrival of Lord De la Warr.

'Well,' mused John, 'I am a free man now. When I feel the urge to explore I need not consider whether it is wise for me to leave. I may go when and where I will.'

He believed now that as an explorer-adventurer he would have been more successful than he had, working in a community, for he was essentially an individualist.

I'll warrant, he thought, I was not an easy fellow to live with. Yet some were fond of me.

His eyes grew soft as he thought of Pocahontas. She was waiting for him, and if he asked for her, he knew, Powhatan would give her to him.

If he married Pocahontas he might one day become the greatest of all Werowances in the land of Powhatan for he was already a legend in that land. He thought of her, half civilized, half savage and felt a yearning to be with her.

What could be more fitting than a marriage between them – the marriage of the King's daughter and the man whom the Virginians would always believe to be the greatest of all Palefaced chiefs!

As he lay there one of his men came aboard smoking a pipe; and the strong wind caught the burning tobacco from the pipe's bowl and blew it on to the powder bag. John started up a second or so before he heard the deafening explosion.

As he saw the flame running up his coat, he sought to tear off the garment but his doublet was now ablaze; in a few seconds he was alight from head to foot.

He cried out in his agony and half fainting with pain he was aware of the river. Realizing that it was hopeless to extricate himself from his burning clothes he leaped over the side of the boat and into the water.

Several of his friends had stood aghast watching what had happened; this was fortunate for John was unconscious as he struck the water and could do nothing to save himself. They got him aboard and tried to take off his charred garments, but when they did so his skin came off with them. John lay still, uttering no sound, and his friends stood round him, their heads bowed.

Dr Russell had not accompanied them on this trip and there was no doctor in the party who might have alleviated his sufferings; he lay mercifully unconscious most of the time but now and then waking to agony and fainting again during the painful journey of seventy miles back to Jamestown.

When they brought him into the settlement many of the colonists crowded about the improvised stretcher to look at him. His poor burned body was covered, but they saw from his face that this man, who was surely very near death, scarcely looked like the vigorous Captain who had left them a short time before to go up-river.

George Percy was filled with grief. He had been eagerly awaiting the return of John, for he found the role of President an exacting one, particularly now that those trouble-makers, Ratcliffe, Archer and Martin were back in the colony.

Indeed every man who wished well to the colony was plunged into melancholy. Those three trouble-makers, however, were delighted at this turn of events.

John was put to bed and his wounds dressed, and although most men would have died from the shock alone he gradually began to recover.

One evening, shortly after John had been brought back to the settlement, Ratcliffe asked Archer and Martin to take a walk with him, and he led them to a quiet place in the woods where they could talk.

As soon as they were out of earshot, Ratcliffe said: 'I verily believe the Captain is going to cheat death again.'

'What has the man which the rest of us lack?' demanded Archer.

'I believe him to be immortal,' said the nervous Martin.

'Nonsense!' retorted Ratcliffe. 'He is merely lucky. A pistol would put an end to him.'

'Would you fire that pistol?' asked Archer.

Ratcliffe hesitated. 'It would be traced to me, or to you immediately. We should be foolish to commit such a deed. But I think I know of two men who hate him well enough and the promise of a reward would tempt them. I speak of Coe and Dyer. Do you remember them? Smith punished them for some petty offence some time ago, and they are vindictive men.'

'It would be murder,' ventured Martin.

'We live in dangerous times,' replied Ratcliffe. 'There will be an inquiry into the management of the colony when De la Warr arrives. There will be further investigation in London. How do you think *we* are going to fare then! And who do you think will be the chief witness against us?'

'John Smith,' cried Martin.

'If he lives,' added Archer.

'My dear fellows,' said Ratcliffe, 'we must see that his luck does not last.'

'Is it possible?'

'Indeed it is possible. He is lying in his bed, a sick man, scarcely conscious of what goes on around him. This is not the John Smith who slew the Turks, nor the man who held Opechancanough by the hair before seven hundred savage warriors. This is a sick man with one foot in the grave. Life could be more pleasant for us if both of his feet were safely there.'

'And you propose . . . ?'

'To sound Coe and Dyer. Leave this to me.'

It was quiet in the cold bare room in which John lay sleeping. His body was swathed in bandages; his face and head had been almost untouched.

He did not hear the two men creep into his room, for they came with the utmost caution because they knew it would go ill with them if they were discovered.

They stood by the bed looking down at him, their pistols in their hands.

He was completely at their mercy.

'Now,' whispered Coe. 'It will soon be done. Why do you hesitate?'

'Why do you?' hissed Dyer.

Coe did not know; nor did Dyer.

Coe lifted his pistol unsteadily, but the sound of their voices had roused John from his sleep. He opened his eyes and looked at them, and a look of understanding flashed into those vivid blue eyes.

The men stared at him and as they did so unconsciously stepped back from the bed.

John's eyes did not stray from their faces and before that sharp gaze they backed out of the room.

'Why did you do that, you fool?' whispered Dyer.

'Why did you?' demanded Coe.

'There is something about him . . .' began Dyer.

Coe nodded. 'To kill him would be more than killing a man . . .'

'Let's get away from here. Let Captain Ratcliffe do his own dirty work. I'll have no hand in the murder of John Smith.'

John lay still, thinking. They had come to kill him as he lay. He felt the pain of his bandaged body and he thought: My days are done in Virginia. What use can I be here now? How could I go to Powhatan, a maimed man, and ask for the hand of his daughter in marriage? Or what use should I be to any or to myself in a wild and savage land?

He knew that beyond the settlement the ships lay anchored in the bay.

He also knew he had not come to his end yet; there was one course open to him. He would return to London. There he could place his poor body in the hands of doctors who might do something for him. Here he could not hope to recover.

He felt at peace, resigned. This was his fate and he could not avoid it. He must say goodbye to Virginia which he had loved as men love their wives and families, for Virginia had no further use of him.

*   *   *

It was October when the ships set sail for England, and with them went Captain John Smith.

George Percy watched until the ship which carried John was a speck on the horizon. Then he turned to two men who stood beside him, Master Fettyplace and Master Pots and said to them: 'So we have lost him – he who was our great leader. He was always just, and hated pride and sloth. Did he not suffer with us any hardship which had to be borne! He is the greatest among us. His adventures were our lives, and his loss may well be our death. Mourn with me, my friends, for we have lost our father and our guide.'

XVI

Rebecca

Wrapped in her cloak of deerskin, her blue beads glistening at her neck, came Pocahontas. Her eyes were wide and her brown fingers clutched nervously at her cloak.

Certain colonists, who remembered how she used to come to the settlement with baskets of food, looked for her followers; but Pocahontas came alone.

'I beg you,' she said, 'to tell me true. Is Captain Smith here?'

'No, my little maid, Captain Smith is no longer here.'

She said: 'Then I beg you take me to one who is a leader among you.'

The men looked at each other, and at that moment Ratcliffe appeared in the company of Archer.

'Why,' said Ratcliffe, 'this is John Smith's *inamorata*. Let us go and hear what she has to say.'

Ratcliffe approached her with some ceremony and, taking her hand, kissed it, treating her with the deference due to a princess.

'I have come to ask you what has happened to the great Captain,' she said.

'You mean Captain John Smith, I believe,' said Ratcliffe.

'Yes. I do mean the great Captain.'

Ratcliffe said: 'Walk a little way with me, for I fear I have bad news for you.'

Archer walked on one side of her, Ratcliffe on the other; and when Archer was about to speak Ratcliffe silenced him with a look.

'John Smith is dead,' said Ratcliffe.

Pocahontas stood still and looked from one to the other as though entreating them to tell her that this was not so.

'I heard he had been hurt by gunpowder,' she said. 'I heard he sailed away to be made better. That is true, please?'

Ratcliffe shook his head. 'Nay, he died of his wounds. The powder-bag exploded, and his flesh was torn from his body with his clothes. He died in great agony.'

She did not speak.

Fearing she did not believe him, Ratcliffe took her to that spot where they had buried their dead and showed a cross on a mount. She could not read, so it was easy to deceive her.

'There,' he said, 'lies what remains of Captain John Smith.'

Pocahontas stared at the little cross; then suddenly she ran and did not stop until she was deep in the woods and far from the settlement.

She threw herself on to the grass and lay there, and when the night came she was still lying there.

Her women came to find her, and when they saw her they said: 'Matoaka, why do you lie here? See, the night has come. Did you not notice?'

She said: 'Yes, the night has come. Now it will always be night, for the daylight has fled for ever.'

The news spread through the Powhatan country. 'John Smith is dead.' Powhatan laughed exultantly. There was no longer need to keep the peace. He sent his men to prowl about the settlement and take any opportunity to pilfer arms; they had orders to surround and torture, kill or take prisoner any Palefaces they found; they might bargain, but not accept beads and trinkets as they did from Captain John Smith, but must demand arms in return for corn.

Meanwhile, in the settlement Ratcliffe laughed to scorn the idea that the colony had relied on John Smith's trading with the Virginians to tide them over the months of scarcity. It was nonsense to worry. The colony was well stocked.

George Percy had become very ill and was unable to keep the rebels in order; therefore Ratcliffe was in fact the ruler of the settlement. Having a fancy for pork or lamb now and then he ordered that animals should be slaughtered, for he did not see why he should deny himself these pleasures. Thus the slaughtering of animals went on to give this important man and his cronies a rich diet.

But even Ratcliffe had to realize at length that food stocks were alarmingly low.

Powhatan, watching carefully, knew exactly what was happening in the settlement, and one day he sent a message to Ratcliffe. 'I traded with Captain John Smith and I will trade with Captain Ratcliffe. Let him meet me at Orapakes in Pamaunke and there I will load his ships with corn in exchange for copper and hatchets of which I am in great need.'

'There!' cried Ratcliffe. 'You see it is not so difficult. You men believed that Captain John Smith was the only man capable of trading with these savages. I will show you that all Captain Smith did I can do as well or better.'

As he was selecting the men who should accompany him, one of the latest arrivals begged to be allowed to join the expedition. This was Henry Spelman, son of Sir Henry Spelman, young and eager for adventure.

'You may certainly join us,' said Ratcliffe, 'but do not look for the kind of adventures which you have heard befell Captain Smith. I am of a firm opinion that these never happened outside the great Captain's imagination.'

The party set out and travelled by the Chickahominy River to the Powhatan territory.

When they left the barge and went into the village Powhatan was waiting for them. He received them with courtesy, but Ratcliffe found it difficult to bargain with him and was greatly disappointed with the amount of grain he was able to procure.

At length, realizing that Powhatan would not give him all he needed, he said that they would return to the barge with what they had managed to procure and go farther afield.

Powhatan bade them farewell, and they set out through the woods. They had not gone very far when they heard the sound of the Powhatan war-cry and realized that a party of Virginians in full war-paint had encircled them.

Ratcliffe lost his head and prepared to fire his musket, but before he could do so his body was pierced by ten or twelve arrows and he fell groaning to the ground. The rest of his party attempted to use their muskets and scored some hits among the Virginians, but they were so few and their attackers numerous.

Henry Spelman, who had had little experience of savage warfare, was crouching on the ground with the rest when he saw that he was lying close to a clump of bushes.

The arrows were falling thick and fast and the whooping of the savages was bloodcurdling; and Henry, thinking to take cover, crawled farther into the bushes. In doing so he lost his musket and lay there saying his prayers because he believed that his end was near.

Now the Virginians had closed in on the little band. Henry could see through the bushes that the members of his party were all either dead or wounded, and that the savages were examining the dead bodies, stripping them of their possessions.

'Now it is my turn,' thought Henry, and closed his eyes.'

But it was not his turn, for the bushes completely hid him and, although he saw the savages drag the bodies of the Englishmen away from the spot, they overlooked him.

He realized then that he had been fortunate, as he was the only surviving member of the party. He lay still for a long time, listening to nearby shouting; he heard the cries of triumph and when he saw the thick black smoke rising to the sky he knew it came from the burning bodies of his companions.

Then a great fear came upon him; he was alone in hostile territory. If he reached the spot where they had left the barge he did not believe he would find it there because the savages would have forestalled him; moreover they might be waiting for any stragglers to return. He shivered to remember the stories he had heard of how these savages had been known to torture their captives. Captain Ratcliffe and the others had died mercifully compared with some.

For a long time he lay shivering under this bush. He grew hungry and when darkness fell came out of his hiding place. Cautiously he made his way back to the river, but the barge was not where he believed they had left it. What could he do, miles from the Settlement, in hostile Powhatan territory? He believed that he could not live long; for if the savages did not find him he would die of hunger.

He crept back to the forest and at length, worn out with fatigue and apprehension, he fell asleep.

It was early morning when he awoke, and a cold shiver ran down his back, for he knew that he was not alone. A savage was bending over him. Feeling sick with fear, he scarcely dared open his eyes, for he had no musket with which to defend himself.

Then a voice said: 'Do not be afraid, Englishman.' And when he opened his eyes he saw that it was a girl who bent over him. Her long dark hair fell over her shoulders; her dark eyes held an expression which he believed was pity.

She said: 'I know what happened. Your friends have all been killed and you are alone.'

'Yes,' he said.

'Be careful you are not seen. If you are, they will kill you.'

'I shall die of starvation in any case.'

'No,' she said. 'I saw you come from your hiding place. I saw the battle. So I bring you food.' She had brought a basket. In it was the roasted flesh of deer, and corn cake, which he ate ravenously.

She said: 'Once I had a slave who was a god. But he was too great to stay on Earth. The gods took him. You have blue eyes and you are an Englishman. Have no fear. I will bring you food and tell you when it is safe for you to walk the woods by day.'

'Are you real,' he asked, 'or do I dream?'

'I am Pocahontas the daughter of Powhatan,' she told him. 'Perhaps I will make you my slave, and you shall make copper beads for me. He was to be my slave and make beads. But he was a god and it was not to be. Perhaps he watches from the great hereafter and tells me to save you. I like to think he watches. You will be safe.'

She left him, and he would have believed that he had been the victim of delirium, but that there was the food in his hand.

She came again that day and for many days. She talked to him in his language, and he spoke in what he had learned of hers.

And a few days later, for she said he would die if he were continually exposed to nights in the forest, she led him into her father's village and told great Powhatan that he was her prisoner and slave. He would live among them and make beads for her.

And Powhatan, whose anger rose at the sight of any Englishman, was subdued by the will of his daughter; so very soon they seemed to forget that Henry Spelman was not one of them. He hunted with them, he fished with them; he would bring in a deer as easily as any of them. He could speak with them and tell them tales of England. They accepted him and forgot that he was not one of themselves.

*   *   *

The winter had come and starvation, such as had never been known to them before, stalked the colony.

'If Captain Smith were here,' men said to one another, 'we should not be in this sorry state. Always when we approached it, he would go off into the forest, and did he ever return without food for us? It was a different matter when Ratcliffe went, and we shall never see Ratcliffe again.'

The situation seemed worse because with the Third Supply women and children had come out to the colony. In the summer the population had been some five hundred, but men, women and children were dying every few days.

Men such as Martin and Archer killed off the rest of the livestock and ate it, and little of this found its way to the humbler colonists. For a little grain they frantically bartered weapons and tools which were essential to their existence.

Powhatan was delighted. He was like a great vulture watching. He told his warriors: 'Soon it will not be necessary for us to take weapons from the English, for soon they will all be dead.'

The three Dutchmen and Henry Spelman were still with him.

'Great Powhatan,' cried the Dutchman, 'what did we tell you! Soon there will be no colony. We were right. Soon the whole of the Powhatan territory will have but one ruler again, and that will be great Powhatan.

'It is true,' said Powhatan. 'Oke is with me. He will drive the English from my land and all will be as it was before the coming of the white man.'

Meanwhile conditions in the settlement were getting worse. There were no animals left; they were living on roots and herbs and a few nuts; occasionally a little fish was caught.

'The greatest starving time of all time is upon us,' said the people of Jamestown, 'because this time we have lost Captain Smith.'

Martin and Archer died of a sickness which was born of starvation. In every house men and women lay dying. Of the five hundred inhabitants of Jamestown only about one hundred were left.

One day the smell of cooking meat again came floating along the line of houses. In a few moments men and women were pushing each other aside to reach the house from which it came. There, stooping over a steaming pot, they saw a man and woman; in their hands they held lumps of meat, and all those who could crowd into the house soon had their hands in the pot.

When there was nothing left the owner of the house began to laugh hysterically.

'You have eaten the body of that Redskin we slew the other day,' he cried. 'I could bear my hunger no longer, and if pig tastes good, why should not man!'

There was a deep silence, and many of those who had rushed into the house and fed themselves slunk shame-facedly away.

But hunger is a very potent urge and in a few days the living were feeding on the dead.

It was noticed that the pinnace, which had been left behind when the ships had sailed away, was missing. This meant that some of their number had left the colony and escaped to sea.

But starving men and women were too lethargic to care, and the starving time went on.

The cannibalism ended abruptly when it was discovered that a man had killed his wife and salted her body. He had eaten a certain part of it before this became known.

'What has happened to us!' the people asked each other. 'We have lost all decency, humanity and honour. What would Captain Smith do if he were here?'

They had no doubt. They took out the man who had killed his wife and hanged him.

Each day those who had the energy strained their eyes

for the sight of a sail on the horizon, for they knew that only the coming of the promised supply ships could save them now.

The winter had passed; May had come, and soon the heat would be upon them. They consoled each other: 'We shall not be here to feel it.'

Sometimes they looked towards the forest. 'In the old days,' they said, 'we were saved by the coming of a beautiful savage. She came with her handmaidens, and they carried baskets of food.'

'She came for Captain Smith,' was the rejoinder. 'She comes for no other.'

So they looked to the woods for Pocahontas, and they looked to the sea for the coming of Lord De la Warr; and it seemed that they looked in vain.

Now there were but sixty of their number left, and very soon they would all be dead.

Then on the horizon they saw the ships.

They tried to cheer, but they had not the strength to do so. And when Sir Thomas Gates and Sir George Summers brought their ships into Chesapeake Bay sixty starving people, who were little more than skeletons, huddled together on the shore to greet them.

'God be praised,' cried one of them. 'The great starving time is over.'

News of the arrival of the ships reached Powhatan and his anger mounted. He sent for the three Dutchmen.

'You tell me that soon the English die and there be no more English.'

'But the ships have come, Great Werowance.'

'You not tell me truth. Now there are more English and they will be strong again. Big ships have come. They bring more devil-machines than we have here. How shall we drive the English from Powhatan territory?'

'Great Powhatan, we will work with you as we have

done before. We will spy for you now that the English will have a new Werowance to take the place of Captain Smith.'

Powhatan cried out: 'I know not whether Captain Smith be dead. Some say he is. The English lie to me. He was your brother and you betray him. You would betray me as you betrayed the great Captain.'

'We would never betray great Powhatan. Powhatan is our brother.'

Powhatan called for mats that his three brothers might sit with him. They sat and feasted; then Powhatan called to a woman to bring water and feathers that they might wash and dry their hands.

And when this was done he had three great stones brought in; and on these the heads of the Dutchmen were laid while the executioners beat out their brains.

Powhatan called his daughter to his side and spoke seriously to her.

'You are no longer a child, my Matoaka. It is time you give children to the tribe. It is time you marry.'

Pocahontas shook her head.

'Captain Smith is dead,' said Powhatan. 'The spells of the dead no longer bind.'

'Some bind for ever,' she told him.

He looked at her sadly. 'You love these Palefaces because Captain John Smith was one of them. You love them more than your own people. There is the boy you saved.'

'He has been our friend. He has worked with us.'

'He will one day turn against us. He is of them, not of us. Marry, my daughter. When you have children you will have broken the Paleface spell.'

'It can never be broken,' she answered sadly.

'I cannot keep you here unmarried. You know that full well.'

'Then I will go away, as is the custom for unmarried daughters.'

Powhatan nodded sadly. Even he would not think of disobeying the custom.

'Do not go far from your father, Matoaka,' he said.

She replied: 'I will go and stay with the Werowance Japazaws. He loves me well, and his wives will be my friends.'

Powhatan looked sorrowful. 'That Werowance was a friend of John Smith. He sold him much corn.'

'For which,' answered Pocahontas, 'he was well paid. He possesses much copper which came from Captain Smith.'

'And you would go to him. My daughter, I am grieved to lose you. But you must go, or take a husband from among us.'

'Then,' said Pocahontas, 'to Japazaws I go.'

With Lord De la Warr's fleet of ships, men, women and children had come to reinforce the colony. The Company, with the co-operation of men such as De la Warr whom it had appointed Governor of Virginia; Sir Thomas Gates who was Lieutenant-Governor; Sir George Summers who was Admiral; Sir Thomas Dale, High Marshal; Sir Fardinando Wainman, General of the Horse; and Captain Newport, Vice Admiral, had the backing of great wealth. Moreover there was the experience of the pioneers to draw upon, and the colonists had at last learned that if they were to survive they must rely on the cultivation of the land and their own hunting for provisions.

However, with a larger and more prosperous colony, the Company was prepared to send out more supply ships, and in the following years the terrible starving time was not repeated.

But the natives continued to give trouble. Powhatan had changed his headquarters from Werowocomoco to Orapakes, which was farther from Jamestown. He was dismayed to see that when the English lost Captain Smith they had replaced him by great numbers of people and the constant arrival of big ships.

All he could do was refuse to trade, send his pilferers into the settlement by night and attack the English wherever he met them.

Clearly what was needed, said many of the oldest settlers, was the treatment which Captain Smith used to give them.

But the leaders of the colony reminded them that the Company's orders were to live on friendly terms with the natives and, because of these orders, they must strive to do so.

With a few fleet of supply ships a certain Captain Argall arrived and, as he had visited the settlement during the days of John Smith, he was appalled to find how relations had deteriorated between the English and the natives. He had been some time in Canada, and therefore had experience of dealing with the natives.

'Why,' he told the Governor, 'what we did in Canada was to capture some of the people and hold them as hostages. Then we would demand what we needed in exchange for the return of these prisoners. It was invariably effective. You must, of course, make sure that you kidnap the really valuable people.'

One of the old settlers said: 'Powhatan has a daughter for whom it is said he cares more than for any other person. She is not living in his house now, but for some reason – an old custom probably – lives with an old Werowance on the banks of the Potomac River.'

'That is interesting,' replied Captain Argall. 'We will kidnap the girl and hold her as a hostage.'

'Who will do this?' asked Sir Thomas Gates uneasily.

'I will,' replied Captain Argall. 'It is my idea, and I am very ready to carry it out.'

So, armed with presents, he set sail up the Potomac River and came to that village over which the Werowance Japazaws reigned.

Captain Argall ingratiated himself with Japazaws, who was a peace-loving chief and whose eyes gleamed at the sight of the copper goods which Captain Argall brought; there was one larger copper kettle which Japazaws particularly coveted.

'What do you ask for that kettle?' he wanted to know; but Captain Argall shook his head and explained that it was a very special kettle with which he could not bring himself to part.

Japazaws was regretful, and Captain Argall lingered in his village. It was thus that he met Pocahontas; he thought her charming, for she seemed apart from the women among whom she lived. There was a fire in her, and yet a brooding melancholy. She was friendly with him. She told him: 'I have a special love for the English.' And he spoke English in a manner which surprised the Captain.

He could well see why she was highly prized by her father.

Captain Argall talked privately with Japazaws.

'You long for this kettle,' he said, 'and it shall be yours on one condition.'

'What is this?' asked the chief eagerly.

'I wish Pocahontas to be brought aboard my ship.'

Japazaws looked startled. 'She is the daughter of great Powhatan!'

'I know it, and I swear by my god that no harm shall befall her. I merely mean to detain her until my people have been able to make peace with her father. If she is with us it will be easier, and everyone in the forest will be the happier for it.'

'She is the daughter of Great Powhatan,' repeated Japazaws trembling.

But his desire for the kettle was too great, and he said: 'Tell me what you wish.'

*　　*　　*

The chief wife of Japazaws came to Pocahontas.

'I wish you to do something for me, Matoaka.'

'Then I will do it,' replied Pocahontas. 'I will gladly repay you for your hospitality to me since I left my father's house.'

'I wish to go and see the Paleface ship in the river, but I am afraid to go alone. Will you come with me?'

'There is nothing to fear,' said Pocahontas, 'and of course I will come with you.'

'Then I may go. Old Japazaws will not let me go among the Palefaces alone, but if you come he will not say nay to me.'

So they went on board the ship – Japazaws himself deciding to accompany them – where Captain Argall was waiting for them.

He received the women with the utmost courtesy, and they were all given food and shown the ship, and when it was time for them to go the Captain said gently to Pocahontas: 'I am afraid I cannot allow you to leave.'

She looked startled.

'You are my prisoner,' he told her. 'Have no fear. I shall allow no harm to come to you. You will merely be my hostage until your father agrees to come to terms with us.'

Japazaws and his wife began to wail but Pocahontas, who knew them well, thought she detected a note of something like triumph in their wailing; and when Captain Argall said to the chief: 'Take this copper kettle. It will compensate you,' she understood.

She had been betrayed for the sake of a copper kettle. Old Japazaws and his wife had done this. She had trusted them. There was no one in the world whom she could trust as she would have trusted John Smith; and he had been a Paleface – the enemy of her race.

She was resigned, as the barge made its way towards Jamestown.

*   *   *

The news was brought to Powhatan. His daughter, Matoaka, a prisoner of the Palefaces! She would be returned to her people when he, Powhatan, made peace and promised not to molest any Palefaces he found in the woods; he must return to the settlement all the weapons which had been stolen by his braves!

Powhatan stamped through his new house in the woods and called curses on all Palefaces.

He wanted his daughter.

Then he went to look at the store of weapons which he kept in a wigwam close to his own, and which was guarded day and night. He picked up swords and hatchets, knives and muskets.

They were very dear to him. Through them he saw the eventual triumph of the natives of Virginia over the intruders, and to return them was too big a price to ask even for his favourite daughter.

'They will not harm her,' he told herself. 'She was put under a spell which made her almost as one of them. Let her stay with the Palefaces, and I will keep my treasures.'

Meanwhile Pocahontas was received at Jamestown. She was a Princess, it was said, for she was the daughter of the ruler of all Powhatan, and she was unlike the other natives whom they had seen. She was quiet and a little sad in her demeanour; she could speak a little English and she had acquired certain English manners.

'But she is charming!' said the women.

They began to make her a pet among them. They were eager to help her and teach her their ways; and Pocahontas, who since she had met John Smith had felt a great admiration for the English, began to lose a little of her melancholy.

It delighted her to be among English ladies; to learn their manners; to sit with them at table and learn to eat as they ate; to watch them at their embroidery and learn to use the needle.

She felt that in this way she was a little nearer to John. He must have known women such as this in England; she therefore found great pleasure in modelling herself in the ways of the English.

Many of the women gave her dresses and helped her to make some for herself. So she was now dressed as an Englishwoman and spoke continually in the English language.

One day Lady Gates said to her: 'Pocahontas, what would your feelings now be, if you father decided to redeem you? How would you feel about returning to your people?'

She answered: 'These are my people. Here I stay always. Here I am most happy . . . happier than I have been since . . . since a long time. My father cares more for his machines than he cares for his daughter. Therefore he shall have no longer this daughter. They have said goodbye.'

Lady Gates was a little taken back. 'Do you mean, my dear child,' she said, 'that you will stay always among us?'

'I will stay,' answered Pocahontas.

Lady Gates was thoughtful; and shortly afterwards she suggested that some of the women should talk to Pocahontas about religion. 'For,' said Lady Gates, 'she grows more English every day, and if she is to be as one of us she should have a chance of adopting our religion. It is not meet that one who lives among us should continue to be a heathen.'

So Pocahontas learned the story of Jesus; she listened attentively and asked many questions.

This, she thought, is the God *he* served. If I become a Christian I shall have John's religion. And after death Christians meet in the Hereafter.

She went to Lady Gates and said: 'I make this decision. I wish very much to become a Christian.'

Lady Gates embraced her and wept. 'My dearest child,' she said, 'how can I express my pleasure? You shall be baptized and received into the Christian Church at once.'

This was done, and at her baptism Pocahontas received a new name – a Christian name; and henceforth she was known throughout Jamestown as Rebecca.

It was now five years since John Smith had left Virginia. Rebecca rarely spoke of him to anyone; she could not trust herself to do so, and she believed that she could be happier by never speaking of him; for merely to mention or hear his name brought his image so clearly before her that she must suffer again all the anguish she had felt when it had been broken to her that she would never meet him again.

She had taken to the Christian religion because she had been taught that, in the Hereafter, one was reunited with loved ones whom one had met on Earth, and she longed for the time when she would find John in that far-off land; she could be happier now because she believed that one day, in the green meadows of the Hereafter, she would be once more with John Smith.

There had come to Virginia with one of the supply ships an earnest gentleman of serious demeanour named John Rolfe. He was a widower and had recently suffered a great tragedy. His brother and sister-in-law had settled in Virginia, and he had come out with his wife to join them; but the hardship of the journey had proved too much for her and she had died before reaching Virginia.

John Rolfe was therefore a sad man when he arrived. He was fair-haired and blue-eyed, and although Rebecca had seen many people with that colouring, she always told herself that no eyes were as blue as John Smith's had been. She was attracted by this quiet gentleman, and he by her; no less attracted because, in his quiet and gentle way, he was quite different from that other John.

The fact that his name was John pleased her. He had lost his wife, and she had lost John. They were two people who had suffered a bereavement and, although she did not believe that he could have loved his wife as she loved John Smith, her sympathy went out to him.

He had come to grow tobacco and, when he took her to his plantation, proudly showed it to her and talked of his future plans, she was interested.

'I shall go to England every few years,' he told her. 'One grows homesick for one's own land.'

'I long to see England,' she replied.

'Who knows,' he answered, 'perhaps one day you will.'

Always when he came to the settlement he sought Rebecca, and always she was delighted to see him and was sad when he did not come; and gradually she began to realize that she was happier since she had known John Rolfe than she had been since the loss of John Smith.

It may be, she thought, that I have years to live before I reach the Hereafter and see John Smith again. There must be something for me here on earth, something to make the waiting seem less long.

John Rolfe came to her one day and said: 'You do not marry, Rebecca. Yet there must have been many willing to marry you.'

'I would never marry with my own people,' she answered. 'I am no longer one of them.'

'You could marry with a man of your adopted people?'

'Perhaps none would wish to marry me,' she answered. 'I am a stranger yet.'

He took her hands and said: 'You are not a stranger to me, Rebecca.'

Then a gladness came to her, for she thought: This is the answer. I will marry this John and be a good wife to him. I will make him happy and be happy, and the journey to the Hereafter will seem less long.

'Will you marry me?' he asked. 'You know, do you not, that I had a wife whom I loved dearly.'

She nodded. 'I know it well,' she said. 'Let us not think of the sadness of the past, of the loss of dear ones. Let us say, We will go together now ... until the call comes from the great God, and we leave this world for the Hereafter.'

Rebecca was married to John Rolfe in the church at Jamestown; and this was an important wedding, for it was the first between a native girl and an Englishman.

The Governors of the colony were delighted, because they believed that this, more than anything else, would bring peace between the two peoples.

When Powhatan heard the news he was astonished. He was angry because his daughter had deserted her people, but at the same time he was proud because she was to have a ceremony in their church and be treated with dignity. He imagined it would be similar to the coronation which he had once enjoyed, and he would have rejoiced to witness it.

But how could he be sure that the whole thing was not some cunning plot to lure him to Jamestown? He was not going to his daughter's wedding. But he sent her brother, Nantaquaus, to represent him.

'Forget nothing,' Powhatan warned his son. 'I would hear of all that the Palefaces do at the wedding, and if my daughter does not have all that a Paleface woman has, I shall make war at once on Jamestown. Tell them this.'

Powhatan could not make up his mind whether he was pleased or angry. He missed his Matoaka, yet he was proud of her. She had ever ruled him, and it was not good for great rulers to be ruled by women. Henry Spelman, who had once been content to live among them, had long since deserted and returned to Jamestown. He had only cared to serve Powhatan because of the debt he owed Powhatan's daughter.

She was no daughter of his now, mused Powhatan; she had had too great an influence on his actions; so it was well that he was rid of that influence, well that he was rid of the impulse to act without reason because his affection for her demanded it. But he missed her. He would have been happy to see her bringing children into the world here in his house, as did other members of his family. For them he cared little, and for her had cared much.

'Tell them that I will come against them unless they give her the best wedding any Paleface ever had!' he shouted.

So in the simple church Rebecca stood with John Rolfe, and the light through the fan-shaped windows shone on her dress of Dacca muslin – a present from the Governor himself – and caught the jewels mingling with the plumage of birds which decorated her hair. The church had been made festive with many flowers; and after the ceremony there was a feast, during which the health of the bride and bridegroom was drunk with great enthusiasm. Nantaquaus thought he could return to his father and tell him that nothing had been spared by the Palefaces to give Powhatan's daughter a wedding worthy of her.

To Nantaquaus it seemed strange to see his sister thus united in marriage to an Englishman from over the seas; but to those English who had come to know and love her and to whom she had become Rebecca, it seemed less strange.

Rebecca was quietly happy. She was proud to be able to call herself an Englishwoman; she had heard that women took the nationality of their husbands. John Rolfe was a gentle husband, but ten years older than herself, and she was proud of him.

She was continuously grateful for the tender courtesy with which he treated her, a quality which she knew would have been construed as weakness in her father's ménage; but she had realized there was much that Powhatan and his people did not know of the world.

John Rolfe had started the first tobacco plantation in Virginia, and he was kept busy; Rebecca was equally busy caring for his house as she had seen the English ladies do. There were frequent visits from the ladies of the settlement who had become her friends, and the days passed harmoniously.

She gradually learned about her husband's background in England. He talked of his home at Heacham in Norfolk and of Heacham Hall where he had spent his boyhood. He told of his twin brother, Eustacius, who had died when they were boys, and how he had always wanted to explore new lands.

Sometimes he talked of his first wife, and it delighted her that he could do so without great anguish now that he was happily married a second time. He told her of the voyage from England, of the wreck of the ship and their being picked up and taken to Bermuda where their child – a daughter – was born.

'We called her Bermuda,' he said sadly; 'but alas, she did not live. How could we expect it? It was asking too much after all her mother had suffered.'

And the mother had died shortly after the birth of the baby. It was a sad story, thought Rebecca; and she wanted to make him so happy that he ceased to regret.

He was happy when she told him that she herself was expecting a child.

He would not allow her to work too hard; she laughed at his care of her. She remembered how the women of her race had their babies in the meadows or in their wigwams. They did not rest; nor were they cosseted by their husbands.

Poor John, she thought. He had lost one child. He does not wish to lose another.

There came a day when her child was born and she held him in her arms . . . a strange child, she thought, because he was born of two races. He was dark of hair, yet his skin was light. She loved him dearly.

'What shall we call him?' John asked her. 'Shall we call him John?'

She looked at her husband and in his place she saw another John – blue-eyed, invincible, a demi-god.

She said sharply: 'No. Do not let us call him John. You are John ... that is enough. We do not wish two Johns, for how shall I know which is which? Let us call him Thomas. Sir Thomas Dale has been good to us, and he will be pleased.'

'Indeed he will,' answered John Rolfe. 'Let us call him Thomas then.'

So her son was Thomas, and she called him little Tom. And for a year, while she watched him grow from a baby to a little boy, she was happier than she had been since John Smith had passed out of her life.

When the child was a year old, John Rolfe seemed a little withdrawn as though he were keeping some secret to himself.

Rebecca asked him to let her share his secrets, and then he smiled at her, and a gleam of excitement came into his eyes.

'Rebecca,' he said, 'there is something you said you always wanted more than anything else. Do you remember?'

She was silent, her great eyes questioning.

'To go to England,' he went on.

'Yes, John.' Her voice was calm, but her heart had begun to flutter.

'The plantation is in good order. I could leave others in charge. We could afford a little holiday. What would you say if I said "We will take a holiday. We will go to England"?'

She whispered: 'And little Tom?'

'Well, you don't imagine that we should leave him behind! You, I and little Tom shall go to England. Would you like that?'

She was too emotional to speak. She was thinking: I shall see streets and houses. I shall sail across the sea as he sailed, walk in streets in which he has walked. It has been said that he did not die. Is that because he is immortal? What if I should see *him*?

XVII

New England

For two years after he returned to England John Smith had lived a life of great suffering. He had been examined by the best doctors in London and the use of their unguents had at length succeeded in soothing his burns.

He had spent a great deal of time on the farm with Francis and his wife. Francis was glad to have him home, and proud, too, for John was famous as the stories of his adventures were becoming well known in Europe.

John was disappointed that Francis' wife had had no children.

'I had no time, Francis,' he said. 'I had intended Virginia to be my child. But you . . .'

'It is a disappointment to us both,' said Francis' wife. 'But what is to be, will be.'

There was something else which alarmed John. He believed he detected traces of that disease which had killed his father, mother and Alice, showing in Francis' face. It was slight as yet, and John prayed that he might be mistaken.

News from Virginia came as the various ships docked in England. When they heard of the terrible 'starving time' and the trouble with the natives Francis was gleeful. 'Why,' he said, 'this will show your critics that they were wrong. If the Company had given you the support you needed, there would have been no "starving time" and less trouble with the natives.'

But John had never been a vindictive man. To have been right meant little to him; he could only feel sorry to think of the terrible sufferings of the colonists.

He was fêted in London, now that he was proved to be right, and as his health was improved he was able to enjoy these treats. Francis had a ballad written about his brother in which the three Turks' heads were not forgotten; and this was sold and sung about the streets of London.

It was pleasant for a time but, as soon as John began to feel well again, the old spirit of adventure returned.

He was delighted to meet in London that Henry Hudson who was working for the Dutch; they had agreed to finance his venture and it brought joy to them both that they were in the Capital at the same time.

They sat in Henry's lodgings poring over maps, some of which John had sent him, of Chesapeake Bay.

Henry pointed out a great tract of land, north of Virginia, from which he had just returned.

'I have named this river the Hudson River,' he said, 'and I have taken possession of this land in the name of Holland.'

'A pity,' cried John, 'that you must work for the Dutch!'

'Explorers must work for those who will provide the money for their expeditions. Think of Christopher Columbus; he sought help from his own country but finally had to go to Spain.'

John stared at the maps before him. 'I have always wanted to discover new lands ... for England,' he said.

'Well,' replied Henry, 'the fact that England has a foot in Virginia today is largely due to you. Will you return thither?'

John was thoughtful. 'I am not sure,' he said after a pause. 'Now there are great gentlemen there. They do not want a plain Captain. The colony is no longer a handful of men. It must be self-supporting by now. Providing the Company at home do not make too great demands upon it, all will go well.'

He was thinking of the early days, of the arrival in

Chesapeake Bay; and into his mind there came a hundred images of Pocahontas.

She had been constantly in his thoughts these last two years, but as he had lain in his bed, too sick to rise, he had said to himself: 'Of what use should I be in Virginia, a sick man?'

Now he thought: It is too late. She will have changed. She will have married one of her own people. I should only make trouble if I returned.

He looked at the land which lay to the north of Virginia. Why should he not found a colony for England there?

He watched Hudson sail away that April.

He did not know then that it was to discover Hudson's Bay, the inland sea four hundred miles long and one hundred miles wide. He did not know that Henry Hudson's treacherous crew were to mutiny and set him adrift in a small boat on that bleak and uncharted sea, and that no one would ever know what had become of him.

His head was full of his own plans. He was going to found a new colony for England.

Two more years passed before he was ready to sail. There had been the same difficulties which he had experienced before; he must persuade people to provide the money; then he must fit his ships. On this voyage he commanded his own ship, realizing an ambition which had long been his; and what he lacked in experience for this task he made up for by intuition and that amazing resourcefulness which had never deserted him.

When he arrived on the shores of that land which he had come to investigate, the weather was gloriously fine, and he found the air so good that he declared: 'Of all the places I have ever visited, this is the most beautiful, the climate the most delightful.'

It was a great pleasure to him to make maps and charts of the coast and to name points of interest. He named three islands, 'The Three Turks' Heads', and one cape he called 'Cape Tragabigzanda'.

And the country which so delighted him he named New England.

When he returned home he brought with him a valuable cargo of otter and beaver skins as well as salt fish, and this cargo aroused the interest of enterprising men, so that King James' son, Prince Charles, sent for John and talked to him about founding a new colony.

Charles was interested in the idea of colonizing, and John's maps absorbed him. He would not allow a cape to be named after a Turkish lady as it struck him as heathenish, so he changed the name of Cape Tragabigzanda to Cape Anne, his mother's name.

'But,' he said, 'I like well the name New England. We will keep that; and since this place is henceforth to be known as New England we will bestow upon it some of our own place names. Why should we not have a Plymouth or a Boston and a Cambridge in New England?'

John was a little regretful that he could not immortalize Charatza in Cape Tragabigzanda, but he said: 'I can think of nothing more suitable, Your Highness, than transplanting our names as well as our people in New England.'

John immediately set to work to begin the colonizing of New England, and in the spring of the year 1615 he set out with two ships. However, before they were many miles at sea, they came into conflict with storms and it was necessary to return to Plymouth. John managed to acquire another ship and he took with him two men, Chambers and Miller, as master and mate that they might bring the ship back while he stayed in New England. It was not long before John discovered the calibre of Chambers and Miller.

A few miles out at sea they saw a pirate ship bearing down upon them, and these two men were thrown into panic.

'We must surrender,' they told John. 'What chance has a ship of sixty tons against one of one hundred and twenty?'

'By God!' cried John. 'You would surrender without a fight! What manner of men are you?'

'Sailors,' replied Chambers ironically. 'I believe, Captain Smith, you were a soldier.'

'Soldier or sailor,' cried John, incensed, 'I do not give in without a fight. Heavens above, I see our pirate is an English ship.'

'There are English pirates, Captain Smith, as you will find when you have had a little more experience of sailing the seas.'

'Let us engage the pirate with all speed. We'll give a good account of ourselves.'

'The men would not obey your orders, Captain Smith. They're sailors, all of them. They know a ship of our size hasn't a chance.'

John was in a dilemma. He knew that if the crew mutinied he could do nothing. Therefore, with one of those swift decisions which had saved his life many times, he decided that he would send Chambers and Miller to row over to the pirate and ask his terms.

'But,' he added, 'if they are not what I consider fair, tell the Captain, small as we are we'll fight and sink her.'

The Captain of the pirate ship was a certain Edward Fry and, when he heard John Smith's message he put his hands on his hips, threw back his head and laughed immoderately.

'Your Captain must be mad,' he said.

'Mad! Of course he's mad,' answered Chambers. 'He's Captain John Smith.'

'What!' cried Fry. 'Not *the* Captain John Smith?'

''Tis so.'

One of the pirate crew said: 'I was with him in Transylvania.'

Another added: 'I was with him in Virginia.'

'Well?' said Edward Fry, looking at them impatiently.

'We'd not wish to harm him or any ship he sailed in,' said the first man stubbornly.

'Nay,' said another, 'I am with you there. I sailed with him out to the land he called New England. He's the finest captain I ever sailed under; ay, the bravest and the best. He never hesitated to do his share of the work, and he'd eat the food his men ate, and if they were sick, it was the dainties that went to them, not to his own table. If all captains were like Captain Smith there'd be no pirates.'

Edward Fry studied the faces of his men. He knew they spoke the truth; as for himself, if he had been fairly treated he would not have stolen his ship and turned pirate.

He said: 'Go back to Captain Smith. Tell him this. He has naught to fear from us. We'll sail with him and protect him on his journey. Let him board us if he will. I'll put myself and my crew under his command till we come to his journey's end.'

Chambers and Miller stared at the hardened pirate captain. 'You joke,' the said.

'No,' he answered. 'I've a rough and mutinous crew. Mayhap they can be called to order by this Captain Smith whom they all seem to worship.'

'We will take him your message,' said Chambers, and they went back to John.

John was sorrowful to hear that some of his old friends had turned pirate.

They were right, he knew: the conditions accorded seamen were appalling, and it was small wonder that they mutinied and turned robbers on the high seas.

But his answer was: 'I do not come to terms with pirates.'

And the pirate ship turned away and went on her course, leaving John to go on unmolested.

They had not gone many miles, after parting from Fry and his crew, when they met with two French pirates.

Chambers and Miller wished to surrender, but John threatened to blow up the ship if they did so. He was certain that he could escape the two vessels, each of which was twice the size of his, for he knew that small craft could manoeuvre more easily than larger vessels. The wind being favourable, he had the sails skilfully set and was soon proved right, for the larger vessels could not keep pace with the smaller one.

But John was fated not to reach New England; and one morning with the coming of dawn he found himself at the mercy, not of one or two ships, but a fleet of French warships. When John was commanded in the name of the King of France to surrender, he shouted in French to the Admiral on the nearest ship: 'From whence do you come?'

'From Rochelle in France,' he was told. 'We are commanded to seize all pirates of Spain and Portugal.'

'We are English and no pirates.'

'Then come aboard and prove it.'

As John was the only one of his company who could speak French, he rowed over to the French flagship. No sooner had he set foot on the French vessel than he realized his mistake, for the commander, a Monsieur Poyrune, immediately made him a prisoner.

Poyrune was at heart a pirate, and it was the easiest thing imaginable to sack a ship and swear it was a pirate, at the same time keeping much of the prize for himself, and he made a practice of this. But when he and his men went aboard John's ship it was so clearly a supply ship that Poyrune decided to send it on its way after all.

But Chambers took him aside and said to him: 'Do you know whom you have taken prisoner? It is Captain John Smith. He is a man of rigorous code, and he will not let an incident like this pass. He will report you as nothing more or less than a pirate yourself.'

The Frenchman was thoughtful. He left the English ship and held up formalities until nightfall, so that John was kept aboard the French man-of-war.

Suddenly the ship began to move off and John, on asking the reason, was told that a Spanish pirate had been sighted.

'How can you chase it at night?' asked John.

He received no answer, and in the morning when he looked about for his own ship it was nowhere to be seen. He realized that he had been tricked and was a prisoner on board the French man-of-war.

Chambers and Miller, now believing themselves to be rid of John, divided his more valuable possessions between them and took the ship back to Plymouth. There they explained that John had been captured by pirates, killed and buried at sea.

The colonists in the ship had little idea of what had happened; all they knew was that Captain John Smith had gone aboard the Frenchman and had not come back; so there was no one to deny this story, and the country mourned for John.

'He is dead,' it was said. 'And that is a great loss to England, for he was a rare man.'

John soon discovered that he had fallen into the hands of a commander who, while posing as an honest seaman, was nothing but a pirate. Poyrune was clever enough to see that in John Smith he had a man of astonishing and brilliant resourcefulness; he therefore treated him as an equal and consulted him on some occasions, and John, who had never railed against his fate, was ready to bide his time until he could return home and start out for New England once more.

So, when it was a Spanish ship to be attacked, John was ready enough to help, for he regarded the Spaniards as the natural enemies of England; he was not averse to helping in attacks on Dutchmen either.

Poyrune was delighted, for it happened that again and again John's action made victory possible.

'We should sail together,' suggested Poyrune. 'You would soon become rich, John Smith. 'You know, do you not, that I am an honest man who would share my prizes with you.'

'Then give me a taste of your generosity,' said John. 'The cargo we took from the Dutchman must have been worth 200,000 crowns.'

'It was, and you shall have your share,' answered Poyrune.

'I ask for something else in addition; at the first port I shall be put ashore. On these terms I shall help you to take as prize any Spaniard, Dutchman or other enemy of England which crosses our path.'

Poyrune agreed to this; but there were occasions when the prizes to be won carried the English flag. Then it was necessary to keep John Smith battened down in the hold while the action took place.

It soon became clear to John that Poyrune had no intention of putting him ashore, and when it was time for the vessel to return to Rochelle, Poyrune called John to him and said: 'During the three months we have sailed together I have come to know you very well. You regard yourself as an honourable man, and me as a pirate. I believe that, when we land, you might well consider it your duty to denounce me. As you would do this I intend to forestall you. I shall take you to Rochelle, and there explain that I caught you in an act of piracy.'

'That would be a lie,' retorted John.

'In Rochelle they will believe a worthy captain like myself rather than a wanderer like you.'

'I shall denounce you as a cheat and a liar.'

'If you attempt to do that, it will go hard with you. Admit the charge and I will have you quickly released. All

I wish to do is to prevent your charging *me*. Think about it, Captain Smith.'

John went away to think. He had visions of himself lying in a French prison, waiting for miserable death. It would surely be his fate if he tried to defend himself. On the other hand, if he acknowledged the charge it was possible that Poyrune might get him released, for he was eager that they should sail together again.

He could not sleep. He lay turning over this problem in his mind, so preoccupied with his own dilemma that he scarcely noticed the rising of the wind. The storm broke over the ship and the Captain gave orders for all who were not needed on deck to get under the hatches.

It occurred to John that in the tumult which followed he might have his first opportunity to escape. The ship was close to the coast of France; it was just possible that, if he cut loose one of the small boats, he might reach the shore. In any case he was ready to risk it; it appealed to him more than years in a filthy French prison.

Cautiously he crept on deck. He could hear Poyrune's voice growing more and more anxious with every second, trying to make itself heard against the roar of the storm. John let the boat down into the water and leaped into it. He rigged the sail – almost an impossible feat in that wind – and made an effort to steer in the direction where he believed the shore to lie.

It was soon clear that he could not fight against such a gale; this time he believed he had really come to the end of his life as desperately he fought against that seething sea while his little boat was rocked on the waves and tossed hither and thither as though it were a feather.

Desperately he sought to steer, clinging to life as a man who has had repeated evidence that the determination to live has often defeated death.

And as he fought with the storm he was suddenly thrown

to the side of the boat, on which he hit his head with such force that he collapsed unconscious.

He lay in the bottom of the boat, unaware of what was happening to it.

In the morning some fowlers, working near the Île de Ré at the mouth of the River Charente, saw a boat drifting towards them and in it they discovered the body of a man.

'He is dead,' they said. 'He must be a victim of the great storm.'

They bent over him, and one of them cried out: 'There is life in him yet.'

They took him into a hut on the river bank and there they built a fire and fed him. In a short time he opened his eyes, and told them that he was an Englishman who had escaped from a pirate ship, and that it was necessary that he should reach Rochelle without delay. If they would provide him with the means to do so he would give them in exchange this boat in which they had found him.

It was an excellent bargain, the fowlers decided; and very soon John was on the way to Rochelle, there to lay his account of what had happened before the administrators of that city.

Reaching Rochelle, the first people he encountered were some members of the crew of Poyrune's ship. They were astonished when they saw John and thought he was a ghost.

He explained what had happened, because he knew that these men had not approved of the way in which Poyrune had treated him.

'Why,' they said, 'we thought you were swept overboard. The ship was lost and Poyrune with her. You were fortunate, Captain Smith.'

John reminded them that he had been deeply wronged and that he had been kept a prisoner against his will for three months, for which he was determined to be compensated.

The crew advised him to go immediately to the Court of Admiralty at Rochelle, whither they would accompany him and confirm his story; for, as usual, John had managed to win the respect and liking of the humble sailors.

The Admiralty Court listened to his account and declared that he had indeed been wronged and should be recompensed. That meant he must stay a little while in Rochelle, and John was wondering how he could do this when a messenger came to him, as he left the Court, and said that his mistress offered lodging to Captain John Smith.

John accompanied the messenger to a comfortable house and there made the acquaintance of Madame Chanoyes, a comely lady a little older than himself.

'I have often heard of your exploits, Captain Smith,' she told him, 'and I regard it an honour to meet you. I trust you will make use of my house while you find it necessary to stay in Rochelle.'

John accepted her kind invitation; but it soon became clear to him that if he did not pass on, his relationship with Madame Chanoyes would become similar to that which had existed between him and Madame Colombier.

He was older now; he had suffered a great deal and his body was disfigured by the burns he had received; but it appeared that that charm he held for women had not diminished in any way.

John was gallant and charming. He was grateful to the lady, but he had no wish to be embroiled in an emotional relationship.

'I wonder you never married,' said Madame Chanoyes archly one day.

'Madame,' he answered, 'I never married because when I was young I lived for adventure, and when I grew older, Virginia was as much to me as a wife would have been.

Now there is another colony which claims me.'

She sighed and came close to him. 'Captain, you have had adventures enough. Why do you not choose a more comfortable way of life? The hearth could give satisfaction beyond that of strange new lands. Danger is for the very young. Peace is to be preferred when one grows older.'

When he looked into her beautiful, glowing eyes he knew that the time had come for him to leave Rochelle.

John returned to England as soon as possible. He was to receive a portion of the prizes which Poyrune had taken, for some of the cargo had been salvaged; but he knew that it would be a long time before he received it, and he was impatient to set out again for New England.

His return to Plymouth was greeted with great joy and, when he explained what had happened, Chambers and Miller were arrested and sentenced to terms of imprisonment.

John's one aim was to prepare for another visit to New England, and for this purpose he went to London.

XVIII

Pocahontas at Gravesend

When the report that his daughter was to visit England was brought to Powhatan, he sat for a long time on his mat, staring into the fire in contemplation of this news.

He felt proud of his little Matoaka. He had heard that she had borne a son, a son who was half Virginian, half Paleface; and that her husband treated her as though she were some precious object on whom the rain must not fall for fear she should catch cold.

And she was happier, he understood; in her quiet way, she was content, as content as she could ever be since Captain John Smith had left Virginia for the Hereafter, as some said, for England as others said.

She was to visit England. She was to sail on a ship with the English, as one of them; they had made his daughter one of their people. He was bewildered, yet he was proud and pleased.

He called one of his servants to him. This was Uttamatomakkin, a brave whom he trusted, not perhaps as he trusted Rawhunt, but Rawhunt was a man he needed to keep beside him, and he wanted a man whom he could send with Matoaka into a foreign land.

He would not wish the English to look at hunchbacked Rawhunt and say, That is a man of Powhatan. No, he must send them one of the tallest of his braves; and he should be decked in fine feathers, and Powhatan would lend him his ostrich cloak.

Uttamatomakkin stood before the ruler of all Powhatan and murmured the greeting: 'I serve Powhatan.'

'My daughter is to sail on the big ship with the English. She goes to their land. I give you to her. You go as her servant. You will come back and tell me all you see. Here is a long staff. I wish to know how many English there are in that land across the ocean. When you come to their village, cut notches on this stick. It will tell me when you return with it how many there are in the land.'

Uttamatomakkin took the stick and assured Powhatan that he would serve him with his life. When he came back, there should be a notch in the stick for every Englishman he set eyes on in England.

So Rebecca went aboard the ship which had for so many months been lying off Jamestown. It was the month of June, and she felt an exhilaration which she had known since those days when John Smith had been her friend.

She was going to embark on a great adventure; she would be at the mercy of the great sea whose many moods she had often marvelled at, but she would be with friends. There was Captain Argall, whom she had long forgiven for making her his captive; there was Sir Thomas Dale, who had been so good to her; there were many other friends; and there was her husband and her little son.

The others talked of England in awed whispers as though it were the promised land, but when she thought of it she called it to herself, John Smith's country.

The journey had begun, and she stood on deck looking back on her native land until it became but a smudge on the horizon.

'Farewell, Powhatan!' she murmured. 'Farewell, oh my father. It may be that we shall never meet again.'

Then she thought of that great day in her life, the beginning of the change, the day she was no longer a thoughtless child, the day they brought him into her father's house and placed his head upon a stone.

There had been a wild unspoken wish in her heart ever since, and it had so nearly come true.

Now she felt the salt spray mingling with the tears on her cheek.

'John Rolfe is such a good husband to me,' she whispered. 'But he is not that other John.'

There were the usual trials of a long voyage. The storms raged and it was feared that the ship might be lost; but the calm came in time, and then the hot sun beat down on the deck of the *George*.

Ships were sighted on the horizon and shivers of apprehension overtook all on board for fear that pirates might be racing towards them. But all these terrors came to nothing, and at length land was sighted.

There was great joy among all the passengers. Rebecca stood with them on deck and shared their awe and emotion.

This was England, their native land; and one woman turned to Rebecca and threw herself into her arms.

'I never thought I should see my home again,' she murmured. Then she drew herself up and stood smiling.

'They're crowding on to the Hoe to welcome us in!' cried John Rolfe. He stood beside his wife, and in her arms she held little Tom.

And thus the ship *George*, with that Rebecca who had been Matoaka and Pocahontas, came sailing into Plymouth Sound.

Rebecca had never seen so many people. They came to greet her; they embraced her; they called her 'Princess'.

There were banquets given in the City of Plymouth, and the people came out to cheer her, for they had been told that one of their Englishmen had married the daughter of the King of Virginia.

They stared at her strange looks, and they found her

beautiful. She became known through the town as 'The Beautiful Savage.'

The Vice-Admiral of Devonshire, Sir Lewis Stukely, who had been responsible for bringing Chambers and Miller to trial, was charmed by Rebecca whom he called the Lady Rebecca Rolfe.

He took little Thomas in his arms and gave him his blessing.

'My dear fellow,' he said to Rolfe, 'you have a charming wife. And you have done much good for the colony. What could be more calculated to bring about better relations between our two peoples than marriage! And yours is the first mixed marriage, and this child here is the first child to be born of such a marriage. If all the Virginian ladies are like the Lady Rebecca I could wish to see all our young men married to them. But, my dear fellow, there may be a little trouble in store. You have married into the Royal Family, and the King and Queen are sticklers for etiquette. Did you not know that royalty should not marry with commoners without the consent of the King?'

John laughed. He was thinking of Powhatan in his wattle wigwam which had been his home before his coronation when he demanded a house with glass holes. If King James could see what the ruler of Powhatan was really like he could not take offence because an English gentleman had married into Virginian royalty.

Sir Lewis insisted on entertaining the pair while they stayed in Plymouth; he gave a great banquet to which he invited Captain Argall and Sir Thomas Dale, but the guest of honour was the Lady Rebecca, the King's daughter, and it was she who sat on the right hand of her host.

He was enchanted with her; she looked strange in the costume which had been procured for her by her friends. Her black hair was taken back from her face and caught up with jewels; the lace ruff about her neck was in the new fashion open at the front like a collar and exposing her firm throat; the bodice of her dress was encrusted with gold-coloured embroidery, and the skirt was divided to show a magnificent petticoat laced with gold. But the dress of an English lady seemed to accentuate her high cheekbones, her large black eyes with a hint of sadness in them.

Sir Lewis was attentive to her. Clearly he was of the opinion that she was accustomed to being treated as a King's daughter.

Over roast sucking-pig he said to her: 'I have always been interested in your country since I heard stories of it from a friend.'

'So you have friends who come to our country?'

'One above all. Virginia meant so much to him. Indeed I sometimes think that, but for him, there would have quickly ceased to be any English in Virginia.'

Rebecca's heart had begun to beat very fast; the room seemed close and she found it difficult to breathe; from the moment of landing she had found the air of this country very different from her own, but this was nothing to do with the air.

She heard herself say: 'Tell me of whom you speak.'

'I speak of Captain John Smith.'

'I knew him,' she said.

'Ah, all would know him. There is no one quite like John.'

'No,' she said, 'there is no one like him. When he died . . .'

But Sir Lewis laughed. 'Dead! John's very much alive.'

'So?' she said faintly.

'Why, yes. I saw him but recently. We thought he was lost at sea. Well, John has been given up for lost many a time.'

She said faintly: 'In Virginia we gave him up as lost.'

'Ah yes. I remember. He was in a bad state when he came home. We never thought he would be his old self again. He had to take to his bed for months. His injuries were terrible. But now ... he is the same as ever. Allow me to fill your goblet.'

She said nothing. She tried to listen when she was spoken to, but she could not attend; and when they rose from the table she found her husband at her side. He said: 'My wife is over-tired. This has been too much for her. She has never been accustomed to such banquets, you know. She needs rest.'

Sir Lewis was alarmed, but John reassured him: 'There is nothing wrong with the Lady Rebecca. Let her rest awhile, and she will be well.'

So she took her husband's arm and said goodbye to the guests; and when she reached the bedchamber which had been allotted them in the house of Sir Lewis, John made her undress and go to bed.

She obeyed and he sat beside her bed. She turned her face away, and when he stood over her he saw that the tears were slowly streaming down her cheeks.

She is over-excited, he told himself. It is too much for her. We forget that although she is looked upon as a King's daughter, she is but a simple woman from the Virginian forests.

He put little Thomas in her arms, and she lay still, holding the child against her.

But she continued to weep quietly, and John Rolfe, not knowing what comfort to offer, sat silently by her bed until he thought she slept. Then he undressed and crept in beside her.

She was lying still, her eyes closed, and the baby slept.

There was no sleep for Rebecca. But she was no longer Rebecca. She was Pocahontas, as she had always been to John Smith; she lived their lives together over and over again, and she whispered to herself, 'Why did you not come back for me? Were we not always to be together?'

*   *   *

John Smith was in London hoping for an audience with Prince Charles. He was impatient once more to fit up an expedition and sail to New England. One day, as he was walking through the London streets, he saw a crowd gazing at a strange figure, and in that moment John thought he must be dreaming, for there, striding along the street, a long cloak wrapped about him, and wearing the costume of his own country, was a tall brave such as he might have expected to meet in the forests of Powhatan.

John hurried to the figure and stood staring at him.

Then he cried: 'We have met before. You are one of Powhatan's braves.'

'I am Uttamatomakkin, Captain John Smith,' was the answer.

John could not restrain himself. He embraced the Virginian, much to the amusement of the spectators.

'Now tell me how you are ... why you are here.'

Uttamatomakkin held up the staff he carried; it was notched all over, and he looked very worried.

'For Powhatan I mark, to tell him how many people I see.'

John laughed. 'Powhatan cannot imagine what London is like, let alone England. You can throw your stick away, Uttamatomakkin, and tell Powhatan, when you return, that you would need the trees of his forest to make enough notches. But how came you here?'

'With Lady Pocahontas, who is now the Lady Rebecca Rolfe. Powhatan sent me to guard her and to mark the stick.'

'Pocahontas!' cried John. 'She is here?'

Uttamatomakkin repeated: 'She is here. She stays at a place named Brentford, with a Bishop. Pocahontas is a great lady here. She is the King's daughter, and they do not forget. They all offer honour to her, but there is one whose honours would mean more to her than those of the Great Werowance of England himself. That is you, Captain John Smith.'

John said abruptly: 'I must know more of this. I shall ride forthwith to the house of Sir Thomas Smith, for he will tell me what this means. And, Uttamatomakkin, do not tell the Lady Pocahontas that you have seen me. Rest assured that I shall lose no time in seeking her out.'

They parted, and Uttamatomakkin went on his way, happily discarding the stick which had given him such anxiety; and John went forthwith to the house of Sir Thomas Smith, who was treasurer of the Virginian Company and would be sure to know if a passenger as unusual as Pocahontas had travelled in one of the Company's ships.

Sir Thomas received him readily, for it had long been realized by the Company that John Smith had been much maligned by his enemies, and that the Company had a great deal for which to be grateful to John.

'Why, Captain Smith,' he said, 'you look as though you have received a shock.'

'I have met a Virginian in the streets of London, and he has told me that Powhatan's daughter is in this country.'

'It is true. She has become the wife of a tobacco planter, and there is a child.'

John felt waves of emotion sweeping over him. Pocahontas with a child – the child of a white man!

He wanted to cry out: No. It is impossible.

But he knew that it was true. He knew that he had refused to analyse his feelings; glibly he had said: 'Virginia is my wife and family.' But Virginia was lost to him now ... even as Pocahontas was.

'I knew her well,' he said gruffly, because he realized that Sir Thomas was regarding him strangely. 'She saved my life and later the lives of us all. But for this woman first *I* should have perished, then the whole settlement.'

'Then it is well that we treat her with great respect.'

'Now that she is here,' said John, 'I shall write an account of all she did for the English, and I shall address it to the Queen. She must be received by the King and Queen, not only because she is the daughter of the overlord of all the Powhatan territory, but because of what she did for the English.'

'Write it, John,' said Sir Thomas, 'it's a good move. We have always been eager to establish good relations between the English and the Virginians.'

'I shall tell all,' said John; and his voice shook as he recalled it – that moment when the clubs were raised above his head, and her soft, warm body lay between him and death.

'She is now staying at the house of the Bishop of London. We are eager that all homage should be paid to her. She has become a Christian, and what more fitting than that the Bishop of London should receive her in his house at Brentford?'

'Yes,' mused John, 'I shall tell the story to the Queen . . . but first I must ride out to Brentford to see her.'

John Smith was coming. Her husband had told her so.

'Rebecca,' he had said, 'there is a surprise for you. An old friend of yours has heard that you are here, and he will ride out to see you. It is the famous Captain John Smith himself.'

'Yes,' she said.

'You do not sound over-eager. Have you forgotten him? I had heard that once you thought highly of him.'

'No, I had not forgotten. Yes, I thought highly of him,' she answered.

'Of course it is so many years ago . . .' murmured John.

'Oh yes, it is many years ago.'

She prepared herself to meet him. It would be hard to remember that she was an English lady now, for the lady Rebecca would disappear and in her place there would be only wild Pocahontas.

How could she stand before him; how could she curtsy and say what an English lady would say to an old acquaintance: ''Tis long since we have met. I am happy that we should meet again.' How could she?

The calm English lady would disappear. There would be a wild savage in her place. She would run to him and beat on his chest with her fists and cry: 'You left me. You left me all alone. You were a god who put a spell upon me so that there was no happiness for me without you. And then I think you die. But you do not die. You live and . . . you forget . . . you forget all that happened in the forests of Powhatan.'

She stood, clenching and unclenching her hands; she wanted to tear off the satin petticoats, the gold embroidered farthingale. She wished to stand before him, with nothing on but her buckskin apron, her hair wild or perhaps adorned with the down of birds, her copper beads, her white beads, the blue glass beads which proclaimed her the daughter of a great Werowance about her neck.

There was a tight feeling in her chest; it was a reminder of the pain she had felt when the wicked men of Jamestown had told her that he was dead. The pain had been there ever since, and she knew what it meant because the women of the forest knew such things. It meant: My life is over, for it belonged to John Smith, and he went away and left me and there is nothing I wish for when he is lost to me.

And now she was the wife of a good, kind man; and in the cradle in this very house lay the fruit of their union, a brown-skinned light-eyed baby whom she loved.

But she loved none as she loved John Smith, and there was nothing in her life which could take away the pain in her heart, which was a longing for death, so deep that it could only be the herald of death; for all the women of the forest knew that if one of them longed for death and called to death, death would come.

John Rolfe came to look at her. He could not see behind

her eyes; he did not know what happened in her heart.

He said: 'Come! You should be there to greet him.'

And he led her down to the oak-panelled parlour in the house of the Bishop of London, there to await the coming of John Smith.

In the parlour others had assembled. There was Dr King himself; and there were some of the ladies who had accompanied Pocahontas on her journey to England; there were one or two Virginian girls whom Powhatan had sent with her as he wished his daughter to travel regally with her little court.

This was a great occasion. All those present had heard of the fame of John Smith; so his visit to the house was no ordinary visit.

But we should have been alone, thought Pocahontas. Not only must we meet in this closed-in room, but others must be present.

She stood waiting for him, her fingers playing with the richly-embroidered material of her skirts. But when he entered the room she scarcely dared look his way.

She saw that he had changed. He was older. He too had suffered; she saw the scars on his hands; his face had scarcely been touched by the fire. But suffering had scarred it. There was the brightly coloured hair and beard; the alert eyes of that deep shade of blue. He was dressed as she had not seen him dressed in the forest; he wore a velvet cloak, rich with embroidery, and his silken doublet was puffed and slashed.

Eagerly he looked about him, and she knew that he looked for her and that in those first quick looks he failed to find her, for he did not recognize Pocahontas of the woods in this stiffly farthingaled Lady Rebecca Rolfe.

Dr King had greeted him. He was saying: 'I am sure, Captain Smith, that it will be a great pleasure to see again the Lady Rebecca.'

'Take me to her,' he said, and Pocahontas, listening, felt that her emotions would overwhelm her.

Now he was standing before her. Now he was looking, not at the rich garments of fashion, but at her face; and there he found her, and he knew that no English garments, no English customs, could change her.

He was an Englishman and he could control his emotion so that none in this room but herself would guess what he felt.

But she was a Virginian and, in moments such as this one, all that she had learned since she gave up the life of the forest for that of the settlement dropped from her.

She was a woman who would love until death; she was the savage of the forest.

She wanted to cry out: I belong to you, and you to me. Without you I will not live. John Smith, I had thought you dead, and ever since I have mourned you.

But she was in this strange, alien room and she was surrounded by strange and alien people. The weight of their manners and their customs oppressed her so that she was neither Englishwoman nor Virginian.

She could not speak. She dared not, for she feared that if she did she would betray herself. She turned from him and, burying her face in her hands, she ran from the parlour.

John stared after her in dismay. Then John Rolfe came and laid his hands on his shoulder.

'She thought you dead,' he said. 'The shock of seeing you alive has been too much for her. She thought highly of you, and she mourned you long. She will recover; then she will wish to have speech with you.'

'You,' said John, 'are her husband?'

'That is so,' answered John Rolfe. 'It has been a happy marriage. Rebecca and I have a little son, Thomas. She adores him.'

'Rebecca . . .' murmured John. 'To me she was always Pocahontas. She will always be so.'

One of the ladies said: 'Shall I go to the Lady Rebecca? Shall I ask her what ails her? She is not sickening for something, is she? I notice she has a cough.'

'She is overcome by the sight of a friend whom she believed dead,' said John Rolfe. 'Leave her for awhile. She will soon recover.'

Dr King joined them. 'You two will have a great deal to talk about,' he said. 'I am sure the Captain will be interested to hear how things go in Virginia.'

'Yes,' said John Rolfe quietly. 'Let us walk in the gardens for a while. Later you will wish to talk to Rebecca.'

It was more than an hour later when John found Pocahontas in the garden.

'Go out to her,' John Rolfe had said. 'She awaits you there. But she would see you alone. She has been emotionally disturbed.'

So in the garden of the bishop's house, with its lawns and flower beds so different from Powhatan's forest, John Smith talked with Pocahontas.

'They told me you were dead,' she said.

'They were far from the truth,' he answered.

'Why did you go away without a word to me?'

'Because I was so wounded that I thought I was to die. I did not wish to grieve you.'

'Yet I grieved.'

'Dearest Pocahontas, my skin was burned from my body. Beneath these fine garments I am disfigured by many scars. I am not the John Smith whom you saved from your father's executioners.'

'Are you not always John Smith?'

'I thought I should have been of no use in the forest, no use to the colony . . . no use to you.'

She shook her head, and the tightness in her throat prevented her from speaking.

'And now you have a husband. He is a good man. I rejoice, Pocahontas. John Rolfe is the best type of Englishman. He is kind and gentle to you, is he not? And you have your son.'

She spoke then, and her voice was full of accusation. 'You rejoice!'

He answered: 'It is best for you.'

'Nay,' she cried, her eyes flashing, 'there was but one thing which would be the best for me.'

'Our lives do not run together,' he told her.

'That is not true.'

'Pocahontas, you will go back to Virginia with your husband. You have your child. Your life is there. Mine is elsewhere.'

'My life on Earth was with you . . . always with you . . . from the moment you entered my father's house, it was so. I know this because I am a woman of the forest and these things we know in the forest. But for me you would have died, and that meant that my life could only be lived if it was with you.'

'My dear Pocahontas, you are John Rolfe's wife; you are the mother of his son.'

'And you are my Father,' she said; and he knew that she used the term as the people of her tribe used it. It meant – you are that person for whom I have the greatest respect. You are my chief, and you only do I serve.

'Nay,' he said. 'Why, are you not the daughter of a King! I am but a commoner. You must not call me Father. You must call me plain John Smith.'

'I shall call you my Father,' she repeated.

'But the King would be displeased if you did so. You must not forget, while you are in England, that you are the daughter of a King. They set great store on such things in England. I should be afraid of the King's anger if he heard you, who are a King's daughter, call a commoner like myself Father.'

'When were you ever afraid, John Smith?' she asked. 'When you were in my father's house you knew no fear. You are my Father, and that I shall call you. Do you not see it is the only thing left to me?'

'Pocahontas,' he said, 'let not our thoughts dwell on what cannot be. Let us talk of what may be. You are in England, and I wish you to see some of the splendours of our country. When you go back to Powhatan you must tell him I think of him often; and I want you to tell him of the marvels you have seen in England.'

She smiled at him a little sadly. 'You think of the colony,' she said. 'Yes, always you think: Powhatan must know of the mighty nation from which the Palefaces come.'

'I am going to make sure that you enjoy your stay here,' said John, and he would not meet her eyes. 'I am going to write to the Queen and tell her how you saved my life. I am going to tell how you came with baskets of food when the colony was about to perish. I am going to ask that homage shall be done to the daughter of Powhatan.'

'You speak as though you think this will make me happy.'

'And so it shall.'

'And you?' she asked.

'I shall see you often. I shall ride over to Brentford each day. We will talk together. We will remember the old days. Perhaps I myself will present you to the Queen.'

'So then we shall be together?'

'While you are in England, yes. But, Pocahontas, you will go back to Virginia with your husband and your child.'

'And then,' she said, 'I must say goodbye to John Smith for ever?'

'We shall be constantly in each other's thoughts.'

'And in the Hereafter we shall meet again, John Smith. I am a Christian now, and the Christian religion tells us this. It is not only great Werowances who go to the Here-after. It is all those who lived good lives on Earth. We shall meet there, John Smith. For you there will be a place of honour in Heaven and, since I have been a Christian, because I believed I should find you there, I too have done all that the Christian religion asked of me.'

'Oh, Pocahontas, do not speak so. You are young to talk of death.'

'Yet since I lost you I have longed for it.'

'Lost! I am not lost. See, I stand beside you.'

'And when you pass from my life again, that will be death for me,' she said.

'I am going to make you happy while you are with us. Ah, here comes your husband. He is concerned. He thinks that the excitement of coming to England has been fatiguing for you.'

'He does not know me. I am strong. Should I be fatigued?'

John Rolfe had joined them. 'Rebecca, my dear,' he said, 'a cold wind has risen. This is not Virginia. We must take care of you.'

He put his arm about her and they went into the house – John Rolfe on one side of her, John Smith on the other.

John Smith went back to his lodgings and wrote to the Queen. He told her of all Pocahontas had done for him and Englishmen in Virginia. He implored the Queen to show some favour to this Virginian Princess, the daughter of the ruler of all Powhatan, whom she would find a charming English lady, now the wife of Englishman John Rolfe.

When he had written this he was restive. He had forgotten his urgent desire to go to New England. Instead he rode every day to Brentford, and there he walked and talked with Pocahontas.

Her fame had travelled through the capital, and gentlemen of the Court asked Smith to allow them to accompany him to Brentford that they might meet this lady who John had declared was the Nonpareil of Virginia.

So there were gay occasions at the house in Brentford, and one day John brought news that Pocahontas was to be received at Court.

Pocahontas – she could not think of herself as Rebecca now, for John Smith had always called her Pocahontas and refused to do otherwise – took her place serenely in the centre of this activity; she stood still while seamstresses fitted gowns upon her. She seemed unmoved because she was to meet the Court.

Queen Anne was delighted with her, and gravely Pocahontas accepted her success. When she went to Court people stood aside for her to pass, and they called after her: 'Long live the Indian Princess!'

The Queen was kindly and homely, and she asked Pocahontas to sit beside her and talk to her about Virginia.

'You have made a great success,' said John Rolfe, and he was pleased that she should do so, although he himself, being a commoner, could not always accompany her to Court.

Pocahontas learned to dance the English dances; she attended the masques and banquets. It was a strange life of colour and brilliance; but she only lived for those days when she saw John Smith.

Her husband was alarmed about her health, for she was coughing a great deal. She did not tell him that when she took her kerchief from her mouth it was often stained with blood. That would have made him unhappy; but she felt exultant, for she understood what it meant.

John Rolfe said: 'I must take you down to Heacham. It will be more healthy in the country. There you will recover your spirits, and you will be as you were in Virginia.'

So he took her to the big house which belonged to his family; and there she met his relations who were startled that their John should have married a Princess and feared she would find their way of living too simple.

She was amused, and tried to explain what living in a Virginian village was like, and how their house, with its great open fireplaces and its gabled windows, was like a palace compared even with that which the Palefaces had built in the woods for Powhatan.

But she did not recover her health in the country, and she told John Rolfe that she wished to return to London.

Thinking she pined for the gaiety of the capital, he took her back there, where she was received once more at Court. Her picture must be painted, she was told, and Simon de Passe painted her. She wondered what Powhatan would have said, could he have seen a portrait of his daughter. An Italian artist also painted her picture.

One day he said to her: 'Lady Rebecca, you change even as I paint. You grow more and more remote from the world, and it seems as though you look beyond this life to another to which you are growing nearer and nearer. I believe you are yearning to be home in your forests.'

She smiled but did not answer.

Christmas came and Pocahontas was enchanted by festivities such as she had never seen before. She attended the Twelfth Night masque at Whitehall and herself danced. She noticed that she was more breathless than she had been when she first arrived; but she told no one of the blood-flecked kerchiefs. Not yet, she thought; there will come a time when I can no longer keep this secret. But the time is not yet.

When they had returned from Heacham they stayed for a while at an inn near Holborn. Here she would sit at her window while many famous people came to talk to her. But there was only one she wished to see; and when he came, which he did frequently, she was happy.

John Smith sat with her at the window of her room in

the inn, and they would look on to the inn-yard and talk of Virginia.

One day he said to her: 'Pocahontas, this country is not kind to you.'

'It is kinder than any other country could be.'

He refused to understand her meaning. 'This dampness in our air makes you cough. You cannot hide from me the fact that you grow thinner every day. You must go back to Virginia while there is yet time. I have seen illness such as yours. You are young and you need the hot sun and the dry air of Virginia. Our damp air does you no good.'

'You talk to me like a doctor, John Smith.'

'I would be your doctor. I would see you strong and well, as you were once in the forests of your father's land.'

He talked to John Rolfe about her and, as a result, they found lodgings at Brentford; but her health did not improve and now she could not hide the blood-stained kerchiefs.

John Rolfe said one day: 'It is folly to remain here. We are going back to Virginia. Only thus can we bring you back to health.'

He had expected her to protest, for she had once said that she would never go back to Virginia.

Now she bowed her head, and her husband kissed her tenderly, delighted, he said, to find her so sensible.

A few days later he came riding back from London.

'I have seen Captain Argall,' he told her. 'He is preparing to leave for Virginia, and the *George* is even now anchored at Gravesend. He will be sailing within a week. It is little time, Rebecca, to say goodbye to all your friends.'

'Yes,' she said, 'there is little time.'

'My dear wife, you shall not go to London. They shall come to you to say their farewells.'

She did not protest.

'Oh, dear God,' thought John Rolfe, 'how weak she is!'

*   *   *

The jolting coach took her from Brentford to Gravesend. She had said farewell to John Smith.

He knew, of course. How could it be otherwise? In those last moments he did not pretend.

In the few minutes that they were alone he held her in his arms. How frail she was! No bigger than that small child who had sat astride his body when the executioners' clubs had been held above him.

She did not need to tell him that she would never go to Virginia, because he knew.

'Farewell, my love,' he said.

'Farewell, my only love,' she answered. 'Farewell, my slave, my master, my friend and Father.'

'It could not have been otherwise,' he said.

But she shook her head. 'We shape our lives, John Smith,' she said. 'That which we wish, if we wish it fiercely enough, it will come to us.'

'Your life lies over the sea, and mine lies – God knows where.'

She answered: 'I have come home, John Smith, for your home is my home. It was so since the day when I offered my life . . . when I would have died with you, had you died.'

'You will feel better when the ship sets sail, when you see your native land.'

She shook her head. 'I have come home,' she answered.

Then he embraced her once more, holding her as though he would never let her go.

'Now,' she said, 'in this short moment I am happy. In this small moment I shall live until I reach the Hereafter. There I shall wait for you, John Smith. In the lands beyond the impassable mountains.'

'That is the Hereafter of your people. You have become a Christian now.'

'The Hereafter of my father's people, the heaven of yours . . . it is the same place, John Smith. It is the waiting place.

I am going there now . . . very soon I go. And there I shall wait for you.'

He could bear no more. He took his final leave of her and hurried away.

At the door he turned to look at her small, dark face as she lay back on her cushions. Thus he would remember her for as long as he lived, tender and wise . . . with the wisdom of her people. He knew that she would never return to Virginia.

She had gone aboard the *George*, and in a few hours it would sail away from England.

She lay in her cabin, waiting . . . but not to sail.

John Rolfe sat beside her, holding her hand in his.

'The ship rocks so,' he whispered. 'Does it disturb you, Rebecca?'

She did not answer. She was unaware of the rocking of the ship.

She was thinking of the smell of the forest, of the rushing of the falls of the Powhatan River. There she had played with her brothers and sisters, happy, careless of time, her father's beloved daughter, the favourite of all his children.

She saw the smoke rising from the wigwams; she heard the whispering of voices mingling with the rustling of the pines. 'The Palefaced men are among us.'

Then she was in her father's house, and the heat was great. She could smell the paint on the women and the warriors, the sweat on their bodies, the oil on their hair.

She saw him enter, the man who had come to bring her the utmost sorrow, the utmost joy.

But it was over now. She was going to that land beyond the impassable mountains. She called it Heaven now, because she had taken his religion. His people were her people, his gods her gods.

She smiled and said: 'I am going now, John.'

And the man who was not John Smith threw himself on

his knees and buried his face in his hands. She saw his shoulders heaving and she thought: He weeps for me.

Her thin hand reached out to stroke his hair.

'Farewell, John,' she whispered so quietly that he could not hear. 'Farewell, my slave, my master . . . It will not be for long.'

They carried her body ashore and buried her at St George's Church there at Gravesend. All over London there was mourning for the death of her whom they called the Indian Princess; and outside that inn where she had stayed in the city of London, the innkeeper put up a new sign. On this was a reproduction of the portrait which Simon de Passe had painted of her, and beneath it was printed 'La Belle Sauvage'.

XIX

The Last Years

By a tomb in St George's church in the little town of Gravesend a man stood. He was no longer young, for he was fast approaching his fiftieth year; but since Pocahontas had died, thirteen years before, he had often visited this spot.

His blue eyes were embedded in wrinkles, and they were not so alert as they had once been; his back was a little bent; the gait less sprightly. John Smith, the adventurer, had become John Smith the writer.

When she had died his life had changed abruptly. He had never again gone to New England, though he had at first believed that he could again take up the threads of his adventurous life; he had told himself that Pocahontas had been merely one of the threads in the pattern of that life – a vital thread, it was true, without which at one time the tapestry would have fallen to pieces; but that was past. She had gone and he had his life to live.

He would dedicate it, as he had always said he would, to the making of colonies for England. Virginia would be as his first-born; New England, his second beloved child; and there would be others.

For those weeks following her death his only solace had been to throw himself into preparations for a new voyage; but the difficulties this time were insuperable even for a man of his driving energy.

Investors shook their heads and said: 'You set out before, Captain Smith, and what happened? You did not reach New England.'

They looked away from him. They believed him to be unlucky.

And so, although he was known as Admiral of New England, still he remained at home in frustration, unable to raise the necessary money to equip an expedition.

Francis died, followed shortly by his wife. They had had no children and, although John had seen little of them, he felt suddenly a lonely man. He had no near relations, but he had enough money to live on comfortably, and he made the discovery that he could relive his adventures by writing about them.

He wrote a book which was called *A Description of New England*; he had made a map of the territory which was the only one in existence at that time. He followed this with *New England's Trials* which contained further maps of Virginia and New England.

All this time he was hoping to equip an expedition that he might continue with his work which he felt to be his real vocation. He received with intense interest any news which came from the New World. He followed with great joy the success of colonists, and mourned their failures.

When in the year 1620 he heard that a band of pilgrims was about to leave England in the *Mayflower*, to settle in the New World, where they might be allowed to worship God as they wished, he was struck by their courage, and offered to accompany them and place himself at their service. 'For,' he said, 'you go to a country of which you know little and of which I have some experience. While I applaud your courage I fear what hardships may confront you in that land.'

But the pilgrims rejected his offer. He was not a member of their Church, and they felt that all the good he could bring them could not compensate for that.

So they refused help which would have been invaluable to them, and once again John lost a chance of sailing to the New World.

Back he went to his writing and produced *The General History of Virginia, New England* and *The Summer Isles*.

Bad news came from Virginia. Opechancanough had become ruler of all the tribes on the death of Powhatan and, perhaps because he remembered the humiliation he had once been subjected to when Captain John Smith had held him by the hair in front of seven hundred of his warriors, he staged a great massacre of the white men; hundreds of them were slain, their goods stolen and their houses burned to the ground.

John presented himself to the London Virginian Company. 'Let me go out there,' he begged. 'Let me avenge this massacre. Let me show Opechancanough that he cannot treat white men so with impunity.'

But again there was not enough money for an expedition, and a year or so later the Company went into liquidation and the settlers of Virginia were left to themselves.

John secretly rejoiced in this, because he realized that when the colonists need not think of satisfying the people at home, when they could concern themselves only with making their own way, they would prosper. This proved to be the case.

It was some years now since he had ceased to think of voyaging. He had never really recovered from the shock of almost being burned to death, and he had begun to realize that the pen could serve him even as once did the sword.

So now he stood in the churchyard at Gravesend and thought of Pocahontas and what might have been.

Her little son was being brought up in England, and John Rolfe, back in Virginia, had married a certain Jane Pierce with whom it was said he lived a happy life; he had a family to help him forget those brief years when Pocahontas had been his wife.

King James had died, and that Prince Charles who had

been so interested in John's voyages in New England, was on the throne. And there was trouble brewing between King and Parliament.

John remembered that once he had said to Francis: 'Virginia is my wife, my family, my home.' And Virginia would flourish; Virginia would grow as perhaps would that other love of his, New England.

As for himself, he had his friends. He had not returned to Lincolnshire, but had made his home in London; and here there were frequent visitors. There were soldiers who had served with him in Europe, and men who had been to Virginia and New England with him. There were others, such as the friend in whose house he was now staying – Sir Samuel Saltonstall, who had helped in the printing of John's latest book.

He was happy to have such friends. Their houses were always open to him, so he could not be lonely. He had his writing, his friends and his memories. It seemed a great deal.

He left the churchyard and made his way back to Sir Samuel's house.

The June sun burned down hotly and as he came into the city the stench from the gutters rose to assault him. He scarcely noticed it.

He thought: Times are changing now. It is not the London I came to, to see Captain Ley when I hoped to join his expedition to Guiana. There was trouble brewing in this dissension between the people and the throne.

But, he told himself, I shall see none of it; and he ceased to think of it. Indeed, as he walked along those narrow streets, he found that he was making his way through Holborn, and he came to rest before the inn on which the signboard creaked.

The picture had been blurred by weather, but there was a faint likeness there; and as he watched it, it seemed to him as though the dark eyes smiled at him.

'She believed we should meet in the Hereafter,' he murmured to himself.

'Are you feeling well, sir?' It was the innkeeper.

'Yes, yes. I'm well.'

'Why, 'tis Captain Smith himself. Come in, sir, and take a tankard of ale.'

John thanked him. 'No,' he said. 'I must be on my way.'

He left the inn and did not look back at the sign, yet he had the strange feeling that she was there watching him.

'What has come over me?' he murmured, and he laughed at himself.

He reached the house of his friend, a mansion far more grand than his own lodging, for he had never amassed a great deal of money.

He went into the cool hall, and as he did so one of the servants came to him and said, as the innkeeper had: 'Are you well, sir?'

He did not answer. He was sitting in the chair they had brought for him; he was unaware of the hall and the servants and Sir Samuel himself, whom in some alarm the servants had brought to him.

He thought that she had come down from the sign, that she had walked beside him and that she was leading him, not across the hall of Sir Samuel's house but through the forests of Powhatan.

A few days later he died; and he was buried in St Sepulchre's Church in the parish of Holborn. It had been his wish to be buried there, not far from that creaking sign which had seemed to him to hold more of Pocahontas than the tomb at Gravesend.

The Pleasures of Love

Jean Plaidy

She was ready to endure all – for the pleasures of love.

Newly married to King Charles II, Catherine of Braganza has left her sheltered upbringing in Portugal to become part of the notoriously licentious English court. She soon falls deeply in love with her charming, witty husband – but brought abruptly face to face with the true state of affairs at court she becomes overwhelmed by despair.

Catherine finds enemies are everywhere: rivals for the King's affection such as Barbara, Lady Castlemaine, beautiful, simple-minded Frances Stuart and merry Nell Gwynne – and more deadly adversaries, like the venomous Titus Oates, determined to destroy her.

Despite all this, and despite Charles's humiliating neglect, Catherine's love prevails through disillusion and despair – to triumph in the end.

ISBN 0 00 647200 1

Madame du Barry

Jean Plaidy

She could dazzle King and commoner alike - but not for ever...

Marie Jeanne Bécu began life as the illegitimate daughter of a humble cook, but by the time she was twenty-three she had become Madame du Barry, the official mistress of King Louis XV of France. By virtue of her exceptional and seductive beauty, her enchanting wit and her unfailing good nature, she came to govern the monarch and all around him.

While the King is alive, she can endure the jealousy and resentment of others who are constantly seeking to usurp her place. But once King Louis is dead, it is clear that she is no longer welcome at the French court. Yet there is far worse to come, for in 1789 the French Revolution casts its long shadow and Madame du Barry's life is in mortal danger...

ISBN 0 00 649619 9

In the Shadow of
the Crown
Jean Plaidy

Young and inexperienced, her life was shaped in the
shadow of the crown.

Mary Tudor found her once assured future devastated
by the perilous and dramatic events of the reign of her
father, Henry VIII: the break with Rome, the
suppression of the monasteries, the execution of two
Queens.

Longing for marriage and children, Mary became
convinced that she was preserved for a divine purpose:
to restore the Church of England to Rome. And one
man had the power to satisfy all Mary's ambitions –
Philip of Spain . . .

ISBN 0 00 617739 5

Seven for a Secret

Victoria Holt

When Frederica Hammond comes to live with her Aunt Sophie in Wiltshire, she quickly becomes fascinated by the mysterious House of the Seven Magpies. Through her acquaintance with the strange sisters, Flora and Lucy Lane, who live there, and through her friendships with Rachel of the forbidding Bell House, with Tamarisk St Aubyn and Tamarisk's brother, Crispin, she is drawn into a web of evil and intrigue that leads eventually to murder.

Her hopes of happiness threatened, Frederica flees to the remote Casker's Island. But she becomes determined to find the answer to the riddle that is darkening her life. Only Crispin can help her, and only he can tell her the secret buried at the House of the Seven Magpies...

ISBN 0 00 647307 5

The Black Opal

Victoria Holt

Imprisoned by the past, she is determined to uncover the mystery of those last tragic days of her childhood...

Carmel is the unwanted one at Commonwood House. A gypsy foundling, she is treated as an outsider by her unhappy adopted family. And, when an horrific tragedy occurs and the household is quickly disbanded, she is determined to leave these unhappy days behind her.

Her beloved Uncle Toby takes her far away to Australia, a land full of adventure, where the sundowners mine for black opals and an exciting new life awaits her. But she is constantly haunted by the mysterious happenings at Commonwood, and she knows she must return, to discover the truth about the dark secret that has overshadowed her life...

ISBN 0 00 647930 8

Daughter of Deceit
Victoria Holt

In her 30th bestseller, the inimitable Victoria Holt spins a mesmerising tale of passion and intrigue, family fortunes and deadly betrayals.

Noelle Tremaston has led a charmed life. Daughter of Desiree, the darling of Drury Lane, she has grown up amid a flurry of opening nights and elegant parties, basking in the fatherly affection of her unconventional mother's devoted admirers. But, when kind-hearted Desiree opens her home to Lisa Fennell, an adoring fan and ambitious ingenue, Noelle's carefree existence is changed forever.

Desiree dies after a sudden illness and Noelle turns for solace to the man she loves, but the revelation of a dark secret threatens to separate them forever.

As Noelle tries to rebuild her life, she meets many people who are not as they seem, from the English aristocracy to the bohemian artists of Paris's Latin Quarter. Mystery and murder stalk her, keeping happiness just out of reach until an ironic twist of fate brings her tantalisingly close to the happiness she thought was lost forever.

ISBN 0 00 647113 7

The Captive
Victoria Holt

From shipwreck on a desert island, to the cloistered and exotic intrigues of the harem of a Turkish pasha, and a stately and secretive house in Cornwall, Rosetta finds her fate irrevocably linked with the lives of two men.

Lucas Lorimer is attractive, wordly and cynical. Simon Perrivale is a wanted man, a suspect in a much publicized murder case. By chance, they are country neighbours and, while visiting the crippled Lucas, Rosetta has the opportunity to prove Simon's innocence.

Her self-imposed mission is as dangerous as any bizarre adventure they have shared so far . . .

ISBN 0 00 617803 0